SHOOTING
STRAIGHT
IN THE DARK

SHOOTING
STRAIGHT
IN THE DARK

*Watch out for
Jackie in this one.*

~~RICK BLECHTA~~

Rick Blechta

M&S

National Library of Canada Cataloguing in Publication Data

Blechta, Rick
Shooting straight in the dark

ISBN 0-7710-1534-8

I. Title.

PS8553.L3969S5 2002   C813'.54   C2001-903811-9
PR9199.3.B49S5 2002

We acknowledge the financial support of the Government of Canada through
the Book Publishing Industry Development Program for our publishing
activities. We further acknowledge the support of the Canada Council for the
Arts and the Ontario Arts Council for our publishing program.

Designed by: Kong Njo
Typeset in Sabon by M&S, Toronto
Printed and bound in Canada

McClelland & Stewart Ltd.
The Canadian Publishers
481 University Avenue
Toronto, Ontario
M5G 2E9
www.mcclelland.com

1 2 3 4 5   06 05 04 03 02

This book is fondly dedicated to Jo-Anne Yale, Lori Kernohan, Roger St. Louis, and Checkers, who taught me that being blind is not the same as having only four senses.

ACKNOWLEDGEMENTS

I owe a huge debt of gratitude to the following people (and they know why!): my editor, Pat Kennedy; my copyeditor, Adam Levin; James Dubro; Leslie Watts; André Leduc; Kim Lee Kho and Kal Honey; Gerry and Marilyn Cornwell; Gary Greenland; Marian Misters; Leslie Wang; Judy and David Mungovan along with the redoubtable Wilbur; and last, though *certainly* not least, my best critic and biggest fan, Vicki.

Author's note: Detective Constable Brent Patton is a real person – although he's not a policeman. He won a raffle prize several years ago at Dixon Grove Junior/Middle School here in Toronto to be in "Mr. B's next book." Here it is, Brent! Thanks for being patient.

PROLOGUE

So it's August 3rd, and I'm having a party for my big 2-1. Legal-the-World-Over Kit. I'd talked my mom into letting me use our cottage on Georgian Bay, just me and my current boyfriend, my four best friends, and their guys. We'd built a bonfire on the beach, roasted wienies and marshmallows, and were hard at work on a couple of two-fours of Molson Golden. During the festivities, my guy and I slipped off into the woods for a little fun.

To keep this story short, he stuck a particularly bright flashlight right in my face to screw up my night vision, then ran off with all my clothes – just to be cute. What happened after was anything but. I had a hell of a time finding my way back. Took me about an hour. Everyone was worried, but not as worried as I was. Lately, I'd been getting these weird blank spots in my eyes, especially from bright lights, and my night vision had always sucked. But in the darkness of the woods with only a sliver of moon out, I couldn't see a thing. Nada. After bumping into trees and tripping over rocks and roots, I wound up crawling a good part of the way. It scared the hell out of me. The party ended early.

A couple of days later I went to my doctor. She sent me to a specialist. He sent me to another specialist. That guy, after doing a truckload of tests, sat me and my mom down in his cushy office one blazingly hot afternoon. "Miss Mason," he said, peering over his glasses, "you show a marked deterioration in both optic nerves."

"You're saying I need glasses?"

"Oh no, no! It's much worse than that, I'm afraid. You're going blind."

No gentleness, no careful laying of the groundwork to prepare me. Just, "You're going blind." Goddam idiot got his bedside manner from K-Mart.

I didn't hear much more of what the doctor said after that. Apparently, he told Mom all these complicated medical things about what was happening to me and how he could do more tests, and "research is moving at the speed of light these days," but the end result was, "Your daughter's eyesight is rapidly failing and there's not a whole lot we can do for her at the present time."

Mom fought like a tiger. She went everywhere, bent everybody's ear, read about anything to do with my condition, but in the end she had to admit defeat. She had to admit it because thirty-seven months later I couldn't see her slumped shoulders or sad eyes. I couldn't see anything.

Want to know what it's like to be blind? Think of it this way: what do you see out of the back of your head?

PRELUDE

THE MAN JOGGED EASILY DOWN THE gentle slope. With each footfall the gravel on the path gave a satisfying crunch. Taking a deep breath, he glanced up through the bare fingers of the wooded slopes of the ravine park. Hard to believe that houses sat at the top. The way it felt down here, you could be miles from anything, not in the heart of Canada's biggest city. A few of the overwintering birds flitted from tree to tree, singing happily in the warming air. Perfect. Even though he was enjoying himself, every observation registered on his consciousness, as things to be noted, sorted, and analyzed.

Ahead, a lone runner also ran on, not altering her pace, legs, arms, and body moving like a well-oiled machine. She had a good figure. An especially nice ass. Girls in good shape always looked great in Spandex. He remembered someone who'd once told him that wearing Spandex was a privilege, not a right. His internal laugh escaped as a gentle snort.

The girl could motor. He had to give her that. But speed would never save her. He was faster and he was the stalker. She'd never know about him until it was too late. The man idly contemplated how he might take her out.

First of all, she was stupid. Plain stupid. He mentally ticked off the reasons. Never jog with a headset on; never jog alone; don't follow the same route every day. Like most of them, though, she did all these things. She made it almost too easy. He'd only have to wait for the right opportunity, wait until no one was around. Without tapping his memory, he could think of at least four quick and silent ways to carry out his assignment. Maybe a quick snap of the neck from behind, or a knife slipped between the ribs. A bullet in the brain. The wire. It all depended on the point his employer wanted to make. He'd only have to pick the location to carry it out. Simple. Keeping things simple was the key to his extraordinary success.

Deer. He often thought of deer when he worked, it helped keep his mind detached, aware yet emotionally uninvolved. You had to be that way. Hunting deer. *They* seemed to know when they were being stalked. It was part of their lives, and they seldom made it easy for the hunter. Humans were just the opposite – even those who should know better. But in the end it came down to the same thing: eyes. Deer and humans. They stared back at that ultimate moment with huge, sad eyes – the only difference being that deer accepted what was happening to them. Humans looked at you as if to say, "How can you do this to me? It isn't fair!" At that point he'd always end it quickly.

The man in the olive-green sweatsuit took another deep breath, which he expelled as a sigh of resignation. Keeping his eyes fastened on the figure a hundred feet ahead, he sped up a bit, carefully matching his pace to hers.

Since he didn't have to do anything about the girl at the moment, maybe he'd catch a movie this evening. When he needed her, she'd be here.

Same time. Same place.

CHAPTER I

—✺—

> Attractive, SWF, 5′7″, slender, dirty-blond hair,
> heavily into music, baseball, and what really
> matters in life, needs help with some things,
> looking for a regular guy between 30 and 45 who's
> sensitive, sensible, and unattached. Let's arrange
> to meet and talk. Photo definitely not necessary.

"What do we put down for a phone number?" I asked. "I don't want any of these bozos calling here."

After almost an hour of hysterically funny and incredibly ribald repartee, my friends had refined the wording of the companion ad to something that made me only *slightly* uncomfortable. Put it down to too much beer that they'd talked me into this in the first place. It was Susan who'd brought up the subject. She thought that I was spending too much time on my own, brooding about my problems, that I needed to get out more, meet new people, in short that I needed a "steady guy." Everything had started off playfully enough, but now that we'd produced hard copy, the project was rapidly losing whatever meagre lustre it had held for me.

"Heavens, Kit! They're not bozos," Susan corrected. "One of them could be Mr. Right."

"That's no problem," Carolina said, actually answering my question. "We'll use the voice-mail service the newspaper offers. Anybody whose interest you pique can leave a message. All you have to do is call in and play it back. If you don't like the sound of the guy, erase him! You never have to come into contact with anyone you don't want to."

Jackie shifted on her favourite beanbag chair. "And if you decide to meet the guy, one of us should go along."

"Are you going to do a financial and police check, too?" I challenged.

Marion giggled. "Only if you get serious." She definitely sounded two sheets to the wind.

We'd gone to see the Blue Jays play a spring-training game at the SkyDome. Afterwards, since I lived nearby, we'd come back to my place to finish the evening in what *I* thought was going to be some idle chatter about the upcoming ball season.

I've known these women since our days at the University of Toronto. Carolina had posted an inquiry about forming a team to play in a girl's fast-pitch softball league. The Ruthless Babes had been the result. The five of us had bonded permanently, because of our love of the game. The team's still going strong eleven years later, and we're the last of the original members. I used to be a solid shortstop and occasionally pitched, too, but these days all I'm able to do is keep score and go out for beer after the game. I'd gladly give a year of my life to be able to hit and catch and throw in just one more game.

We'd ordered pizza from Guido's joint down on the first floor of my building, an old, four-storey walk-up on Queen Street, west of Spadina Avenue in downtown Toronto. As the pizza arrived, the Babes sprang their brilliant idea on me. Several beers later, they were still hard at work trying to convince me their new scheme was a really terrific idea.

By the time they wobbled down to the communal taxi and I wobbled to bed, four out of the five of us thought everything would work out beautifully. Susan had already begun planning my wedding.

I was the only one with doubts. And they were *big* ones.

The next morning I wanted to dismiss the previous evening's she-nanigans as a bad dream, but after I got back from taking Shadow, my coal-black Newfoundland guide dog, for his morning constitutional, I found matters had progressed in my absence. I played back a phone message from Carolina as I removed Shadow's harness.

"Kit, I hope you're feeling better than I am this morning. It's dangerous having the five of us together. Know what I mean? My body isn't up to it any more. Edward could barely pry me out of bed to go running with him. Anyway, you'll be glad to know the ad is all arranged. It'll be in this week's paper. I can't wait to see what transpires! Talk to you later. Bye."

Glad *she* felt so excited. Every time *I* thought about the whole endeavour, a little voice inside my head started sing-songing "Dumb-ass, dumb-ass . . ."

I sat in the kitchen brooding over a cup of coffee while Shadow chowed down, but my reverie was soon interrupted by the phone. Walking into the living room, I flopped down on the sofa and picked up the receiver. "Talk to me."

The voice at the other end sounded startled at my abrupt greeting. "Uh, Kit Mason?"

"That's me. Who's this?"

"It's Nick from Complete Sound."

My mood blackened further. This whole companion-ad thing was the bitter end of something that had begun at Nick's place of employment about five days earlier.

I'd thought my songwriting career might finally be getting off the ground when a mutual friend introduced me to Robbie Newman. He'd listened to my material, then told me he had connections with some big-shots in L.A. We could put together a demo with a couple of musicians and a singer he knew, and he'd use that to get a deal. Bells should have gone off when Shadow growled at Robbie the first time they met. Come to think of it, the Babes had growled, too.

No, I'd gotten good and suckered, that's all. It was my own fault. I had believed what Robbie told me – and besides, *I* had liked him. So, over the objections of guide dog and friends, I'd decided to work with him. Talk about dumb-ass moves.

Nick continued. "Look, Kit, I'm calling about what happened the other night."

"There's no need. Robbie's a slimeball. You were only doing your job. I wouldn't want you getting in trouble with your boss. Robbie didn't pay his bills and you had to kick us out. I would've done the same thing."

"Thanks for understanding. But that's not the reason I called. I've been listening to those tracks, and Robbie left one of your home tapes here, too. Your material is really good. It deserves to be recorded."

"That's very nice of you, Nick, maybe someday it –"

"You don't understand. I'd like to approach my boss and see if he'd be willing to back production for the rest of the demo."

That stopped me short. "Really?"

"Yes, really," he said patiently.

"But where are we going to get a singer? I'm sure as hell not going to use that little twit girlfriend of Robbie's."

That was the part of this dirty misadventure that *really* hurt. Besides trying to help me get my songs considered in the City of Angels, Robbie had been trying hard to get into my jeans, and I'd been seriously toying with the idea of letting him. When Nick informed Robbie the previous Monday that he couldn't let us continue since Robbie hadn't paid for any of the time we'd used, I'd been pretty upset. Especially since Robbie had told me his connections in L.A. were picking up the tab. But that was nothing compared to the way I felt after the next little revelation slipped out.

"C'mon, Nick," Robbie had whined, "we're just about done! If you like, we'll can the rest of the overdubs and just do the lead vocals. I can have Leslie out here in twenty minutes, ready to go."

Nick obviously didn't know about Robbie putting the make on me, because he said, "Leslie? Give me a break! You're not still trying to get your old lady a recording deal, are you? She may be a pretty good painter, but she sure can't sing!"

You could have heard *half* a pin drop. I was dying to see the expression on Robbie's face. He tried on a few lame explanations before Shadow and I *both* growled at him. After airing it out for about five minutes at high volume, I grabbed the handle on my trusty guide dog and stormed out of the control room. Since I didn't know precisely where the studio was and didn't feel like wandering the streets looking for a bus stop, I fell back on Susan, my surrogate mommy, and talked her into driving in from Mississauga to pick me up. That also gave me over an hour to get myself pulled back together. Robbie must have ducked out a back door, because he certainly didn't come through the lobby. Which was lucky, 'cause

I'd given Shadow permission to eat him. And to think I'd almost offered him the keys to the kingdom. Using *my* songs to get his bimbo-girlfriend-I-didn't-even-know-about a contract! *Bastard*!

Nick interrupted my thoughts. "Kit? You still there?"

I shook my head and sighed. "Yeah. I was just thinking."

"About my offer?"

"Among other things."

"Well?"

"There's still the problem of the vocals. Who do we get to sing?"

"You," Nick said simply. "You sing your own material on those tapes I heard."

"That's different. We're talking about something that record execs will listen to. I sound like a frog with a sore throat!"

"So do Kim Carnes, and Rod Stewart, and Joe Cocker, and they make a pretty good living."

"Yeah, but they sing blues or bluesy stuff. What I write is hardly like that. I hear my material sung by someone with a light, clear voice, more feminine-sounding, less Kim Carnes, more Jann Arden. Besides, the purpose of the demo is to sell my songs, not me!"

"That's where I think you're wrong. You're not hearing what I'm hearing. There's something there in your voice, Kit, and I think it *does* suit your material – which could use a bit of toughening up, truth be told."

"I don't know . . ."

"Think about it, Kit. I'll call back when I get a chunk of free time here, and we'll get those vocal tracks down so I can play them for the boss. Okay?"

"But I'm a songwriter," I persisted.

"Think about it."

Naturally, Sue had told the other three about what'd happened with Robbie. Tickets to the ball game miraculously appeared over-night. And would you believe, for the first time since Christmas, every one of the Babes had nothing on their social calendars? When I lost my sight, they seem to think I'd also lost my wits. At least they had the decency not to ruin the game for me. We'd all gotten settled back at my apartment, beers in hand, before Jackie, in her usual fashion, had gotten the discussion rolling with all the subtlety of a runaway bulldozer.

"You know, Kit, I never trusted Robbie. That little –"

"Jackie!" Carolina said. "Can't you see Kit's upset enough?"

"I'm not upset! I'm just down about the whole thing, that's all. Aren't I allowed to be depressed now and then?"

"No!" they all said in unison, and broke up laughing.

"You really crack yourselves up, don't you?"

Marion moved over next to me on the sofa and took my hands. "Kit, you know how you get when things go wrong. We don't like to see you hurt." She paused, then asked gently, "What happened? You didn't tell Susan very much."

I gave them the dirty details.

"Robbie has a *girlfriend*?" Marion asked when I finished.

I nodded. "A live-in. For the past two years." I decided I didn't want to talk about it any more. "Who wants more beer?"

After taking orders for four (and red wine for Carolina), I went to the kitchen and couldn't find the damn bottle opener. Jackie insists on bringing these obscure European brands, and they haven't heard of twist tops over there. Then, adding insult to the injury of a freshly corrugated hand, she doesn't hang up the opener in its usual spot.

While I pawed around the counters looking for it, I heard a *sotto voce* conversation from the living room. I raised my eyes heavenward – a habit that hasn't died yet – wondering what my friends were cooking up now. They view themselves as my protectors, something that, even though it springs from the best intentions, can be a royal pain in the backside. I scooped up the bottle caps, dumped them in the garbage, and carefully navigated the drinks into the living room. Conversation ceased the moment I appeared in the doorway.

After handing things out and downing half my bottle, I asked, "Okay. What are you guys up to now?"

"I *told* you she'd hear us," Marion said.

"Come on, out with it! I didn't hear any more than whispering."

Susan said, "We know you never thought Robbie was the answer to your dreams, but you really enjoyed being with him. We were just talking about helping you find a guy that, um . . ."

"That I could have a long-term relationship with?" I interrupted testily. Silence greeted my comment. I'd complained about just that thing far too often, and it was only because they got me angry that I blasted off at them. But we all knew it was true. I never could seem to find a decent guy. My theme song should be "Unlucky in Love." I took another swig of beer. "Do you know any single guys I might like?" Silence again. "No? Well, what the hell am I supposed to do? Take out a companion ad?"

Marion laughed delightedly. "What a great idea! Kit, you're brilliant!"

"I wasn't serious!"

"Oh come on, Kit," Susan said, "Who knows what nice things could happen? At the very least, it'll be a real hoot."

"It sounds to me like an idea worth pursuing," Carolina added.

Jackie belched loudly. "Go for it. At least it'll keep you off the streets."

Like I said, sometimes I make dumb-ass moves. I remember thinking that too much beer after the first ball game of the season and then letting the Babes talk me into their hare-brained scheme might make this another in an ever-lengthening line of DAMs.

———ɷ———

FROWNING, THE MAN REPLACED THE BARBELL on the stand above his head and got up from the bench. He should have let the answering machine do its job, but he had a feeling the call might be important.

Crossing the living room, he picked up the receiver. "Yes?"

"It's me," said the voice at the other end. "We need you to look into something for us."

"Is it part of this job?"

"Yes. Check the girl's place. We think she's been collecting information and it may be stored there. How long will it take?"

"How big an area do I have to search?"

"Not big, a few rooms, bath and kitchen. There's a computer and a ton of books, though."

"Depends then. If she hid it well, maybe eight, nine hours."

"We don't think she'd do that. She has no reason to expect anyone knows."

"Maybe three hours, then. Four, max."

"Okay. We'll make sure she's out of the way for, say, five hours, then give you a call."

"Will it be today?"

"I doubt it, but stay close to the phone. And remember: this job has to be discreet. We can't let her know that anything is going on."

The man smiled. "Should be no problem at all. Money?"

"Will five thousand do?"

After a pause, the man countered, "Make it seventy-five hundred."

"All right. Now, here's what you're going to be looking for . . ."

When he hung up, he crossed back to his exercise area. Grabbing two twenty-pound dumbbells, he began doing bicep curls, all the while thinking about what he'd need for this new task. He hoped they'd call back soon and tell him they were ready for him to do the girl as well. This assignment was taking too long. He had other things he'd rather spend his time on.

CHAPTER 2

—⟋⟍—

The night after the ball game, Jackie and I went to an Irish pub for a wee bit o' the old sod on St. Paddy's Day. You can imagine the silence that greeted our entrance. First came me, with a dog that looked like a stand-in for Smokey the Bear, closely followed by a fugitive from a headbangers convention.

If she wanted, Jackie Goode could be quite pretty – in a conventional sense. Generally, though, she wears her hair short and jaggy, variously coloured purple, blue, or even green, and she currently sports a ring in her nose. From the way she acts, you might think she's a dyke, then find out *very* differently if she's in the mood. Jackie's the youngest of the Babes, just turned twenty-nine. She's my height, but all muscle, which comes from being a bicycle courier. It's not a good idea to crowd *her* plate when she's pitching, because you're risking a fastball in your ear.

Jackie can be pretty hard to get along with, and if you only knew her casually, you'd probably think she's perpetually angry. She'll always take a contrary viewpoint in any discussion. One year, for a joke birthday present, we gave her a two-foot pin to help her puncture everyone's balloons more easily. Jackie laughed louder than anyone over that.

That's only part of the story, though. Say you're moving and need someone to slug countless boxes up and down stairs, Jackie's there. Grumpy, maybe, but she'll work until she drops. When I was at my lowest ebb over my impending blindness, I could always count on her to show up at the right time, distracting me from something that was pretty overwhelming to deal with, usually by getting me angry at something she'd said. In short, you could always count on Jackie Goode when you needed help, and I'd go a long way to do the same for her. All the Babes would.

We found an empty table in the corner, and I made Shadow curl up under it. Waitresses tend to find his black hide difficult to spot in the dim light of a bar – and even harder to scramble over.

As we were leaving my place, Marion had called to say she'd been putting in some weekend work and was on her way downtown, so could she join us? Jackie and I had just ordered two pints of Guinness when she arrived.

"Hi, Kit! Jackie. Top o' the evenin' to ye!" she chirped in a miserable attempt at an Irish accent, and sat down, causing Shadow to shift against my feet. "I hope you don't mind me barging in like this, but Tony's off playing hockey with some of his buds, so I had nothing to do. God! I've had the worst day in a long time."

"Working on what should be your day off will do that to you." I smiled, hoping she wouldn't go on.

Marion worked just north of the city, up in Richmond Hill some place, and she took her job very seriously – too seriously sometimes. She told everyone that she was an executive secretary, and I suppose she was, but basically the place wasn't large enough for her to have that kind of title. Carolina thought they'd given it to her so that she wouldn't leave, because even though Marion could be a pain in the butt, she was also exceptionally conscientious and hard-working.

The place was a laboratory with about twenty employees, which did contract work for various firms around Southern Ontario that didn't do enough work to have a lab of their own. Everything Marion told me about it generally went in one ear and out the other, but I'd gathered they did some sort of chemical testing.

Marion constantly told us that the guy who owned the place was a brilliant scientist, and at one time we all thought she might be harbouring a crush on him. Not that she would have acted on it.

Marion would find it unthinkable to have anything to do with a married man, which her employer was. All I knew was that she'd really liked working there – until about a month before.

That was when her boss had been killed in a car accident on his way home from work late one night. Everyone at the place had been devastated, especially Marion, who'd worked with the good doctor closely. I can't describe the state she was in when she called to tell me the sad news. The funeral was terrible but I'd been the only one available to go with her, and poor Mar needed all the moral support she could get. It hadn't been a fun experience.

"It's not working overtime," Marion snapped, and her tone made it clear that she was pretty tense behind her falsely cheerful front. "Things have been simply awful at work since Dr. Sloane passed away."

"In what way?" I asked. Jackie just grunted, showing that she was sort of listening. Jackie finds Marion's talk about work exceptionally tedious. Hell, she finds anyone's talk about work tedious.

"The day after the funeral, these businessmen no one had ever seen before showed up at the lab and said they were taking over the day-to-day running of the place. Claimed that they actually *owned* it."

"What?"

"They called all the employees together and told us that Doc Sloane had come to them for some investment money a year or so back, and now that there was no longer anyone there to run the business due to his tragic death, blah, blah blah. . . . The long and short of it is that I have a new boss."

"Can they just do that?" I asked. "What about Sloane's wife?"

"I called her up as soon as they arrived and dropped their little bombshell. Mrs. Sloane's lawyer says that these people *do* have the controlling interest. Seems the Doc needed more money than he originally planned to put in that new testing equipment last year – a lot more – and went to this investment group for venture capital. He never even told his poor wife about it. You can imagine what a shock that was on top of everything else! She doesn't know whether to try to sell out her share or hang on, the poor thing."

Jackie took a swig of her beer. "At least you still have a job. They could have just closed the place down."

"Gee, *thanks* for that, Jackie," Marion fired back, but she sounded like she was smiling. The two of them enjoyed lobbing verbal grenades at each other.

"How are things running?" I asked.

"It's pretty much business as usual, I guess, but a lot of the fun, the camaraderie, has gone out of the place. Doc S was like everyone's older brother and he always made sure we got along. You know how hard that can be when you put a bunch of pretty intelligent people together in a small place. He made us all feel important. We always discussed things together and came to a consensus. Now we're just told to jump and we're expected to do it without complaining – even when it's pretty unreasonable. The worst thing is the new boss. Talk about micromanaging! This jerk brings a whole new level of meaning to the term!"

A waitress coming over to take Marion's order interrupted the story, but Marion continued as soon as she'd left. "So I went in today to try to get caught up on some work I haven't been able to do because of other things they've been giving me. Quite often I used to do the bookkeeping-type things right in Doc Sloane's office, because it was easier than having to run back and forth from my office to his. He was usually in one of the labs anyway. I'm sitting there working, minding my own business. The place is nice and quiet, just a few people around finishing up some overdue reports and the like, when the guy who's been acting as the manager since this all went down storms in and tells me to clear out. He said I had no right to be in *his* office without *his* permission. You wouldn't believe how rude he was!"

"Did you try to explain?" Jackie asked.

Marion sounded exasperated. "He wouldn't give me a chance! Part of the problem was that one of the first things he did was change the lock on the office door. Doc S never even bothered to shut the darn thing, let alone lock it! Today it was open and I just walked in like I used to. I thought that maybe this new guy was loosening up a little. Boy, was I wrong! The man just stood there screaming at me about how, if I couldn't be trusted, then I'd have to be let go. It was just awful!"

I asked, "What happened then?"

"He actually grabbed me by the arm and led me out of the office!"

"I would punched him out," Jackie growled.

"I'm sure everyone in the place heard him airing me out, but they didn't say anything in my defence – not that I think it would have done any good. Everyone's scared of him. The whole thing was just *awful*," Marion repeated yet again. "I'm still shaking."

"You need another beer."

While eating big plates of corned beef and cabbage, we listened to a duo of button accordion and guitar the pub had hired for the occasion. They did quite a good job with various traditional Irish songs, but they must have gone through "Danny Boy" three times before finishing their set. Throughout the meal, Jackie and Marion surreptitiously fed Shadow, something I usually don't allow. They're like children sometimes, thinking that, because I can't see them, I don't know what they're doing. I didn't bother to say anything.

"If I have to listen to that damn song once more, I'm going to puke," Jackie said loudly as she pushed back her plate. That must have earned her more than her share of ugly stares from the largely Irish crowd. She lit one of those awful French cigarettes and blew out a noxious cloud. Normally, my friends know better than to smoke around me, but I guess she felt safe because of the already thick atmosphere. "Look, can we go somewhere else?"

Since my apartment was only a few blocks away on Queen Street, and Marion was bagged anyway, we headed there. Marion held onto my free arm all the way, her tension transmitting itself to me loud and clear. I began to be concerned. She's seldom anything other than relaxed and happy, but lately there'd been something bothering her, and not just this mess with her job. I can be pretty sensitive to a lot of unspoken things these days. Uncharacteristically, though, Marion hadn't been yammering on and on about it. My guess was she'd run into a rough patch with her boyfriend, Tony.

Shadow, eager to make an early night of it, hustled us along the last two blocks. Jackie stumped along silently behind, puffing furiously on a cigarette.

"Does anyone want coffee?" I asked as we came through the door. Receiving two positive answers, I went to the kitchen and plugged in the electric kettle, I heard the TV being switched on – Jackie catching up on the fortunes of the Leafs. I keep the set around for my friends. For electronic companionship, I prefer the radio or my stereo.

A whiff of Chanel No. 5 from the doorway told me that Marion was standing there. "Kit?"

I closed the fridge, put the milk on the counter, and sighed. "Okay, Marion, let's talk."

"Well, you know how I hate confrontations. That man had no right to speak to me like that, and I couldn't do a thing about it!"

"Well, you *were* in what should have been a locked office," I pointed out. "Some people tend to get pretty upset about incursions into their territory."

"That's what makes *me* so upset. Everyone else who works at the lab is really nice and Doc Sloane used to rely on me quite a bit. This new manager treats me as if all I should be doing is typing letters and bringing him coffee!"

As if on cue, Jackie called from the living room, "Where's that coffee?"

Marion and I both laughed and got busy making it. I took Jackie a mug, finding her sprawled on the sofa. "Mar and I will join you in a minute."

"No rush. The period just started."

I went back out to the kitchen. Marion slid my mug over as I sat down on one of my two kitchen chairs. "Thanks."

She sighed heavily. "I was just trying to do was what I thought was my job! All sorts of records haven't been updated in quite a while – to be honest, my old boss wasn't as good about paperwork as he should have been – and I was just trying to get everything organized. All kinds of things had been moved around."

"Look, the guy's obviously a total jerk. Just be thankful you aren't stuck in the job if you don't choose to be. There are lots of places that could use a person with your abilities."

"I've already thought about that."

What I didn't say was that Marion Joseph couldn't bring herself to stand up to anyone, and that's probably all this guy needed. Bullies are always like that. But I kept my mouth shut. No sense opening *that* can of worms again. I've watched people walk all over Marion since the day we met.

After she passed thirty about a year back, though, there had been a change, and she'd seemed more in command. Part of it had to do with the fact that, through a ton of hard work and dieting, she'd lost over thirty pounds. On a person who's only five-three that's a lot of baggage. With her frizzy brown hair, which she usually wore pulled back, the total effect would, I imagine, look pretty cute. That cute package had recently snagged a boyfriend at her health club, whom Carolina described as "dangerously handsome." But deep down, Marion was still what we used to call her: Short 'n' Sweet. And that was the problem. She wouldn't think badly of someone until they stabbed her in the back. Come to think of it, she might think they had stumbled and the knife slipped in by accident.

"What should I *do*, Kit?"

I leaned back in my chair. "You have to make up your mind whether you want to work there any longer or not. Don't think you're going to be able to make this guy behave like a decent human being. He doesn't sound the type to me. Weigh the working conditions against what they pay you and then decide if it's worth it."

"Damn!" Marion said, "I used to really believe in what I was doing up there. It was a good job."

"Is that the only thing that's bugging you?" I asked, hoping that, since she was in a gabby mood, I might get some info on whatever else had been bothering her for far longer than this present bump on the road of life.

"No," Marion answered far too quickly. "Nothing else is bothering me. Why do you ask?"

"No reason."

Oh well, I thought. *It will come out sooner or later. It usually does with Marion.*

We went into the living room and sat with Jackie until the end of the game. I don't know how much Marion concentrated on it, but my mind wasn't on the game or her problems. I stewed over Nick's recording offer the whole time.

Before they left, I made arrangements with Marion to dogsit Shadow the following Tuesday when I had my weekly coffee-house gig. I can't take my mutt, because the hole-in-the-wall place I play has no dressing room, and the woman I accompany has a voice that hurts his ears. A howling dog doesn't do much for a folk duo.

On Sunday nowadays, I get up around 9:00. Actually, I always get up by 9:00. If I don't, Shadow will come in and yank off the covers: potty-time. I wish I could paper-train the big dope, except that I'd need at least one copy of the *Sunday Times* for each dump.

So, up betimes, to hie myself to the coffee shop down the street (with a poop stop on the way), where I enjoy a cup of fresh-brewed and a croissant or a Danish and hear the local news. If I'm feeling expansive, I occasionally break my rule and buy Shadow a little something, too. I have to feed him surreptitiously, though, because the Noviks, who own the place, just barely tolerate him. They tried to refuse us entry the first time we came in, until I loudly said that, if they did, I would report them to the authorities. Always use the word "authorities" when dealing with people from the Eastern Bloc. It works wonders. It also didn't hurt to flash my guide-dog ID which prominently says "Violators may be fined up to $1,000."

Mrs. Novik brought me one of her apricot Danishes (my fave) and coffee the minute I sat down. She'd come to like me, but her husband remained sulky. "Kit, dear, I make special for you. Maybe eat two. You look very thin lately."

I smiled. Mrs. Novik thinks that anyone who isn't as fat as she is, is too thin. "Thank you, Mrs. N, but no. One is enough." Even if I can't *see*, I want to *look* good. Just to make sure that I didn't gain any weight, Shadow scored half the Danish. I prayed that Mrs. N's back was turned.

While we munched away, someone walked up to my table. "Well, Kit, how are you on this fine morning? Mind if I join you?"

It was one of my downstairs neighbours, Gerald Davies. Quite often on Sundays our paths cross at Novik's. He's addicted to their cinnamon coffee cake. Gerald's about fifty (he won't admit his exact age), a successful advertising exec, and gay. He didn't tell me that himself. He'd figure it doesn't have anything to do with our friendship. Know-it-all Jackie told, not that it bothered me. She tends to be a little touchy on the subject, though.

Gerald often reads my mail for me, helping to sort the wheat from the chaff, as it were, but the best part of our relationship is that he reads me the Sunday paper. He swears it isn't because he feels sorry for me. He says he *likes* to read out loud.

I spent the first seventeen years of my life in the States – Westport, Connecticut, to be exact – and only came to Canada when my mom returned after she and dad called it quits. The *Sunday Times* had always been an important part of my youthful weekends, once I outgrew comics. So, we usually pick up a copy at the variety store on the corner, go back to his place or mine, and enjoy the news from New York. Gerald also makes a mean café au lait.

"You girls had quite a wild time the other night," he said.

"Sorry if we disturbed you. We got rather silly, I'm afraid."

"May I inquire as to the cause?"

"They talked me into putting a companion ad in the paper. All the noise was us trying to come up with the perfect wording." Putting down my coffee cup, I stuffed the final piece of Danish into my mouth. "Know what a BC/LD is?" I asked around the crumbs.

"I have no idea."

"Neither did I. It means Big Car/Little Dick. You see, Carolina has this theory that the size and expense of a man's car is in inverse proportion to the size of his pecker. That's the kind of important stuff we were discussing."

Gerald laughed uproariously. "Women can be more crude than men sometimes. Well anyway, I wish you luck in your search, my dear." His chair scraped on the floor. "Have time for the paper?"

"You bet."

Gerald and I spent the rest of the morning at his place finding out about the past week's happenings in the Big Apple, drinking coffee, and talking about life, the universe, and everything. One of the subjects that I brought up was Nick's offer to finish the demo.

"You used to be involved in the music biz. What do you think of my singing, Gerald?"

He was silent for a moment – probably trying to think of a tactful way to put the truth. "It's more suited to hard rock or heavy metal, I think, but there's something in the way you sing that's attractive despite the gravelly quality. You should trust this engineer's judgment, if he's as good as you say."

"How come nobody else was interested in my singing before? An agent actually laughed at me one time. I couldn't stand that happening again."

"Kit, I wouldn't lie to you about something this important. Try it. The worst you can do is fail – and you just might surprise yourself. If you don't try it, you fail for sure."

Gerald had to go out for lunch, so I headed upstairs shortly after 11:30.

I pulled out one of my acoustic guitars and put in some time practising scales and modes just to keep the old fingers strong. Eventually my mind started to wander, and I began fooling around with a neat little chord progression. Before long I also had a melody to go with it.

My hands were pretty tired by that point, but I was energized and wanted to keep working. So I went into the bedroom and pulled my rowing machine out of the closet. I don't seem to be able to create unless I'm moving. When I was younger, I used to think up lyrics by going for a walk and letting things turn over in my brain. Nowadays I can't do it that easily. Even with Shadow watching out for me, I have to keep my mind on where I'm going. It's kind of embarrassing to suddenly realize you have no idea where you are or how you got there, and that makes it difficult to lose oneself in the creative process. So, two Christmases ago, I got my dad to buy me one of those rowing machines, complete with a timer to let me know when I'm exhausted.

By the time my muscles were toasted, I had the bare bones of a dynamite song taking shape. This wouldn't be a doe-eyed tear-jerker. It was an uptempo rocker, one of those tunes that really kicks butt. I got out my electric, a Fender Telecaster my old teacher had grown tired of, and experimented with a few different things using my original chords, settling on a chunka-chunka rhythm that seemed to fit pretty well with the melody and lyrics I had. Then I recorded the whole thing on my four-track home-recording studio and felt that I'd done a good day's work – that is, if I still liked the song when I played it back the next morning.

After a dinner straight from the kitchen of some frozen-food maker, I took Shadow for his evening walk, gave him a thorough combing, and yakked on the phone with Carolina for a while.

She told me about a convicted serial killer, a real sick puppy according to the accounts of his trial two years earlier, who had been brought into Toronto for some kind of psychiatric examination and managed to just walk away from the hospital. The public, whose sentiments were being fanned by some highly inflammatory reporting and editorials, had its shorts in a major knot, and the administration of the hospital, as well as the cops, were working overtime to cover their butts. Not very good bedtime conversation, I'm afraid. It was Carolina's way of telling me to be careful. But even with her warning, the apartment felt more claustrophobic than ever. I let Shadow sleep on the bed with me.

I'd been backing up this folk singer at a coffee house in the west end of Toronto on Tuesday nights for almost a year. Carolina had called to ask if she could go with me. So two nights later, since neither of us drive, we hopped on the streetcar and eventually a bus, and she babbled throughout the trip. You must understand that Carolina Graf never babbles. I often think she goes over what she wants to say two or three times in her head before she actually spits it out. Something had to be making her unsettled.

The gig went the way it usually did. Glynis sang her dopey songs about unicorns and butterflies and guys who've run out on her. Now I don't claim to know this woman very well, but I can sympathize with the poor suckers who take up with her. From what everyone tells me, she's drop-dead gorgeous, blond hair to her waist and the kind of body men admire and other women hate. She does have a decent voice, and the melodies of her songs aren't bad. It's just the sentiments she expresses are so – I don't know – *cloying* might be the most charitable word. Unfortunately, Glynis is also that way in real life. I met her through Marion. She and Marion are very close and it's obvious why Marion likes her. She still has all her stuffed toys in her bedroom, too.

From the lack of noise in the club, I could tell that we didn't have a very good house again. It would only be a matter of time before they either got a new Tuesday-night act or the place went belly-up. It had been growing in my mind that I'd reached the end of the road with Glyn, anyway, and that night settled it for me. I told her after the last set that I wouldn't be back the next week and offered to find a suitable stand-in. She cried a little, but I think she'd seen it coming. We parted on good terms, and I felt as if a big weight had been lifted – but it was only the one on my foot, not my chest. I still had to come to a decision about the demo.

Carolina sat impatiently through our three sets and breaks, but steadfastly avoided discussing whatever was bothering her. It wasn't until we got out the door and stood waiting for the bus that she said softly, "Kit?"

"Ready to talk?"

"Am I so obvious?"

I nodded and smiled. "Yeah."

"I've done something very stupid."

"In what way?"

"Well, it involves you. You know how I'm chairing that committee to fight the big development near my neighbourhood?"

Carolina lives with her man at the bottom end of Cabbagetown, an old neighbourhood just east of downtown. At one time it had been down-at-the-heel. Then the yuppies started moving in during the seventies and fixed up the old houses. Now it costs dearly to buy there. Just two blocks away, on the other side of Gerrard Street, is Regent Park, Toronto public housing at its not-very-good: drugs, gangs, the kind of place where you don't want to bring up your kids.

Some developers had got hold of a huge parcel of land to the south and east of Regent Park, the site of factories and warehouses, long since closed. They proposed to move the Regent Park denizens into new digs that they'd build down there. In turn, the city would trade a section at the north end of Regent Park and allow them to build high-rise luxury condos, office towers, and the like, one of those multi-purpose developments cities are so fond of nowadays.

What was the problem? First off, the Regent Park people didn't want to move. Home wasn't that swell, but the proposed site at the crotch of two major expressways would leave even more to be desired, regardless of the fact that the buildings would be brand new. The Cabbagetown folk living just north of the proposed development would probably never see the sun again with huge buildings blocking it, so they weren't pleased either – and *they* had big-time political clout.

Carolina had been volunteered to chair the local Action Committee, and I could see why they'd wanted her. She'd already scored major points debating the media flack for the development on a cable TV show two weeks earlier. Carolina's performance had been so good, in fact, the local newspapers had said she could become a serious roadblock in the path of the developers. It probably hadn't hurt that she looked the way she did, either.

Everything about Carolina oozes elegance, even the way she pronounces her name: *Caroleena*. It comes from her breeding, I guess, fifth-generation blueblood and all that. She'd look great on TV: tall and slender, with penetrating hazel eyes and a smile that can be devilish and light up the world at the same time. I think she's working on degree number four now, and living with Edward, her former faculty advisor, who's trying to turn her into a long-distance runner, like he is. At thirty-two, C's the *grande dame* of our group. They tell me her long brown hair is showing the slightest inklings of premature grey, and she had to get glasses last fall. Probably comes from slaving over all those theses. With her height (5'11"), you can see why she's the Babes' regular at first base.

I could picture her standing on one foot, waiting for me to answer, so I said, "Spit the whole thing out."

"We're going to hold a big rally to stop the development and, ah, I sort of volunteered you to write, ah, to write a song for it."

"You *what*?" I shrieked.

"Now don't get mad, Kit," she interrupted. "I know I should have asked you first, but you know how it is. We all got a little too enthusiastic about the idea. The rally's in three weeks." She grabbed my arm. "This is really important. The Regent Park people need your help. Their backs are against the wall. The city should be improving where they live now, not shuffling them off to some godforsaken corner. We've uncovered other things about the development that are making us very uneasy, too. It must be stopped!"

"And then there's the matter of no sun on lower Cabbagetown . . ."

"Goddammit, Kit! You know me better than that!"

"Sorry. Look, C, you know I can't write songs to order."

"And you won't even try?"

I shook my head vigorously. "Absolutely not."

"I suppose," she said slowly, "I could ask Glynis. She might do it."

"*Glynis?* Are you kidding? She'd give you a song about elves living under mushrooms. You need something hard-hitting, something with punch. Glynis would get you laughed at." I shut my mouth suddenly. Carolina was only trying to push my buttons. She thinks Glynis is a goof, too.

"See, Kit? You know what to do. I just thought that it would be a great opportunity for you. One of the guys on the committee works for CTV and he's promised some big coverage, maybe even an exposé on their current-events show."

"The answer's still no."

Carolina leaned close to my ear. "Coast-to-coast coverage, Kit."

I turned my back and thought it over until the bus arrived. We got on in silence. It wasn't until a few blocks later that I said, "Okay, I'll help you out of this mess."

"That's great! I know you won't regret this."

Yeah, right.

—⁄⁄⁄—

AFTER SLIPPING ON HIS GLOVES, THE MAN tried the door. Locked. Not too many people were careless about that any more, but it was worth a try. Oh well, he thought, pulling a set of picks from his pocket. Looking around to make sure he was unobserved, he went to work. In a matter of seconds, he opened the door and stepped inside.

Knowing that he had three hours for certain, he began searching each room methodically. With luck, he would have enough time to find what his employers required. But this couldn't be one of those slash-and-smash searches, either. No one could know he'd been there. That would be too dangerous for the hit he had set up.

The man didn't often perform this type of service. It was not his specialty, but he was good at it and enjoyed the change it provided. Several years ago he'd honed his skills by methodically breaking into every apartment in his building. No one had ever known someone had invaded their living space, violated their privacy, sometimes even while they were at home.

Searching the computer took the longest time. He detested the things. You could hide a ton of information on them, and almost every file had to be opened and inspected, because they were the most logical place to store the information he'd been dispatched to look for. At least he'd been provided with the password, so he didn't have to waste time figuring that out or using his special hacking software.

One hour and forty-eight minutes later, the man looked up from the screen and rubbed his tired eyes, but he was smiling. A mere fifty-one minutes after that he was smiling again, this time in the bedroom. Okay, he knew exactly where he stood, and where she had put the things he'd be removing. When the time came, he'd be ready to move in fast.

Checking to make sure everything was shipshape before leaving, the man allowed himself to wonder at how a person's life was not always reflected by the way they furnished their living space. On the surface they might appear to be one way, but if you searched underneath, behind things, rummaged through their drawers and closets, a totally different picture often emerged.

As he went on his way, the man felt thoughtful, contemplating what her friends and family would think if they knew the kind of things that went on here when no one was around to see. What would *she* think of him knowing?

CHAPTER 3

—〰—

Between talking things over with Carolina, getting her and Marion the Dogsitter (enthusiastic to the max about Carolina's proposal) out the door, and trying to quiet my cluttered brain, I barely managed five hours' sleep before Shadow rousted me from bed for his morning constitutional. Afterwards, I tried crawling back under the covers, but it didn't work.

Right about the time I managed to nod off again, the phone rang: Nick from the studio calling to tell me they had an opening that night – if I wanted to take him up on his offer. "I know it's short notice, but we've had a late cancellation. You interested?"

Decision time. I held my breath and took the plunge. "I guess. . . . Yeah, sure, Nick. When do you want me?"

"How 'bout 7:30?"

I said I'd be there and hung up. That put an end to any thoughts of sleep. My stomach started twitching right away. I knew I shouldn't be so nervous about singing my own songs, but I couldn't help it.

Playing guitar wouldn't have fazed me in the least. Other than writing songs, it's about all I've done since I lost my sight, and I'm pretty good at it, if I do say so myself. Not too many girls can play hot licks note-for-note with the guys. That ability used to land me some interesting part-time and summer work. When I turned twenty, for instance, I got a gig with an all-girl topless country band called Eight of a Kind. You know – there were *four* of us in the group. I lasted a week. Mom and Dad ganged up on me and that was it. Dad punched the manager's lights out when he tried to tell the old boy I'd signed a "legal and binding contract." That was also the last time I saw my parents agree on anything.

Shadow and I kept our trips outside as brief as possible that day due to the fact that T.O. was suffering through a late-winter storm. The weatherman had forecast only two inches, but a bitter wind off Lake Ontario blew right through my buckskin jacket and swirled snow in my face and down my neck. Everything taken together, spring never seemed further away. People hurried silently by as I waited on the sidewalk, shivering while my doggy did his thing. Afterwards, I had to scoop, something that ain't easy when you're cleaning up a small mountain of poop you can only smell, and everything around it is slushy. None of this improved my mood.

By five o'clock, I was tempted to phone Nick and call the whole thing off. Sue, whom I'd again commandeered to drive, blew in shortly after with food she'd picked up in Chinatown, a few blocks to the north.

Susan Quinn was the real "babe" of the Babes: blond hair she used to wear long and free (it's apparently cut in a more parental-looking bob now), an oval face with deep-blue eyes, and a body men would die for. Perhaps that explained why she was the only one who'd gotten married. Or maybe it was her June Cleaver Syndrome, as Carolina called it. You know: house in the 'burbs, 2.75 kids, a dog, a minivan. Sue used to write a lot of poetry, most of it bad, but she possessed the soul of an artist and understood my lyrics better than anyone else. She also still played a dynamite third base. Her husband, Paul, couldn't understand why a thirty-one-year-old mother of two would still find diving headlong to snag a hot grounder so enticing. He didn't get it. Softball was the only slightly outrageous thing Susan still allowed herself to do. It was kind of sad to see her rein in that way.

"I went to your special place and got all your favourites: barbecue pork *lo mein*, shrimp with lobster sauce, spring –"

"I can't eat. I'm so nervous right now, I feel like puking," I interrupted from where I sat huddled in the corner of the sofa.

She stopped in mid-bustle. "Kit, I just don't understand how you've become so insecure."

"I think I've done pretty well, all things considered!" I shot back.

"Then where's that devil-may-care attitude you used to have? Weren't you the one who took the dare to break into that frat house –"

"That was ages ago! You make it sound as if I'm afraid of everything now. I *know* I can play guitar. And I think I write pretty good songs. It's just that singing on this demo has me shitting a brick."

"Oh, Kit, dear Kit. If you play the guitar so well, how come you aren't doing it more? If you believe in your songs so much, why aren't you out there getting them recorded? The Kit I used to know would have kicked somebody's door down if she had to do it to get what she wanted."

"You're saying I don't try any more?" I asked angrily.

"Well, maybe . . . yes." Sue sat down next to me and took my hands in hers. "We've been talking, all of us. Your mom even called me a few weeks ago and –"

"My *mother*? What did *she* want? Probably for me to come home with my tail between my legs, if I know her."

"Kit, I know you two have had your differences, but she's worried about you."

"I don't need any more *mothering*. If I hadn't got out of that place, she would have smothered me – and you know it! I know she's still pissed off at me for going to Dad for the money to get my apartment, but tough."

Susan tried to sound understanding, but the telltale sigh before she spoke gave her away. "Kit, we've been through all that. You know I agree you made the right decision. We're all your friends. We care about you. It's just that everyone feels . . . You seem to have given up hope."

"Oh."

"Just 'oh'? That's all you can say?"

"What do you want me to do? Punch you in the nose?"

"That might be a start." I knew she was smiling. "Look, it's as plain as a pikestaff that you're ready to call off this recording session tonight. Don't do it!" She dropped my hands, got up, and walked over to the window. She stood for a long time, apparently thinking while watching the traffic pass below. "I have to say something and I don't know where to begin."

I wasn't about to give her a lead-in.

"Kit," she said, "you've been blind for six years now and you still haven't accepted it." I started to object but she cut me off. "Let me finish! You might *tell* all of us that you have, and heaven knows you handle the day-to-day things pretty impressively, but it's like your life's on hold, like you're still waiting for some miracle to happen. It won't! You're blind today and you're going to be blind tomorrow and the next day and the day after that. Accept it!" Susan's voice sank almost to a whisper. "Please. Accept it. And live with it."

I sat stunned. Every time I started to form the words for a denial, the sentence died on my lips. I'd never outwardly admitted to believing that my long darkness would ever end, but I had never completely given up hope. Worse though, she was right, I hadn't done anything with my life. Oh yeah, I wrote songs and backed up a semi-talented folksinger, but I hadn't *really* gotten on with my life. What was I going to do? Sit on my butt in an apartment my father paid for and write songs that no one but my friends heard? Oh Christ! No matter how much I tried to wriggle off Sue's hook, she had the barb stuck in real good.

"Kit? What are you thinking?"

I sighed. "Is it that obvious? Am I that much of a cripple?"

"You're not a cripple! It's simply harder for you to do certain things. But you have to face facts. Get on with your life! You still have the power to grab the brass ring, to soar with the eagles."

"Those are pretty hackneyed metaphors," I pointed out.

"Kit, be serious for once!"

We remained silent for a few minutes, while I sifted through the dusty remains of my dreams. What *did* I want? I wanted . . . I wanted my songs to be heard. Maybe I wanted to play in public again. Not whole nights of finger-picked acoustic bullshit, but real turn-up-the-volume-to-eleven, kick-the-audience-in-the-ass playing. I wanted a band. A good band that would inspire me, make me want to play better every night.

"What time is it, Sue?"

"Almost 6:00."

"Get your coat." I raised my voice. "Shadow! Get off your butt. We've got a session to do! Sue, would you grab my Telecaster while I get Shadow's harness on? I can do the solo on the first song better than that guy Robbie got to play it."

"That's the spirit, Kit!" Susan said delightedly, then stopped. "But what about the food?"

"Throw it in the car. We'll eat on the way. Do you want to drive or would you like me to?"

We were soon on our way. As I ate lukewarm *lo mein* out of an aluminum pan, my euphoria began to seep away. And while Sue chattered on about her kids, her house, and the upcoming ball season, doubts about my singing again slithered out of their dark holes. I made her stop at an LCBO to get a bottle of Southern Comfort.

Almost eight hours later, Susan poured me back into my apartment, helped me off with my clothes, and tucked me into bed. If nothing else, I'd accomplished one thing that evening: I was thoroughly and comprehensively pissed.

As the unseen room rotated around me, I grabbed for her arm. "Susan, please tell me. Was it any good?"

She stroked my hair with her free hand. "Kit, I don't think I've ever seen you work that hard. I was only hoping to get you going again; I didn't want you to burn out right before my eyes."

"No, no, no!" I said shaking my head. "Don't give me any of your nice mommy crap. Was my singing any good? I have to know!"

"You have no idea what it sounded like?" She sounded flabbergasted.

"Okay, I know I sang mostly in tune and I got the lyrics right, but I have no idea what my voice sounded like."

"That engineer, what's-his-name, thought it was good."

"Engineers are paid to say that stuff to the customers. They do it automatically."

"Kit, you always tell me to wait a day or two before deciding whether something is good or not. It's that way with my poetry. I always think something's awful when I first reread it." She laughed. "It isn't until a week later that I *know* it's awful!"

"Sue, you're sounding like me now."

"Maybe. Look, we're both exhausted. Get some sleep. I'll lock up on my way out."

Two late nights and a bottle of Southern Comfort had caught up with me and I suddenly felt incredibly sleepy. "Thanks for the food tonight . . . and everything else."

Susan's reply came from the doorway. "No problem." As she crossed the living room to the front door, she added, "I hope you don't feel *too* rotten in the morning."

I did.

My day got off to a great start with a warm, moist tongue about a mile wide, slobbering over my face. I pushed the big hairball off me and smacked the top of my talking clock radio. "The time is 10:44 a.m," it screeched at the top of its little electronic lungs.

"Oh Christ. Come here, baby," I said to Shadow. "I'm so sorry! Your poor bladder must be bursting." Which reminded me. Mine didn't feel very good, either.

After we'd both taken care of business, I opened three cans of his favourite food to make amends for the late hour and Shadow chowed down with gusto. The sound was enough to make someone with a cast-iron stomach queasy, so I decided to escape to the bathroom for a much-needed shower. While I luxuriated in its steamy embrace, I tried piecing together my blurred impressions of the previous evening.

For most musicians, being in a recording studio is like going back to the womb, creatively speaking. Usually built windowless, with carpeting on the walls as well as the floors, and a ton of other acoustic-deadening materials, they seem designed to cut you off from the outside world. Not a bad idea if you have trouble concentrating. On the other hand, if you're like me, it can be intimidating at best and downright scary at worst. I'm cut off from the world enough as it is.

Complete Sound Studios was pretty high-end as Toronto operations go. Their main room, while not overly large, had a nice sound, warm and open. It also helped that the place was loaded with analog equipment, if you prefer that kind of thing. And the control room, well, I'd spent enough time sitting next to that idiot Robbie while he'd played producer to know that the recording console was huge. Nick could make it do anything.

Problems arose when Nick wanted me to use the vocal booth. They're soundproofed to the nth degree, so a singer's voice is totally uncoloured by "ambient sound." But they're always cramped, the musical equivalent of solitary confinement. By prowling the perimeter with my hands, I discovered this one had a wall of thick glass that looked out on the studio and a smaller window looking into the control room. Altogether it measured about five feet by five feet. My only connection with the outside world was through the cord of my headphones.

Incarcerated in my vocal tomb, I listened to the bed tracks of the first tune, "Dance Hall Girl." It's always weird having music thundering through your head when nobody's playing anywhere nearby. You have to create a spontaneous-sounding performance, make it feel like there's the give-and-take of musicians feeding off each other's energy. I tried singing it through, but stopped well before the end. Nick didn't say anything and rewound the tape. The next two attempts were even worse. I began to freak out.

Finally he said through the talkback mic on the recording console, "Something wrong?"

"Just run the song again," I snapped.

My voice barely came out in a croak on the fourth try.

"Maybe we should try this another night, Kit."

That comment really shook me up. But it also made me even more angry with my inability to produce under pressure. "No! I can do it. This booth makes me feel all closed –"

"Hey," Nick interrupted with a laugh, "no problem. Just give me a minute to set up a mic in the main room."

I groped my way back to the control room and sat down on the floor next to Shadow. My spirits were down there with him too. "Sue?"

"Right here, Kit," she said as she came in from the lobby. "I retrieved this from the car." She pressed the bottle of liquid confidence, still in its paper bag, into my hand.

I felt like a rubby as I unscrewed the cap and took a tiny sip of the booze, rolling it around my mouth. "That sounded like total crap! My voice was shaking from nerves." I sat silently for a moment, then tipped the bottle back and took a healthy swallow. A glowing rivulet of Southern Comfort traced its way down to my stomach.

"Just be yourself, Kit. You'll do fine."

Nick came back through the double doors out to the studio. He put his hand on my shoulder. "Come on, Princess. Time to turn this pumpkin of a tape into a swan."

"Isn't that a bit of a mixed metaphor?"

"Do you want good engineering or good grammar?" he answered, then laughed. I reached out a hand, and he pulled me to my feet. "Can I have a hit of that?"

"Sure."

Nick took a swallow and handed the bottle back. "Who are you trying to be, Janis Joplin?"

"Something like that."

"Well, my dear," he said as he led me out to the studio, "if this tape turns out half as good as some of her stuff, you've really got yourself something." He put the cans – that's what engineers call headphones – on my head and showed me where the mic was, so I wouldn't bang my nose on it. I had another big swallow while he went back to his star-pilot's seat behind the console. "Can you hear me?" I winced as Nick's voice thundered in my ears. "Sorry," he said after turning down his mic. The tape ran for a couple of seconds. "How are the levels?"

"Could I have more of the guitar and less of the drums?"

The tape ran some more, and things evened out to the way I wanted.

"Better?"

I gave Nick a big nod, and after he adjusted the balance of the instruments further anyway, I tried another run-through:

How would you like to spend the night with me
Dancing and pretending that our lives are free
From all the ugly things that happen and only bring us down . . .

By the time we got a usable take, I was halfway through the bottle.

As the booze did its job, though, I began worrying less about what I sounded like and more about what the songs needed from me to sound good. A couple of times, after a take, Nick just sat there before playing it back. The first time, the silence made me incredibly insecure. I figured they were in the control room laughing. As I took off the cans so I could go in, Susan hurried out.

"What's going on in there?" I demanded.

"We were discussing the take."

"It was that bad?"

"No, silly. It was that *good!* We were just wondering how much booze you could consume and not be too sloshed to sing. I think your Joplin technique is working."

Nick joined us. "Kit, stop worrying. You're doing a killer job. Now, let's get back to it while you're still hot."

He probably meant while I could still stand up. I never did that guitar overdub. I may have proved I could sing when I've had a snootful, but I knew I couldn't play guitar, so I didn't even try. We did get all but one of the vocal tracks down, though. Nick said he'd let me know when there was another open space, so we could finish off the last vocal, cut the guitar solo, and start on the mix-down. Well, actually, I don't remember that part. Susan told me later. I was too far gone by the time we packed it in.

Having parboiled my body to the point where my throbbing brain felt partially alive again, I dried myself vigorously with the rough side of the towel, went back to the bedroom, and lay down on the bed. The cool air from the open window felt nice on my skin.

Reaching over, I grabbed the phone and put it on my stomach. Feeling too lazy to go to the answering machine in the living room, I dialled in my code to play back any messages remotely. There were two.

The first was from Sue's husband, and he sounded really pissed off. "This is Paul Quinn. It's after midnight. If Susan's there would you tell her to get her butt home *now?* I have a breakfast meeting with a client, and one of the kids has been vomiting all night."

Oops. Susan was going to get major crap about this. She'd really had to twist Paul's arm to get him to babysit, since it had been his night to play squash with his lawyer buddies. She didn't drop me off until after 2:00 a.m., and it was still another half-hour to her place. He must have gone right through the roof when she got home.

Feeling guilty, I dialled her number and caught her as she was leaving for her morning run.

"Sue, it's Kit. I just played a message Paul left last night. Is everything okay?"

"No," she said. "He let Marty eat a huge candy bar right before bed, and of course it made the little guy sick. He's okay now, though."

"But how's Paul? He sounded really pissed."

"Still that way, I'm afraid. We had a *huge* argument. He said I'm always off doing other things when I should be home taking care of my family."

"Look, Sue, I'm sorry I caused all this trouble. I should have taken transit."

"It's not your fault. If it wasn't this, it would be something else. Lately we only seem to talk to each other at a scream and Paul's become so . . . different. I hardly feel as if I know the man any more. He's almost never home, and when he is, it's almost as if he wishes he wasn't." She sighed heavily. "So now we're not talking at all, and this time I'm not going to be the one to apologize. Look, I've got to be going. Maybe we can talk later. Okay?"

"Sure. Just call or come over any time you want to talk or simply hang out. I'm here for you. And thanks again for all your help last night."

I heard the smile in her voice. "Don't mention it, Kit."

After Sue clicked off, I checked the remaining message – Carolina's gorgeous contralto. I'd kill to have a voice like hers. "Kit, I was just talking to Jackie. Has the ad attracted any attention? We're all dying to know. Phone me up in the morning."

As I began dressing, I thought about finally giving the number that went with the ad a call. I'd been avoiding it, but after my success of the evening before, I was feeling more confident.

"Who knows?" I said to Shadow. "It might turn out to be interesting."

THE MAN CROUCHED LOWER IN THE BUSHES, cramped and cold, but happy to be finally on the hunt again. He always went through a period of doubt whenever he started an assignment, but, as he worked things out, he'd feel his confidence rising until he couldn't wait to see how smoothly everything would go. Flexing the muscles in his legs, he tried to keep the blood circulating.

Tired hands rubbed weary eyes. He'd worked hours the previous day at a microfilm reader in the library doing research, then stayed up most of the night staring at his turned-off television, visualizing his plans, almost as if they were being played out on the black screen. The man subscribed wholeheartedly to Murphy's Law. Overlook one tiny detail and *pow*! Game over and the cops got you. Or worse, your intended victim did. His entire night had been consumed with attempting to anticipate every possible weakness in the game plan.

From the beginning, this had been an odd commission. The man had never talked to the person in charge, just a go-between. It had never been face-to-face either, not that this kind of thing hadn't happened before. No, it was the way he'd been spoken to. The arrogant voice on the phone had talked to him as if he was some kind of servant, not the hired expert who'd be getting these dough-heads out of a tight corner.

Then there were the instructions: nobody must know anything, that her place had been searched, that she'd been murdered. He'd had those kinds of instructions before, too, but never in such detail and with so many reminders. As if he were some amateur!

The man had puzzled for a while over how to carry out his commission, but then an incredible opportunity had dropped right into his lap. He would make this hit look like a murder, *but not the murder it was*. He'd dump the blame for it on the Back-Door Strangler. Through their own stupidity, the cops had let the poor bastard walk, anyway. He loved the irony of it. The cops would go screaming off after the poor joker, never suspecting they'd been set up. Even if they caught the guy, who'd believe him when he said he hadn't done it? The plan required the necessary knowledge of the sicko's *modus operandi* to trick the cops, but a few hours' research had supplied that.

The man's gloved hand drifted to the pocket of his sweat-shirt, where he felt the coil. He would have preferred a length of piano wire, or better yet, one of his knives, but this hit required rope. The length of dirty clothesline he'd found that morning was the perfect solution. Couldn't be traced. No cop was going to find some overly observant sales clerk who'd be able to point at him in court and say, "Yes, Your Worship, that's the man who bought the clotheslines."

He gave a disgusted shake of his head. This had started happening lately. No matter how much he went over things, planned everything down to the smallest detail, the doubts, the things that could go wrong, still rose up accusingly in front of him. If he'd been stupid enough to buy new rope, he deserved to get fried. But the cops wouldn't get far enough even to begin to know what had actually happened. They'd never get the slightest inkling.

He hunkered lower, partly for cover, partly for warmth. A brisk wind had sprung up, along with a mist of light rain that slightly obscured the gravel path. He would have pre-ferred being concealed by something more than the few scant boughs of a small fir tree and some dead weeds that winter hadn't managed to flatten, but hell, you couldn't have everything. The colour of his sweatsuit had been calculated to help.

He couldn't complain about the miserable weather: foggy, a cold drizzle falling continuously, melting slush from yesterday's snowfall. With each moment, darkness crept closer. No normal person would come out in this.

A slow smile crossed the man's face.

She would.

CHAPTER 4

—ɱ—

It took me almost three hours to work up the guts to call that stupid electronic mailbox.

First, my stomach distracted me by growlingly announcing that it was now feeling well enough to require filling, so I headed for the kitchen.

I have to know where everything is in my apartment down to the centimetre. For that reason, I keep my interior decorating to a minimum. The bedroom has only my double bed with night tables and a low dresser. In the living room I've limited myself to the sofa with an end table for the phone, a coffee table, the shapeless beanbag thing Jackie loves, and a rattan chair my mother brought back from one of her jaunts – a peace offering after one of our major fights. My stereo and recording equipment, along with the old TV, sits against one wall, on shelving made of old boards supported on bricks. The bedroom is carpeted and I have a small imitation-Oriental rug in the centre of the living room. That's it, and my friends are well aware they shouldn't move anything around under pain of death. If they take something out, it had better be put back in the right place immediately. They all listen – except for Jackie.

The booze might have made the previous evening go better, but it wasn't doing much for the morning after. For some odd reason everything seemed to be about four inches from where it should be, with the result that, as I crossed the living room, I caught my shin on the edge of the coffee table and fell sprawling into the kitchen. My forehead smacked the linoleum with a hard thud that really stunned me. I pictured little cartoon birdies circling my head.

This is the toughest part about blindness – at least for me. I never know when I'm going to get whacked. I spent the first year of sightlessness with permanently bruised legs, arms, you name it. After a while (a long while for me), a person tends to develop a kind of a sixth sense, though. It's hard to describe. You feel the *presence* of things. Maybe it's a subtle shift in air currents or something scientific like that. I don't know. What you are sensing might be anything from a television set to a large houseplant, but you generally know *something's* there – unless overindulging in booze causes things to shift around erratically. Even so, I still always move in strange places like there are eggs underfoot. I hate those stupid white canes, probably because I'm not very good with them.

I lay on the floor cursing the coffee table, the makers of Southern Comfort, the Armstrong Flooring Company, everything I could think of. Shadow came over and planted a sloppy kiss on my ear, but I angrily shoved him away. He was probably only making sure I wasn't dying and would be able to feed him at dinnertime.

Thoroughly miserable, I lay for another few minutes, considering the situation. The fall had finally knocked the truth into my thick head. I was the source *and* solution of my problems. Nine years ago I'd been dealt a bad hand, but so what? Everyone has rotten luck at one time or another. Case in point: why curse everything but the obvious cause of my fall – me? If I hadn't been such a weak baby and been able to do the job at the studio, I wouldn't have been hungover that morning. My resolve, set in Play-Doh the night before, needed a truckload of concrete mixed in.

Rolling onto my back, I touched the growing goose egg on my forehead. A salty taste and stiffness in my lower lip showed that I'd also inflicted some damage there. I gingerly stuck out my tongue and found the cut. Sensing my softening mood, Shadow came back across the kitchen and lay down with his head near mine. A scratch behind his ear let him know that all had been forgiven.

Time to see to my injuries. I didn't want someone to come barging in and find me with blood all over my face. After carefully washing the cut, I stood leaning against the counter, contemplating my navel, one paper-towel-wrapped ice cube pressed on my lip and another against my head.

My loud snort made Shadow jump. I'd been thinking of that stupid companion ad. I couldn't invite someone else into my life until I got the damn thing pulled together.

I had to get out for a while, calm myself down, so I hitched up Shadow's harness and we hit the street. The temperature had gone up, but now it was drizzling, which turned the wet snow into a morass of slush. A car driving too close to the curb drenched us with a slurry of half-frozen water and gutter garbage. That led to a full-volume exercising of my extensive four-letter vocabulary and an immediate about-face back to the apartment. But yelling at someone had made me feel a lot better, and I spent the next hour wrapped in a bathrobe in the middle of the living room, calmly trying to get the crud out of Shadow's coat. Once again I saw the wisdom of having a black Lab or a Rhodesian Ridgeback for a guide dog. Grooming's a cinch on those shorthair critters.

After fortifying myself with a late lunch (or maybe it was an early dinner) of chicken soup and peanut butter on crackers, I went to the stereo and threw on the tape of the new song I'd made Sunday. Listening to it with the volume turned way up confirmed the feeling that'd been growing the past few days. My concept of the song was solid, but my execution had been too fast. It shouldn't be an uptempo butt-kicker. I grabbed the acoustic off its stand, tried a slower version of the rhythm and, sure enough, everything fell together much better. So now I had a down 'n' dirty song on my hands. It reminded me of Robert Cray's "The Forecast (Calls for Pain)" or one of those Memphis soul songs.

With my confidence somewhat bolstered, I sat awhile, trying to think of something positive I could do. I tried Carolina, but talked to her answering machine instead. Considering the weather, I hoped she hadn't gone out running after her last class. Susan wasn't home either. Marion ditto – probably still working or possibly also out for her *après*-work run. Jackie doesn't have a phone. That left me with the alternative I'd been studiously avoiding all along: The Ad.

I sat with the phone on my lap for several more minutes before actually dialling. What if there hadn't been any inquiries? But then I sneered at myself. That was the old Kit talking. The new one was fearless – sort of.

I felt fourteen again: sweaty palms, fast heart rate, the whole nine yards. I remembered that the Babes, possibly sensing my unease, had made the exercise of writing a personal ad sound like a game.

Yeah, and I was the prize.

With a slightly unsteady hand, I punched in the number the paper had provided, followed by my mailbox code.

The first guy sounded like a real nerd. "Hello. Ah . . . I'm calling in response to the, ah, ad you placed in the, um, you know, paper? I just thought that you and I, um, might get together and, you know, for coffee? And, like, get to know each other?"

With a sigh, I erased that one. The next guy was even worse. "Listen. I just read your charming ad in the paper and you sound like someone really super. You say you have difficulty with things. Bet I know what it is. You've got a husband and you want a little fun on the side. Well, I'm the guy for you, babe. I've got all the equipment any woman could want. Know what I mean? And do you know what I'm going to do with it? Well, first –"

Taking the phone away from my ear, I poked Shadow, who was lying at my feet. "I hope the assortment is better than this."

That second sucker also got erased fast. Then the third message began. He had a nice voice: deep, kind of lazy, with a hint of country air. For some reason I felt certain he hadn't been brought up in a city. His accent sounded American, possibly West Coast. He also seemed unsure, but not like the first guy, stumbling all over the place. It was almost as if he was rehearsing what he wanted to say and didn't realize he was being recorded. It was cute. Well, that's the way it struck me.

"I don't usually call these things. Hell, I *never* call these things but, well, I thought your ad sounded intriguing. What's the next step? Are you supposed to call me? Maybe we could get together someplace and talk. Would that be okay with you? Here's my number –"

I engraved those digits in my memory and put the phone back on the end table. Leaning forward, I scratched Shadow behind his ears. "Do you think I should call this guy?" He let out a groan of contentment. "Should I take that as a yes?"

It took me a long time to decide what I really wanted. Was it possible to meet somebody worthwhile through a companion ad? With my confidence in the ascendancy, I was tempted to call. But something inside, having insulated me for the past several years, began waffling: what if he's a jerk; what if he isn't honest; what if . . . It suddenly struck me that I needed to do something really daring, something like calling up this man whose voice resonated with me. No waffling! With that I picked up the phone again, though a little voice inside my head started sing-songing, "Dumb-ass, dumb-ass . . ."

"This is Patrick. Please leave a message and I'll get back to you." His phone machine caught me by surprise, knocking whatever ill-formed words I had right out of my head. So I hung up, collected my thoughts, and dialled again.

"Hello. You called about my ad in the paper . . ." I stopped and took a deep breath. "I think it might be fun to meet. How would Saturday afternoon be? Ummm . . ." *You're starting to sound like an idiot, Mason. Come out and say it!* "Look, I have to be upfront with you. It says in my ad that I have trouble with things. Actually, I have trouble with only one thing. I'm blind. If that makes a difference, then I guess we shouldn't meet. If it doesn't, give me a call at the number in the ad. As I said, I'm free Saturday. Oh, and by the way, I hope you don't mind dogs. My guide dog's part of the package. 'Bye."

At least I'd remembered Jackie's caution about not giving someone I hadn't met my home phone number. Tomorrow I could call up the paper and see if Patrick (I liked the sound of his name. Nice and friendly) had left an answer – a positive answer. I wasn't sure if my tender ego could handle a negative one. But on the whole I felt really good about the two forward steps I'd taken in the last twenty-four hours. All I needed was several healthy kicks in the *derrière* from my friends, along with a knock on the head from my kitchen floor, and look what I could accomplish!

"Well, Shadow," I said, nudging him again with my foot to make sure he was paying attention, "the die is cast. Let's hope this whole thing doesn't blow up in my face."

I wished one of my friends would call. I needed to tell someone what I'd done. To pass the time, I went to my special tape cassettes, which I keep in four piles on the stereo: happy, sad, reflective, or sassy. The tapes contain compilations I've made of songs that fit each mood. Depending on what I feel like listening to, I grab whatever's on the top of that particular pile. Tonight definitely called for sassy.

But someone (probably Jackie) had messed up the piles, and what I got was the old Eagles tune "Lyin' Eyes." The second try produced Mary Chapin Carpenter's "When She's Gone." Being a firm believer in bad omens and not willing to tempt three in a row, I flipped off the power, stomped to the bedroom, and hauled out my rowing machine. By the time I quit in a puddle of sweat and aching muscles an hour or so later, I'd rowed across Lake Ontario at least three times.

Nobody had called back in answer to any of my recorded summonses, and I got tired of waiting, so even though it was only 7:32, I unplugged the phone and hit the pillow.

Was anyone alive out there?

THE MAN LOOKED AT HIS WATCH FOR the third time in five minutes. His calves had begun to ache from crouching for so long, but with little foliage to hide behind, he had to stay low or risk being seen. A person coming by might not acknowledge his presence overtly, but later would certainly remember someone skulking in the bushes. It would be lunacy to chance that, so he stayed where he was and tried to put discomfort out of his head.

Where the hell was she? Could he have been wrong?

No. He knew for certain that she didn't have anything special on today. But maybe she was sick. Maybe the weather really was too miserable, even for her. He cursed emphatically under his breath.

Thirty minutes behind her usual time. Not good. The forecast called for clearing skies and fair and more spring-like weather for the next three days. After such a miserable winter, the runners would be out in droves. She *had* to come today. He didn't want to hang around idly waiting for a weather change, and he didn't want to come up with a whole new plan. This one was too good, too safe. The lack of passersby while he'd been waiting showed the validity of that. Everything pointed to a clean, safe operation, an opportunity handed to him on a silver platter by the escape of the Strangler, and he meant to take it. At least the increasing darkness would help. Nobody could see down into the ravine now.

Forty minutes. The man began to worry seriously about his legs being too cramped for the swift, sure movements his attack required. Just as he hunkered down again after a good stretch, he heard the light footfalls of someone running down the hill from the main park into the low bushes and trees of this marshy ravine area. Feet sounded hollowly on the first of the short plank bridges followed shortly by the second. A moment later, she flashed into view, running faster than usual, her breath a ragged plume trailing behind her.

She's making up for lost time, he thought. *Well, her time has run out.*

He let her get a short way ahead before moving from his hiding place. As she'd gone by, he'd noticed the volume of her headphones. She had them way up. Good. A quick glance in both directions showed that they were quite alone.

Sprinting up behind his quarry, the man got the rope from the pocket of his sweatshirt and wrapped it carefully around each hand. He couldn't afford to have it jerked loose at the critical moment. Soon, she was approaching the gloom under the bridge arching high overhead. The man had picked this spot carefully. It afforded excellent cover on both sides, and masked noise from the cars and trucks using the bridge.

He waited until the last possible moment before lunging. The rope crossed as it looped gracefully over her head, and he'd already begun pulling it tight before the girl realized what was happening. The secret was to jerk the rope in quickly, so the victim couldn't get at it before it dug into the meat of the neck.

So far so good. He had his quarry secured, and already

the rope had begun its deadly work, cutting off breath to the lungs and blood to the brain. The girl did respond quickly, though, after the initial shock. She tried to free her neck, but the man had chosen his weapon well. The thin diameter of the clothesline made it impossible to grab with gloved hands and she had no time to take them off. Realizing that she had to get at him to free herself, she kicked back with her heels, hoping to meet his leg or tromp on his instep. She'd obviously taken one of those self-defence courses. Too bad he was a pro. He only had to have his legs apart and back and she couldn't reach him no matter how much she struggled.

It was dangerous to stay on the path, though. As unlikely as it might be in this rotten weather, someone could come along. Or she might get lucky and land one of her kicks, so the man just yanked the rope back and down, and the girl had to follow. After that, it was a simple matter to drag her farther into the undergrowth.

The end came quickly. He rolled the girl over onto her stomach and put his knee in the centre of her back, pulling the rope up, forcing her to arch and making movement impossible. The girl's face turned purple and her mouth moved as she fought to get breath into her lungs to scream, but all that came out was a watery gurgle. Her movements soon grew feeble.

The man leaned into her field of vision. There they were. Deer eyes. Big, almost luminous, with that puzzled "Why me?" expression. They already had a surface glaze. Someday he hoped to see eyes that raged at him in death, gave up life with something more than shocked puzzlement.

He held the rope tight for another minute after she stopped twitching. No sense taking any chances. That was him. Never take the slightest chance if you could help it. He looked down again. She had been quite pretty in a delicate way. Forcing all feeling from his mind, he dragged the body through the broken glass and litter that covered the ground under the bridge, junk heaved off the bridge or left by kids partying in the warmer weather. He looked at one of the massive concrete supports. Yup. A ton of graffiti. He bet the place crawled with kids on hot summer evenings, chugging beer, with perhaps the more adventurous ones going off into the bushes for a quick screw.

The man snapped out of his daydream. He had to finish this off. After stowing the rope back in his sweatshirt pocket, he reached down, unzipped the girl's windbreaker and removed it. Underneath she'd been wearing one of those one-piece winter running outfits, mostly black with swirls of light blue on top and down the legs. It was a simple matter to slip her arms out and peel it down over her body. She hadn't worn panties. His eyes lingered on her breasts and the V of hair between her legs. Pretty. Too bad. A waste really. He wondered what kind of person she'd been. He thought about the "toys" he'd found in her closet.

After binding her hands with the shipping tape in his pocket, the man turned his back and quickly walked away. Rock and roll spilled from the broken headphones dangling loosely from one of her ears. Returning to the main path, he looked around carefully, then took off at a leisurely jog up the hill that the girl had run down brief minutes earlier.

A few sparrows and pigeons flitted noisily around the underside of the bridge, quarrelling over possible nesting sights. Far below, the body of the girl lay, seeming to observe it all through amazed eyes. Water leaking through a crack in the pavement high above began to spatter her face as the gloomy day darkened completely to night.

CHAPTER 5

That Friday somebody stuck a large stick into my life, stirred it violently, and dumped it out all over the ground.

The morning started just fine. No, *better* than fine. The sun had burst triumphantly through the cloud cover of the past three days. When I took Shadow for his morning walk, I could already feel its warmth and strode along happily with my jacket wide open. The air even *smelled* warm, with that hint of green you get when things are about to start growing again. People stopped to pet Shadow (something I don't like because it distracts him), but I smiled tolerantly, agreeing with their compliments about his rugged good looks.

After breakfast, Nick called and told me he couldn't squeeze anything in again until well into the coming week. "Some perfectly awful band just booked a series of marathon session. Looks like five days of sex, drugs, and rock and roll for me."

"That'll be a real hardship," I commented dryly.

"Kit . . ." he said, then stopped.

"You don't have to say it, Nick," I answered quickly. "I know I wasn't that good."

His reply was sharp. "When are you going to get over this complex? What you laid down the other night was solid; it has a few warts, but it's pretty damn solid. The boss is out of town, but as soon as he gets back, I'm going to play him what we've got."

"Do you think it's ready?"

"I'll make it sound ready. Look, Kit, when we get this band cleared out of the studio, I'll give you a call and we can get together with the boss."

So far, so great. *Wow*!

Full of the cockiness unexpected good news can bring, I felt brave enough to try the voice-mail number for the companion ad, though I have to admit to another attack of the shakes as I dialled. It may have been a bit early to expect an answer to my message, but I could hope.

For once I wasn't disappointed. "It's Patrick. Thanks for the call. You sound even more intriguing. Saturday should be fine. Where and when would you like to meet? Looking forward to hearing from you. I'm out all day, but I'll be picking up my messages. By the way, what kind of dog do you have?"

This time I had little trouble leaving a message. "Hi, Patrick. This is Kit. How about Saturday afternoon at Hazelton Lanes? Three o'clock? I'll be sitting in the café area in the basement. Do you know where that is? And I'll have Shadow with me. He's a Newfoundland, coal-black and big as all get-out. You can't miss us." I paused, trying to think of something personal to close with. "I'm looking forward to meeting you. 'Bye." A bit lame, but serviceable.

The warmth of the sun earlier had felt so great that I took Shadow out for another walk along Queen Street. Once you get east of Spadina, you're in the heart of Soho, a sort-of rundown, artsy-fartsy neighbourhood that has pretensions to being "someplace." I was on the hunt for a certain hot-dog wagon, and Shadow knew it. I'm sure the nostrils on both our noses twitched when we caught that elusive fragrance wafting down the wind. He dragged me directly to José at his usual spot on Queen across from Peter Street.

"Caterina! My beautiful, young friend. You want a dog on this first spring day?"

"No thanks. I already have one," I answered, giving Shadow a pat on his side.

José laughed delightedly, even though we went through this little two-step almost every time I stopped by. He's more than satisfied with his lot in life, even though the hours are long and the weather often makes his street-corner site pretty miserable. Everyone greets him by name, he has a steady flow of regular customers, and he makes enough to get by. "What more could I want? A mansion in the most fancy part of your town?" he answered when I quizzed him on the topic one winter day. "In this country I have what I always want: peace and security for my family. What is a little hard work and cold weather, eh?"

I sensed my friend hovering with his tongs at the ready, glinting in the spring sunlight. Maybe his teeth were glinting, too. I always imagined José as having a sun-baked complexion, even in the dead of winter. It went with the accent.

"José, I want a sausage. Just short of burned, please."

"What can I be putting on it for you?"

"Hot mustard and some of those special onions your wife makes."

He held it while I got out my money. I keep each denomination in specific places in my wallet, and I've had to learn to memorize scrupulously exactly what I'm carrying at all times. I learned the hard way that some people will take advantage of anyone. For that reason, I was taught at the Canadian National Institute for the Blind (I lasted there about four weeks) to try always to get my change in coins if possible. Maybe I should get one of those electronic bill readers. Don't get me wrong, though, I trust José – about money, that is. While I dug out a five, he fed Shadow at least one hot dog.

I found a bench nearby and, with my pooch at my feet, I enjoyed the sunshine, warm breeze, and my sausage. Even though he tried his damnedest, Shadow didn't score another crumb.

Everything was great.

We took our time strolling back. After retrieving my mail from my box in the lobby and trooping up the two flights to my place, I kicked off my runners and picked up the towel I keep by the door to clean Shadow's paws. The last thing I want is for him to have problems because he's picked up chunks of rock salt or something. As I hung up my jacket, I heard somebody rushing up the stairs. Still, I jumped involuntarily at the sharp rat-a-tat on my door.

"Kit? Are you there?" It was Gerald, but his voice sounded strained, not just out of breath.

I opened the door. "Come on in. Do you have time to look over my mail for me?"

"Sure, sure," he said distractedly. "Kit, I have some bad news. Very bad." He stopped as his voice caught. "I was passing an electronics store at lunch and a news report on one of the TVs caught my eye. She was discovered this morning by someone whose dog got away, and only identified an hour ago."

"What, Gerald? For God's sake, spit it out!"

"Your friend, the short one with the frizzy hair . . ."

"Marion?"

"Yes, that's her. I rushed right over, so you wouldn't have to be alone." My heart stopped as Gerald gripped my hands in his. "I'm so sorry, Kit. I'm so sorry. Your friend Marion's been murdered."

My mind sort of spun loose for the next day or so. I tried very hard to get some kind of a grip on what had happened, but the more I tried, the more things slipped away.

Gerald had sat while I held on to him and cried. I don't cry often. It's not that I don't feel things strongly; it's just that crying isn't me. But that afternoon I couldn't hold it in. Gerald simply held me tight. Shadow, sensing something was wrong, paced the floor in front of the sofa and whined. As usual, Jackie stormed in first – probably alerted in the same way Gerald had been. She was closely followed by Carolina and Susan. Gerald, who didn't seem surprised to see those two, quickly excused himself, and I got the feeling he'd sent out an all-call. I hadn't even been aware he had their phone numbers.

Death isn't that familiar to any of us. Carolina had lost her mom a few years back, and we'd all had grandparents pass away, but not anyone our own age, not one of *our friends* – and not like this. It was . . . incomprehensible. It didn't, wouldn't, *couldn't* sink in.

As the day ground on, the news only got worse. A special TV report at 4:00 announced that the slaying was sex-related and hinted strongly that it might be the work of the escaped serial killer. Our response to that further blow was absolute stunned silence.

Jackie finally broke it. "I'll kill the bastard," she hissed.

We sat miserably in my living room all afternoon and into the evening, about as low a group of people as you've ever seen. We had two radios and my TV on so we could catch any bulletins as they were issued. About 6:00, just as the evening news with its tragic lead story began, the buzzer from the lobby sounded, making us all jump.

"Cops, I'll bet," Jackie announced from the beanbag chair.

She was right. Carolina did the honours, eventually ushering in two officers: Ron Morris and his sidekick, Brent Patton, both detectives.

It made sense that the cops would want to speak to Marion's friends, and they seemed pleased to find us all together. After the requisite meaningless apologies for bothering us, they started by asking about any contact we'd had with Marion the past few weeks, whom she'd been seeing, trouble she might have been having, the kind of stuff you'd expect in these situations. We tried to answer as best we could. The questions went on interminably.

"May I ask a question?" Susan said at one point in the conversation. "The news reports say that Marion had been assaulted, you know, um, sexually. Is that true?"

Morris answered with surprising gentleness. "We won't know that for certain until we get results from the autopsy, but yes, we do have reason to believe the attack was sexual in nature."

"Was it the Back-Door Strangler?"

"It's too early to say. It might have been, then again it might not. We wouldn't want to spread panic by saying anything before we're sure."

Jackie couldn't resist sticking in a pin. "But doesn't it concern you that, if it was, he may strike again?"

"Of course it bothers us! That's why we're here. The Strangler always stalks his victims carefully. Maybe you know something, saw something. But even if it wasn't him, we need every shred of information we can get. Certain things don't completely add up at this point."

The other detective, Patton, who had so far barely spoken, started to say something, then stopped. I got the feeling Morris, in his anger, had told us something he shouldn't have.

"Ms. Mason," the senior detective continued, noisily flipping pages in his notebook, "what did you mean when you said earlier that Ms. Joseph never attracted any attention? I quote, 'She didn't feel comfortable having people notice her.' That's an interesting thing to say about someone."

"No, no. What I meant was that she was quiet; she didn't create waves. You know, she shied away from things that might be confrontational or make her stand out."

"What she was wearing when she was found doesn't follow then."

"I suppose you're going to try to convince us she was dressed like a hooker," Jackie growled.

The detective sighed before answering. "She was wearing a rather colourful, tight-fitting running outfit. That doesn't sound like someone who's uncomfortable with attention."

"So you think Marion *asked* for what she got?" Jackie again.

"No!" Morris snapped. "And let's make one thing perfectly clear, ma'am, do you want to help us or just give us a hard time? Make up your mind! You say you knew your friend well and saw her frequently. You might have that shred of knowledge that helps us apprehend the person who murdered her."

"Detective Morris, we're all upset," Carolina said soothingly, "and I think that's colouring what's being said. I would like to apologize for my friend. Of course we'll do *anything* we can to aid your investigation. Do I speak for all of us?"

The answer was unanimously positive, although rather grudging from the direction of the beanbag chair.

Morris and Patton stayed over two hours, probing into little corners of every contact we'd had recently with Marion. We all wracked our brains, dredging up every memory we could, but all of it seemed useless as far as I could tell. I didn't see the point. If it was the Strangler, the cops should have been out looking for him in every dark hole in Toronto. By the time the officers left, each of us was exhausted, annoyed – and, surprisingly, famished. Somehow it didn't feel right to be hungry.

Susan said she had to be getting home. "It's well past 8:00 and the babysitter can only stay until 8:30. I'll call you first thing in the morning, Kit."

Jackie, Carolina, and I decided on pizza, not a hard choice considering Guido's Pizza-to-Die-For downstairs and the fact that I didn't have enough food for the three of us, even if we felt like cooking. For the first time I can remember, though, we didn't finish it. We stayed up late, talking quietly, remembering our friend. The tears flowed freely. It only struck me later that Jackie had been uncharacteristically silent through it all.

After crashing for a few hours, I had to get up with Shadow, and we glumly went through the morning ritual. It took everything I had to work up the interest in doing even simple things like feeding him or making coffee.

I don't know if it's usual in situations like this, but I felt so incredibly helpless I couldn't stand it. How had something like this happened, and why wasn't anyone *doing* anything about it? Oh yeah, I could rationalize that the whole thing was in the hands of experts, but weren't they the cause of this tragedy in the first place? If they hadn't bungled and let a convicted sex maniac get away, Marion would be alive and in love and happy and still with us. It wasn't fair!

Susan, as she'd promised, called around 10:00, but didn't feel any better than I did. We went through the motions of making innocuous small talk and, in the end, both of us started crying again.

Around 12:30, Jackie buzzed up from the street door. "Kit, do you feel like company? I need to talk to you."

"Sure. Come on up," I said into the wall panel and pressed the door release. As I let Jackie in, I asked, "Want coffee? I just made some."

"I guess so." I brought two mugs out to the living room and we sat silently on the sofa, neither of us touching our drinks. "Kit, I need your help." The stress in Jackie's voice was quite noticeable.

"What's wrong?"

"I think I know something about Marion's death, and some of it may be my fault."

"*What?*"

"It's been eating away at me all night. When those cops were here, one of them said something that shook an idea loose in my brain. The more I thought about it, the more it began to make sense."

"Why didn't you say something to them?"

"I . . . I couldn't. I mean, I didn't want to. Oh shit! You just wouldn't understand."

"Jackie, you're talking in circles. What do you know about Marion?"

She took a deep breath and expelled it noisily through her mouth. "Remember Marion talking about problems she was having at work?"

"When?"

"On St. Patrick's Day."

"Oh that!" I shrugged. "Her new boss is obnoxious. What of it?"

"It was more than that."

"What do you mean?"

"Be glad you only had to listen to it once. She's been yammering to me about it, too – for the past month! That's why I turned on the Leafs game when we got back here. I didn't want to listen to Marion bitch and moan yet again. It was your turn. You know how Marion is . . . could be."

"Like a broken record sometimes," I said, smiling wistfully.

"I got sick of hearing about this latest problem after about the third time, and told her to can it, which didn't make her very happy, but I thought that would be it. A few days later, maybe two weeks ago, I had to deliver a parcel to City Hall, and guess who I run into coming out of an elevator?"

"Marion?"

"Right on the first guess!"

"What was she doing there?"

"That's exactly what I asked her. 'Hey Mar! You're a long way from Richmond Hill. Shouldn't you be up at that lab supervising soil tests or something? Wouldn't want that new boss getting mad at you.'"

"That was a really low blow, Jackie. You know better than to say something like that!"

Jackie's answer did sound a bit contrite. "You're probably right. I just couldn't help needling her sometimes."

"I'll be she was pretty angry."

"That's where you're wrong. She *was* pissed when we talked later, but the words were hardly out of my mouth when Marion turned absolutely white. It looked like she was going to pass out on the spot. The guy she was with gave her a pretty strange look, too. When Marion tried to pretend she didn't even know me, I got the feeling I'd really put my foot in it, and scooted into the elevator before the doors could close."

Jackie took a noisy sip of coffee. "Jesus, that's hot! Anyway, I made my delivery and was barely out the door again when Marion pounced. She'd been lying in wait for me. 'So what's up, Mar?' I asked, expecting to get reamed out for my little indiscretion. 'You looked like you swallowed a fly a few minutes back.' Without saying a word, she drags me across Queen Street to the lobby of the Sheraton, sits me down on a chesterfield in the corner, and gives me a real good airing out. When she gets to the end of her little tirade, she said something pretty strange. 'You could have just ruined the whole thing, too, with your smart mouth!'

" 'Ruined what?' I asked her.

" 'I was down here doing some investigating. That man I was with works in the Housing Department, and I didn't tell him about where I worked. Now, thanks to you, he knows and he told me to get lost.' "

"What was Marion investigating?" I asked.

"Something to do with her work at the lab."

"What could all this have to do with Marion's . . . murder?"

"Jesus, Kit! I'm getting to that," Jackie said sharply. "Marion told me she'd found a record about something in an odd place, something about a project the lab had done a year or so ago. She said it was very mysterious and she decided to follow it up."

"And that's what she was doing at City Hall?"

"Exactly. She thought that this guy knew something and she was accusing me of queering the whole thing with my smart comment. How was I to know?"

"The whole thing sounds pretty ridiculous."

On the other hand, Marion's book collection included a complete set of Nancy Drews. She probably checked under her bed for spies every night and firmly believed many of those ridiculous conspiracy theories: the Kennedy assassination, flying saucers, you name it.

"That's what I thought, too, and I told her so," Jackie said immediately.

I could imagine the result of that comment. Even though they were total opposites in so many ways – Marion neat as a pin, organized, careful; Jackie unrepentently sloppy, totally disorganized, and completely reckless – their friendship had been the closest of any in our group. They were very much like sisters. Go figure.

"So Marion either clammed up on you or walked out," I commented dryly.

"Right on both counts."

"Why do you think this has something to do with her death?"

"That wasn't the end of it. On her way out, with that little red face she used to get when she was really hot, Marion told me she was certain something was going on and she'd prove it. I just shrugged it off. After all, it's not like we hadn't heard stuff like that before from her. Anyway, next morning, Marion's waiting for me at the agency when I show up to get my walkie-talkie and the day's first run.

" 'Hi, Mar. What brings you down here?' I ask innocently.

"She has this smug expression and says, 'Okay Miss Smarty-Pants, I found out something really big.'

"I drew a blank. 'About what?'

" 'What I told you yesterday. Remember?'

" 'Oh, that.'

" 'Well, last night I stayed behind at work until everyone had gone home and did some digging and the trail does lead down to that guy in the Housing Office. He knows something!'

" 'Is it illegal?'

" 'Yes!'

" 'So? Fry his ass!'

" 'It's not that easy,' she answers. 'It doesn't look good for Doc Sloane.'

" 'So? He's dead. How can it hurt him?'

" 'You're right, I suppose. It just doesn't seem very loyal of me, that's all, and besides, I could be wrong. I'm not sure yet. All I know is that there's something going on and I'm going to find out what it is. Do you want to help me follow it up?'

" 'When?'

" 'Tonight, maybe, if I can arrange it.'

"I had something to do that night, and I really didn't want to change it to run around with Marion Joseph, Junior Detective, so I told her to count me out.

"Marion got her shorts in a major knot and told me she couldn't do that yet, that she just had suspicions, strong ones, but still only suspicions, and she couldn't take something like that to the police.

"I admit that I was getting a little impatient by then, so I told her that she should bother me about it again when she actually had something concrete, but that I really had to be going. Marion just said, 'I'll show you, Jackie. I'll show you all! This is important and it could be dangerous. If you don't want to help, fine; I'll do it myself!' That's the last time I spoke to her about it. I didn't bring it up the other night with her, because I didn't want to upset her again. When she didn't bring it up, either, I figured it had all petered out and she'd gone on to a new conspiracy theory – aliens living among us or something." Jackie gave a bitter laugh that said a lot about the way she was feeling.

I took a sip of my now-lukewarm coffee. "You seriously think all this may have something to do with Marion's death?"

"Doesn't it seem strange that Marion finds out something she said was important and maybe dangerous –"

"Marion *was* given to hyperbole," I interrupted.

Jackie's words came out in a torrent. "If I'd only taken her more seriously! If I had, maybe this awful thing wouldn't have happened. I think I'd lose my mind if the person who did her in got away with it, not when I can do something about it!"

"Calm down, Jackie! The media are really pushing the idea that it was the Strangler and the cops ain't denyin' it."

"And what if it wasn't? What if someone else killed Marion to keep her quiet?"

"It's got to be the Strangler. Wouldn't it make it instantly easier on the cops if they could say that they hadn't blown it when he got away from them, that Marion was murdered by someone else? And yet they aren't denying the rumours. That's significant."

"Then why not find out for sure? Remember that cop, Morris, said some things weren't adding up? This morning I went to see where they found Marion. It's all roped off, but if we could get in there we might find out what he meant. Then we would know if what I just told you has any bearing on Marion's murder."

"Why not just get in touch with Morris and tell him what you suspect?"

"And be given a pat on the head and told to go away because we don't know what I'm talking about? No thanks!"

"But right now the crime scene is probably crawling with police. What makes you think they're just going to let us waltz in and look around?"

"They won't even let pedestrians on the Bathurst Street bridge which crosses right overhead. You couldn't slip a mouse in there at the moment, but if we go tonight, there won't be so many gawkers around. The cops on the lines might be willing to chat a bit, too. It gets pretty boring out there in the dark. What do you say?"

Like I said earlier, I'd go a long way to help Jackie Goode. She'd been there for me too many times for it to be any other way. Besides, even though this sounded like a pretty dumb idea, I would be doing *something* – not just sitting at home feeling completely impotent.

"Okay, Jackie," I said slowly, "let's do it."

CHAPTER 6

L ate that afternoon, we reconnoitred the police lines around the perimeter of the spot where Marion's body had been found, coming to the conclusion that it would be best to tackle the problem of getting in from the northwest end of the ravine. At the southeast end, just past the fluttering yellow crime-scene tape, was a steep path leading down from street level, and, since it was right at a subway stop, there were more people there. The sides of the ravine were also way too steep to attempt, unless we wanted to sneak through the yards of several wealthy people who owned property on the north slope – not a good idea since they probably had alarms out the wazoo. If we were going to sneak in, the northwest end was best.

By the time we sauntered back through the posh neighbourhood that perched around the north edge of the ravine, I had the beginnings of cold feet literally, but also about the whole enterprise. After the heat of deciding not to sit around but to actually *do* something, I was coming back to my senses.

We waited for a while at the police line, part of the group of rubberneckers who show up at the scene of any tragedy. "Did you get interviewed by that TV guy who was here earlier?" "Any news from the cops?" "Is it true what they're saying about that Strangler fella?" Jackie moved against me uncomfortably when someone said, "I hear she was dressed real skimpy, and that's what attracted the killer."

We retraced our steps back up the ravine, found a bench where Jackie could keep an eye on things, and sat quietly talking for an hour or two. The temperature plummeted, and people slowly drifted past as the crime scene lost its interest in the chill night air. I hunkered down into my coat in an effort to stay warm, regretting that I hadn't put on winter boots instead of my runners.

"Looks like some of the cops are leaving and it's pretty dark," Jackie said finally. "Now's our time to move."

We got up and walked back down the gravel path. At the line, the one cop still on duty showed no interest in chewing the fat and only told us in the bored tone of a thousand repetitions to move on.

"All right, what do we do now?" I whispered to Jackie, hoping she would vote to give up and find a nice warm restaurant where we could thaw out and fill our empty stomachs.

"There are some thick bushes way off to the right. I might be able to sneak in through there without being seen. I can see a whole bunch of arc lamps underneath the bridge. That must be where they found . . . where Marion must have been."

"And you're seriously proposing to sneak in there?"

I could feel Jackie shrug. "Sure."

"What am I supposed to do?"

"Wait around here for me."

"Don't you think that's going to look pretty suspicious? A blind person standing around at a police line?"

"Good point. I shouldn't have asked you to come along."

"Now you tell me!" I waited for a few moments. "Well?"

"You could wait back up the hill on the bench."

"No! It's freezing up there in the open. And what if you get into trouble?"

"Then come with me as far as the bushes and wait there. It's far enough away, and the wind's in our favour. The cop on the line shouldn't hear us. How's that?"

"Pretty dumb, but it'll have to do."

Okay. Anyone sane would think that we're dumber than should be allowed, but I could counter with the fact that we'd had a major shock, and I, at least, wasn't thinking too well. Fact is, though, I'd have to agree with you. It *was* a dumb idea.

Things went all right at first. We made good progress and, thanks to Shadow and Jackie, I didn't trip over anything or step on any twigs. After a few tense minutes, Jackie got us to the bushes.

"Now you wait here for me to come back," Jackie said. "I shouldn't be too long."

She moved silently off before I could ask her what to do if she didn't come back. In my rapidly chilling enthusiasm, I fully expected her to get arrested.

Time dragged on and Shadow got fidgety. I whispered sharply to him to lie down and shut up. Flipping up the lid on my wristwatch, I felt the hands. Jackie had been gone almost forty-five minutes. When an hour had crept by, I decided that I would have to do something. First of all, it was downright frigid by that time and, second, I couldn't do much to help Jackie by hiding in the undergrowth. Unfortunately, I had only the barest idea of where I was.

"Shadow, do you know the way back to the path?"

Getting the message that we might be going home, the old furball roused himself up, but just stood there. He never had shown much natural ability as a trailblazer.

I waited another five minutes and then mentally tossed a coin. It came down heads, so we slowly crept off to the right. We got about ten feet before I stepped on the driest branch in the history of the world. You could probably have heard the *cra-a-ck* five blocks away.

Immediately someone off to my right shouted, "*Who's over there?*"

I panicked. It wasn't hard to imagine a squad of policemen wading through the undergrowth, flashlights scything this way and that, with me eventually pinned under the multitude of beams. I wasn't going to wait around for it.

Taking an extra-firm grip on Shadow's harness handle, I said in a brisk voice just below the edge of hysteria, "Hop up! Now!"

Shadow took off like a runaway freight train.

Guide dogs need to understand all kinds of commands, and "hop up" is the one most often used for "Pay attention! Something important is going to happen." "Now" is my emergency command, and when used with "hop up" means, "Get me the hell out of here!"

Footsteps pounded after us from the right – where the path probably lay – and I heard more shouts off to the left, but we stumbled on.

I had no clear idea what I hoped to accomplish. I guess I had it in my brain that I might be able to outrun them if I got into the open, which couldn't have been too far ahead. Of course, it would have been a simple matter to scour the surrounding streets for a blind person with a Newfoundland guide dog. We wouldn't have gotten very far in any event.

We got a lot less far than I might have hoped.

Shadow suddenly swerved to the right, probably to avoid the tree I ran right into. A shattering pain split my forehead in half, and the world winked out.

Consciousness returned slowly in a big jumble of voices and smells. I think I remember being carried and I definitely remember something lumpy being put under my head as I lay on a hard surface. Somewhere in the distance, Shadow was barking frantically. My strongest impressions, though, were of dust and that cigarette-like smell you get from strong coffee that's been heated too long. My head felt like a broken melon. As the aural fog began drifting away, I put my hand to my forehead. I had a lump the size of Mt. Everest.

Someone knelt beside me. "Are you with us, Ms. Mason?" I knew the voice, but couldn't place it.

I licked my lips and took in a careful breath.

"Just barely. What happened?"

The name that went with the voice clicked in.

"You had an unscheduled meeting with a tree," Morris said. "We carried you back here to wait for the ambulance."

"Where's here?"

"Our command post. It's a trailer we keep for site investigations. It's warmer and drier than leaving you on the ground." I started to get up, and his hand on my shoulder gently but firmly pushed me down again. "Just wait there. The ambulance shouldn't be much longer."

As things got more clearly in focus, embarrassment started replacing my earlier confusion. "I don't need an ambulance."

"That's quite a knock you took. You have to be checked for concussion."

"How long was I out?"

"About five minutes."

"Where's Shadow?"

"Your dog? Don't worry. One of our constables is taking care of him. He used to be assigned to K-9. Is your neck okay?"

I checked. "Yeah. Look, I feel stupid lying on the floor like this. Can't I get up? I promise I won't fall over."

Morris sounded slightly amused. "Do you feel up to sitting in a chair or would you prefer to lean against the wall?"

"Chair, please."

He helped me into a swivel chair and handed me a cup of something cool. I realized then how hard I'd been whacked, because I couldn't even identify it at first. Lemonade.

"Now, would you tell me precisely what you thought you were doing?" Morris asked, as he sat down next to me and turned my chair to face him.

"What do you mean? Someone started chasing me."

"They chased you because you were creeping around in the bushes. What were you doing there?"

"I . . . ah . . ."

"Precisely," Morris answered simply. "For your information, we'd already caught your friend, Ms. Goode, who refuses to answer any questions. One of my officers reported he'd seen her with a blind woman and a bear. We were looking around for you when you had your little adventure. You know, you're lucky you weren't killed, the way you hit that tree."

"I have a hard head," I said bitterly.

"Now, are you going to tell me what I want to know?"

The jig was up. I squeezed my eyes shut for a few moments before answering. "We wanted to find out what was going on, why you haven't said for sure whether it was the Strangler or not. That was our friend who was murdered, and we don't know why or by whom and I guess this was our lame-brained attempt not to feel so damned useless!"

"Lame-brained is right. All you had to do was wait. We've called a press conference for 10:00."

"A press conference? Why?"

"I suppose it won't hurt to tell you now, because you're going to be at the hospital and your friend is going downtown."

"Why is Jackie going downtown?"

"Because she went berserk and slugged one of my men when we carried you in."

"You shouldn't arrest her! She was only trying to help me."

"Don't worry. We're not going to charge her. I know she was upset at the time and she didn't hurt him anyway, but Ms. Goode needs a bit of shaking up. We can't have her assaulting constables and think she's getting way with it."

The door to the trailer opened with a blast of cold air. "The ambulance is pulling up, sir. Do they need the stretcher?"

"It might be a good idea, constable."

"I don't want a goddamed stretcher!" I said. "I can walk just fine."

"You'll use the stretcher. Have them bring it," Morris said to the cop at the door.

To tell the truth, I felt pretty wobbly. It's just so embarrassing to be hauled around on a stretcher. And, as I knew damn well, there'd probably be some news photographer or cameraman around to document the whole thing for the entire world to see.

As they were strapping me onto the thing, I asked Morris. "You didn't tell me what you're going to say at the news conference."

I was already on my way out the door when he replied. "That it was the Back-Door Strangler."

Carolina and Susan retrieved me from the hospital a few hours later. When I told them that the doctors had X-rayed my head and found nothing, they both laughed at the old Yogi Berra–ism anyway, glad that I was feeling okay. On the way home, we picked up Jackie and Shadow at the main cop shop on College Street. Jackie was so bent out of shape she couldn't even speak coherently. C and Susan were beside themselves to know what had happened, but I refused to tell them until we got back to my place and I had a whole bunch of headache pills and some food inside me.

About an hour later we were deep in conversation, wine, and pizza with double cheese and anchovies – and Jackie was still majorly grumpy at the way she'd been treated. I guessed the cops had really made her sweat. Striking a police officer can be a heavy-duty charge.

"So, after all that, you didn't find out anything useful?" Carolina asked.

I popped a loose piece of anchovy into my mouth. The intense saltiness made me pucker involuntarily. "Well, I found out how much I dislike connecting with tree trunks at a dead run, and, other than the fact that I could have scooped the media on what Morris was going to say at his press conference, I came up with zippola."

"I didn't get anything, either," Jackie said, "except marks where they put the handcuffs on too tight. Those bastards!"

"Jackie, you can't go around hitting policemen," Susan told her, sounding very much like a mother.

I distinctly heard a muttered, "Fuck you."

Nonetheless, after we told the other two what we'd been up to and why, Carolina the Brain remained firmly unconvinced about Jackie's theory – in the light of zero evidence. Susan felt as I did, that we had to follow up what Jackie had been told by Marion.

"But you all heard the press conference on the radio," Carolina said. "The assistant chief was quite clear that they're searching for the Strangler as being responsible for Marion's murder. Why do you think that is? They have all the facts. You have only Jackie's suppositions."

"I still want to know what Morris was bothered about, and why it took them so long to decide it was the Strangler they were after," Jackie said.

"I don't see how you're going to accomplish that. And look what happened to Kit when you tried. She could have been killed! I still can't understand how you let yourself get talked into something so stupid, Kit. You're usually quite sensible."

"It was *her* stupid idea to make a run for it!" Jackie said indignantly.

"Whatever. I think you ought to let the police handle this. Tell them what you know, and they will take it from there."

"C has a point," Susan chimed in. "It can't hurt, can it?"

"The cops are all jerks!" Jackie grumbled.

Everyone but Jackie left shortly after. She remained, nursing a beer she'd found in the back of the fridge, and continued bitching. My feeling after all was said and done was that Carolina had a good point. I made the mistake of telling Jackie so.

"Ha!" she said, pouncing. "The cops aren't going to believe us. You wait and see. They think it's the Strangler, and have already made a public statement to that effect. They won't back down now. They can't! How many innocent people are in jail because the cops wouldn't admit they'd made a mistake? Don't make me laugh! They'd look even dumber than they are, and they know it."

I finally got Jackie out the door about 1 a.m. Shadow needed his evening constitutional, so we walked her over to the Spadina streetcar stop.

As the streetcar pulled up, Jackie grabbed me tightly around the waist. Normally, she doesn't lunge at me, something I naturally find extremely disconcerting. But tonight, because of an over-abundance of wine and beer, coupled with everything that had happened and her strong emotional wash, she forgot herself. It's a tremendous shock when someone does that, *especially* when you can't see it coming.

I tried to take a step back, but Jackie held onto my arms. "I'm not blowing smoke here, Kit. I thought this out carefully and reasonably, and I believe I'm right. Don't we owe it to Marion to make sure?"

With that comment, Jackie disappeared onboard, leaving Shadow and me standing on the corner in a blustery wind.

That wind also whistled desolately through my soul.

After cleaning up the dinner mess, I took a shower, got into bed, and pulled the covers over my head, but no matter how hard I tried, sleep eluded me. Toronto has some good late-night jazz shows, so I turned on the radio and tried to let my mind drift into more peaceful channels. But no matter what I did, my thoughts kept returning to Jackie's story.

It was no problem for Jackie to get people going. She could be so intense that her mood sucked you right in. Once, she got involved in some typically inane campus struggle for "the rights of the student body." I can't even remember what it was about, and probably Jackie wouldn't either, but an awful lot of people remember the results. I sure as hell did. By the time Jackie'd finished whipping us all up into a frenzy of righteous indignation, we marched down to the university president's office and took it over. Unfortunately, he had a lot of work to do at the time and needed his office rather badly, so he called in Toronto's Finest, and every single one of us got carted off to the hoosegow – all except Jackie, who, as it turned out, was being interviewed by the campus radio station.

With that kind of history to make me wary, I should have been able to brush her theories aside. I did solidly agree with her on one point, though. Finding out that Marion had been murdered for a real reason was far preferable to her death being the random act of a lunatic. And I know we all wanted the person who had done it to be punished. It would make it far worse for us if the murderer got away.

Some time after 4 a.m, I finally dozed off, but the tortured dreams to which my tired brain treated me made me wish I hadn't bothered.

When I first lost my sight, I ached to be asleep, because in my dreams I could still see, life still had colour and movement and purpose. I'd sleep twenty hours a day if I got the chance, and if I remembered only one brief dream, it was worth it. Mom finally sent me to a shrink, who told me I had to take hold of what had happened to me, to fight back. Easy for him to say.

Sight is even fading from my dreams now. It used to make me angry, because I was still clinging desperately to that last vestige of my old life. Now I'm only wistful about it. My memory of visual things is becoming fuzzier and fuzzier as the years pass, too. I still occasionally have sighted dreams, but more often dreaming mirrors reality; there's no sight, but in place of that my dreams, like life, are filled with a myriad of subtler things: smells, sounds, textures, even movements in the air. All of these communicate to me in ways I would have thought impossible before.

When I do have a visual dream, it's a special treat – if it's a good one. Maybe I'm up at our family cottage or hiking in the Rockies or even playing ball again, things indelibly etched into my psyche. Everything's wonderful. I can't understand why I was so worried, and I tell myself, "See? Things worked out after all. Your sight came back." Even after I wake up, the sweetness of being sighted again, if only for a short while in a dream, makes the hard reality less depressing, odd as that may sound.

But sometimes these dreams become twisted. I have a recurring one where I'm swimming way out in Georgian Bay like I used to do, when suddenly blindness strikes. I wake up screaming from those suckers. Swimming in Georgian Bay is scary enough when you can see.

That morning my dream was something new. I was searching through bushes, clinging, scratching undergrowth that tore at my clothes and face and arms. Even though I kept glimpsing Marion ahead in the distance, flitting in and out of sight, and called to her, she wouldn't stop. After what seemed like hours, I found her – and wished I hadn't. She lay on the ground, her clothes torn off, her eyes staring lifelessly at the sky. At that point my sight vanished, as if a light had been switched off. I was about to scream when I realized that *he* was lurking out there, waiting to pounce, and I was absolutely helpless.

I woke up standing on my pillows, back pressed against the wall. Shadow was halfway on the bed, whimpering with worry and licking at my feet. I stood for a few moments, my heart going about ninety miles an hour, then sat down and tried to get my bearings. My doggy put his head comfortingly on my lap.

"Poor Shadow. Did I frighten you? I sure scared the crap out of myself." I told him the whole dream from beginning to end, but he couldn't shed any light on it, not that he needed to. Jackie got a good cursing-out for bringing it on. Too bad she wasn't around to hear.

CHAPTER 7

F irst off, I really loathe funerals. Funny thing is, a funeral would have been preferable to what actually went on the following Monday morning. We had to settle for a hastily thrown-together memorial service for Marion because they wouldn't release her body. Seems she was "evidence." God! It was enough to make you sick. They'd stuffed our friend into a refrigerated filing cabinet somewhere until they decided she wasn't needed any more.

The service was held at Marion's family church in Guelph, about sixty miles – excuse me, 100 kilometres – west of Toronto. Since I was driving out with Carolina and Edward, I decided to leave Shadow behind, which made me a bit uncomfortable. I'm not very good with a cane, but there wasn't really room in Edward's car for the big furball. Gerald offered to stop by at lunch to take Shadow for a walk, and Carolina promised to keep a firm grip on me.

Funerals – or a memorial service in this case – should make people feel better. Marion's only made me angry. I just sat there, desperately wanting her back. Carolina seemed totally withdrawn. Only Susan was handling things well. She'd been busy helping Marion's mother. Marion's mom, as you might imagine, had completely fallen to pieces. The rest of the family wasn't much better. Sue had organized all the cooking and a great deal of the arrangements for the service and reception afterwards in the church basement. Maybe it's her way of dealing with grief. You know, keep yourself too busy to think about things.

Jackie was nowhere to be seen.

I've never been in a situation where everyone seemed so afraid to speak. You know how it is at funerals. You talk about the person's funny habits, or remember something you did with them. Maybe you comment on what a shame it is that they're gone, but you say *something*. The group that assembled at the church seemed nearly mute. Any talking was carried on in whispers, as if we couldn't acknowledge why we had all shown up.

The organist wheezed through a couple of nondescript hymns in a thoroughly lugubrious fashion, then left the compressor on the organ running, which made the place sound as if a noisy air conditioner had been turned on two months early. Someone to my left blew their nose loudly, and, as if that were his cue, the minister began speaking.

The man had an infuriating tendency to mumble, then break out for a sentence or two before subsiding to a mumble again, giving his words the feel of rising and falling waves. It was hardly something to give one comfort, especially me with the way I feel about open water.

The minister obviously had no idea who Marion had been, and the information given to him had been filtered through family members. He made no mention of baseball, of the recent improvement in her physical shape (something she was most proud of), of how she'd been basically quiet, except when she saw injustice, which brought out the bulldog in her. He went on and on about her commitment to Girl Guides, of all things. I didn't have any idea she'd ever been a Girl Guide. She certainly never talked about it to us. If I'd wandered in off the street, I would've had no idea who was being eulogized. It was sickening.

Anger helped the three of us keep our composure until right near the end.

The minister said, "Let us remember our dear sister Marion by listening to a song she loved."

I heard a click, and then the hiss of tape noise before the sound of a finger-picked acoustic guitar washed through the church. *Not*

"Four Strong Winds," I thought. *Oh God, not that song*! Immediately, my throat closed up and the tears sprang from my eyes.

About eight years earlier, just about the time my eyesight had started to fade to black, the whole bunch of us had come out to Guelph for a huge picnic at Marion's family farm. She'd made us practise the old Ian and Sylvia song "Four Strong Winds" for a week so we could perform it at the party. I worked out the harmonies and patiently taught the Babes how to hold onto their pitches and not drift into someone else's part (Jackie had been the worst at that). Marion proved to have such a beautiful, clear soprano that I'd given her Sylvia's part. As I sat listening to that tape, Marion's was the only voice I could hear, and it tore me up. Carolina and Susan lost it, too.

After the mercifully brief reception concluded, I stood outside the church in a cold rain while Edward went to get the car and Carolina moved off to talk to someone.

A male voice spoke from off to my left. "Excuse me, but you're Kit, aren't you? We've never met. I'm Tony, Marion's . . . I was dating Marion."

I stuck out my hand in the direction of the voice. A large, warm fist enveloped it. "I'm sorry we have to meet like this," I said. "Marion spoke about you quite a lot."

"It's been just horrible. I feel so sorry for her parents. And you girls. I know how close you were."

"You should feel sorry for yourself. Marion was quite a person."

"I just . . . I'm finding it very hard to accept all this. I'd like to have a few minutes alone with the bastard –"

"We all would," Carolina interrupted as she came up the steps. "Have you heard anything new from the police?" she asked.

"No. They've completely lost interest in me since Saturday."

"They want to get this one solved in a big hurry, especially since it's turned out it was the Strangler."

"Yeah, that Safe Cities Coalition is really piling on the pressure."

We'd all been worried on the drive out that a bunch of protesters would show up at the service and turn it into a media event. Sure enough, Safe Cities was there. A dozen or more protestors circled on the sidewalk in front of the church, carrying placards and chanting, but they'd been relatively quiet. Other than them and a couple of camera crews, we'd been allowed to mourn in peace. That was a big difference from the noisy demonstration that had taken place the previous evening in front of police headquarters. Thank heavens for small mercies.

"I'm just glad the cops decided *I* wasn't involved," Tony said. "They really gave it to me. I had to come up with a list of names as long as your arm of people who would attest that I was on my way to Kingston to play hockey when the attack occurred. They had me down at the station for four hours the other day because of some, ah, stuff they found."

I was about to inquire what that was, when Tony asked if he could bum a lift back to Toronto. We tried making small talk on the way back, but had fallen into depressed silence by the time we arrived home an hour or so later.

And Jackie had never shown up.

Later I found out why. She arrived at my door some time after 6:00 and in the worst state I'd ever seen her. She was totally incoherent with rage, pacing up and down my living room like a caged tiger. I knew her well enough to sit tight and wait for the storm to pass. Finally she flopped onto the beanbag chair with enough force that I thought it might explode, embedding flying beans into the wall.

"Want to tell me what's wrong?"

"That asshole! That *asshole*! He laughed at me!"

"Who?"

"*Morris*! I went to see him this afternoon. I did like you said and told him my story."

"And he didn't take you seriously?"

"Of course not! What he basically said is that I didn't know what I was talking about. I should have known better than to bother with the cops!"

"They must have a pretty strong case against the Strangler to be so definite," I said carefully.

"They *think* they do, but there are holes."

"What holes?"

"They have no semen sample – and there are no other indications that a rape took place."

"No rape?"

"That's right. Morris even admitted it. You see, I know a courier whose brother is a cop. He's not working on Marion's murder, but he does know what's going on. He told me that's why they held off so long deciding it was the Strangler. Whoever killed Marion didn't rape her."

"So? Maybe he got scared off."

I waited for the explosion, but it never came. Jackie replied softly, sadness plainly in her voice. "Kit, I saw the actual place where Marion died. The cops have packed up and gone now. They found her body way off the path, and that was only because somebody happened to stumble upon it. If you remember, the weather Thursday evening was absolutely rotten. Unless a person enjoys tramping through mud and underbrush in the dark, the murderer would have been completely out of sight and undisturbed. He would have had hours to do whatever he wanted. So why'd he stop?"

"How should I know?"

"I'll tell you. The killer stopped because he never intended to rape Marion. Marion's death was made to look as if the Strangler had done it. That's what the killer wants the cops to think so they won't look any further. Besides, the cops have the Strangler's DNA profile. They'd know in a minute if it wasn't him."

"And you pointed all this out to Morris?"

"That's when he said I didn't know what I was talking about." Jackie suddenly laughed bitterly. "I'm afraid I lost it. I started calling him names and he had me escorted out. I've been walking the streets ever since."

"That temper of yours . . ."

Dumb thing to say.

Jackie blew up again. "Me? *My temper*? You talk me into going to see those fools and I'm supposed to keep my temper when they don't even *consider* what I'm saying? Well, if that's the kind of support I can expect from you, you can just *go to hell*!"

She was out the door before I could even begin to think of an apology.

Carolina called about 9:00 the next morning to ask if I wanted to meet for coffee at Novik's. I arrived early, and, opening the door, received the customary blast of warm, moist air heavy with the aroma of freshly baked bread and pastries. Carolina came through the door about ten minutes later, also early.

Mrs. Novik went on and on about Marion, someone she'd liked a great deal. In her pudgy incarnation, Marion would often stop by for a pastry when she was in the neighbourhood, and even after she'd sworn off all sweets, she would still drop by for herbal tea and a chat.

"The poor, poor dear," Mrs. N clucked as she refilled our cups. "How could such a thing happen? Is this whole city gone crazy? Imagine! Little Marion who wouldn't hurt a fly. My heart is broken!"

When Mrs. N finally left us alone, I asked Carolina why she wanted to see me.

Carolina sighed. "Jackie. Quite frankly, I'm worried about her. She's not handling this well."

"You ain't heard nothin' yet." I spent the next five minutes filling Carolina in on what Jackie had told me the previous evening. "You're right about her being totally out of control," I concluded.

"What do *you* feel about Marion's death, Kit?"

I played with the handle of my coffee cup as I thought the question over. "I don't know . . . confused, angry, numb. Her loss hasn't completely sunk in yet."

"That's normal. I find myself very blue at times. I'll read something for example, and I'll think about telling Marion; then it hits me."

"Yeah, that's a lot like me. My eyes fill with tears and I try to push them aside."

"You shouldn't do that. Let your feelings out."

"But what about Jackie?"

"For all her toughness, Jackie has trouble dealing with heavy emotional issues. It's one reason she doesn't form any kind of serious relationships with men, for instance. I think she simply couldn't face going to Marion's service yesterday. For all their arguing, Jackie and Marion were very close. You know that. Marion saw herself as Jackie's big sister, always wanting to help, and on a certain level I think Jackie acknowledged that. She simply responded like a little sister and they fought. The Babes are the only family Jackie has, after all."

"That thought has crossed my mind, too."

"She feels guilty that she let Marion down somehow, and now she wants something to strike out at. That's why Jackie is desperate to believe this story."

"What do you think about Jackie's theory, C? You're the smart one."

"I find myself agreeing with her on several points," Carolina said slowly. "She makes a certain amount of sense."

"Then why aren't you pushing to help Jackie?"

"Jackie's response is what I'd expect from her. She will not accept that Marion died for so little reason. What will it do to her mental state if we find out Marion *did* die for very little reason? I'm not certain that going along with her mania would be good for Jackie in the long run. Surely, that's obvious."

"Maybe to someone like you."

"I know, I know. Because I'm the smart one! The whole group of you always says that about me. *I'm* the smart one. *I* have all the answers. It gets pretty damn wearing after a while! Why do I always have to be the intellectual? Why can't *I* be the one with an emotional reaction now and then?"

Boy, had I hit an unsuspected nerve ending. "C, are you okay? This isn't like you."

"Maybe it should be!" She reached across the table and gripped my hands tightly. "Kit, I feel totally overwhelmed. All of you seem to think I'm this big brain with all the answers."

"Well that certainly is your background . . ."

"I'm not *that* smart! I know how to study, that's all. Why the hell do you think I'm still in school?" I didn't answer. "It's because I have no idea what to do! Big brain Carolina is too stupid to know what she wants to do with her life, so she just continues collecting degrees and staying where it's safe."

"I think you're being unfair to yourself."

"How can the truth be unfair? Maybe that's the best thing to come out of what's happened. It's forced me to face reality. Life is too short to be always hiding from it." She paused then gripped my hands even tighter. "What do *you* think of me, Kit? When you think 'Carolina,' what crosses your mind?"

A loaded question if I ever heard one. I wondered if Carolina's grip on my hands was a subconscious effort to keep me from answering. She was pretty damn strong. "Well . . ."

"Kit, I want an answer! The unvarnished truth! I don't care how much you think it might hurt me."

"I . . . I see a person who is smart and clever, sensitive and –"

"Cut the crap and answer my question. I'm serious!"

"All right – but you *are* those things, C. If I thought about negatives, let's see . . ." I was stalling for time. Carolina's grip tightened and my anger flared about being put on the spot like this. "Okay. I think you're right about hiding out in university. I also think you're too aware of your background, even though you seldom mention it. So your father runs one of the biggest corporations in Canada and gets to hang out with prime ministers and the like. What does that really have to do with you? The way you speak is infuriating sometimes. It's like you chew every thought three or four times before you spit it out. Sometimes I think you were born with a stick up your butt. Is that the kind of stuff you want to hear?" I smiled at her to take some of the sting out of my words. "And who else do you know would actually say 'the unvarnished truth'?"

Carolina let go of my hands and sighed deeply. "Am I really that bad? Is that what everyone thinks of me?"

I snorted. "No. Everyone who's ever said *anything* thinks that you're a pretty great person. And what's wrong with being good academically? I'm sure that once you've decided what you want to do . . . Well, the world had better look out, that's all I've got to say!"

Carolina patted my hand. "Thanks, Kit. I really needed to hear all that." She laughed and sounded a lot less tense. "So I act like I have a stick up my butt?"

"Only sometimes, C. Only sometimes."

We paid our bill and headed out onto the street. The wind had kicked up a bit and it smelled like a storm was brewing, so I shook up the reins on my old doggy and we moved along at a better clip.

"I know you probably aren't in much of a mood to think about it right now," Carolina said, "but what happened with the ad?"

A wave of embarrassment hit me. With everything that had gone down, I'd totally forgotten the meeting I'd arranged with Patrick. I had a vision of the poor slob still waiting for me at Hazelton Lanes. As we walked along Queen Street, I told Carolina about the messages and what I'd arranged. "The whole thing went right out of my brain when I got the news about Marion."

"Don't you think you should call him?"

"Why? It's too late now. Besides, I just don't feel like it at the moment."

I let Shadow stop to sniff a fire hydrant. He's not supposed to do stuff like that, but old habits die hard, and like me, he's not very good at following rules.

"Kit, I don't mean any disrespect to the memory of Marion, but life has to go on. I think you should at least check for a message. Part of this was her idea too, you know. I think she'd want you to find someone." When I didn't respond, she continued. "That first night after, you know . . . when I got home, Edward was waiting up for me. We went to bed and he took me in his arms and stroked my hair until I fell asleep. You could use a little of that right now. You've been alone too long."

"Would you guys just *back off*? Let me handle this my own way and in my own time!"

Carolina's voice was subdued, "Okay, Kit. Anything you want."

"And tell the others to leave me alone, too!"

It didn't surprise me when Carolina said her goodbyes at the door of my building. I wasn't being fair. She was only trying to help. They all were. Maybe my way of dealing with Marion's death was to just get upset at everyone and everything. Thursday night I'd been so hopeful, with a possible recording deal and new guy on the horizon, but that fragile house I'd been building turned out to be made of rubber cards. So what if I *had* screwed up? I couldn't summon the energy to care right then.

Even the ringing of the phone sounded angry as I unlocked the door to my apartment.

—m—

THOUGH NO ONE COULD OVERHEAR, the man spoke softly and stood with his ear pressed against the phone receiver.

Repeat business never bothered him as a rule. Hey, if somebody wanted his services again, that spoke volumes about the quality of the work. As expected, the public, led by the Safe Cities Coalition, had taken a hairy fit, and after an initial nerve-racking delay, the cops had committed themselves to following the wrong trail. No, it was the heat from this job. Cops under public pressure had the tenacity of bulldogs, and that could mean big trouble, if they ever cottoned on to what had really happened.

The man had spent the past few days going over and over the whole operation. The cops would never come up with the rope. Maybe it was taking things too far, but he'd cut it into half-inch sections and flushed them down about fifteen different toilets around the city. His clothes had been burned and the ashes buried forty miles from downtown. In a stroke of good fortune, he even had the same shoe size as the Back-Door Strangler, something he hadn't picked up in his careful research. He'd followed the criminal's *modus operandi* almost to the letter.

That deviation had always been the one weak point in his plan. The Strangler would have raped the girl for sure, but, because of DNA testing, something like that was out of the question.

The man, though, *had* toyed with the idea of . . . well . . . abusing her a bit, leaving some sort of marks that would indicate that it might have been the Strangler. It had happened once when the Strangler had been interrupted in the middle of one of his crimes, but the man hadn't been able to force himself into following through on that part of his plan. He felt a revulsion bordering on nausea when he even thought about it. He wasn't an animal like the Strangler. Leave that sort of thing to the animals.

Still, he was certain that was why the cops had hesitated over whether it had been the Strangler or not. Nobody had seen him at the crime scene; he was sure of that, and besides even if someone had, what had they seen? A guy of average height wearing some sort of green sweatsuit. Big deal. With the suit's hood up, they couldn't even say what colour his hair was. No, he felt safe as far as this hit went, but he still wished he hadn't taken the job. It was no good working in the city where you live. Too dangerous. New rule: from now on only whack people out of town.

But despite all the man's care, he still had a problem – from an unexpected source.

"No. I'm sorry. I won't do it," he said firmly into the phone. "Get yourself another boy."

The voice at the other end of the line went silent. When it spoke again, there was something in it that made the man's skin crawl. "You will do this additional service for us."

"I thought I made myself clear. I'm not doing any more work for you. It's too dangerous right now."

"The person who's poking around might get lucky. Your ass is on the line, too."

The man stood with almost-bared teeth, an animal reaction to stress, stress he wasn't used to. How dare they treat him like this? As if he were some common *hoodlum*! "Let me think about it. I'll call you in –"

"No. Now. You will give me your answer now. We are willing to pay you an additional twenty-five thousand, even though we feel this is an extension of the original commission."

Dammit. The man had two options left. One was obvious, even if it went against everything he felt he should do. The other he liked far less: cut out for parts unknown, set himself up in business all over again, and hope that these guys weren't serious in their threats to retaliate. But that option presented too many problems. He really *didn't* have much of a choice. "Okay," he said after a deep sigh, "I'll do it, but it will cost you an additional fifty thousand."

"Out of the question!"

"Take it or leave it."

The voice on the phone told the man to wait, and he spent the next three minutes cooling his heels on hold. He was about to hang up when the voice returned, not sounding particularly happy.

"We are prepared to meet your price, provided the commission is carried out within four days, same restrictions as before: it must not be a suspicious death."

Four days? All his experience cried out against attempting such a tricky hit within that kind of limit. "I'd suggest you allow more –"

The snarling reply took the man by surprise. "Four days. No more. We are anxious to have this matter taken care of. Several important transactions hinge on it. We cannot have *anyone* throwing a monkey wrench into our plans. Too many questions are being asked already."

"All right, all right! Don't get your shorts in a knot." The man smiled. He knew the person he was conversing with would be distinctly put out by his choice of words. Even if he'd been forced into something he didn't want to do, he could at least have fun at this clown's expense. "What's the name of my, ah, commission?"

"A loud-mouthed bitch named Jackie Goode . . ."

CHAPTER 8

It was Nick on the line. "Kit. Sorry I've taken so long getting back to you, but things have been crazy."

"That's all right. Things haven't been very good around here." I told him about Marion.

"Look, maybe I should call back another time."

"No. Life has to go on. How was the dreaded headbanger band?"

"Interesting," he replied, standard engineer-speak for "I'd rather not be honest." "But that's not why I called. My boss would like to meet you."

"You played him the recording?"

"Sure did, and he loved it. He's already counting the dollars we're going to make on this." Nick laughed. "So can you come?"

"When?"

"Today. Around 3:00?"

"I'll be there! He won't mind my dog, will he?"

"No problem. See you at 3:00."

I hung up with my emotional yo-yo on the upswing for the first time since Friday. All right! I stopped with the phone still dangling from my hand. My words had inadvertently echoed Carolina's: "Life has to go on." A wave of remorse washed over me, taking some of the sweetness I was feeling with it. Poor Marion. God, I missed her, but I had to reluctantly agree with Carolina. Life *did* have to go on.

While I took a shower and washed my hair, I couldn't help thinking: what does an aspiring singer/songwriter wear to a crucial interview? What did I want to project? Good question.

Marketability. I had to make Nick's boss feel that he could peddle my recording or this would go no further. I'm pragmatic enough to know that it's a lot easier if you have looks as well as talent. Since I couldn't do much about the talent at this point – unless I could dash off a few sure-fire number-one hits in the next two hours – I settled on looking good.

I've always had a nice figure, and it's stayed that way thanks to my rowing machine. Okay, tight jeans to show off my butt. My calf-length rawhide boots would go well with that. The problem remained the top. A T-shirt? No, that would be too rock and roll. Something frilly? Yeah. Show him my soft, feminine side.

Wait a minute! Back up the dump truck! What in God's name was I thinking? My music was going to sell me, nothing else. Obviously my voice hadn't turned this guy off, but my real strength was my music, *not* the way I looked. I went over to the dresser and took out a turtleneck sweater. I reached inside the collar. Good. No label. My mom had made the mistake of buying me two sweaters that felt identical, one deep green and the other black. I'd had a difficult time telling them apart, until practical Marion had suggested I take the label out of one. Trouble was, I usually can't remember which sweater doesn't have the label. I wanted the green one. Oh well, black wouldn't be bad, either. Shadow and I could go as twins.

While I brushed my teeth, Carolina's damned comments floated through my mind. I had treated that Patrick guy pretty badly, regardless of the reason. I at least owed it to him to offer an apology. I didn't have to leave right away, so I picked up the phone and dialled his number, getting the voice mail.

"Patrick, this is Kit. About Saturday . . . I'm really sorry, but one of my close friends was, um . . . died, and things have been kind of hairy around here. I didn't remember our date until today. Would you still like to get together, maybe for a drink? You just name the place and I'll be there. 'Bye."

He'd probably already deep-sixed the newspaper's answering number, but at least I'd done the proper thing by apologizing. Oh well, maybe next time. Right now nothing could dampen my spirits. I quickly touched wood, remembering the last time I'd thought that.

With my jacket thrown over my shoulder, my pooch and I headed off in the warmth of the strengthening sun on the long transit ride into deepest Scarborough, or Scarberia, as some local wags call it.

The meeting went very well.

Nick's boss, Arnold "Call Me Arnie" Richards, sounded as if he was a nice man, though a little on the greasy side. I could *feel* him giving me the once-over as he took my offered hand over his desk. "Well, Kit. I have to say that Nick is certainly impressed with your material, and after listening to it, so am I. You should be quite marketable."

"Thank you. I think –"

"Nick tells me you can really wail on the guitar."

"That's very kind of him to say that, although –"

"Excellent! A blind artist *and* a girl who plays guitar like a guy, if you don't mind my saying so. Good angle. And good-looking, too, very good-looking. Now, I think the arrangements on the tape are all wrong for these songs. Musically, they're stale. I hear your songs with a tougher sound. Less country-sounding, more up-to-date, urban, harder. It would fit the lyrics of your songs better."

"I agree, but Robbie, the guy who was originally producing, thought that he –"

"We should throw out the tracks you've done and start from scratch. We'll get new musicians, too. Tell me, Kit, do you have any more material we could use?"

"As a matter of –"

"Super, super! We'll have to do this properly, you know, a signed contract and all."

I was doing a slow burn, but I got the feeling that the man's interruptions were not out of the ordinary when Nick verbally stepped between us.

"Arnie, slow down! Tell Kit what we have in mind, and then let her answer."

"What? Oh, sorry. I get a little overenthusiastic sometimes. Kit, what we want to offer you is this . . ."

I liked what they had in mind: a fully produced album. They'd want input on the material, and Nick would produce as well as engineer. In the event that the tape was sold to a record company, Complete Sound would be reimbursed for studio time as well as the producer's cut of the royalties. It all sounded fine to me.

"What about backup musicians?" I asked.

"We have people you can use, or you can supply your own," Nick said.

Things were soon settled. Nick knew a keyboard player and a guitarist whose style would be a good fit with what we wanted to do. I knew a drummer and a bass player I wanted to use if they were available. We listened to the recording I'd made of my new song, and talked about a schedule. On my way out of his office, Arnie handed me an envelope.

"This is our agreement. It's the standard type of thing. Read it over . . ." He stopped. "Um, get your lawyer to read this over; then you sign it and give it back to us. We can get started next week. I'll clear some studio time for you. Stick by the phone. We'll talk soon."

Arnie's offer and his verbal style left me breathless. Thankfully Nick offered Shadow and me a ride downtown. En route he almost blasted me out of my seat playing a rough mix-down of what I'd recorded the week before. He had used it to sell the production idea to Arnie. Shadow only howled a little.

He let me off at the corner of Avenue Road and Yorkville because he had an urgent appointment nearby. My confidence was soaring. My singing *was* acceptable. I'd done all right. Who'd've thunk it? Kit Mason, Singer.

Shadow's tags jingled merrily as he scratched himself while we waited for the light to change. The sun felt gloriously hot on my back, and birds twittered from someplace nearby. The acrid smell of a car burning oil wafted over me, but I didn't care. Life was on the upswing.

Being near Hazelton Lanes made me think of the guy I'd stood up, so I went into the big hotel on the corner of Yorkville and asked someone to point me towards a pay phone. I dialled the number at the paper, followed by my secret code, and lo and behold, there was a message from Patrick.

"Hello, Kit! Glad you called back. I'm really sorry to hear about your friend, and I certainly don't blame you for forgetting our meeting. I'll be home all afternoon. Give me a call if you get a chance."

With nary a tremble of my index finger, I dialled Patrick's number.

The man himself answered. "Hello?"

"It's Kit," I said with more bravado than I felt. "I got your message."

"Where are you?"

"At a pay phone in the Four Seasons on Yorkville."

"Are you available to have that drink?"

My pulse rocketed upward. "Um, yeah . . ."

"Wait right there. I'll be over in fifteen minutes."

He hung up before I could respond. I had Shadow guide me to a chair, and I sank down heavily into its upholstered comfort. "Well, the die is cast, old friend," I told him as I scratched his neck to keep my hands busy.

Twelve minutes later – and believe me, I counted every second – someone stopped in front of me. "Kit?"

I leaped to my feet – too quickly as it turned out, because I bumped right into him. "Oh God! I'm sorry. I guess I'm a little tense."

"That's okay," he said, then added magnanimously, "so am I." He didn't sound tense in the slightest. "Why don't we go into the bar?"

He found seats at a table in a quiet corner. I ordered a glass of wine. Patrick ordered Scotch.

"That's some dog you have," he said while we waited for our drinks.

"Yes, he is," I managed to reply. "Newfoundlands are generally considered too big to be successful guide dogs, although they are very intelligent." *What are you saying, you idiot! You sound like a goddamed brochure.* "Um, his name's Shadow."

"I guess we should introduce ourselves. Patrick Donnelly's my name, originally from the States. Santa Barbara, California, to be exact. Currently residing in Toronto."

"Katherine Isobel Mason, which I can't stand, so you'd better call me Kit like everyone else," I answered, sticking out my hand for shaking.

"Why Kit?" he asked, taking it. "Why not Kate or Kathy?"

I smiled at a pleasant childhood memory. "Because when I was seven I was crazy for cowboys and Indians. Actually, I made the kids play cow*girls* and Indians, and I always got to be the outlaw. So my dad started calling me Kit, as in Kit Carson. It just stuck."

"I'm a bit of an outlaw, too, sometimes," Patrick said, laughing. "Your accent tells me you're not Canadian either. Where do you hail from?"

"I was brought up in Connecticut."

"So we have two things in common, don't we?" The waiter came with our drinks. I held mine out and he clinked it with his. "Kit it is, then. Now, tell me how you wound up in Toronto."

"Dad's from the States. He owns a big engineering firm. Mom is originally from Harriston, Ontario. It's a little town about two hours from here. They met in Banff, and he took her back to Connecticut after they got married. They split up when I was eighteen, and I came back to Canada with her. That's it. Nothing special I'm afraid."

I felt comfortable enough to let Patrick talk me into a dinner of *bœuf bourguignon* at a little bistro around the corner. We gabbed almost nonstop, and by dessert I'd found out that Patrick had been married and divorced before he reached twenty-five, and hadn't had a steady relationship in a long time. "Too busy working. I'm a financial consultant. I help people with too much money make decisions about how they're going to protect their investments and make even more." His job allowed him to travel, which he really enjoyed. "It's hard for me to stay in one place for long." His age was forty-three. "The age difference doesn't bother you, does it?" Patrick had a nice way of speaking, clear and direct. Just like the rest of his personality – I hoped.

I sat there taking it all in, swept away by what was happening, wondering what he looked like and trying desperately to sound as relaxed and confident as he did. I told him about my music career, and that I enjoyed baseball.

"Do you get to many games?"

"Some. But it costs a lot, and I don't have much to spend."

"I have season seats on the club level, right behind the plate. Great seats. Want to go to opening day next week?"

"Really? I'd love it."

Patrick was quiet for a moment, then said gently, "I hope you don't mind my saying this, but I keep forgetting that you can't see. I haven't been around many blind people, but I thought they always, you know, stare. Your eyes seem so normal."

I laughed. "That's vanity mostly. When I first lost my sight, I desperately wanted to seem normal. I knew how sighted people use their eyes, and I could still fake that pretty well. Now it's not so important, but it's become a habit."

"How long have you been blind?"

"I've been totally blind for six years, but my eyesight began failing when I was twenty-one."

"Can you read Braille?"

"Enough to get by on elevators and things. To tell the truth, I don't have the patience to really learn it."

"It must have been tough losing your eyesight so late. No. Rewind the tape. That was a pretty stupid comment."

I smiled at the sweetness of his momentary embarrassment. A warm hand covered mine and gave a gentle squeeze. The world fell away. I began to feel normal again. Not the way I used to, exactly, but I didn't feel as if I was encased in yards of protective cotton any more.

Patrick and I dawdled over coffee, talking about the blues scene – of all things. It turned out he was a big fan, and we compared our favourites, who was hot and who was not. Our conversation had an easy flow. We laughed a lot, too. It surprised me how natural every-thing seemed.

Eventually, with all the drinks, I had to pee.

"Patrick, could you point me in the direction of the lady's room?" I asked.

"Want me to take you?"

"No, that's not necessary. My glutton of a dog should do something other than sitting under the table eating the scraps you've been feeding him."

"You knew?"

"I'm blind, not deaf."

"*Touché*!" he laughed as his chair scraped back. "Okay, let's find the facilities you requested. No, I insist! Think of me as your guide male."

I grabbed hold of Shadow's harness handle anyway. Patrick and I were both laughing as we headed off on our search. It felt good when he held my hand.

Patrick got me home around 8:00. He had a Mercedes two-seater, and we almost had to resort to a crowbar to cram poor Shadow into the back, from where he drooled on the gearshift and enjoyed the ride mightily. I gave Patrick my phone number at the downstairs door. I didn't want him to come upstairs – not yet.

"My apartment's disgustingly dirty," I said by way of excuse.

"How can you tell?" he teased.

"By the smell. When the odour gets to a certain point, I get the firehose from the hall, flush the place out, and start all over again," I shot back, laughing, then stopped. "I had a really wonderful time, Patrick. Thanks."

"I did, too." He kissed my cheek. "You're not what I expected." Then he laughed again, a sound I could get used to hearing. "I'll give you a call. Don't forget about our date for opening day." His car door slammed and he took off into the night. Judging by the way the engine sounded, he had one hot car, and it impressed me that he had resisted the urge to squeal his tires. Some guys think that's the quickest way to a girl's heart. Well, maybe it is in high school. My first boyfriend drove my father nuts, doing that in front of our house every time he dropped me off. With a satisfied smile, I turned the key and went into my building.

Surprisingly, Carolina was waiting upstairs, watching what sounded like a Chekhov play on television. I stood by the door with my jacket still on.

"Well, are you going to stand there like a dummy all night?" Carolina asked. When I didn't answer, she clicked off the television. "Where have you been?"

"What are you, my mother?"

"What's that smug expression on your face?"

Hanging up my jacket, I went out to the kitchen. "Want coffee? A beer? Some wine?"

"I shouldn't . . . but sure, maybe a glass of wine," she said from the doorway.

In between sips, I fixed Shadow a double helping of his favourite dog food. Carolina said nothing, but I knew I had her thoroughly puzzled. The time-out gave me a chance to reflect on exactly what had just happened to me. Clearly, it had been my best day in too many years. As we stood there listening to the disgusting sounds of Shadow enjoying his long-overdue meal, I started to talk, telling Carolina about the deal from the studio. I didn't mention Patrick. For now, I wanted to keep that information to myself.

Carolina embraced me when I finished. "I'm so happy for you, Kit. Things are finally going to work out. I can feel it!" She stopped, then said in a softer voice, "Sue told me what she said to you the other night when she came to take you to the studio. She said you were petrified that you'd fail. We've wanted to help you for so long, but didn't know how to do it. Sue figured the only thing left was to yell at you."

I smiled, in spite of what she was saying. "I have been under-achieving for the last little while, haven't I?"

"And now things are looking up." Carolina stopped, and the shy smile I knew was on her face was apparent in her voice. "Do you think you could get that studio to –"

"Front the recording of the song you've been pestering me about?" I finished for her. "I'll ask first thing tomorrow morning. I'll suggest to Arnie that he it would improve his image to help worthy causes. We couldn't get him a tax write-off, could we? And before you ask, I promise to try to come up with something. Maybe even tonight."

"My, you certainly are a ball of energy!"

"Now, C, why am I graced with your presence this evening?"

"Jackie asked me to meet her here," Carolina said, sounding surprised. "Don't you know anything about it? She said she had something to tell us about Marion's death. She was supposed to be here over an hour ago." I heard the swish of her coat. "I have a lot of assigned reading to do before I hit the sack, so I guess I'll be going. Tell Jackie I'm really annoyed about having to wait for nothing."

As Carolina turned to leave, we heard the sound of someone charging up the stairs.

"Three, two, one. Cue Jackie pounding on door," I said, and sure enough the force of her knuckles on the wood was enough to rattle the hinges.

"You're late," said Carolina pointedly as she opened the door.

Jackie sounded distracted. "Oh, yeah, right. Sorry. I couldn't call to tell you." She dumped her coat on the sofa as she passed by on her way to the beanbag chair. The beans settled noisily as she stretched out with a groan of contentment. "God, I'm tired! I never realized how tension can take it out of you."

"*Jackie*! What have you been *doing*?" Carolina said.

I was in shock. From the moment Jackie walked in, my nose told me something momentous was happening. I went to where she sat and reached down. My hand touched soft fabric and a hem that ended above her knees. "God in heaven, Jackie. You're wearing perfume – and a dress!"

Her tone dripped smugness as she replied, "You know how I told you that no one was going to make me give up about what I *know* happened to Marion? Well, I spent most of the afternoon and evening doing some research."

"But the dress!"

"*And* a wig," Carolina said.

Jackie laughed. "Kit, dear, a girl has to look her best when she expects to spend time necking with a guy who might be a murderer."

CHAPTER 9

—〰—

"**W**hat?" Carolina and I screeched in unison.

"Well," Jackie admitted, "I might be exaggerating a tad, but the fact remains that I've been out *doing* something about Marion's death while everybody else sits with their heads up their –"

"In God's name, tell us what you've been doing!" Carolina's tone brooked no argument, and I think it took even Jackie by surprise. It shocked the hell out of me, but my jaw was already on the floor.

"I was out with a guy who works in the Housing Department and who I have reason to believe figured into whatever Marion was investigating."

"How did you find him?"

"From a person on one of the other teams in the softball league. She works at City Hall and told me about a guy in Housing who thinks he's God's gift to women. If it has a skirt, he'll chase it. I found out he spends his evenings at a place over on Church Street. Figuring that a person like that wouldn't be too difficult to get information from, I was waiting for him and we struck up a . . . conversation of sorts. When you're doing that sort of dance, there's a lot of room for 'idle chatter.' I didn't get everything I think he might be able to tell me tonight, so I let him know I'd be back tomorrow evening and that I was interested."

"In what?" I asked dumbly.

"What do you think? Look, if you want to get a man like this to tell you anything, you have to play up to his ego, and part of that is also playing to his agenda."

It wasn't a stretch to imagine Carolina holding up her hands in a T for a time-out, something she does with regularity. "Just stop for a second! What in heaven's name are you talking about?"

Jackie laughed loudly. "Even if no one else does, *I* want to find out what *really* happened to Marion. I figured that the best place to start would be where I knew she was looking. She said she found out some stuff at the city's Housing Department. I only needed a way to get in, and this goof I've been telling you about is perfect for that. The man thinks with his gonads. If you have any better investigative suggestions, I'd like to hear them."

"So you've been out with this man, trying to find out if he knows something?"

"Yeah. Beats sitting around here with a long face."

"And you promised you'd have sex with him?"

"Give me a break! Not in so many words. He can think what he wants. I just sort of led him on. Even if you don't take what's happened seriously, *I* do. Besides, if you know how to handle the situation, you can get a lot of information with a few kisses and a quick grope." She laughed, but I thought I detected an underlying nervous edge.

"And what precisely have you found out that makes you think it's wise to continue?"

"It wasn't hard to casually bring up a murder that's on everyone's mind. He actually said he'd seen Marion! She'd been in his department not that long ago. How dumb is that?"

"Jackie, this is dangerous. What if he does know something? What if he actually were the murderer? Do you think you can handle anything that comes up?"

"It might be dangerous. What of it? I have to do *something*!"

"Jackie, I have to be honest. You're being pretty obsessive about this."

"Thank you, Carolina Graf, Amateur Psychologist," she sneered. "It's easy to stand on the sidelines and give advice. If it does get dangerous, I can deal with it. I'm not walking around with absolutely no protection."

"You mean you're carrying a weapon?"

"Sure."

"Jackie, this is nuts! You can't –"

"So what did you find out?" I asked, verbally getting between them.

"This guy knows something. I'd bet on it. You've got to see the way he throws money around. Plus his car costs a lot more than what you'd expect somebody in his position could afford. *And* it's new."

Carolina said, "Maybe his favourite aunt died. There could be any number of simple explanations."

"And maybe a complicated one."

"Do you think he killed Marion?"

"How should I know at this point? You don't expect him to say, 'You'll never guess what I did last week,' do you? I have to do more probing, but my gut reaction is that he's involved."

"Are you going to tell the police?" Carolina asked.

"*The cops*? Fat chance of that!"

"Why are you so against them? What have they ever done to you?"

It was such a seemingly innocuous question that Jackie's reaction astounded us. First she went silent, and I could almost feel the white-hot anger vibrating through her. After a few moments she began pacing up and down the floor, breathing like a winded bull. Then, she walked over to the wall between my front windows and punched or kicked the wall hard enough to make the windows rattle. Carolina and I held our breath, waiting for the eruption.

It never came.

Finally, she answered quietly, through gritted teeth. "All right. I'll tell you since you've decided to be so nosy."

"Jackie," Carolina said, "I . . . Please don't think –"

"No! Don't . . . Just *don't*, Carolina!" Jackie strode around a bit more, then stopped as if she'd come to a decision. "The cops . . . The fucking cops wrecked my life!"

"How did they do that, Jackie?" Carolina asked gently.

"I never told you guys the truth about why I left home."

It had taken Jackie about three years from the time we met for her to tell us anything about her past. We'd only known that she'd hit out on her own, but we hadn't wanted to pry. When she eventually told us a little more, the story had been that she ran away when she was fourteen because she couldn't stand her parents. She hadn't said why. Hitchhiking, she'd made her way from a small town outside Calgary to her great-aunt's place in Port Colborne, down near Niagara Falls.

"I walked to a truck stop on the Trans-Canada and hitched a ride on the first rig heading east. My aunt almost didn't let me in when I showed up on her porch. I was pretty scruffy-looking," she'd told us, smiling slyly. "Not like now."

The "now" had looked pretty outrageous to me even with my failing eyesight: long hair on one side of her head with a crewcut on the other, two rings through her left nostril, army surplus fatigues, and black Doc Martens. She's mellowed more from those days – although I don't worry she'll ever dress like Susan.

The aunt took her in and, under her firm hand, Jackie had managed to graduate from high school with honours and got accepted into the University of Toronto, where we all met. However, when her aunt died, whatever stability Jackie had regained disintegrated, as did her stay at university. Since then, she's put in time as a cab driver, a cocktail waitress, and, most recently, a bicycle courier.

"I lied to you about why I left home," Jackie repeated defiantly.

"In what way?" I asked.

Jackie paced a bit more, too full of nervous energy and tension to stand still. Eventually she sat down in the rattan chair and from its creaking I could tell that, even sitting, she couldn't hold still. Carolina and I planted ourselves on the sofa, waiting silently.

"It was my dad," Jackie began with quiet intensity. "He was a drunk, a brutal, savage drunk. He used to beat us: my mother, my brother, me. One night, I was the only one there when he came home really pissed and . . . and he raped me."

"Oh dear God!" Carolina whispered.

My stomach gave a heave. "How old were you?" I asked.

"I'd just turned eleven. He said he'd kill me if I ever told anyone. After that, any time he got the chance, he did it to me again. It was . . . terrible, and I wanted to die. I think my mother knew about it, but she was probably just as happy not to have him bothering her.

"My brother stumbled in on us once, and when my father threatened to kill him, he just walked right out the front door and we never saw him again. I have no idea where he went. Aunt Peg said once that someone told her they think he's out on the West Coast some place. I don't know.

"One day, my father forced me to do something . . . Anyway, I had to stop him or I felt like I would've exploded. I didn't care any more what he did to me, but I had a nine-year-old cousin and he'd started looking at her the same way."

"So you went to the police?" Carolina offered.

"Yeah. I went to the *goddamed* police. You've got to understand that we were living in a small town. Everybody knew each other, and my father was an important, *respected* member of the community. Hah! What total *bullshit*! Anyway, the cops didn't believe me or they didn't care. I even offered to show them where he'd . . . the marks from what he'd done.

"Can you believe they got right on the phone to my father and told him what I'd been saying? He asked them to hold me there, that he'd come right down and explain to them about my severe emotional and social problems. He actually told them that he'd been trying to get help for me, and this was the thanks he got for all his trouble! It was easy to see that the cops were completely snowed by his story.

"I was only fourteen! It was like I was stuck inside a Kafka novel. I needed help, and no one would give it to me. The goddam cops treated me as if *I'd* done something wrong for Chrissake!" Jackie stopped to pull herself back together. "I asked them to let me use the washroom. While I was in there, I climbed out the window and started running. I knew my father would kill me or . . . worse if he got his hands on me, and I couldn't face that again. Even after Aunt Peggy took me in, I lived in mortal terror that one day, on my way home from school or when I was alone in the house, he'd come after me. I still have dreadful nightmares about it."

"Did you tell your aunt what happened?" Carolina asked.

"Not past what I couldn't avoid. I think she knew more than I told her, though, because she didn't make a move to contact my folks. When I eventually did tell her what forced me to leave, she said I should learn to 'forgive and forget.' I challenged her on that, and then she admitted that my father had died three months earlier, but she hadn't wanted to tell me at the time. I think the whole family conspired to keep me and my story out of the picture. My aunt said something about 'family honour.' She went down in my estimation after that. Family honour . . . What a crock! My family's a dungheap!'"

Jackie's story explained *so* much. My heart went out to her. "Jackie, I don't know what to say. The whole thing's just too horrible to contemplate. I know it sounds lame, but is there anything we can do?"

"You need help," Carolina said.

"Do you mean psychological help?" Jackie spat back, sounding more like her usual self. "No thanks!"

"No, no. I mean we have to help you find out if your theory about Marion is correct."

Now it was Jackie's turn to sound flabbergasted. "You're kidding."

"We need concrete information, solid evidence for the police. Kit? I think you should go down and see Detective Morris. I bet he'll talk to you. See how much you can find out and maybe put another bug in his ear about Jackie's ideas. Jackie, as soon as we find out anything –"

Jackie perked up amazingly. "No way! I'm not sitting around waiting. I plan on seeing that guy from Housing tomorrow evening. We'll get all cuddly. He'll talk. They always do after –"

"You're not seriously considering going to bed with this bozo, are you?" I exclaimed.

"It won't get that far. This guy likes to brag. I only need to string him along."

"That all depends if he actually knows anything useful," Carolina pointed out.

"I'll bet you a hundred bucks he does. You gotta see this guy operate. It's enough to make you puke. His life is one long trying-to-impress-the-next-girl-he'd-like-to-screw. If there are other people involved in Marion's death, they should be worried about this turkey."

"Why don't you just wait to see what Kit finds out from Morris?" Carolina suggested.

"I can't stand sitting around doing nothing."

"How can you *stand* sitting?" Carolina pointed out, in a very poor attempt to be funny, but it backfired badly.

Mount Jackie finally erupted. "So *that's* what's going on! This is all fun and games to you, is it? I never should have told you anything! You don't really want to help me. You just led me on and said all that so I'd do what you want! You don't want me to be right; you just want to play shrink." She grabbed her jacket and stormed to the door. "Carolina Graf, you're not as goddamed smart as you like to think you are!" The door crashed shut, and Jackie disappeared into the night. Talk about a one-woman emotional roller-coaster.

Carolina sighed. "Oh Christ! I shouldn't have bearded the goat. We're in for it now."

"Yeah," I agreed. "Why does it always make me uneasy when Jackie gets like this?"

"History."

"You were serious about helping Jackie."

"Absolutely."

"Why the sudden change?" I asked.

"Now that we know what she's been through, it's pretty obvious what a knife-edge Jackie's on emotionally. *We're* her family now, and she and Marion were closest. In her mind, it's all her fault that Marion is dead, because she didn't offer to help when Marion asked. Whether that's accurate or not doesn't matter. Jackie *believes* it, and she won't be able to walk away from this until she finds out the truth for herself. We can help by supporting her in her quest. And that's exactly what it is to her: a quest in the classic sense of the word. If we don't stand behind her, she has no one. So we help. It's the only thing we can do for her." Carolina picked her coat up off the sofa and went to the door. "Call Morris. It might speed things up."

"We should have got the name of the club where she's meeting that guy."

"I was just thinking the same thing."

I had a lot to think about, and kept putting off calling Morris until it was too late. That gave me something else to beat myself up about that whole evening. To take my mind off it, I tried working on

Carolina's damn song, then attempted to practise a bit, before finally taking out the rowing machine. Nothing worked. I couldn't stop images of Jackie's horrible childhood from flashing through my thoughts. I went to bed early, thoroughly depressed – but incredibly grateful that my parents had both been good people who tried hard.

Surprisingly, I woke up the next morning with a lot more – I don't know – *hope* might be the best word to describe the way I felt. Energy flowed through me as it hadn't in a long time. I felt ready to do things, not be done by them.

Humming to myself, I took a shower and, as I combed out the after-shampoo tangles, I wondered how my hair looked. Susan had been cutting it for the past couple of years, using the skill she'd gained at the expense of her kids' appearance. Nobody'd said anything bad about her work, so I assumed it was okay, but now the way I looked mattered to me. What *did* I look like? More importantly, what did I look like to Patrick?

It was a pretty distracted mistress who took Shadow for his morning stroll. I visualized myself walking down Queen Street in my own private sunbeam. Shadow, sensing my distraction, began to take liberties, stopping to do doggy things like sniffing at hydrants. He even barked at something across the street. Generally, he's all business when we're out, even when we're out for his business. Shadow's mind wandering at the wrong time could obviously prove disastrous to me, and I have enough scars to keep me always aware of it. That morning, though, I just let him do his thing, and I did mine. I felt invulnerable.

When I returned to the apartment, I called Morris at the number he'd given us after that first interview. It took a few minutes to get him on the line.

"Ms. Mason, how's your head feeling?"

"Pretty good – the hospital agreed that I have a very hard one. It was only a mild concussion."

"You know, you're lucky. That was a pretty stupid stunt you two girls pulled," he said, but chuckled regardless. "What can I do for you?"

I bridled inwardly at his "two girls" comment, but since I wanted info, I kept my thoughts to myself. "Would it be possible for me to see you?"

"I can't get away from the office right now. I'm sure you understand we're rather busy."

"No, no. I'll come to you."

"When?"

"Soon as possible."

"Do you have information?"

"I'm not sure. I *think* I might," I lied. "I can be there in about
an hour. Is that okay?"

"An hour would be fine. Just ask for me at the information desk.
They'll get you to my office."

Morris worked out of Police Headquarters on College Street.
He must have alerted the front desk to watch for me, because
Shadow and I got hustled across the echoing lobby, into an elevator, and along a rather winding trail through a series of rooms. The
noise of phones ringing, people talking (and shouting), accompanied by the reek of old coffee, stale sandwiches, and a faint whiff of
surreptitious cigarette smoke made us both uneasy. We were then
deposited in a room and left alone. The closing door cut off the
outside noise like a knife sliding into soft flesh. Sorry for the
metaphor, but police stations make me uncomfortable. Shadow
crawled under the big wooden table that seemed to fill the room,
while I sat perched on one corner of it, leg dangling lazily as I tried
to look as if all this was normal for me. We waited at least fifteen
minutes. Typical officialdom: hurry up and wait.

When the door burst open, I jumped a mile. Shadow did as well,
slamming his head on the underside of the table.

"Sorry to startle you – and for keeping you waiting," Morris
said and paused awkwardly. Figuring he might be used to shaking
hands with people at the start of a conversation and might be at a
loss on what to do with someone like me, I stuck out my hand, and
he gave it a perfunctory shake. Then I sat down on one of those
moulded plastic chairs and he pulled out another. The table
stretched between us. "So, what do you think you have for me?"

"Actually . . . I mean . . . ." So much for being prepared to snow
the man. "Could you answer some questions?" I finally blurted out.

"Does this have anything to do with Ms. Goode's story?"

"Well . . . yes."

"Look, Ms. Mason –"

"Why don't you call me Kit? 'Ms. Mason' makes me think my mother just walked into the room."

"Okay, Kit, let's get one thing crystal clear. Your friend's story doesn't hold any water. That lunatic we let escape – I'll admit we're to blame for it – committed the murder we're investigating. All the facts point in that direction."

A light bulb went on in my head. Maybe if I took a different tack . . . "I certainly understand that, but my friend Jackie is having a tough time with this. She's got some unresolved issues from her past –"

"Just what are you asking?" I got the feeling that Morris was watching the clock, sorry that he'd given me some of his time.

"I'll cut to the chase. Jackie thinks that, because you hesitated for forty-eight hours before you said it was the Strangler who murdered Marion –"

"– that we aren't really sure it was him and we're just caving in to the pressure groups?" Morris finished for me and he did not sound happy. "She said as much yesterday, before I had to have her thrown the hell out of here. I should've charged her," he added under his breath.

"Look, if you could answer a few questions for me, I could probably satisfy Jackie. You wouldn't want her to go spouting off to the media, would you?" I crossed my fingers as I said that last bit.

"God no! We have enough trouble as it is." He was silent for a moment. Shadow stretched, then groaned contentedly under the table. "Okay. I'll answer if I can."

"When you interviewed us at my place, you said that something about the case was bothering you. What did you mean?"

Morris came to a silent decision before continuing. "When we started the investigation, we discovered certain, ah, things in Ms. Joseph's apartment. For a while it made us think she might have been murdered by someone she knew."

"What things?"

"Are you aware that your friend engaged in some odd sexual practices?"

"*Marion?*" I asked, totally flabbergasted. "Get out of town!"

"It surprised us, too, after what everyone had been saying about her."

"What did you find?"

"An assortment of sex toys, whips, and restraining devices."

"*S&M? Marion?* Are you sure?"

"They were definitely hers."

"I don't know what to say. I had absolutely no idea. None of us did."

Morris breathed deeply. "Her boyfriend certainly did, but it took a bit of pressure to get him to admit it."

"What did they do?"

"Pretty harmless stuff, really."

"But Tony certainly didn't kill her. He was in Kingston at the time, and you knew that. Why did you think Marion knew her murderer?"

"Let me put it this way: You all said her friend Tony was the first person Ms. Joseph had gone out with in almost three years."

"Positively. I don't think she had one date in that time. She was always complaining about it."

"Do you think it's possible she was seeing someone on the side? Someone she didn't tell you about?"

I shook my head in bewilderment. "After what you've just told me about the sex toys, I have no idea *what* Marion was and wasn't doing."

"We have reason to believe that she was seeing someone with short, blond hair. Her boyfriend has brown hair and it's long. There were also oblique references in a journal she kept, but she didn't use a name or even an initial. One of her neighbours also thought she remembered seeing a blond man with Ms. Joseph sometime in February.

"But in the end, we couldn't come up with anything, and the evidence the other way was too strong. True, the Strangler usually enters the houses of his victims by an unlocked back door, but he did kill several times out in the open. He's a creature of habit, meticulous in his own way. These killers often are. No, it's definitely the Strangler. We're sure of that. But that's why there was the preliminary delay. We had to follow up that first lead." Morris's chair scraped back and he got to his feet. "I hope that's enough information to keep Ms. Goode out of our hair. And I hope you realize that what I've told must not go any further than this room. Sorry to have to rush you out of here, but as you can imagine, we're really busy. We must get fifty sightings of the Strangler every day, and naturally they all have to be followed up."

I couldn't leave without giving it one more try. "Detective Morris, don't you think *anything* we're saying merits investigating?"

"Ms. Mason – Kit – please understand, our resources are stretched to the limit right now. If you had something more concrete, something other than the suspicions of a woman you yourself have told me has problems, we would certainly look into it. Believe me, the department has to get this one right." He gave a short, sardonic laugh. "Even at the risk of having to say we were wrong."

I rose and slung my purse dispiritedly over my shoulder.

"Thanks for coming down," Morris said. "I appreciate the fact that you want to help. Your friend's death is a horrible thing." He stooped to scratch behind Shadow's ears. I knew from the groan of utter contentment that he'd found just the right spot. "I had a Newf when I was a kid. They're great animals, but I've never heard of one as a guide dog."

"You probably never will again. As far as I know, I've got the only one, and they trained him only under extreme duress."

"How so?"

"The place I went for my guide dog also breeds Newfs. When I got out of the car, this big idiot, who was still pretty much a puppy at the time, came charging up and knocked me over. The owners were appalled and started to drag him off, but something had clicked between us. I guess you'd call it love at first sight." I smiled. "To make a long story short, I asked if he could be trained and they said flat-out, 'No. He's too big and clumsy. They tend to be too short-lived. His hair's too long. Blah, blah, blah.' So I got my dad to make them a financial offer they couldn't refuse. This is the result. And don't let him fool you, he's actually very good at his job – most of the time. Aren't you, Shadow?"

Shadow, at the mention of his name, soaked my hand with his tongue.

"Why Shadow?" Morris asked.

"It should be obvious, considering what he's trained for and by the colour of his coat." When Morris made no response, I added, "Don't you get it? Me and my Shadow?"

"Oh."

Some people have no sense of humour.

Shadow and I stopped at the local variety store on the way home to pick up something for lunch. I'm pretty good with cans, and soup or spaghetti is generally good enough for me. Shadow likes cans, too, because sometimes I open one of his dog foods by mistake. If he's already had his dinner, then he scores a second one, which is all right by him.

I checked the voice mail when I got home: two messages, neither from Patrick. Damn!

Mom, who was currently in the south of France, left the first one. "Hi, Honey. Just called to see how you're doing. The weather here is atrocious: cold and wet. Next year I'll go to the Caribbean. I hope you're out doing something exciting right now. You sit at home too much, but then I say that all the time, don't I? Well, since you're not home, I won't waste my money. I'll be back in about two weeks. Why don't we go out and have dinner? I'll call. Love you."

Carolina had left the second message – using a cellphone, no less. She absolutely abhors the things. It has to be a real emergency for her to use one. Considering she'd called when she was so pressed for time made it doubly obvious the call was important.

"Kit? It's Carolina. I've only got a few minutes between my class and another stupid seminar I'm leading, so I'll make this brief. I've been thinking about everything Jackie's been saying, and I'm beginning to believe that she may have something. It's just so hard to imagine Marion mixed up in something that got her killed. She was such a mouse. Maybe the three of us can get together with Susan and talk it over, but anyway, I'm worried about Jackie getting herself into trouble." She laughed. "No, not that way! I'll call back after 3:30. Got to run. 'Bye."

As I kicked off my boots, I said to Shadow, "Wait till C hears what Morris had to say."

Carolina's call made me feel guilty about still having no idea of what to do for that song I'd been snookered into writing. I hauled out the acoustic and strummed around for a while, hoping I'd be struck by some brilliant idea, but other than deciding that the guitar needed new strings, nothing much happened. After I'd got some canned soup, peanut butter on crackers, and a banana into my stomach, practised for a while, and rowed to Detroit and back, it was almost 3:30. So I stretched out on the bed with the phone at hand to wait for Carolina's call.

The damn thing ringing on my stomach blasted me right out of a deep sleep. Try it sometime. It's a real adrenaline rush.

"What is it?" I barked.

"Kit? It's Patrick. Is this a bad time to call?"

That got the cobwebs out real fast. "Um, no. I fell asleep and the phone startled me, that's all."

"Sorry I woke you. Look, I'm calling to find out if you'd be available to go to a concert on Saturday. I just got tickets for Bonnie Raitt."

"Bonnie Raitt? That show's been sold out for weeks!"

"I've got a friend who owed me a favour. Want to go?"

"You bet!"

"I'll pick you up around 6:00. We can have a spot of dinner at one of those places along Queen Street, then toddle over to Roy Thomson Hall."

I told him my apartment number, hung up, and sat there on cloud nine. Bonnie Raitt was one of my all-time favourites and a guitarist of the first water. I had most of her CDs, and I'd even gone as far as learning a few of her slide-guitar licks, something I seldom bother doing with most guitarists. Actually, about the only other guitarist who interested me that much was my old teacher back in Connecticut, Link, who passed away several years back.

My euphoria lasted through doggy duties and the ritual can-opening for dinner. Then there was a knock on my door.

"Well, Shadow, want to take bets? Carolina or Jackie. Which one do you think it is? My money's on Carolina." Shadow only continued to chomp disgustingly on his food. I hoisted myself off the stool and went to the door. "Who is it?"

"Carolina."

Bingo! "Shadow, I win," I called out as I opened the door.

As Carolina breezed in, she gave me a quick peck on the cheek.

"Sorry, I didn't get a chance to call, but I figured I'd just stop by on the way home instead. Are you talking to that furball again? You've been cooped up in this place too long."

I couldn't hold in my big news. "I won't be on Saturday. I'm going to see Bonnie Raitt."

"Really? I thought the show was sold out." Then she stopped. "Say . . . wait a minute! Who's taking you?" When I didn't answer, she walked over to me and took my chin in her hand, tilting my head up. "You're holding out on me, young lady! I can tell from that smug look on your face. C'mon, give!"

I just continued smirking. "I met a guy the other day."

"What do you mean you met a guy? Why didn't you tell me last night?"

I grabbed her around the waist and squeezed, my happiness bubbling over. "I don't know. For some reason I felt shy about it. Then Jackie came over, and her antics pushed it right out of my head."

It took Carolina half an hour to complete her cross-examination. "Well I'll be damned!" she said at the end.

"It just kind of fell into my lap."

"This sounds very encouraging. The phone call proves it. Oh Kit, I'm so happy for you!" Now it was her turn to squeeze me. "What do you wear to a concert at Roy Thomson Hall?"

"I don't know – clothes. I hadn't thought about it," I lied.

"Well, dear, it seems to me you need to make a definite impression." She fiddled with my hair for a bit, then had me stand up and turn around for her. "Okay. This is what I think you might want to consider. First off, we have to get that hair fixed up. The length isn't bad for your face – you've always looked better in longer hair – but the cut doesn't do much for you. Some highlighting maybe, too. Now for clothes . . . I've got it! That scarlet silk blouse Edward gave me for Christmas would look great on you. And those black jeans; they really show off your bum."

"Carolina! Are you trying to get me laid or something?"

She chuckled. "Wouldn't *that* be nice!"

"What if I'm not interested?"

"The way you've been talking?"

Funny, but considering how I used to be, I hadn't thought about Patrick like that – well, not *too* much. It had just been nice to have someone male to talk to. Carolina's comment projected this just-born relationship about three light-years down the road, and I wasn't sure I wanted to take that step right away.

Someone leaning on the street-door buzzer shattered our girlish reverie. I walked over and said into the panel, "This had better be important."

"Kit! Kit! It's Jackie. Let me in!"

—⚹—

"THIS IS A REAL MESS!" THE MAN muttered under his breath.

He was sitting in his car on the shady side of King Street, just west of Parliament. In the sun it had become almost warm, but a remainder of winter still held sway where the sun couldn't reach, and his toes had gone numb from the effects of the now – he consulted his watch – two-hour wait.

He had been unhappy at being pressured into taking this job. It had always been his rule to pick over offered work, then choose the surest and safest assignments. That approach had made him the success he was. His specialty had always been the subtle affairs. Leave the drive-by shootings and the bombs under cars to the coarser practitioners.

He'd been taught his craft by the U.S. Army. They'd developed a pretty good system for training expert killers, and he'd quickly shown himself to have the Right Stuff to be recruited for one of the elite fighting groups. He hadn't proven to be much of a team player, though, and that eventually got him into so much trouble he'd had to leave. No CIA or FBI job for him, either. He'd had enough of being ordered around. So the man had found himself, like many others, back in the real world with an expertise he wasn't allowed to use. He went back to school on the GI Bill, thinking that becoming an accountant would be the way to go, but the experience had only lasted a year. Next, he tried life as a hunting and fishing guide – closer to what he was really good at.

He had become bored again and just about to chuck it all

to try something else when two businessmen he was escorting on a moose hunt got him talking about his experiences in the Army. He told them that it had been the most enjoyable period in his life. Whenever his sergeant needed someone to do a nasty or dangerous job, he could always be counted on to volunteer. Once, he'd taken out five members of a terrorist cell who would have cut his group to ribbons if he hadn't gotten them first. He thought the businessmen would be shocked when he frankly confided that what he was really best at was killing people.

But they hadn't been shocked. In a fantastic turnabout they'd proposed something that shocked *him*. A competitor was about to put them under. Everything they'd worked so hard to attain would go right down the toilet. The target was a blight on society, anyway, according to them. They'd hired a detective to dig up dirt they might use against him, but the only result was to learn that their competitor had a weakness for women, other men's women, often wives. It wouldn't take much cleverness to make his murder look like a crime of passion, and the field of suspects would be wide open. The more the man talked about it with the two businessmen over drinks around the campfire, the easier the job looked. If the affair was handled right, the cops would never find anyone to pin it on. A quick bullet in the brain, and it would be all over. It had been a breathtaking realization that he would actually enjoy carrying out something like this.

The man stretched his legs and wiggled his toes to get the blood circulating again.

Remembering that first assignment, he shook his head. Never having had to plan any of the military operations he'd been a part of, he had no idea of how much planning something like this took. And he was so green about police procedures! He'd made enough mistakes that a Boy Scout could have nailed him, but fortunately the local police had only had eyes for the obvious motive: half the men in town hated the victim. The one thing that all the mistakes did do, however, was to make him realize the inescapable value of thorough planning.

But that was long ago now, and reminiscences of past successes didn't make up for the fact that he felt cold, hungry, and frustrated. He couldn't remember an assignment that had brought him less pleasure. He'd already half decided to pack up quietly and head out for parts unknown. These guys wouldn't go after him if he split. They couldn't afford to. Anybody they hired would know how difficult he'd be to take out, and they'd charge accordingly. Why bother?

He knew why he *was* bothering, though. His reputation for reliability. That didn't come easily in his line of work, and if he cut out now, it was an asset that would be destroyed. People would think he'd lost his nerve, and that would make him a liability.

He sighed for about the tenth time and looked across the street. Where the hell was she? Was this going to be another wasted day?

The voice on the phone had told him she worked for the bicycle courier service that had an office on the second floor of the rundown building opposite. It had been a simple matter to discover that the couriers stopped by every morning to pick up their walkie-talkies and the day's first run from the dispatcher. Her description seemed accurate enough, but this girl would stand out in many crowds. Not too many people had purple hair and a ring in their nose.

His plan was simplicity itself, the perfect hit, one he'd held in reserve for many years. Too bad he could only use it once. He would admit to killing her! What had suggested it to him this time was how reckless bike couriers could be, weaving in and out of traffic, breaking just about every law in the Highway Traffic Act. One flick of the wheel as he drove behind her, and she'd be dead meat. How could anyone fault him? "Officer, she just rode out right in front of me! I couldn't stop in time! Oh God! It's so awful, but I couldn't help it! I just couldn't . . ." He'd practised his little speech until he wasn't sure he could still make it sound spontaneous.

He'd missed her the first day, though. She'd been one of a large crowd to arrive at the same time, but it had been the purple hair that'd done him in. It hadn't been there. She now had it dyed bright orange, and arranged in rather jagged clumps, instead of a brush cut. She'd been out the door and away before he could be sure that it was actually her. After cruising the downtown core for hours, he hadn't been able to catch sight of his target.

And this morning she hadn't shown up at all. He'd spent the best part of it waiting, but she just never appeared. After that he made some attempts to find out where she lived. The result? No person with that name listed in the usual places: phone books, voting lists, stuff like that. Her last known address turned out to be a now-empty lot waiting for redevelopment.

Not wanting to have the job drag into the weekend, the man had taken a step he'd rather have avoided. He called the courier agency and fed them a line about owing the girl money and wanting to pay it back before he left town. "When will she be in today? This afternoon, to get her pay? Great! I'll try to meet her at . . . 5:30? That's perfect. Thanks a lot!"

Now he'd had contact with someone the cops might speak to, but he'd just have to risk that. Dammit all! It would have been so easy just to crush her under his wheels. What was he going to do now? Come up with a whole new plan, that's what. Once he spotted her tonight, he wasn't going to let her out of his sight. Maybe she'd be co-operative and use her bike when she picked up her pay. Then he could follow his original plan and *whammo*! Quick and clean. He'd spent too much time on this already. Besides, he had something planned for the weekend.

But in any event, Jackie Goode would die that evening. The man would make sure of it.

CHAPTER 10

—⟁—

I opened the door and waited. Jackie practically flew up the stairs. "Shut the door! Shut the goddam door!"

"My God, Jackie! *What happened?*" Shock was plain in Carolina's voice.

With my hand still on the doorknob, I asked, "Would somebody tell me what the hell's going on?"

This type of situation makes me more frantic than anything else. When the shit hits the fan, nobody has time to stop and give the blind person a running commentary. You stand there like a dummy, while everybody runs around. For all I knew Jackie had shown up at my door with her head shaved and a Santa suit on. Carolina's next comment made me aware that matters were rather more serious.

"Kit! Do you have disinfectant? And we need bandages. Oh shit, Jackie, we should get you to a hospital!"

"No!" she answered from the bathroom. "No doctors. No hospital. It's not that bad."

I moved to the middle of the living room and shouted, "If one of you doesn't tell me what's going on, *I'm* going to call the goddamed police and let them sort this out!"

"Somebody just tried to kill me!"

After that news bulletin, neither of them took the slightest notice of me, and I had to lump it. Someone turned the faucet on full blast in the bathroom sink. Eventually, Carolina spoke over the noise. "Jackie's right knee and arm are badly scraped and there's a big cut on the back of her head. C'mon, Jackie! Lean over and let me look at it. Stop squirming!" A few moments of silence ensued. "No, you're right; it's not as bad as it looks. Here, hold this wad of toilet paper over it. I'll get some ice."

Carolina rushed by me on her way to the kitchen and in short order had the bleeding from Jackie's scalp under control. I had the softball team's medical kit in my closet, and she used some of the stuff to get the cuts on Jackie's arms and legs taken care of. The scalp wound took some trimming work with scissors on her hair and a couple of butterfly bandages. My job boiled down to getting Jackie a stiff belt of the only hard liquor I had in the house, some junk my mother had brought back from one of her European forays.

"What is this shit?" Jackie asked after a healthy swallow.

"It's called Cloudberry Liqueur. From Norway, if I remember correctly."

"Do the reindeer piss on the berries before they're picked?" she asked. I knew she was feeling better.

After switching to beer, Jackie told us what'd happened. "I didn't ride today, but I wanted to pick up my paycheque, so naturally I took my bike. By the time I got there it was almost 6:00, and I was in a hurry."

"Your heavy date with that guy from City Hall?" I asked.

"Yeah. I had to get dressed and over to the bar by 8:00. At any rate, I was peddling up Sherbourne back to the place where I'm crashing, and this car cruises up next to me. When I got to a row of parked cars, he tried to squeeze me out."

"Maybe he didn't see you," Carolina said.

"Not likely! This was deliberate or I'm a fool. The guy boxed me in, and when I started to speed up, he kept pace. As we approached a parked truck, he swerved right into me. I mean, if I wasn't used to dodging this kind of bullshit driving every day, I would have been plastered all over the side of the truck or under this jerk's wheels; it was that close! Anyway, my bike's a pile of scrap now. It went right under the car. That thing cost me over seven hundred!"

I shook my head. "How come you aren't dead?"

"I bailed out just behind the truck. That's where I got these cuts. Fortunately there was space between it and the car parked behind, and I just dove for it. Next thing I knew, I was under the rear of the truck. The car stopped, but when the driver got out he didn't know where I was – and I wasn't about to tell him. As soon as I'd got my brain scraped back together, I wormed my way through the crowd and took off."

"Jackie, do you mind if I play devil's advocate?" said Carolina.

"What do you mean?" she asked suspiciously.

"Could we look at possible alternatives? Now don't get upset! I just want to be logical about this. Okay?"

"Well . . ."

"Could this have been just bad driving?"

"No way! He was staring right at me when he did it."

"Could you identify him?"

"No," Jackie said sourly. "There wasn't that much light, and I was too busy trying to stay alive."

"But if he were drunk . . ."

I could imagine Jackie shaking her head violently. "Absolutely not! Bernie, my dispatcher, told me someone called this afternoon saying that he owed me some money."

"Oh," was all Carolina said.

The idea that Jackie could have loaned money to anyone (besides us) was totally out of character. Because of her lifestyle, she has to struggle for every penny. On top of that, she's basically a cheapskate.

Jackie continued, "Now why would someone call the courier service, ask when I'd be there, and say they'd meet me to pay back dough I hadn't loaned them? Tell me that!"

Carolina and I remained silent, probably thinking the same thing: how could somebody have gotten wind of the fact that Jackie had started asking questions? Could she have blown it with that guy from City Hall?

"Are you sure about everything you've told us?" Carolina asked.

"You're saying I'm lying?"

"Oh, come on! We know each other better than that. You have to admit you have a tendency to exaggerate. I want to be sure what you've told us is accurate, no added colour."

"The goddamed, complete truth!"

"Then we phone up Morris and tell him."

"No!"

"Jackie, be reasonable –"

"I think we should discuss this some more," I interrupted, "before any calls are made."

"What do you mean?" Carolina asked.

"First, do you feel that Jackie may be right about Marion?"

"Yes, that seems an increasingly strong possibility."

"Thanks for the ringing endorsement," Jackie said sourly.

I ignored her. "Okay. Jackie, exactly who did you speak to about Marion – other than us and Morris?"

"No one – by name anyway. With Morris, I only told him what I suspected. No names. And I didn't really get much from that guy from City Hall. When I saw him yesterday, I only tried to set up a situation where I might be able to get information."

"What about the person who put you onto this guy?"

"Oh, right. I see what you're getting at. I don't think we have anything to worry about from her. She only told me about Rex – that's his name by the way – who's been acting like a big shot lately and seems to have more money than he should. It's that way with any government bureaucracy. Half the people are on the take and the other half are envious about it. I just thought Rex sounded stupid enough to get information from."

I sat back and considered for a moment. Now was probably the best time to tell them what I'd found out at the police station. "I went and talked to Morris today."

"I knew it! That guy looked crooked from –"

"Aw, Jackie, give it up! You can't possibly think Morris is involved in this. Anyway, he told me some things about Marion, and they just . . . blew me away. I still can't believe it."

"What, for Chrissake?"

So I told them – as close to word-for-word as I could remember. When I finished, you could have heard a pin drop.

Finally Jackie said, almost laughing, "I don't believe it! Sweet, innocent Marion . . . Kit, blown away is too modest a description."

"This certainly complicates matters considerably," Carolina said, massively understating the obvious. "It seems to me that there could be more than the one solution to the matter of Marion's death."

"Not really," I answered. "If Marion was murdered by this blond guy Morris told me about, that would be one thing, but what does Jackie have to do with that? She wasn't even aware that Marion *had* a blond lover – and certainly hasn't been out investigating something like that. Let's stick to our original assumption, since it looks as if something about what Jackie *has* been doing the past few days has stirred up the trouble she had tonight. We have to figure out what that is."

Jackie summed up all her feelings in one word, "*Morris*!"

"Not necessarily," Carolina answered slowly. "I see what Kit's getting at. It looks as if somehow, Jackie, your interest and your belief that Marion's work had something to do with her death got to the ears of someone who has reason to be concerned."

"So where does that leave us?" Jackie asked.

Carolina said, "We have to contact Morris. No, no! Hear me out, Jackie. We need help from the police right now and it would be stupid not to use it. How are we going to find the man who tried to run you over? Only they have the resources for that." She walked over to the phone. "What's the number, Kit?"

She got someone from Morris's office on the line and said that we had important news. "Stay put," she was told. "Detective Morris will be in touch within fifteen minutes."

We received a return call before the Chinese food we'd called out for had arrived. Morris asked to speak to me. "What've you got?" He sounded peeved. We'd probably broken into his once-a-month poker game or something.

I approached the subject obliquely. "Someone tried to run down Jackie Goode earlier this evening."

His manner became more businesslike. "Tell me about it."

"I'd prefer to tell you in person. Do you want us to meet you at headquarters?"

"No." He hung up after saying to expect him within an hour.

The rest of the evening was quite comical in some respects. Carolina and I coaxed Jackie into shelving her antagonism, and Morris was obviously trying hard to do the same. On the surface they behaved politely, but you could tell what was bubbling underneath by the tightness in their voices and the curtness of their answers. It reminded me of two lions circling the same carcass.

As a peace offering, Jackie had asked Morris if he'd like the last of the Chinese when he arrived. He declined and started out by asking her to tell him what had happened. She kept to her task admirably, even when Morris, too, asked whether she had considered that the driver might have been drunk. After he'd heard all she had to say, Morris immediately got on the phone to headquarters and asked them to check out if there had been an incident reported at the corner of Sherbourne and Wellesley that evening. Within minutes he had his answer: nothing. He then asked to have a unit sent around to look the area over.

"If there wasn't an injured party, police assistance might not have been requested," he explained. "You'd be surprised how many things happen in that neighbourhood that we never hear about."

"But do you believe my story now?" Jackie sounded almost resigned.

Morris didn't speak right away, and I could feel the tension escalate in the room. "I think that what you've reported requires following up."

"Well, thank God for that."

Jackie did the best she could, providing Morris with information. Big deal. She couldn't describe what the guy looked like. He drove a dark-coloured late-model car. She didn't know the make. I could have done about as well. The detective dutifully scribbled down the meagre information.

A great deal of the conversation centred on what Jackie had to say about this Rex character from City Hall. Fortunately, she left out the part about being halfway willing to jump into the sack with the guy to get him to talk. I couldn't guess how he would have responded to that bit of news.

Finally, Morris said, "I think I'll speak to him first thing in the morning."

"And what about the fat bankroll he's been flashing?" Jackie asked.

He dutifully wrote that information down.

When Morris's second call came, he ah-hmmed into the phone several times before saying, "Thanks," and hung up. "Well, ladies, the bike is leaning up against a telephone pole at the corner. The frame's bent and the back wheel and brakes are missing –" He was interrupted by a string of graphic obscenities from the bike's owner. "There's an apartment building on that corner. We might be able to get information from the tenants." Morris stood up. "We'll get to work on it. I'd like to thank each of you . . ." He paused at this point, and I felt sure he had fixed Jackie with a jaundiced eye. ". . . for taking the time to call me. I'll let you know if we turn up anything. And in the meantime, I'd advise you to stay away from further amateur detecting, Ms. Goode. Good night all."

The door had barely shut before Jackie muttered, "Cocky bastard!"

Jackie spent the night snoring in my living room. I think the incident had shaken her up more than she'd admit. At any rate, she asked if she could crash on my sofa, to which I agreed under the circumstances. She'd slept on it plenty of times before and not always alone (which makes it hard to use the bathroom discreetly). About six months ago I arrived home unexpectedly early and caught her in the act with some guy I'd never met. That was when I took away her key to the apartment, although I'd left her with the outside door key so she could at least stay warm if she arrived when I wasn't around to let her all the way in. All the other Babes have both keys. Anyway, it amazed me that she fell asleep so easily. Come to think of it, how come Jackie was the one who'd almost died and I was the one who couldn't sleep?

I woke up next morning well after 11:00, which meant that Jackie had seen to Shadow's needs. Lying in bed with my hands behind my head, I thought not about Jackie's trials and tribulations, but about the warm feeling that accompanied the name Patrick. I hadn't felt this way in far too long, and I wallowed for another half-hour, tossing things around in my head.

What would the evening be like? I knew the music would be great, although I had doubts about the acoustics at Roy Thomson.

There are plenty of good restaurants between my place and there, so dinner would be enjoyable. But what about Patrick? After all, this was an Official Date. Carolina's comments of the night before surfaced. How should I respond if he wanted to fool around? The warm feeling inside me shifted to a spot lower down, and I knew what the physical part of me was saying. Socially, I had no problems with a roll in the hay with someone who took my fancy. Medically, I knew at least *I* was clean. But did I want to get that involved, especially with everything going on in my life at the moment? Wouldn't a relationship complicate things?

Shadow came into the room and pressed his nose against my bare arm, his way of saying good morning.

"How are you this morning, you old furball?"

A slurpy lick on my arm meant, *Just fine, thanks.*

"Did Aunt Jackie take you for your morning walkies?"

A voice from the living room answered. "Why do you think he let you sleep so long?"

As I padded along to the bathroom, I called out, "How are you feeling?"

"Not bad except for a whopper headache. I stopped at Novik's and picked up sticky rolls. Want some coffee?"

"Sounds great."

While we munched, Nick called to ask if I could get things together for a session Monday morning at 10:00. "I know it's short notice, but the guys we're providing are both free Monday; so's the studio. Think you could round up your people?"

"I'll try."

"I'm afraid this is the way Arnie works. He'll hold off giving away studio time until the last possible second if there's the slightest chance of a paying customer. Call me back before the end of the day, so I can confirm with our people. And Arnie told me to remind you to get that contract signed."

I got on the phone and rousted both Steve the bassist and Terry the drummer out of bed. They said they could do the session, and perked up considerably when I told them that the gig paid. As I hung up, I hoped it actually did. Arnie had intimated as much, but hadn't come right out and said it. Well, if need be, I'd dig into my own pocket. I didn't want to owe anyone anything.

After a call back to Nick, everything was arranged for Monday. I should have been nervous about it, but on this beautiful morning, I couldn't be. I knew, even without seeing it, that the day was going to be warm with a light breeze and lots of sun. Actually, I'd gotten a good whiff of the air coming in my bedroom window while I'd been sogging in bed. Bet you didn't know you can smell weather if you pay attention.

My daydreams of fame and fortune were brought to a screeching halt by Jackie saying, "So you've found a guy. What's his name?" I sat there with my mouth opening and closing and nothing coming out. Talk about being blindsided. Jackie laughed. "I called Carolina this morning to ask if she could come over for a meeting with Susan and us this evening, and she said you had a date with a real live man."

"What exactly did C tell you?" I finally managed to say.

Jackie laughed again. "Everything! I told her we should check this guy out and make sure he's good enough for you."

"That's precisely why I *didn't* tell you anything about him. Nobody would put up with your third degree. Patrick seems nice, and he's taking me to see Bonnie Raitt. Past that, I don't care and neither should you. I never ask who you go out with, do I?"

"But with you it's different."

"Oh, give me a break! Just because I can't see the guy doesn't mean anything. How many men have you gone out with who looked great and were total jerks?"

My friend was silent for a long moment. "Okay. Make your own mistakes."

"Thanks for the vote of confidence."

"Now you know what it feels like." Jackie laughed raucously, and immediately stopped short. "Oh, my aching head!"

"Speaking of which, I wonder what Morris has found out."

"Nothing, if I know the cops. I swear to God we're going to have to come up with all the answers ourselves before this is over."

Aside from going out onto the kitchen fire escape for a smoke a few times, Jackie stayed around the apartment the rest of the day, and I knew why. What'd happened the night before had really spooked her. You couldn't blame her for not wanting to be out on her own. Even though I had no idea where she was crashing at the moment, someone else might.

Carolina arrived about 2:00 to take me to her hairdresser. Under her watchful eye, my hair got washed, cut, highlighted, you name it. I had no idea what Vincent was doing and had to trust Carolina's good taste. I wouldn't have sat so docilely, however, if it'd been Jackie calling the shots.

"You really have quite lovely hair, Kit," Vincent said. "Nice and thick. You should take better care of it."

"That's a little tough to do," I pointed out.

"Nonsense! It's a good length for you to work with. Keep it clean, use a good conditioner, and come to see me every six weeks." He laughed, then turned to Carolina. "I think the idea of Kit having her hair short and off her forehead is good and suits the shape of her face, but it should be layered and longer in the back. Right now her hair looks like something you'd see on a twelve-year-old boy."

"Pretty close," I said. "He's actually around ten," and explained about Susan's ministrations.

After Vincent spent about fifteen minutes clipping and shaping, he put a bit of gel in my hair, combed the sides back and the front up, worked things into place a bit more, then stepped away.

"That's a long way from a boy's haircut now," Carolina said enthusiastically. "This guy's going to know you're one sexy woman."

"Will you just cut it out, C?" I groaned. "You're making me regret telling you about this!"

An hour later, we got back to my place. Carolina asked Jackie what she thought of my hair and, while Jackie allowed that it "looks good on Kit," she also said she wouldn't be "caught dead with something so middle-of-the-road." A typical response, but it showed she was feeling more like her usual obnoxious self.

"Well, I think it looks amazing," Carolina said with real conviction, and the mounting Attack of the Killer Butterflies retreated from my stomach a wee bit.

While I soaked in a hot bubble bath, hair carefully pinned up to protect Vincent's hard work, the basis of Carolina's song popped into my head. I went through the melody a couple of times to make sure I had it solidly and even got a bit of a chorus that I thought had possibilities.

My two friends helped me get dressed and Jackie did the honours with my makeup, something she has a real flair for – when she doesn't decide to become too free-form. By the time they'd assembled me, hair, makeup, and clothes, my nerves were back and more jangly than fifty cups of coffee, and my stomach felt halfway to sick.

"Kit needs something to steady her down," Carolina observed.

"The old whisky-and-mouthwash?" Jackie answered seriously. Since I didn't have any booze other than beer, the cloudberry crap, and a half-bottle of over-the-hill white wine, she dispatched herself to Gerald downstairs and returned with a half-tumbler of bourbon. "Here. Drink this, then rinse with the mouthwash, so he won't think you're a lush."

The effect of the hooch went a long way towards steadying my nerves. At 5:55, Carolina and Jackie declared me "ready for anything."

I wasn't so sure when the downstairs buzzer rang.

THE MAN COULDN'T REMEMBER THE LAST time he'd felt so angry. His rage sent out tendrils in every direction, like some noxious weed: the fucking girl on the bicycle, that smug voice on the phone, but most of his anger he directed at himself and his own stupidity. What in God's name had he been thinking? Never had he done a more slapped-together, un-thought-out job.

The only fortunate thing had been the location. When she evaporated into thin air after he'd managed to crush only her bike, not one person in the crowd seemed overly concerned by the accident. No blood – no interest. Anyplace else, some goody-two-shoes would have run screaming for the cops. At Sherbourne and Wellesley, people were a little more used to violent things happening and it took a lot to impress them. Not wanting to push his luck by asking if anybody had seen the girl, he'd made some appropriate noises, gotten into the car, and taken off – at a discreet speed.

He sat in front of the blank screen of his TV far into the night, brooding. Now she'd be doubly hard to whack. The girl was cagey enough to protect herself, but would she go running to the police? He didn't know.

If she told the cops and they believed her, they would alert body shops to look for cars with damage. If somebody at the scene remembered his plate number, they'd come looking for him directly. Well, he had an excuse for leaving the accident scene: the girl had run off, too. What would he have accomplished by staying? But only one thing really mattered if any of this came to pass: his name would be connected with Jackie Goode, and now he couldn't afford that at any cost. It would tie his hands completely – and that was the ultimate failure. His reputation rested on one extraordinary fact: he had never missed, not once in over twenty years. While the only smart thing now would be to bow out, pride wouldn't let him, whatever the consequences. He'd let the car rot in its garage for a couple of months if need be. If there was going to be heat, he'd know about it before long and could take further steps.

Okay. Hopefully, he had a clearer picture of where *he* stood, what his personal options were, but how should he proceed? Where in a city the size of Toronto could he find this pain-in-the-ass girl in a short period of time? His contact hadn't known where she lived, but the man had been told where her close friends lived. However, he was only one person, and he couldn't watch everywhere at once. She wouldn't go around to the courier agency again. It wouldn't take much to figure out how he'd gotten on her track, and from what he'd been told, she wasn't stupid. No, the only solution was to stake out the friends' places.

The solution to the problem brought a grimace of disgust to his face. Even though it was after 2 a.m, he'd have to call. His employers had to know how much the situation had changed and decide whether they wanted to continue. It was now more dangerous, but the job could still be done. The girl could "disappear." Sure, the cops would be suspicious, probably certain, that she was dead, but if the body was never found . . . He smiled. Hadn't the same thing happened to Jimmy Hoffa?

His employers could probably be talked into helping watch all the locations where she might be, but any contact with them would come with a stiff price: he'd have to acknowledge his failure. Sighing, he dredged the phone number from his memory and, taking a deep breath, dialled. He listened impatiently to the expected we're-not-able-to-take-your-call-right-now message.

His voice was soft and controlled when he finally spoke, the inner rage completely masked. "I've had trouble with the commission. We need to talk as soon as possible."

He gently replaced the receiver and continued looking at the blank TV screen, trying to think better thoughts.

What would be happening tomorrow night at this time?

CHAPTER 11

When the buzzer announced Patrick's arrival, a second attack of possessiveness surfaced, and to the chagrin of Carolina and Jackie, I chirruped happily into the door control panel, "Be right down." Grabbing my buckskin jacket and with a parting "Don't wait up!" I was out the door before they could say a thing, poor dears. Maybe it was childish, but I didn't want Patrick put off by the nosiness of my well-meaning but overly protective friends.

Patrick was waiting at the street door, and lightly taking his elbow, I let him guide me to his car. "You look incredible, Kit, especially your hair. Very nice," he said, following a quick peck on my cheek. "No Shadow?"

"He's being dog-sat," I answered, silently thanking the brilliant Vincent. "You wouldn't want him around anyway. He tends to howl when music gets too loud."

Patrick opened the car door, helped me get my seatbelt hooked up, and, after he jumped in, we took off for parts unknown. I could picture Jackie and Carolina with their noses pressed against the windows of my apartment, watching me disappear into the night.

"Any ideas what you'd like for dinner?" Patrick asked as we waited for the light at Spadina.

"I don't know. Surprise me."

We drove for only a short way before turning a corner and parking in a lot. Patrick put his arm around me as we crossed the street, and we walked about half a block. I felt very comfortable with the way he handled things like telling me where I should step up for sidewalks. Eventually, we passed through a doorway, entering a room filled with low talk, quiet music, and smells that were familiar but somehow different.

"It's not Chinese," I said, breathing deeply. "Korean?"

"Guess again."

"Okay. Let's see . . . Japanese? Thai? I give up."

"Vietnamese. This restaurant is a favourite of mine. I hope it's okay?"

"I'll try anything once. The food smells great."

"Is something wrong?" Patrick asked.

"No. This is just . . . unexpected." I smiled. "I guess I thought you'd take me to one of those noisy pubs. You know, get in the mood for the concert."

"I'm sorry. I thought you'd prefer something a little quieter. We can go to another place if you'd like."

"No, this is great. I'd like to try Vietnamese food. And if this place is your favourite, it must be good."

"You're sure this is okay?"

I laughed. "Shut up and get me something to eat. I'm starved."

Since I had no idea what to order, I let Patrick do the honours. As we were sipping our before-dinner drinks, Patrick asked me the question I knew would come up sooner or later.

"How did you deal with it, you know, losing your sight?" When I didn't respond right away, he added hastily, "I hope you don't mind my asking, but frankly, I've been curious."

I took a deep breath. "About as badly as you'd expect. I felt that life had dumped on me big-time. The injustice of it all nearly drove me crazy, and I hit out at everything. You can't imagine how badly I treated the people around me. Since I had no idea how to get around, I was forced to move back in with my mother. I suppose she meant well, but I felt as if she was smothering me with all her attention, her kindness. I just wanted to be alone in my room with the curtains pulled tight so I wouldn't notice how little I could actually see. They finally sent me to the Canadian National Institute for the Blind." The memory of it caused me to shake my head. "I acted like a Grade-A jerk there. I can't believe they didn't throw me out on my butt the first week."

"If you don't mind my saying so, you seem pretty well-adjusted now. What changed?"

"It was mostly Shadow. He made me feel needed. Isn't that odd? *I'm* the one who can't get along without the big goof, but he made me feel needed. After that, it took a lot of yelling and screaming, but I finally talked my mother into letting me have my own apartment again. My friends have been really great. You can't imagine how supportive they are. Lately, I've been trying to get a songwriting career going." I picked up my drink. "That's the up-to-the-minute report."

When our food arrived, it was obvious Patrick knew what he was doing. The meal he'd ordered tasted great: very fresh and light. While we ate, we talked about music some more. Listening to him, it struck me as odd that Patrick seemed so into the music I'd grown up with. Most people tend to stick with the music they liked when they were young. My dad loves bop, for instance, and my mother still goes gaga over Sinatra and Perry Como. Patrick and I should have been separated by over a ten-year gulf – musically speaking – but we didn't seem to be.

"What kind of music do you *really* enjoy?" I asked. "When you want to lie back and just get lost in the sounds, whose are they?"

Patrick didn't answer immediately. "You're pretty perceptive. I do enjoy a lot of what's happening now – what I understand, at least, but . . ." He took a breath. "All right. Clapton and Led Zeppelin. I was a bit late for Hendrix, but my older brother turned me on to him. If I had to be on a desert island, I'd want their recordings. They could really play."

I nodded my head happily. We were reading off the same page. "For me it's Clapton's stuff when he was with Cream. That live cut of 'Crossroads' on their *Wheels of Fire* album is a killer, and of course Hendrix was brilliant, but to be quite honest, his playing has never done much for me."

"So you didn't listen to Hendrix?"

"Until I wore out the records!" I laughed. "When you want to learn how to play, you study everything. Get me a guitar! I can probably still play 'Purple Haze' note for note."

He seemed taken aback. "You're that good?"

"You haven't heard how well I play it," I answered. "Talk is cheap in the music business. I may be awful, for all you know."

"No," Patrick said thoughtfully, "I don't think you would be. I have a good nose for bull, and there's something about the way you said that. You have confidence. You can back up what you say." He poured me some more tea. "What started you playing guitar?"

"Perversity, I guess. Girls aren't supposed to play guitar. You know that song 'Girls with Guitars'? That was me. My dad was dumb enough to ask what I wanted for my fifteenth birthday – said I could have anything. I asked him for an electric guitar. I wanted to learn how to make an instrument scream like I was screaming inside. You know? Like somebody was trying to pull your guts out through your mouth? Everything about my life frustrated me. My family was falling apart. Everything I wanted to do, I wasn't supposed to do." I leaned back in my seat. "My friends didn't understand why I wanted to play guitar, either. Westport, Connecticut, is a pretty preppy town, after all. The guys thought it was cute and the girls thought I was weird. But that only spurred me on. Luckily, I had a great teacher from the beginning. He didn't quite know what to make of me, but he showed me the road I needed to take. It wasn't until I began to lose my sight that I was able to follow it properly. I would have loved to tell him, but by then it was too late. He was dead."

Patrick put his hand over mine. "Maybe you'll play 'Purple Haze' for me sometime?"

"It has to be really loud, you know, to be effective. You might have to listen from down the block."

The concert was everything I hoped it would be – even the quality of the sound. I don't know how the sightlines were, but from where we sat, I could hear everything, and that's what really counted.

I enjoyed the way Bonnie's band stretched out on some of the numbers, but I didn't realize that she could blow quite like that until she played a tune I wasn't familiar with, which she finished off with an absolutely blistering guitar solo. She didn't have to use a lot of electronic gadgets to make herself sound better than she was, either.

Patrick sat fairly silent throughout, and I got the feeling he was watching my reaction to the music. I couldn't help bouncing in my seat like a kid, as I sang along to the songs I knew and tried to concentrate during every guitar break. I hadn't been to a big show in over five years and I roared my approval of each song right along with the rest of the crowd.

At one point Patrick yelled into my ear, "You really want to be up there with them, don't you?"

"You bet! Maybe I'll get a lucky break, and next time you come it'll be *me* on that stage."

After the last encore echoed off into the night, Patrick asked how I'd enjoyed the concert, and without thinking I threw my arms around his neck and kissed him. "Thank you so much for bringing me."

We waited in our seats until most of the people had gone, then made our way out of the building and walked slowly hand in hand to the lot where we'd left the car. The downtown air smelled clean for once, and the warmth of the departed sun still seemed to radiate from the pavement. On an emotional high from the energy of the music we'd just experienced, I hummed in time to our steps. My whole body tingled with excitement. Life was finally good – both my expanding career and, maybe, Patrick. I couldn't wait to find out what tomorrow and the next day would bring. I didn't want to let go of that feeling. It had been a long time coming.

"What time is it, Patrick?" I asked dreamily, my head resting against his shoulder.

"Ready to pack it in? It isn't quite time for the car to turn into a pumpkin yet." His jacket rustled as he checked his watch and said importantly, "The time is now 11:44."

"I want to do something wild, crazy."

"Want to go to a club? Some dancing maybe?"

"Too tame." Suddenly, I was sixteen again. "Take me up on the expressway and drive real fast."

"Where to?"

"Anywhere. I don't care."

He paused before answering, and his words sounded carefully chosen. "How about my weekend place? It's fifty minutes north of here in the Albion Hills, but if you want to go fast, I'll make it in forty. Would that do?"

We walked several paces as I weighed all the connotations his invitation carried.

"This isn't a come-on, if that's what you're thinking, Kit," Patrick added softly. "I just thought you might like a ride in the country."

My internal voice didn't say *dumb-ass* once as I accepted his invitation.

The drive north progressed on roads that rapidly diminished in size: expressways, two-laners, and finally dirt. Patrick drove them all as if radar guns had never been invented. Our chatter, to my ears, sounded aimless, as if we both had other things on our minds. I certainly did. I had to decide what my response would be if he asked me to stay the night. That age-old question. I sighed and leaned back in my seat and continued humming to myself while Patrick told me about his hundred-year-old farmhouse and the hundred acres of rolling hills and woods that went along with it.

The best part of the trip was the roller-coaster ride along a two-lane highway going up through the middle of the Albion Hills. When you take it at high speed and can't see the dips in the road, it's quite a rush. We only slowed down when Patrick turned onto an unpaved side road, eventually pulling up where he had to unlock a gate. The air that flooded into the car as he opened the door smelled indescribably sweet and earthy. I thought of the ground, recently released from its blanket of frost and snow, where life had begun stirring again, ready to spring from the ground. I could relate.

"Better hold on. I'm afraid the driveway is bumpy. It's gotten pretty washed out the past few weeks."

Patrick didn't exaggerate. Even though he crept along, the bottom of the car scraped in a number of places. Finally he stopped and we got out. The wind that blew across my face, while cold, didn't hold its winter wickedness any longer.

"Describe it to me, Patrick." I said as I slipped my arm around his waist.

"Well, the wind must be blowing pretty well up high tonight because the clouds are moving like freight trains. The moon's almost full, and the clouds look all ragged as they cross it. Ahead of us, in front of the house, are some big maples that were planted when it was built, I imagine. The house is light-orange brick with some geometric decorations built into it with white brick. It has a porch that runs the length of the front and a peak in the middle of the second storey. There are two windows on each side of the door and the second storey matches that with an extra one in the peaked section. The window frames are painted white, and the shutters are black. Around back there's a wing with board-and-batten siding painted grey. That's the kitchen with two more bedrooms above it. Good enough?"

"I can see it perfectly. Are there any flowers or fruit trees?"

"Just a few ancient apple trees back by the barn and some flowers that have gone native through neglect. I don't garden. Want to go in and have a nightcap? I'll drive you back to the city after."

I didn't need 20/20 vision to know what he was thinking, but with a shrug I let him lead me through the front door.

The farmhouse smelled of wood smoke and furniture polish, and our boots heels clicked satisfyingly as we crossed the bare floor. Patrick made a fire in the fireplace that covered a good portion of a side wall in the living room. While he worked, I ran my hands over the rough stones and the thick wooden mantel. I thought of the farmer and his family who'd worked to make this place, and how proud of it they must have been. How many generations had lived here?

When the wood had ignited with a warming crackle, Patrick got us each a snifter of cognac and we clinked glasses. The cognac felt like velvet fire as it slid down my throat.

"Could we sit on the floor in front of the hearth?" I asked.

"Sure. Just a minute." Patrick left the room for a moment, then came back and spread something out on the floor. "Genuine polar-bear rug," he announced. "How's that for corny?"

I burst out laughing. In the wildest recesses of my warped imagination, I never thought for a moment I'd wind up my evening on a bearskin rug in front of a fireplace out in the country. "Just as long as I don't have to park my butt on your bare floor."

Sitting down, I faced the heat of the fire. The sensuous feel of the thick fur under my fingers caused prickly shivers down my back. Despite my bravado, my hand shook slightly as I raised the snifter for another swallow. Patrick sat down next to me and we stayed silent for several minutes, sipping our cognac and toasting away the night's chill.

"May I kiss you?" he asked.

I turned my head. Soft lips brushed mine. The warmth of Patrick's breath caressed my cheek. His second try had more fierceness in it and I opened my mouth as he moved his hand behind my head.

Patrick took the snifter from my hand and we continued kissing for several more minutes. His mouth tasted of mint and cognac, his skin smelled of soap. When Patrick reached out and undid the top button of my blouse, I stiffened involuntarily.

"Don't you want this?" he asked softly.

When I didn't answer immediately, Patrick picked up his snifter again. I began to think that my silence had upset him, but then his lips lightly brushed my neck. *Did* I want this? My body was ready, that was for sure. I mentally stood back and watched my reaction with great curiosity. Who was this person I'd turned into? Nine years ago I wouldn't have hesitated. Things were different, sure, but not *that* different. Hell! Nine years ago, I would have jumped *him*.

"There are a few problems," I protested, stalling for time.

"What problems?"

"Condoms, for one thing."

"It's your lucky day. I just put in a case of them."

We both laughed, and my resolve suddenly burned like a flare lit in pitch darkness. I needed to take this step. And I needed Patrick – at least for tonight.

"I have to phone my dog first," I told him playfully.

He seemed confused. "Your dog?"

"Well, not the *dog* – the dogsitter. Someone's minding Shadow for me and I have to let her know I won't be home when I promised."

He led me to the phone in the kitchen. Jackie answered after one ring and remained surprisingly quiet when I told her I wouldn't be back until possibly morning and asked if she minded staying. I heard her whoop something to Carolina as I replaced the handset on the phone.

We went back to the living room and stood on the rug. The sound of the fire crackling filled my ears. Patrick held me tightly in his arms as we kissed again. When we surfaced for air, I reached up and touched his face for the first time.

Touching is a very personal thing, but the way Hollywood deals with it in relationship to the sightless is a scream. In movie after movie, we reach out to touch the face of everyone we encounter: the mailman, bank tellers, cab drivers, you name it. You just wouldn't do that in real life unless you were intimate with the person. When you're blind, what difference does it make how a person looks? Maybe we're the only ones who can truly see someone, because we're not distracted by their physical appearance. That said, there *are* times when you want to reach out and touch the face of someone special. Everybody does that, sighted or not.

Patrick barely breathed while I got to know him better. I still retain a good memory of how something looks from its shape and contours, and that gives me some advantage. His chin was strong. As I ran my fingers up high cheekbones, I thought of those old black-and-white photos of Indians. His straight nose seemed about the right size for his face, and his eyes were large and wide-set. He had hair cut neat and fairly short and his ears stuck out just a little. His height I guessed at six-one or two. Then there was his generous mouth – something I was already familiar with. But two things remained that my fingers could *not* tell me.

"What colour are your eyes and your hair?"

"Blue and blond," he answered.

"Have you ever worn a mustache?"

"How did you know? I had one for years. I finally shaved it off last summer."

"You have the kind of face that would look good in a mustache."

He kissed me again, then asked, "How much of me can you see?"

"I'd know you anywhere."

As I returned his kiss, he started unbuttoning my blouse. Taking that as a challenge, I undid his shirt. Patrick's hands felt warm against my skin, but I shivered nonetheless.

"Cold?"

"Just a little," I admitted. "Fire or no fire, this room is freezing! Would you mind if I asked you to leave my socks on – or would that look too ridiculous?"

"Anything you want."

I stood with my back to the warmth of the fire while Patrick undressed me. We lay down on the soft fur and proceeded to make the most unhurried, most intense, most wonderful love I had ever experienced. Had I been able to see, the experience would have been blinding.

Afterward, we lay basking, the softness of the fur on one side, the warmth of the fire on the other. Patrick cradled me in his arms.

"Mmmm. That was incredible," I murmured into his chest.

"And you're amazing, Kit." He kissed my face, then chuckled. "Even with your socks on." After gently stroking my hair for a few minutes, he said, "I tried to keep my eyes closed for part of it, trying to imagine how it is for you."

"Didn't remembering to keep your eyes shut distract you?"

"Well, yeah, a little."

"Why bother then?" I reached out and touched his cheek. "I appreciate the effort, though."

He rolled me over on top of him and kissed me hard. "But it was also difficult to do because you look so beautiful in the firelight." His hands drifted down my back to my rear end. "Ready to go upstairs to bed?"

I sat up, resting my hands on his chest. "No. I'm ready for Round Two. Are you?"

CHAPTER 12

Even though we didn't get to sleep until well after 2:00 a.m, I woke up early. Carefully reaching out to the bedside table, I flipped open the lid of my Braille watch with one hand: 6:18. How come I didn't feel the slightest bit tired? Lying on my side with Patrick's body cuddled against my back and his arm draped down my thigh, I luxuriated in the warm closeness. I wanted him to wake up so I could hear his voice and feel his hands and lips . . . and other things. But his steady breathing told me he was still asleep. I tried to convince myself I could do the same, but it didn't wash, so I gave up and lay there thinking.

I liked what had happened between us – and I ain't talkin' about the sex. That I *really* liked. Patrick was different from any man I'd ever met. I think part of it had to do with the fact that he was over forty. He had the inner security that only comes with time. The other guys I'd gone out with always reminded me of big puppy dogs. You know, kind of all over the place, personally speaking. Patrick seemed to know where he was going, but he also didn't need to tell me all about it. In short, he was mature, and I found that very refreshing.

Outside, birds chattered for all they were worth, and I could picture them filling the bare branches of one of those big old maples Patrick had described to me the night before. Like a giant heart somewhere in the depths of the house, the furnace switched on, and its warming breath gently stirred the air in the room. Snuggling back, I felt as if I could happily pass the rest of my life here. Carolina's song about coming home started up in my head.

By the time I noticed Patrick's breathing had changed, I was well on my way to having the damn song finished. I'd gotten two verses and a pretty good bridge, but the killer hook I needed for the chorus still eluded me. With a guitar and a few hours, I'd have the song done – once I had the hook.

"Are you awake?" Patrick asked, his breath tickling the back of my neck.

"For some time now."

"What've you been doing?"

"Working on a song."

"Really? You can do that?"

"Sure," I grinned. "It isn't hard if you're Wonder Woman."

"I used the word 'amazing' if I remember correctly," he shot right back. "Don't take on airs. What's the song about?"

"About home and what it means."

"That's pretty philosophical for this early in the morning."

Patrick nuzzled my neck and pretty soon his hand slid up my thigh and came to rest on my left breast. He tweaked the nipple gently and, as if a switch had been thrown, my body sprang to life, and this time I selfishly let Patrick do all the work. Like a fine musician plays his instrument, he played my body, intuitively doing all the right things the right way at just the right time.

"Holy shit!" I panted, after we were finished. "How do you *do* that?"

"I'll never tell," he said as he kissed my nose. "Do you want to shower first?"

"Do I need to?"

"Yeah," he laughed.

Later, over mugs of black coffee in the kitchen, Patrick asked, "You really wrote a song in bed?"

"Sure. I was waiting for you to wake up and it just came to me."

"Amazing."

"It isn't that hard, really." I put down my empty mug. "Writing songs, I mean. Speaking of which, I should be going. I want to finish off the song and I need a guitar for that. Besides, I can't expect my friends to dogsit around the clock."

By the time we got back to the city, it was after 11:00. As Patrick pulled up outside my door, I felt half-tempted to ask if we could turn around and go back to his farmhouse.

"Well, here we are, Kit," he said. "Remember we have a date for opening day on Thursday. I'll call you tomorrow about it."

"Sure. Well, thank you very much for a wonderful time, Patrick," I answered with fake primness, holding out my hand for him to shake.

"It'd better have been more than that!" Both of us started laughing, and he leaned over and kissed me. A few minutes later, I suggested he help me as far as my door before we did something in his car that could get us arrested.

He sighed heavily. "You're right. Besides, I have to rush. Duty calls and I'm already late for a meeting."

"On Sunday morning?"

"How do you think I pay for all this?" he said laughing.

I stood listening to him drive off, but remained rooted where I was for several more seconds daydreaming. Shaking my head, I made sure my feet were firmly on the ground again before opening the door to the building.

The future would have to take care of itself.

As I walked into the apartment, I called out, "Honey, I'm home!"

Jackie groaned, "You don't have to scream. We can see you just fine."

"That's not true," Carolina continued. "My vision's still double."

Shadow came bounding over, and I braced myself. He's big enough to knock me over if I'm not prepared. Despite his training, if his harness isn't on, he still acts like a puppy when I come home – a major-league puppy. I ended up plastered against the door, with his paws on my shoulders and his tongue all over my face.

"So you stayed overnight, too?" I asked Carolina as I finally pried Shadow off me and removed my jacket.

"It happened, but I didn't plan it that way. Jackie and I got talking, then we decided that something alcoholic might be nice, so we took a cab over to the LCBO."

Surprisingly, Susan's voice coming from the kitchen continued the story. "The two idiots stayed up most of the night drinking and talking. Here's your coffee, my dears. Black, like you asked." Two solid clunks on the coffee table. My largest mugs had been pressed into service. "How 'bout some for you, Kit?"

"Sure."

I found a seat in the beanbag chair, since Jackie lay stretched out on the sofa. Carolina was in her usual place on the floor, attempting to get her Shadow-pillow back into position. Susan remained somewhere over by the kitchen doorway.

The room became so silent I could hear Shadow panting. "Why's everyone so quiet?"

"Aren't you going to tell us what happened last night?" Carolina asked.

Susan added, "*And* this morning. It's pushing noon!"

"C'mon. Give!" Jackie ordered.

"Oh! You mean the concert," I said blankly. "It was really great."

Jackie was outraged. "That's it? That's all you're going to tell us? I give up a Saturday night to nursemaid that walking carpet of yours and . . . and . . ."

"What happened *after*? Carolina demanded. "You stayed out all night!"

"Well, it *was* a long concert," I said, then burst out laughing.

"We noticed that car of his," Jackie said. "*Pret-ty* hot. And it got C and me thinking. This is just for research purposes now, but how big was his –"

"Jackie!" Carolina interrupted in bogus outrage. "For heaven's sake! Show a little class."

"Oh, like you weren't the one who first mentioned it last night."

We'd played kiss and tell many times in the past. On this occasion, though, I told them more about Patrick's farmhouse than I did about what went on while we were there. The announcement that he had a polar-bear rug did get an "Oh my goodness!" from Susan, however.

She gave me a hug. "I'm so happy for you, Kit. What's his name?"

"And how much does he make a year?" Jackie added.

"Patrick, and none of your business," I responded.

"When do we get to meet him?"

"When I can trust you guys around him," I answered, then asked Susan, "Why are you here? I know you wouldn't drive all this way to hear the dirty details."

"No. She'd use the phone," Jackie cackled.

Susan said, "The two lushes here called me up at 7 a.m. to tell me to get my bum over before noon. Can you believe it? Paul was just thrilled to get woken up so early, too. I know as much about why I'm here as you do, Kit. They told me we had to wait for you to get back. Now, you two low-lifes, tell me why you've ruined my Sunday and got my husband completely PO'd by waking him up on his only day off."

Carolina took a noisy sip of her hot coffee. "Kit's heard most of this already, but you need some of the background."

She went on in great detail about everything that'd happened to Jackie during the past week. I listened with half an ear, while my mind drifted between Patrick and the song I'd nearly finished that morning.

"It all sounds pretty far-fetched," Susan told Carolina when she got to the end.

"My feeling was the same, too, at first," Carolina admitted, "but there are things going on that I can't put down to coincidence any longer. Jackie and I sat around discussing it last night, and halfway through the evening –"

"More like halfway through the bottle," Susan interjected.

Carolina ignored the interruption. She sounded as if she was still partially swizzled, and this wasn't like Carolina at all. "We came up with some concrete ideas on what we might be able to do to check the validity of Jackie's theory."

"Carolina!" Susan said. "You can't be serious!"

"I am."

"What does that detective say?"

"Morris?" Jackie said, "Screw him! Carolina and I decided we don't need his help."

"Do you think that's wise?"

"They're off on their wild goose chase for the Strangler. About the only thing that got them interested was Marion's secret lover."

"Secret lover?" Susan sounded really mystified. "What are you talking about?"

"Better fill her in, Kit," Jackie said.

Susan's reaction was identical to the rest of us. Carolina asked Susan if Marion had ever given a hint about any of this.

"No. Not really."

Jackie leaped in. "A-*ha*! That sounds like an 'I'm not sure,' if I ever heard one."

"What did Marion tell you?" Carolina asked.

"She didn't really *say* anything. I just got the feeling a few times in the last couple of months that she was really uncomfortable about something, that's all. Recently, I'd been too caught up in my own problems to get her alone somewhere and ask about it. But I certainly wouldn't have thought for an instant that it was anything like this."

"Yeah," Jackie said, "It's hard to imagine: Marion the Bondage Queen."

"It's not funny!"

"No, it's not," Carolina agreed. "I feel now like I never really knew her. We all probably do."

"So, where do we go from here?" Susan asked.

"We have to try to find out whatever it was Marion stumbled on," Jackie told her.

"But how do we *do* that? If somebody murdered Marion for what she knew – whatever that was – wouldn't they have covered the whole thing up by now, gotten rid of the evidence?"

"I can answer your question with another question," Carolina said. "If what Marion discovered was so important, wouldn't it make sense for her to leave some kind of record or a message?"

I shrugged. "Where?"

"Her apartment?" Carolina suggested. "I spoke to Marion's mom yesterday, and she told me the police said it was okay to go into her apartment now. Then she asked if we could clean it out for her. The poor thing can't face doing it. It would be an ideal opportunity to search there."

"The cops already did that, and, other than the bondage stuff, they didn't find anything."

"But we knew Marion," Jackie said, "so we might have more luck."

"What about work?" I asked. "Could there be something to find out at the lab?"

Carolina said, "That will be a lot more tricky to accomplish, but it's a good thought."

"But that still leaves two big questions," Susan said. "How does all this help us find the person who did Marion in, and how did they find out Jackie's on their trail?"

Carolina took a deep breath before answering. "To accomplish that, I think we need to find the person who tried killing Jackie."

THE MEETING TURNED OUT TO BE everything the man had been dreading and worse. It was bad enough that he'd failed. After his own self-recrimination over the botched job, he didn't need the further embarrassment of someone haranguing him about it.

He'd expected the message he'd left late Friday night to be answered quickly, and even though his phone rang at only 8:24 next morning, the man had worked himself into a state from waiting.

"I got your message," the irritating voice with the overdose of snottiness asked. "We have to meet. The way you've screwed up has made things absolutely intolerable."

"Face to face? I thought you wanted to stay away from that."

"Of course face to face! We're not sure that you're up to this job and –"

"How *dare* you!" the man shouted into the phone, totally losing it – something he *never* did. "You people keep making me rush! That can't be done if you expect success. When I'm allowed to work the way I prefer, there are never mistakes. *Never!* Have there been any repercussions from the last job? That should show you the quality of my work."

The voice on the phone waited until he finished, then said acidly, "You forget that there *was* a repercussion from that job. That's why we've had to ask you to do this! And I don't give two shits about the quality of your work. You bungled *this* job. The message you left last night was pretty vague. Tell me exactly what happened."

Getting his control back with some difficulty, the man reported, leaving nothing out. The monologue, surprisingly uninterrupted, lasted almost ten minutes. The silence when he finished was so complete that he thought his caller had hung up.

No such luck. "You will have to meet with us sometime this weekend, possibly this afternoon. I will call back later and give you directions. Wait by your phone."

This time the line did go dead – before he had a chance to object. He slammed down the receiver. Damn! He had something on for this evening and needed to run a few errands. The last thing he wanted was to sit by the phone to wait for orders. After a few minutes, though, reason took over. There would have been fallout by now if the Goode bitch had gone running to the police. Maybe the situation could still be salvaged. But why the need for a meeting?

Control, the man thought, *I have to get control of myself and the situation*. It bothered him, though, that his temper kept flaring up. That outburst hadn't been good. That was one more dangerous chink in his armour.

He waited most of the day for the return call. When it finally came he was more furious than ever. They were to meet Sunday at 2:00. Why the wait? His whole weekend, the weekend on which he'd planned to relax and have some fun, was going to be a mess now.

"At least it's only the weekend," he said out loud to the four walls of the room.

It could be his whole life that was a mess.

On Sunday, not wanting to use either of his cars, he had taken a long bus ride to an east-end doughnut shop as requested. The clock over the counter now said 2:38, and still no one had approached him. Thursday's Toronto *Sun* sat in front of him, unread. Bored with waiting, his hands itched to turn a few pages, but his contact needed to see the cover to know who he was. The colour picture on the front page showed a man being led away from a crime scene in hand-cuffs. The one-word headline screamed "Caught!" Looking at it gave him an uneasy feeling.

The waitress walked over with a coffee pot and, without asking, filled his cup again. "She's late, isn't she?"

He looked up sharply. "*What?*"

She smiled. "Look, honey, when you've worked in this dump as long as I have, you know how people look when they're waiting for someone – and you're definitely waiting."

The man stared down at his cup. He wanted her to go away, not notice him, forget about him, but she stood waiting for an answer. He cursed the fact that there were only two other customers, both old men, to occupy her attention. Not raising his eyes, he answered, "Yeah. But it isn't a she. Some friends are picking me up. We're on our way to Sudbury to look for work." As soon as he said it, he real-ized how dumb his comment was. People came from Sudbury *to* Toronto looking for work. *Calm down*! he told himself. *You're letting yourself get rattled.*

The waitress put down the pot so she could wipe her hands on her apron, and he finally raised his eyes. She looked in her mid-thirties, small, with medium-length blond hair that showed about an inch of its actual brown at the roots, pretty-though-pinched features, and an underlying look of desperation. The man glanced down at her left hand. The skin at the base of her fourth finger showed pale where a ring had been recently. He again willed her to go away. She didn't, and he internally cursed that nobody had shown up to claim him. He was not in the mood for a woman to be hitting on him.

"You must be pretty desperate to be going up north to look for work," she said as a way to fill the silence. "What's your name?"

At that point the man almost got up and left, but it would have been a stupid move. That would make the woman remember him all the more. "Um, Pete." He forced himself to continue. "What's yours?"

"Julie. If your ride doesn't get here, I get off work in about an hour." She flashed a phony expression of inspiration. "Say, if you want, I could fix you some dinner. I bake a mean chicken, and I only live around the corner."

Even under normal circumstances, the man wouldn't have been interested. At this point her come-on absolutely repelled him. Desperate to get out, he turned around and saw a nondescript brown sedan pull into the parking area. In the front sat two men, both casually dressed. For some reason he'd expected suits. The driver hopped out immediately and yanked open the door to the doughnut shop. Catching sight of the *Sun* on the counter, he started over.

The man stood up quickly and said cheerily to the waitress, "Here's my ride. Sorry I can't take you up on your offer, ah, Julie. Maybe I'll stop by next time I'm down this way."

He left the waitress leaning against the counter, looking more withered than ever.

"Do you know for certain that the police weren't called?"

The man sat in the back seat of the car feeling cornered. He'd tried to answer the questions that had been thrown at him as succinctly as possible. No introductions had been made, but that wasn't unusual. People engaged in this type of business usually preferred anonymity. They'd been grilling him for what seemed like hours, but only because he felt so miserable. It reminded him of being sent to the principal's office, and then having to wait for his parents to arrive before the shit really hit the fan. He only put up with it because he felt he deserved it because of his failure. Failure. The word tasted dirty.

"I stayed for about five minutes after discovering the girl had disappeared. The crowd had already begun drifting away. I think they figured she'd stolen the bike and had cut out. I thought it would be best if I left. If the cops had come I would have had an excuse for what happened, but there was no sense attracting any more attention to myself than I had already."

"We'll have to check into it. See if there have been any inquiries."

Fine. You do that, he thought. *I just want to get out of here, find the bitch who brought me to this state, and fry her ass.* He didn't think he'd ever looked forward to whacking someone as much as he did her.

They'd parked the car in one of the lots near the ferry docks for the Toronto Islands. Something special must have been going on, because the place was crawling with smiling, happy families. Even though the sun had made only sporadic appearances all day, it still felt like a day to be out and about. The man wanted desperately to be walking in the woods, enjoying the fresh air. Anyplace would have been better than where he was.

The driver had done the bulk of the questioning, but obviously the guy on the passenger side was the important one. For the most part, he'd kept his eyes straight forward, but occasionally he'd turn and stare at the man. It made him feel as if he were a bug under a microscope.

The driver had asked his last question. Raising his eyebrows, he looked across the front seat.

The guy in the passenger seat closed his eyes for a few seconds, then reopened them with a shake of his head and a sigh. "It seems to me," he started slowly, "that events have gone too far in the wrong direction. Mistakes have been made." He turned and held up his hand as the man started to protest. "You are not the *only* person I'm speaking about. It does no good to assign blame at this point. If we could cut our losses and pull out, I would push for that option with my associates, but it is absolutely out of the question. What do we do now? First, we must make absolutely certain there are no more blunders." He looked into the back seat. "I agree you were rushed, but that is not the only cause of our problem. We have to patch things up, our position must be re-secured, as quickly as possible, but not so quickly as to cause more mistakes. Too much is on the line. Too much."

He looked across at the driver, "How quickly do you reasonably think you can get things under control?"

"The girl, you mean?" the driver asked.

"No. That's too risky now. I think it's better to cut off all possible sources of information. One of them in particular has me worried. Even if the girl were to keep on, if there's no one to get information from, what harm can she do? We must make absolutely sure that there is no evidence around. You're sure we got everything from the Joseph girl's apartment?"

The man nodded his head. "At that point she had no reason to believe anyone knew what she was doing. Apparently her friends knew nothing about it, because if she had told them something, the cops would be working on it by now, wouldn't they? So if there's any information still unsecured, where could it be?"

The two men in the front seat agreed. The driver started to speak, but the other held up his hand. "There is another source that you felt was not a problem, but that doesn't seem to be the case now, from all I've heard."

The driver sounded surprised. "You mean . . .?"

"You know who I mean." He looked at his watch. "I have other things to do. Drop me at Bay and King."

Nothing further was said until the car pulled over on Bay Street next to the Scotiabank headquarters. The passenger got out, then stuck his head back inside the car and said to the driver, "You know what to do."

CHAPTER 13

Here's how things had finally shaken down by the time I got everyone cleared out that afternoon. We decided to form an Action Committee, as Carolina put it. She nominated herself as the chair. I'm surprised she didn't make us draft a mission statement and adopt a secret handshake.

Jackie's job was to search Marion's apartment. Susan was going to tackle the Housing Department. Carolina got the toughy: trying to find out something about the guy who ran Jackie off the road. Me? I was assigned to pump Morris for additional information, and I was thinking that it might also be an opportunity to see if we could get him to take our allegations seriously.

Personally, though, I thought that Marion wasn't the only one who'd read too many Nancy Drews.

I finally got through to my lawyer, Murray, just as Steve the bass player arrived to drive me to the studio the next morning. I'd met Murray at a charity softball tournament about ten years back. He's a big bear of a guy and a pretty good ball player – though not when it comes to pitching. He tends to bean quite a few people – although that's not a bad quality to have in your lawyer. Since his office is just down the street, I call on Murray whenever I need legal advice. Once, my landlord tried to jack up my rent 60 per cent, figuring I'd roll over and play dead. He got really ignorant when I called him on it. I felt inclined to sic Shadow on the bozo, with instructions to emasculate him as painfully as possible. What I did instead was call Murray, who can really bark when he needs to – professionally speaking. He got great results. Not only was my rent not raised, but the bathroom got remodelled and the apartment door was replaced with something more secure.

"Kit!" he said in the voice he reserved for friends. "What can I do for you?"

"I've been offered a deal to have an album produced, and the guy wants me to sign a contract. Can you look it over?"

"Sure, but I have to warn you I only have general knowledge when it comes to that type of contract. You might want a lawyer who specializes in that sort of thing. When do you need it done?"

"Five minutes ago."

"That soon?" He chuckled, but I could tell he wasn't thrilled. "Okay. Can you bring it right over?"

"No problem. Thanks a lot, Murray. I owe you big-time."

"I know."

When we arrived at the studio, Shadow got parked with the receptionist, who assured me she loved dogs, and Steve and I trucked our equipment in. After introducing Steve to Nick, who took him into the control room to listen to what we'd already done, I sat down on an amp to try and keep my nerves quiet by playing over Carolina's song on my acoustic. I set up a nice easy tempo, strumming softly as I hummed the melody. When I reached the chorus, I started singing:

But a home is more than some place to live.
You fill it with all the love you can give.
When you need some place to go,
You know it'll always be there for you.
Your home will always be there.

146

And there it was: the melodic hook I'd been searching for, that catchy something that would accomplish what Carolina wanted from it. A bit mawkish, maybe, but it got the point across. I sang it again, and this time made the melody twist up at the end, which seemed to add a little more punch to the lyrics. As I wove the pick through the guitar's strings and leaned it against the wall, the door to the studio blasted open and somebody grunted.

"God! This amp gets heavier every time I lift it. I should have taken up the piccolo."

I knew he'd seen me. That's why he'd said something. But it was also obvious he didn't know I was blind.

"Why do you bother to lug around an amp when they have them here?" I asked.

"Because the ones here suck herds of cow dung," he replied quaintly. "I keep telling Arnie to buy something decent, but I think he's emotionally attached to them. Besides, I know how to get the sounds I like out of this mother. Are you the singer we're doing the session for?"

"Actually, I'm more of a guitarist . . ."

"Great! You can play a little acoustic with us."

Five years ago I would have taken offence – well maybe even a week ago – but today nothing was going to rattle me. Besides, you get this frequently with male guitarists. They're all macho men who don't seem to realize that we women can do anything they do – and just as well. They might recognize someone like Bonnie Raitt, for instance, as being worthy of their notice, but they still look on us as oddities, freaks of nature. "A girl who plays guitar. How cute."

By the time I decided not to rise to the bait, I was spared any chance of doing so by the arrival of my drummer, Terry, with his equipment and the keyboard player. Nick came out of the control room to make the introductions.

"Danny and Frank, do you know Terry and Steve, here?"

"Sure! We've seen each other around town," Danny said.

"Kit Mason, this is the guitarist I was telling you about, Danny Kutcher, and Frank Amalfitano, who's going to play some Hammond organ and any other keyboards you might want."

"Hey, Kit, thanks for asking me," said a voice I assumed was Frank's.

Terry came over and gave me a peck on the cheek. I stuck my hand out and found Danny, whose handshake seemed rather stiff. He led Nick off to the opposite end of the studio and asked softly in a surprised voice, "She's blind?"

"I was when I got up this morning," I called out.

Danny huffed and puffed and sounded as if he wanted to come back with something snappy, but nothing emerged.

The rest of the introductions were made. As usual with a group of local freelance musicians, the four guys were either already acquainted or knew *of* each other. It didn't take long for Terry to get out his cymbals and snare and tune the rest of the studio drum kit to his preference. I picked up the acoustic again and fooled around with some background ideas for the new songs. The amp Danny had wheeled in turned out to be an old Fender 4-10 Bassman, about the same vintage as my Telecaster. After tuning his guitar, Danny whipped off a few licks, just to let me know how a real guitarist sounds. He was right; the *amp* did sound good, very ballsy.

In the meantime, Nick was busy getting mics set up. I called him over.

"How do you want to handle this?" I asked. "Steve and I worked together about eight years ago and I've sat in with Terry's band a couple of times –"

"Why don't you jam a bit," Nick interrupted, "and see what happens? Get to know each other. It's going to be a while before I'm ready to get anything down, anyway."

The guys were listening, and Danny asked, "How about some blues in A?"

Before I got a chance to say anything – and this was my session, after all – Danny started playing a nifty bunch of chords with a nice funk groove, and the other guys jumped right in. That was all it took. I dumped the acoustic back in its case and felt around for the Telly. It didn't take me long to slam a jack in, turn on an amp, and do a quick check of the tuning. By then the guys were really cooking, with Danny taking a wailing solo. Nobody took any notice of me. I chunked along on a simple rhythm, not doing anything fancy, while I bided my time.

Danny raced around the guitar like a maniac, and eventually began to run out of gas. I carefully felt my way to where he was standing and shouted over the music, "Wanna trade fours?" That's musician-speak for soloing back and fourth, sort of "you play a lick and I'll try to play one better than yours." "You can go first," I told him.

He whipped out a blistering line, starting at the bottom of the neck and ending with a screaming bent note way up high. What he didn't know was that I'd been hiding in the underbrush waiting for just this chance to bushwhack him. I'd give the little weasel acoustic accompaniment!

Since I became blind, my hearing has naturally improved, but I've always had good pitch and a great memory. It's a little harder now, since I can't cheat by watching the other guitarist's fingerings, but if I really concentrate I can generally play back someone else's lick pretty accurately. Danny had stayed mostly within a pentatonic scale, so I basically had only five notes to worry about. It wasn't hard to repeat his line note-for-note.

I could tell I'd stunned him, because he missed his next entry by three beats, and the lick he played was pretty lame. His third try was better but still didn't give me much trouble. Then things began to get nasty, as he tried harder and harder to leave me in the dust. One thing I had to admit, the lad certainly had chops. I was hard-pressed a number of times in the next few minutes, but I doggedly stayed with him, catching maybe 90 per cent of what he played. We were like two animals, hungry and wary, each waiting for the other to falter. My guitar pick became a jagged tooth I used to bite off chunks of notes and spit them back at Danny as I staked out my territory, daring him to trespass. He circled around the perimeter, not quite sure of the limits of my ability. The tension in the room increased exponentially, as the other guys watched us duke it out.

Danny cried uncle first. "Your turn Frank," he called out, then walked over and said close to my ear, "How the hell do you do that?"

I shrugged and smiled sweetly at him as I kept up some simple chording. "It's not hard." I wondered how old he was. My bet was around twenty.

"Sorry for the comment about the acoustic," he said, then laughed. "I guess you put me in my place. No offence?"

I smiled again. "No offence."

Nick eventually interrupted the jam and asked if anyone wanted to go directly into the console. He got no takers. Most electric musicians prefer using an amp, because it gives us more control over how we'll sound, although a good engineer can still do pretty much what he wants by adjusting the EQ on his mixing console. Terry asked if some of the drum mics could be moved, and he and Nick started in on that.

In an effort to make further amends, Danny spent the time ogling my guitar. You don't see too many Telecasters from the fifties any more, and they're *very* pricey when you do find them. I'd stripped off the old paint job as a "keep busy" project when I started losing my eyesight. The body was a gorgeous chunk of maple, so nice I'd left it unfinished.

"I've never seen strings this high before," Danny said as he played a few notes on it.

I prefer the strings really high off the fingerboard. It makes it tougher to play, but you can't beat the clarity it gives. "My teacher played like that. Try some of the high notes."

"*Je-sus*! You must have the grip of a gorilla!"

I shrugged. "Yeah, but notice the sound? That makes the extra effort worth it."

By that time, Nick was ready to go.

"What would you like us to do now?" I asked him.

"I want you all to get a feel for tunes," he said, addressing everyone. "And if that's all we get today, that's fine. I'm just going to sit back and make producer-type comments, since I don't often get to do that." We all laughed since everyone knew that engineers *always* think they can produce better than the guy sitting next to them in the producer's chair. "As a starting point, Kit, why don't you show the guys the changes to that song you played for me last week."

"The funky one?"

"Yeah, everyone seems to be in that sort of groove today."

"All right!" Danny said. "Kit gets funky!"

I got the feeling that he was still trying hard to bury the hatchet.

I'll never forget the next six hours. Once I showed the guys the changes to each song, they took them and ran. We were absolutely smokin' on everything we tried. Nick said over and over that he'd never seen session guys hook into songs so fast or so completely.

At times, it sounded as if we'd been rehearsing for a month. One of us would come up with a hot idea, and immediately someone else would come up with a part to complement it perfectly. I especially got off on the feel that Terry's drumming added, even if his playing was a bit busier than I would have liked. Each song bounced back and forth around the room, until they were bursting with brilliant ideas. Listening to a playback of the stuff Nick had recorded impressed the hell out of all of us – even Arnie, whom Nick dragged in to listen.

"This is really good!" he said enthusiastically. "It's got that harder edge I was talking about the other day. Kit's material is still there, but what you guys have done to it makes it sound *very* different. I like it!"

"Hey, Kit gets hard. Far out!" Danny said and we cracked up. He'd been repeating variations of that line all day.

I'd begun warming up to him. Despite the way he'd acted at first, Danny was a lot more musically sensitive than I would have thought. The second song we worked on, "Heavy on the Heartache" is probably my most "down" song. Robbie hadn't wanted to record it, saying that it struck him as too sappy. Everyone else who'd heard it, though, said it sounded just like what I was trying to project: someone sitting at a bar about to drown their sorrow over a love affair gone bad. If that's considered sappy, well, so be it. There's many a *chanteuse* who's made her living singing that type of song.

While Nick and Terry did something to the tuning of the kick drum, I picked up my acoustic and started playing the changes to it. Danny went over to the piano and began following what I was playing with some nicely voiced chords.

I stopped. "Sounds good. You play piano too?"

"Nine years of Bach, Beethoven, and the boys. It broke my poor mother's heart when I started playing guitar." He chuckled. "Are you going to record this? It's got pretty changes, and my mother would be ever so thrilled to hear me play piano on something. You wouldn't mind sharing keyboard duties, would you Frank?"

"Be my guest," came the magnanimous response from the direction of the Hammond B3.

"You like the song?" I asked Danny.

"I've only heard the chords so far. What about the melody and lyrics?"

Carefully negotiating my way through the maze of mic cables and guitar cords, I made it to the piano without falling on my face. I sat down on the piano bench next to Danny. "You played a G minor ninth just before the end of the bridge. I liked that. Now if I suspend the fourth in my chord for two beats . . ."

For the next ten minutes we were totally oblivious to everything going on around us, and if you've ever been subjected to the arrhythmic banging of a drummer tuning, you'll know how engrossed Danny and I really were. When Nick finally came over to tell us he was ready to start again, we'd managed to change the crying-in-your-beer sentiment of the lyrics, making it sound more like cool anger at a lover who's rejected you for no apparent reason. The change came in part by the way we restructured the accompaniment, and that in turn forced me to change a few notes in the melody, then we changed a few of the lyrics. When Danny and I played it for the other four, Nick suggested that we might double the tempo in the last verse and give it a kick-ass guitar solo on a long fade.

Danny, bless his youthful heart, wanted to do the solo. I stared him down, something I'm still pretty good at. Still, while we were rehearsing the song, he kept sticking in little guitar "asides," and when we got to the solo at the end, there was Danny "helping out."

I cut everyone off. "Danny, weren't *you* going to play piano on this?"

"I thought I'd do that as an overdub. Besides, weren't *you* going to play acoustic?"

"We're rehearsing right now, in case you haven't noticed. Get your ass on that piano bench and play."

Without another word, he went over and sat down heavily. "Happy?"

"As long as you're at the piano, yes. Let's try this again from the top, guys. One, two, three, four . . ."

The band left as soon as we finished for the day. I wanted to listen to what we'd recorded a few more times and consult with Nick about what we should do on the next session. He said he could drop me downtown, so we stayed for another hour, listening to the three songs over and over, and discussing what we might add with overdubs.

Halfway through a run-through of "Nothing without You" – the funky one – Nick stopped the playback in mid-note. "I still can't believe you talked to Danny the way you did."

"He was being an ass –"

"No, no. You misunderstand. Don't you know anything about Danny Kutcher?"

"Never heard of him before today."

"Boy, have you been leading a sheltered life! Let me tell you something. He has the reputation of being about the toughest guy in the city to work with. People only put up with him because he's so goddamed brilliant. I hired him because of what he might be able to do for this project, but I'll tell you, I'd been cringing over how he might act. The term prima donna doesn't even begin to cover it."

"Really? He doesn't seem *that* bad. A tad pushy, maybe, but he's young."

"Geez, Kit! Didn't you notice how quiet it got when you told him to get his ass over to the piano? And when you started copying his licks, I thought everybody's eyes were going to bug out. Nobody does stuff like that to Danny Kutcher. Ever. He's been known to throw equipment around when he doesn't get his way."

"Sounds like a bit of a baby to me."

"But a baby with heavy talent." Nick paused, and must have leaned back pretty far back from the way his chair screamed in protest. "I'll tell you something else. First, you're one hell of a guitarist yourself. I think Danny's a little scared of you."

"Because of the way I play?"

"There's that. And I hope you don't take this the wrong way, but I know the fact you're blind also makes him uncomfortable."

"Yeah, the thought did cross my mind. Sometimes I get my way simply because people don't know how to deal with someone who can't see. Maybe I pulled a little of that today, but I don't want him screwing up *my* recording because of an ego problem."

"You were impressive. How come Robbie didn't have you playing guitar on the demo?"

I shrugged. "He didn't like the way I play; said it wasn't the right style for what he wanted to do. Since the idea was to get me an opportunity to sell my songs, I didn't argue."

"Your playing *does* have a real R&B/Soul tinge. That choppy chord stuff is right out of James Brown."

"That's a big part of my background. It's all I listened to at one point."

"What got you into writing songs and not doing more playing?"

"Lyrics tell stories, and I like that. Not that guitar playing's not a hell of a lot of fun, too," I added.

"You do it well," Nick said. "Real well. How come I haven't heard about you before?"

I really didn't want to get into all my insecurity and withdrawal problems, so I said simply, "I keep to myself a lot. Maybe too much. I haven't done much the past few years except practise. I'll confide something of my own, too. I was playing for my life out there today. Those guys were really pushing me, and I didn't know if I could hold on." I got up and stretched. "Now, what's the other thing you wanted to tell me?"

"Do you want my honest opinion about what happened here today?"

"Sure."

"Form a band with these guys. Don't let them get away. The stuff you laid down is strong. Things clicked like crazy, and that doesn't happen often."

I shook my head. "The guys all have their own gigs. They wouldn't give that up for me."

"I wouldn't bet on it."

"How do you know?"

"I asked them."

Nick delivered Shadow and me to our doorstep at 5:25, and I walked up the two flights to my apartment with a big smile on my face and a hot CD he'd burned for me in my pocket. I barely had time to get my jacket off before the phone rang.

Jackie. "Do you feel like going over to Marion's apartment with me tonight?"

"Why tonight?"

"Because this is important." She sounded exasperated.

The words "Absolutely not. I'm dead tired," started to form on my lips, but I stopped. Jackie didn't need me along to search Marion's apartment. What good would I be? Then I realized the guy who was after her still had her worried, and she probably wanted my dog around more than she wanted me. With that in mind, it seemed smart to accompany her, regardless of how tired I felt.

"Kit? You still there?"

"Sorry. I was just thinking. Yeah, I'll go, but don't expect me to be too frisky. I'm pretty beat."

"Thanks. I'll be over in about an hour. Carolina said I can use Edward's car. We're just waiting for him to get home."

I saw a way out. "Is Carolina coming, too?"

"No, they have to go to some kind of meeting of that anti-development committee they're co-chairing. By the way, Carolina wants me to ask how the song is coming along."

I sighed heavily. "Tell the slave-driver that the damn thing's written, and I'm hoping to get the bed tracks down on Wednesday."

That would keep her off my case.

Marion's apartment was located just to the west of Toronto's mid-town. She'd adored flowers and always kept the tables and window-sills heaped with plants, cut flowers, and sachets. It had been about ten days since her death, and as we unlocked the door, the fragrances of her life assaulted our nostrils. Jasmine, her favourite, was the most prevalent. Lurking behind the heavy odours, though, like some beast hiding in a dark corner, was the stench of death and decay. None of Marion's beloved plants had been watered. The olfactory effect reopened the wounds we'd suffered because of her death. Jackie and I stood in the doorway, unable to enter.

"Jesus, I never thought it would be like this," Jackie said in a low voice.

"Nobody's been here since the cops searched the place, I'll bet. How does it look?"

Jackie switched on a light. "Pretty much the way I remember it, except for fingerprinting dust all over everything. Just about all the plants have packed it in, but I guess you can tell that without seeing. Everything seems to be roughly where I remember it."

I practically had to drag Shadow into the apartment. "That doesn't mean much."

"I agree. If someone has been here looking for anything, they would've had to be very discreet. If they'd torn the place apart, the cops would have been suspicious." Jackie went over to Marion's desk, and I heard her switch on the computer. "We need a password."

"Try Ruthless Babes," I said absently.

"Bingo!" Jackie shouted. "Kit, you're amazing – although it's a pretty logical choice."

"Then why didn't you think of it?"

"I was trying to build up your self-esteem," she laughed.

Shadow led me to the sofa. I sat back, and immediately began feeling drowsy. What I really wanted to be doing was lying in a steaming bathtub, a cold glass of wine in my hand and my new CD playing in the background, not sitting in a musty-smelling apartment feeling blue over my dead friend. Shadow sneezed so hard I heard his nose smack the floor. I awoke with a jolt when Jackie slammed her hand on the table and said, "Shitbags!"

"What is it?" I asked, disoriented.

"Nothing! There's absolutely nothing here."

"What do you mean?"

"There's nothing to do with the Housing Department or anything else odd on the computer's hard drive or in her files. At least as far as I can tell." The chair creaked as she pushed it back from the desk. "I'm going to check her journals. Maybe I'll find something there."

"Don't bet on it," I answered under my breath and leaned back again, putting my feet up on the coffee table. I'd been wearing cowboy boots all day, and my feet were beginning to feel the effects. As Carolina's song drifted lazily into my mind, I began humming to myself, trying to figure out what kind of accompaniment it should have. It might be an idea to leave that part alone and see what the band could come up with. I liked the sound of that: a band, people I could work with.

My reverie was interrupted by Jackie. "Kit? I think you better come in here."

Something in her voice sent a chill up my spine.

HE'D GOTTEN HIS MARCHING ORDERS FROM the driver – the little snot-nose. These included the necessary information on the new target and (again!) a frigging time frame. He made a disgusted face.

The crash of a glass hitting the tile floor jerked him back to reality. The bar, Dingo's, one more in a growing number of theme-boozers springing up around Toronto, stretched the limit with its Australian decor. Despite the effort, it was still a dump. Judging by the patrons, you came here to tank up, find someone who looked reasonable, and go off somewhere to get laid. This was not the place he would have preferred to spend his evening.

The target sat at the opposite end of the bar. Some blonde bimbo had draped herself all over his shoulder and seemed to be hanging on his every loud word. He hailed almost anyone who wandered in as a long-lost friend, and judging by the way most of them greeted him in return, he must be generous when it came to buying drinks.

The man had followed his target from work, happy to see that he'd parked his car in one of the least-used parking lots on Church Street. Since the Leafs moved from Maple Leaf Gardens to the Air Canada Centre, this area of town died early most nights. Chances were that, by the end of the evening, the car would be alone in its corner of the sea of crumbling asphalt. The only complication would be if his target wasn't alone at the critical moment, and right now the blonde appeared a likely candidate for overnight entertainment.

He breathed deeply. Complications, complications. He hated complications.

Time to go. He knew where his target was, he knew where his target would go (you didn't leave a car like that overnight in an empty parking lot), and he hoped he knew where his target would wind up before morning.

"Bartender! How much do I owe?" The man had had about two sips from the glass of watery Australian beer. Not worth $5.50 plus tip. "The person I'm waiting for isn't going to show up. If she does – short, plain-looking girl with brown hair and glasses – tell her I said to drop dead, okay?"

The bartender grinned. "No worries, mate!" His accent sounded like the only genuine Australian thing in the place – other than the stuffed kangaroo in the corner. He added, "Take care!" as the man left the bar.

Outside, a gentle rain was falling, making the streetcar tracks gleam silvery under the streetlights. The man turned up his collar and headed for his "working" car. He'd parked it across the street from the lot where the target's black Corvette sat in splendid isolation in a dark corner. The shack for the lot's attendant was dark, already vacated for the night.

Taking out a Thermos, the man poured some coffee. He rested the cup on the dash, where it formed a drifting plume of condensation on the windshield while he screwed the lid back on. Slouching down, he sipped carefully, enjoying the scalding heat of the drink. It was 12:55, about an hour to closing time. Good. But the evenings were still too cold to sit comfortably in an unheated car for long, coffee or no coffee.

A raucous laugh disturbed his reverie. Drunken good-nights drifted down the street from the pub, his target's voice echoing the loudest. Now if the fool only came to his car alone . . . The man hoped for her sake that the blonde decided to make a solitary night of it. Normally he would just melt into the darkness when that kind of complication arose, but right now time was of the essence. He sighed. Complications.

Luck was not with him tonight. The blonde, now sporting a cheap-looking white fur coat, clung to the target's arm, each seeming to hold up the other. The man cursed under his breath. His choice now had to be made: whack them both or try again tomorrow. He shook his head heavily. He couldn't take a chance on tomorrows. It had to be now. Damn!

The couple wobbled across the parking lot, dodging the puddles as if *they* were moving. How could this asshole even think he was capable of driving? The man smiled suddenly. Maybe he should let them drive away. In their condition, they'd probably crash within minutes.

He drained his coffee cup, placed it on the seat next to him, and quietly got out of the car, then locked it. Nobody on the sidewalks, not many cars. Good. Crossing carefully, he kept his eye out for anyone who might be nearby. Reaching the opposite curb, he stopped. The target and the woman were locked in an embrace, her coat open and the man's hands all over her breasts. When he started to pull her dress up, she angrily pushed him away.

"Not out here! I don't want to put on a free show."

"Come on, baby. You know it would turn you on. Remember that night at the cottage with those other guys when you —"

"Drop dead, Rex! I was drunk."

"Like you're not now?"

The man stepped back into the shadows next to a building. *Come on, lady,* he said inside his head. *Give this jerk the brush-off! Go home by yourself.*

The target continued to paw the blonde. She pushed him away again, then started across the lot. The target, grabbing at her wrist, slipped and went down on his knees hard. The blonde walked right out to the street, and what drove by but an empty cab! It screeched to a halt as if she had it on a string. The man felt like cheering. There really was a God.

He glided out from the shadows and across the parking lot on soft-soled shoes. The target was standing up now, wiping ineffectually at the mud on his pants.

"Hey buddy, need some help? I was walking by and saw you go down."

The target smoothed back his hair with both hands. "Piss off!"

"Look, I know you're a little embarrassed, so I'll let that pass. You're not thinking of driving, are you?"

"That's the idea."

"If you don't mind my saying, I don't think that would be smart. The cops are all over."

"I won't get stopped. I'm okay."

"That's exactly what a good friend of mine said and now he's hoofing it. C'mon, let me drive you home."

The target looked up with unsteady eyes. "You don't even know where the hell I live!"

"All right, where do you live?" This was going perfectly. No rough stuff needed.

"High Park and Bloor."

"This is your lucky day, buddy. I'm back at Keele and Annette. Be smart. Why don't you let me drive you that far? You wouldn't want to be forced to lock a car like this in a garage for a year, would you?"

The man smiled when his target passed over the keys. Later, as they drove along Lakeshore Boulevard, his smile had reason to broaden further. The target, fallen sideways against the door, had begun snoring loudly.

"This is going to be too easy," he said under his breath, and felt like whistling. Best not to tempt fate.

At Parkside Drive, where he should have turned north, the man aimed the car straight and got on the expressway, enjoying the way the car handled and the power of its engine. His passenger snored away as they eventually drove north, leaving the city far behind. The man knew a convenient dumping ground, a boggy pond he'd found on one of his summer forays into the bush. It would swallow everything, car and all, in its watery embrace. Follow a forest track for about three miles – even in the spring mud, if he took it real slow the car would make it – and there it was. All he had to do was walk out to the highway, make a cellphone call to a friend who could be counted on to drive out, no questions asked, and he'd be back in the city by 7:00 a.m. at the latest to rescue his car from the clutches of the towing brigade.

Everything didn't go that smoothly as it turned out. An especially bone-crunching jolt woke the drunken sleeper just as they arrived at the end of the road.

He stretched and yawned then looked around in confusion. "Wait a minute. What's going on? This isn't High Park!"

"No, it isn't," came the soft voice from the driver's seat.

The target turned to his left and looked straight down the barrel of a gun. He raised his eyes in even greater confusion to the man holding it.

Confusion and gut-wrenching fear.

Deer, the man thought disgustedly as his finger gently squeezed the trigger.

CHAPTER 14

Marion had been living in her apartment for only three years, so I'd never actually seen it. I hadn't been there often, either, since my place seems to be the centre of the Babes' universe. She'd had me over to dinner once or twice, and that was about it. So, when I got up, I had to feel my way carefully along the sofa. Here memory failed me, and I didn't want to disturb Shadow who lay twitching on the floor – probably chasing rabbits in his sleep.

"Jackie, is there anything between the sofa and the bedroom?"

Her voice came from the doorway. "Sorry, Kit. Don't know where my brain is. It's no problem to bring this out to you."

I sat down again and Jackie dropped heavily beside me, almost quivering with excitement. My stomach did a little pirouette. I leaned back, feeling like a convict on her way to the gallows, and I realized there had been a small part of me that hadn't wanted Jackie's suspicions to be correct. It would make everything so messy.

"What have you found?"

Jackie leaned forward and opened something on the coffee table. "This is Marion's journal for this year. It starts January 1st and goes up to the night before she died."

"So?"

"There isn't an entry for March 20th."

"You're kidding!"

"And if you look really closely, you can see where a page has been carefully cut out."

"Oh God . . ."

Jackie, in one of her confrontational moods, had once called Marion "completely on the far side of anal." It had dampened their friendship for several months, as Marion nursed hurt feelings while Jackie carried on as if nothing was wrong. Characteristically, it had been Marion who'd buried the hatchet. Jackie felt she was only being truthful, and while admitting she *may* have been rather blunt, she felt no need to apologize.

The fact was, *I'd* often felt the same about Marion. She wanted everything always to run on the same rails. The unexpected threw her for an incredible loop. Her apartment, like her life, had been totally organized. Everything had its backup, everything had its special place. She also sometimes extended that to trying to organize her friends' lives, too – which is what led to Jackie's comment. Everywhere that Marion went, spotlessness was sure to go. More than once, I remember her using my bathroom, then washing the sink and bathtub while she was in there.

She needed regularity in her life: getting up at a certain time, exercising at a certain time, and *always* before going to bed, writing in her journal. Want to know what you ate at a picnic six years ago? Ask Marion. She couldn't fall asleep if she hadn't scribbled something about the day's events. But only her close friends were aware of this. That's why Morris and his men hadn't found anything suspicious, even if he'd looked in her journals. Something wasn't there and he had no way of knowing. Anyone would've assumed that Marion hadn't gotten around to writing an entry for the 20th – two short days before her death – unless they knew her habits. When I asked, Jackie admitted you had to look mighty close even to see that a page was missing. Marion must have written something in her journal on March 20th that someone didn't want known, and they'd taken it. How the hell were we supposed to figure out what that was?

"Anything else?" I asked.

"Yes! *Another* page is missing and that must have contained her, let's see, February 6th and 7th entries. That's strange . . . Why would somebody remove February entries? She gave me the feeling this thing she was after started much more recently."

"Get out her other journals and let's go through them," I suggested. "Maybe more entries have been cut out."

Jackie wound up reading a number of pages to me that Marion had written during the past three years. I felt rather uncomfortable hearing our friend's most private thoughts; it was as if we were eavesdropping or something. A lot of entries *were* pretty graphic, and we both wound up realizing that Marion's life had been a lot more ... *complicated* than we'd ever suspected. But while her activities were, to my mind, rather bizarre, nothing Marion wrote about seemed to be too excessive or violent. Jackie thought some of it sounded like fun, but I think she was just trying to yank my chain. For all her bad-girl persona, she's actually fairly straitlaced. No other entries were missing.

Altogether we found three small references to a secret lover, starting in January. Neither Jackie nor I could tell who the mystery man was from the scanty information, but Marion obviously felt uneasy about it. What did it all mean?

Jackie spent another hour poking into every corner of the apartment.

"Marion's toys are nowhere to be seen," she called out from the bedroom. "The cops are probably using 'em on themselves downtown."

"Keep your mind on the job and out of the gutter," I told her.

The banging of drawers and increasingly frantic shuffling of papers ended, and Jackie flopped down dispiritedly on the sofa again. Since we weren't in my apartment, she lit a cigarette and took a long drag. "We're no further ahead knowing someone's cut pages out of Marion's journal. Those February dates really bother me, though. Maybe I'm wrong about Housing. Maybe Morris was on the right track with his secret-lover theory."

I shook my head. "No. That person would have no reason to want *you* dead, Jackie. Something you've done stirred up the hornet's nest and you've only been prying into the Housing connection. Somehow, we have to find out what was on those missing pages."

"Well, if Marion hid anything in the apartment, I can't find it."

"Not without pulling up the floor or kicking holes in the walls."

"Wouldn't that make us popular! I'm feeling frustrated and ornery enough to do it, though."

"We've accomplished something tonight." I took a deep breath of smoky air and let it go immediately. "Do you have to smoke those things?"

"Sorry," she said as she stubbed it out. "I thought it would kill some of the stink in here."

"Those cigarettes would kill the smell of anything." I turned to face her. "Anyway, what I wanted to say is this: I'm pretty sure we now have the first concrete evidence that Marion's death was premeditated. But if someone was here to cut out those pages, they might have removed stuff from the computer, too. Wouldn't the cops have been able to tell?"

"Not really. There are programs that will completely scrub any traces of a file and leave everything else intact."

"Maybe. The question is, what do we do about what we've found out?"

Jackie got up. "First of all, we get you home. You look like you're dead on your feet, girl. I'll call Carolina and talk things over with her. Maybe she'll have some kind of brainstorm. C'mon. Let's get out of here. Seeing Marion's dead plants is pretty damned depressing."

"You should try only being able to smell them. It reminds me of a graveyard."

So that was the bitter end to what should have been one of the most amazing days of my life. By 11:00, I was lying in bed with unseen murderers and the ghosts of dead friends waiting for me in every dark corner of my imagination. The weather outside stirred restlessly too, each gust rattling the windows. Only Shadow's loud breathing as he slept next to me kept me from grabbing the phone and calling for my friends. Where was Patrick when I needed him? I certainly could have used someone warm to cuddle against, and Shadow was a poor substitute.

It's tough to be alone when you know there's big trouble on the horizon and you can't see it coming.

Shadow rousted me out at 7:30, damn him. After his potty walk, I put on the new CD and sat down on the sofa to listen while I ate yogourt with a banana and wheat germ for breakfast. The combination made me think of KT Oslin's tune "You Can't Do That," because the first verse talks about what a drag health food is. The lyrics to the whole song are a scream. I've always enjoyed her material because KT has a totally off-the-wall sense of humour. It's a feel I wouldn't mind getting into my songs. The closest I can get to it is snarky. Oh well. I play guitar better than she does.

Listening to my music, I got enthusiastic all over again. Overdub possibilities jumped out in every second bar. It's funny how I'd never really thought about arrangements for my songs. I just wanted to sell them and let the people who recorded them take care of the rest. But the work we'd been doing had totally one-eightied the way I looked at my musical offspring. The public was not going to hear them until I felt they were ready. This recording project had me hooked but good. I wanted it to be tomorrow, because I already needed another musical fix.

But to get to tomorrow, I had to do dirty work today: my allotted job for Carolina's Action Committee. That meant calling Morris. I reached out for the phone several times, only to withdraw my hand and put it back under my chin.

I felt the four of us were about to do something stupid. When Jackie and I got back to my place last night, she'd called Carolina to tell her what we'd found out. My opinion had been that we should call Morris immediately, but they had both adamantly refused. Carolina thought we needed to dig some more, because we still had almost nothing in the way of concrete evidence. So what if some pages from Marion's journal were missing? Maybe her lover, when he'd heard that Marion had been murdered, had snuck in and removed the pages to avoid being dragged into the mess. Jackie wanted to be able to dump the murderer right on Morris's desk. I'd been too tired to know what I thought any more.

By the time I got up and clicked off the stereo, the CD had long since run its course. "Best to get this over with," I said out loud, and finally put the receiver to my ear. I'd have to improvise as I went along. While waiting for the detective to come on the line, I started humming Carolina's song. It was certainly growing on me.

"Morris." He sounded busy.

"It's Kit Mason. I hope this isn't a bad time."

His voice sounded more welcoming when he replied, "No, no – as long as you haven't been doing any more amateur detecting."

I sidestepped that one. "Did you find out any more about Jackie's accident?"

"Not really. We found a few people who said they were around when it happened. The best description we got of the car was "a blue Chevy something." Nobody could give us an even halfway decent description of the driver. One person told us he had brown hair, but two others said it was blond."

"But you do believe us now?"

"What you've told me is worth a little extra digging. That's all."

"You want us to help?"

"No, I *don't* want you to help. You can see from what happened the other night how dangerous that can be."

"Have you looked further into that blond man Marion's neighbour saw her with? Maybe it's the same person who tried to run down Jackie. That sounds like a worthwhile lead."

"Leave that up to me. *And keep your noses out of this!* I don't want anyone getting hurt."

"But we could be helping you."

"You girls are the most exasperating people I've ever had to deal with." Morris's voice had been going up and up in volume. "Trust me! We know what we're doing."

After Morris rang off, I stood there gently tapping my forehead with the handset while I thought. I felt bad, not telling him about the missing pages, but I'd given my word that I wouldn't. The call hadn't produced much, but it hadn't been a total waste, either. Talking to Morris about this blond lover of Marion's had given me an interesting idea.

I punched the numbers for Carolina's. The phone rang four times before a sleepy-sounding Jackie answered.

"Good morning, sunshine," I said. "Have a late night?"

"Carolina and Edward and I sat up talking. You should hear C's theories about how Marion developed this domination fantasy because she had trouble standing up to people. Shows what working on a doctorate in psychology will do for you." Jackie yawned. "I don't know where the two of them get their energy. We got to bed after 2:00, and they were out running at 6:00. I feel like I got hit by a truck." She yawned again. "Sorry. Did you call Morris?"

"Just got off the phone with him."

"And?"

"He's come around a little bit. He agrees that there might be something in what we've been saying. Morris said he was going to do some follow-up."

"Fat lot of good that's going to do!"

"Look, Jackie, unless you want to bring in the crook yourself, you're going to have to trust *some* cop. Why not Morris? I think he plays off the top of the deck."

"Yeah, but you can't see his shifty eyes."

"He has a nice voice. I trust him. And I still say we should tell him what we found out last night." Silence. I sighed heavily. "So what do we do now?"

"C wants to know if we can have a meeting tonight."

"Another one? Do you want to have it here?"

"Sure. Call Sue will you? I've got to get some more shut-eye."

Jackie clicked off. She hadn't been back to wherever she'd been crashing since the attempt on her life. Last night she'd dragged me along with her when I was absolutely no use. I'd never seen Jackie intimidated by anything or anyone. Hell, I once saw her jump all over a guy about eight inches taller and a hundred and fifty pounds heavier than she was. Broke his nose, too, before he knocked her clear across the room. She must be really scared.

I spent the rest of the morning dialling Susan's number every few minutes and singing the songs we'd recorded the day before in between tries. I was slowly gaining confidence in my singing, but I knew I'd need a lot more practice before I could give a smooth and assured performance every time. And it would be one thing to do it in a studio, where I had as many chances as I needed, another to do the job in front of an audience.

The downstairs buzzer went off about 1:30.

"Who is it?" I said into the door control panel.

"Susan. I forgot my keys. Could you let me in?"

I pressed the button, opened the apartment door, and waited. Something gave me a bad feeling about Susan being at my door at this time of day.

"Afternoon, Kit," she said as she breezed by. "What's happening?"

I didn't budge. "Aren't you supposed to tell me that?"

"Tell you what?"

"What you're doing here. Why you forgot your key to the street door for the first time in living memory. Why your answering machine wasn't on when I called you earlier. How are those for starters?"

Susan walked over to the window and stood silently for a moment. "I was going to ask you if you wanted to come with me on my Official Errand to City Hall, but . . . Look, Kit, I have a problem, and with everything else that's going on, I don't know if it's important enough to bother any of you with it."

"How big?" I asked.

"Big," she admitted.

"You've got this far, you might as well go all the way."

"It's Paul. He's gotten us into some pretty serious financial trouble." She said it all in a rush and then snuffled loudly. "Damn! I promised myself I wasn't going to start bawling."

"I'm just in the middle of making coffee. Why don't we sit down with a mug and you can tell me all about it."

"All right," Susan said, blowing her nose. "I've been wracking my brain about what to do since Monday night. I can't talk about this to my parents, and Paul refuses to go to one of those counsellors."

"I don't mind listening," I called from the kitchen – not exactly truthfully. "What happened on Monday?"

Susan came and stood in the doorway. Her voice had a quality that reminded me of a tightly wound spring. "I guess you need some background. I've already told you that things haven't been going well for us lately. Paul's been moody and preoccupied, and we haven't been getting along all that well the past few months."

The coffee was ready, so we parked our behinds on my two chairs.

"What do you fight about?"

"We don't fight. He just seems awfully touchy sometimes. Preoccupied."

"So what's he touchy about?"

Susan took a few noisy slurps of hot coffee. "Mostly money."

"I thought you guys would be rolling in it, what with Paul's job and everything."

It had caught us all by surprise when Susan married Paul. She was only twenty-two at the time, and the whole world seemed open to her: she was good-looking, vivacious, and she really had a talent with words. We'd all had her pegged as a future writer of romantic bestsellers. Then Paul came along, dreadfully handsome, two years older, a law student, and he'd just blown her away. Seven months later, we found out why they'd tied the knot so suddenly. But they seemed really happy together, so we figured everything was okay. It didn't hurt that Sue's parents had given them a house as a wedding present, either – one less worry for the up-and-comers.

I'd always found Paul too intense and self-absorbed for my liking. For example, I once played in a mixed slo-pitch tournament with him, and you'd have thought it was the seventh game of the World Series. I'd actually known Paul first, having gone out with him for a month or so before bringing him out to the ball game where he was instantly attracted to Susan. Luckily, that was fine with me by that point. Jackie detested him; Carolina remained neutral; Marion, he pretty well ignored. After passing his bar exams, Paul had snagged a killer job with a big law firm and seemed well on the way to a successful career.

"So what's wrong financially? I asked.

"Our bank account's at zero, for starts. Paul made a couple of really dumb investments last year. Now he's got a bundle tied up in some real-estate venture and our house is the collateral. Monday night he admitted the deal is in trouble. I really blew my top. I just couldn't believe we might lose the house! Paul wants me to go to my parents and borrow from them, but I can't do that. They've done so much for us already."

"So what's the upshot?"

"Even though he's trying dreadfully hard to be nice, I haven't felt like speaking to him. The kids know that something is wrong and it's affecting them."

"How much dough is involved?"

"Five hundred thousand."

I whistled. Oh boy, they *were* in trouble. My mind couldn't even come to grips with a sum that large. "Seems to me you have three options: bail out Paul's ass by going to your parents; refuse, and lose the house; or pray for a miracle turnaround in this real-estate thing."

"Not much of a choice, is it? My big worry about going to my parents is that Paul won't learn a thing. He'll just go out and do something like this again." She sighed heavily. "This is a side of him I really don't like. Paul constantly goes out of his way to seem more important than he is. I've heard him say the most outrageous things sometimes, total lies, just to make himself look like a big shot. That's what caused this mess and it makes me really uneasy."

"Have you told him that?"

"Yes. He says that I'm too caught up in the safe little world of being a suburban housewife, that the real winners in life are the ones who take chances. Some chances!" Susan took a sip of her coffee. "You know how I used to write erotic poetry when we were in university?"

"Sure do. Remember the night at that frat party we bet that you didn't have the guts to stand on a table and recite some of it?"

"Oh God! I'd forgot!" Susan actually laughed. "That seems so long ago. Anyway, I got some of it out last week. I think it's the best stuff I ever did. At least, I don't wince when I read it. But it made me realize how cut off from that side of my personality I've become. Maybe in some way Paul's right – about the suburban housewife part, I mean. Things never turn out the way they're supposed to, do they?" she ended glumly.

"I don't know what to tell you, Sue." I took my empty mug to the sink. "I wish I could offer you more in the way of help other than saying I'm sorry."

"The past couple of weeks, things had been much better. Paul had actually been encouraging me to help out Marion's mom and come out with the Babes more often. I guess he knew how much what happened to Marion has upset me. First her and now this. Life sure can kick you in the stomach sometimes."

"You've got that right."

"Well . . . getting back to my original excuse for coming here, would you accompany me on my scouting mission to City Hall? I could use the moral support."

"Do you really feel up to trucking over there? Shouldn't you go home and –"

"No! I want to do something useful! I parked the kids with Mom and Dad for a few days, making the excuse that Paul and I need some time alone. I want to help you and Carolina and Jackie. I need to do something positive right now. Besides, if I stay at home, Paul will bulldoze me into asking for that money. This has got to come to a head now."

"Don't you think you should sit down and talk to him like you've been talking to me?"

"It won't do any good! And I just can't bear the thought of sitting at home, totally miserable."

"You're right," I said. "Why do that when you can hang around us and be totally miserable?"

Susan laughed sadly. "What are friends for?"

—ɷ—

FREE AT LAST. FREE AT LAST. THANK God Almighty, I'm free at last!

A great weight had lifted from his shoulders as his target's Corvette bubbled its way down to oblivion in the dark water. He'd been a bit concerned at the amount of late-melting ice, but the car had merely rolled out an additional twenty feet before it crashed through. All the better.

Now he merely had to collect the money owing him, clean up any loose ends, and get on with his life. That was the decision he'd made while hiking down the forest track in the pre-dawn gloom. He knew now that this job had been a sign, a sign that the time had come for him to pack it in. A true artist always knew when his powers had begun to fade. The danger became far too great when you began making mistakes. You didn't last long and he wanted to be able to walk away a winner.

The man leaned against the vinyl back of the restaurant

booth. Life was good again. The waitress hurried over, the coffee pot seeming permanently attached to her right hand like some space-age appendage.

"One more cup for the road, honey?" she asked.

Did *every* waitress in creation call their customers "honey"? But the man couldn't even begin to get irritated this morning. With his belly full of eggs, bacon, home fries, toast, and several cups of strong, black coffee, he felt he could tolerate anything.

"No thanks. I'm sloshing now." He smiled. "Just bring me my bill, okay?"

"Sure thing. I'll have you on your way in no time."

Out in the fresh morning air, the man started whistling as he walked down the street. God, he felt good! Although the air was still pretty cold, the sun was already exerting its power. What did they call Toronto up north? The Big Smoke? How could you call it that on a day the sky was so clear you could almost see heaven?

When he got to the place he'd left his car the previous evening, there wasn't even a ticket under the wiper blade, even though it was well after 7:00 – towing time here in the Big Smoke.

Driving back to the garage to dump his junker of a working car and exchange it for the peppy sports car he greatly preferred driving, he mapped out his day: call the snotty contact and report that his commission had been successfully carried out, then spend the rest of it in some well-deserved R&R. Opening day for the Blue Jays, and he was going. Maybe they'd even roll back the lid on the Dome.

Oh yes, there was one other thing, one other piece of unfinished business. A slight irritation really, and he hoped his contact could help him out there. That guy possessed more information than he'd doled out so far.

Unfinished business. The small matter of Jackie Goode. The stink of the only failure in his career still hung around him like the smell of something rancid. The man abhorred loose ends, and this was one he meant to tie up very tight. He'd reassure his former employers that in no way would their operation be jeopardized. How could they complain anyway when he'd be doing it gratis?

When he called to report, he'd ask. If the contact didn't have the info he needed, he would do the legwork himself, although that would take considerably more time. But he would track her down in the end, and in some dark alley, some hallway, maybe even on a street in broad daylight, he'd get her.

That stupid bitch wouldn't escape this time. It was a matter of principle.

CHAPTER 15

As we walked out the street door, the sun felt so gloriously hot that Susan and I decided to skip the streetcar and walk the seven blocks along Queen Street to City Hall. We could use the time to plan how we would attempt to get information from the people Marion had been after. The whole thing was beginning to feel like looking for a needle in a haystack – when you didn't even know where the haystack is.

The sidewalks hummed with life as everyone tried to cram as much early April warmth as possible into their lunch breaks. Shadow slowed to a snail's pace as he threaded his way carefully through the crowds. I found it interesting that he managed to do his slowest work in the area of José's wiener wagon.

Who said dogs are dumb?

When he spotted us, José shouted enthusiastically, "Caterina! How wonderful you should come along in this nice weather! I have looked for you the last many days now. I am wondering if you find somewhere else to buy your hot dogs."

"No, José. I've been busy, that's all."

"What would you and your most beautiful friend like from me today?"

Who said hot-dog vendors are dumb?

Susan, who'd been holding my elbow, stiffened when the little Chilean called her beautiful, but then, surprisingly, laughed. "Today does feel like the kind of day for a hot dog. What'll you have, Kit? My treat."

So eventually, with Susan's wallet a few dollars lighter, we were again on our way east. If we still had no idea what we were going to do when we got to City Hall, at least our stomachs were full. And yes, Shadow scored a surreptitious dog, too. José's payoff for a job well done.

Not much chatter passed between us for the next couple of blocks, and I began to get fidgety as we approached University Avenue. "Sue, we can't just waltz into the Housing Department and start bombarding them with questions."

We'd crossed the wide street before she replied. "How about this? It just came to me. We go up there and I ask a question they couldn't possibly deal with in that department, but that wouldn't sound totally ridiculous. Something like daycare. Then I could suggest that you wait there while I go to whatever department they send me to. You could try chatting them up. You know how people tend to say unguarded things to you because you're blind. Maybe we'll get lucky."

"You just thought of this?" I asked pointedly.

"Well . . ." Susan giggled. "It's weird enough that it might work."

"Since you're dragging me into this anyway, how about you go up there, ask about subsidized housing for your family, then remember that you left your ID down at, say, the department that deals with daycare. While you're gone, I can pull the blind person routine everyone thinks I'm so good at."

"Brilliant idea, Holmes! Or should I say Holmette?"

"Elementary, my dear Watdaughter."

We were both still chuckling as we walked across Nathan Phillips Square, the open area in front of City Hall. I keep a crystal-clear memory of how it looks, because I spent so many winter days skating on the rink that dominates it – a great place to meet guys. Right now, though, the rink would be serving its warmer-weather function as a reflecting pool. Toronto's City Hall, located at the back of the square, looks as if a flying saucer landed in the space between two skinny, crescent-shaped towers. The council chambers are in the saucer, which is appropriate since many of the elected officials act like space cadets anyway.

The design of the place is kind of nifty, but it must be hell to work there. If you're in one tower, the only way to get to an office in the other is to take the elevator all the way down to the lobby, cross to the opposite bank of elevators, and go up. I know this personally, because with Wrong-Way Susan blazing the trail, we wound up in the opposite tower to the one we wanted. The delay in reaching our objective only made us more nervous.

"May I help you?" a secretarial voice asked when we finally pushed open the glass doors of the Housing Department.

Susan did the honours. The less people in the office thought about me the better. Deaf, dumb, and blind Mason, that's me – all three monkeys rolled into one. (At least that's how a lot of sighted people seemed to think of us blind folk.) "Um, excuse me? Is, ah, this where I find out about subsidized housing?"

The secretary replied in a very bored tone, "Take a number, honey. There are only about five thousand people ahead of you."

"Really? Oh dear. You see, I, um, need a place for me and my kids right now. I was just down at, um, asking about daycare and . . . Oh damn! Can you believe it? I left my ID down there! Without waiting for a comment, Susan turned to me. "Why don't you wait here so you don't have to traipse all over the place? I'll be right back." She helped me to a chair, whispered, "Good luck," and left.

I tried to look suitably vacant and insignificant. Shadow lay down at my feet, and I hoped anyone passing by would be able to get around him. If I'd known we were going to try something this hare-brained when we started out, I would've left him at home.

The secretary fielded a few phone calls, then tried to make some friendly chatter. "That's an awfully large dog. What kind is it?"

"A Newfoundland. And the reason he's so big is because he eats too much, don't you boy?" I said, scratching behind Shadow's right ear.

She laughed. "I can believe it!"

I saw an opportunity in chatting her up a bit. "Bet you get a lot of dumb questions in your job."

"Yeah. We get our share."

"Is it just from people who need a place to live?"

"Mostly complaints or people desperate for a place to live. Some of the stories are pretty heartbreaking."

Just then someone approached the desk and snapped, "Charlene, get me that stack of files on Rex's desk. I'm going to have to try and sort out this mess without him. He hasn't called by any chance, has he?"

"No, Mr. Reynolds. I'll tell you if he does." The person strode off and my new friend said under her breath, "That Rex is such a pain in the ass." I heard her chair scrape back and she left for a couple of minutes.

When she returned, I asked, "Did somebody take an unscheduled day off? I can't say I blame them. The weather is absolutely gorgeous."

"I know. Too bad it wasn't me! Everything's gone wrong today. First a council member shows up and demands information we didn't think we had. Then it turns out that we did, but the person who's working on the file didn't come to work today. I phoned him up, but he wasn't home and the boss is furious. It's amazing he's held on to his job this long."

I had a hard time not smiling. "I worked in a place once where I'm sure one guy had something on the boss."

Charlene said in a low voice, "The thought has crossed my mind."

Just then Reynolds's voice called out from down the hall. "Charlene! Are you sure that this is the whole file? There seems to be some correspondence missing."

"Sorry," she said to me. "Duty calls."

She sped off and left me for quite a long time. No one else came by to liven things up, and eventually Susan returned.

"Have you got anything yet?" she whispered in my ear.

I was about to tell her to bugger off for a few more minutes when Charlene stomped by on her way out of the boss's office. "Oh, you're back. Look, why don't you take these forms home, fill them out, and bring them back when you're done. I wouldn't hold out much hope, though. These things can take a long time." She rummaged for something in a filing cabinet and then her heels clicked off again in the direction of Reynolds's office.

Susan, sounding uncertain, asked, "Should we go?"

"I guess we have to now. If we stay it might look suspicious."

We weren't alone on the elevator, so I couldn't tell her anything until we walked out through the echoing lobby into the open air of Nathan Phillips Square. A group of chattering schoolchildren on their way to the holy of holies for a tour crowded around us wanting to pet Shadow.

"Children," their teacher said, "this is a seeing-eye dog and he is working. You must ask his mistress if it's all right."

"May we please, mistress?" a small child asked, tugging on my jacket sleeve.

I smiled. Shadow always has this effect on little ones. Sometimes they think the big bozo's a bear. "It's okay with me, but please don't feed him or he'll get too fat to walk."

They all giggled and surrounded the main attraction as I got him to sit so he wouldn't knock one of them over accidentally.

The same sleeve-tugger asked another question. "Is it very dark in there?"

I squatted down to answer. "In where?"

"Inside your head."

"Timmy!" the teacher snapped.

Out of the mouths of babes. It got very still around us and I had the feeling that the class's Asker-of-Awkward-Questions was doing his thing. "It's different," I told him.

"What do you mean? How's it different?"

"My eyes don't work, but that doesn't mean I can't see. Take the man reading the paper on that bench over there."

"How do you know there's a man on the bench?"

"Because I remember the bench, I can hear him turning pages, and they sound like newspaper."

"But how do you know it's a man?"

I tapped the side of my nose. "He smells like he's wearing about half a bottle of aftershave."

"Neat!"

It was time for everyone to be moving on. The teacher said to me, "Thank you for being so kind. It's important for the children to understand the affliction of blindness."

I took a deep breath and felt my face turn red-hot. "I hope I just proved to your *students*, at least, that I'm not *afflicted*!" Yanking

Shadow and Susan simultaneously, I strode off across the square, leaving the silent class in my wake. "Let's find a place we can sit and talk and I'll tell you what that secretary told me."

A broad median filled with gardens runs up the centre of University Avenue, and at the corner of Queen there are some fountains which had not yet been started for the season. We parked our behinds on the low wall surrounding the pool, and amidst the noise of the passing traffic, I passed on the little bit I'd found out.

I related the gist of the conversation to her, then said, "So unless we go up there and ask point-blank why Marion was asking them questions – and I'll bet you it was the boss, Reynolds, a slimeball if I've ever heard one – we're not going to find out a hell of a lot. It's just another dead end in what seems to be a long string of them. This is getting damned frustrating! I did find one thing that might be useful, though. It seems this guy Jackie was going to meet at the bar didn't come in to work today. I wonder if he's run off."

"Maybe somebody warned him and he's cut and run. I wish Jackie had left him alone."

"Hopefully it's that and not something else . . ."

On the way home, we called Carolina on Susan's cellphone and left a message, saying that we could meet whenever she and Jackie wanted. We also used Susan's car to go to the big grocery store down by the lake, where I bought about two weeks' worth of food. That accomplished, we struggled our way upstairs to my place, carrying about four bags of groceries each. Shadow didn't offer to carry a thing, the big oaf.

I had a couple of messages waiting, so I listened to them while Susan took the food out and laid it on the counter for me to put away later in the right spots. One of the bothers of being blind is that you have to memorize exactly what's in each box or can and where you've put it. I've opened a can of spaghetti for Shadow and Alpo for myself more times than I'd like to admit. I suppose I should do something intelligent like putting rubber bands around the dog-food cans, but somehow I never get around to it.

The first message was from Nick, saying that the session the next day had been moved forward to 8:00 a.m., because Arnie had booked someone in at 2:00, and Nick wanted to have enough time to do a decent amount of work. He'd already spoken to Steve, who'd pick me up at 7:00.

The second message made my little heart go pit-a-pat. Patrick sounded in high spirits. "Hi Kit! Sorry I didn't get a chance to call yesterday, but everything at work's been going wrong. I hope we're still on for the ball game Thursday. I'll call back to confirm, but I'd like to pick you up at 12:30. Dinner after?" He paused, then added more quietly, "I really enjoyed our evening together."

Susan came out of the kitchen as I reset the answering machine. "Is that him?"

"Yeah. We're going to opening day down at the ball yard."

She came over and hugged me. "He has a very sexy voice. I'm so happy for you." Her voice kind of choked on the last few words.

"Don't worry, Sue," I said, going right to the heart of the matter. "We'll get you sorted out, too. I promise."

"That's a pretty big obligation I'm afraid." She tried to sound lighter when she said, "Speaking of obligations, I'd better call my mother and find out how the kids are doing. Maybe I'll try Paul, too. Do you mind if I use the phone in your bedroom?"

"Be my guest."

The others arrived at 6:00 for our meeting. I'd made a pot of my famous chili – famous because it's the only thing I cook that's any good. And I learned to make it *after* I went blind, just so you know what my skill level is.

Carolina had brought a bag of tortilla chips and a pot of hyacinths for some spring fragrance. Jackie, more practically, had arrived with a bottle of wine. I thought it felt too much like a festive occasion compared to what it was supposed to be: a progress report on finding our friend's killer.

The wine went fast, since I'd used too much cayenne in the chili. To be honest, I think I put it in twice. While I was cooking, I'd been playing the recording of the new songs for Susan, and had been paying more attention to the music than the food. As we sat around drowning the fire in our mouths with glasses of milk (Carolina's suggestion), I played the CD for everyone. They were impressed.

"What about the song you promised me?" Carolina asked. "Have you recorded it yet?"

"Tomorrow," I assured her. "I've already run it through for Nick, and he's excited about it."

"You know we had a meeting of the Save Regent Park Committee last night?"

Something in the way she said it gave me a sinking feeling. If they'd decided they didn't want this song after all, I was going to enjoy shoving one of my guitars up Carolina's –

"Boy, do you have a sour expression on your face," she laughed. "*All* we want to know is if you'll play live at our rally."

"*Live?*" I echoed weakly. The thought was daunting – no backup band for one thing. I hadn't done anything about Nick's idea of talking to the guys about working together on a more permanent basis. Maybe they'd at least do this one gig. "When and where?"

"Monday afternoon, Riverdale Park. We've had to move it up because they're planning on breaking ground by the end of next week, and this is our last chance to stop it without lying in front of the bulldozers or something. It'll mean big media coverage, Kit. Will you do it?"

"I'll ask the guys doing the sessions with me if they'll play, and let you know tomorrow. Is that okay?"

It was time to get down to business. We all related the meagre amount we'd discovered, and the further we got into discussing things, the more it seemed that I'd been the only one to come up with anything really useful so far. The other two had spent most of the day scouring the Wellesley area for any information on Jackie's accident.

Jackie said, "We pounded on all the doors in that apartment building at the corner where it happened and nobody except the superintendent, who happened to be sitting on the front steps at the time, had actually seen anything."

"What did he tell you?" Susan asked.

"Not a heck of a lot. The guy who ran me into the back of the truck was tall and drove some nondescript car, probably a Chevy. The super didn't think he'd recognize him again, but said he was definitely blond."

They were all interested in what I'd found out from Charlene in the Housing Department as well as what Morris had told me over the phone that morning. After that our resident academic took over and spent some time organizing her thoughts on paper. During this intermission the phone rang.

Jackie, who was coming out of the bathroom, beat me to it. "Hello, Mason residence . . . Just a moment, sir. I'll see if she's available." The phone got thrust into my hand. "I think it's The Guy," she whispered.

"I'll take it in the bedroom," I said, "and if any of you listens in, I'll remove a vital organ – with a dull spoon!"

They all went "Ohhhh," and laughed as I shut the door. I lay back on the bed, picked up the phone, and waited until I heard a definite click from the living-room extension. "Patrick?"

"Was that your butler?" he chuckled.

"No," I said, "just one of my friends, and don't ever call her that if you meet her. She'd probably cut off something I love."

"Having a girls' night?"

"Sort of. We uncovered some information about my friend's death. Remember I told you a little about it when we were driving back to town on Sunday? Well, it's looking more and more like somebody silenced her."

"What makes you think that?" he asked.

"Two pages from her journal are missing. Somebody must have been in her apartment after she died."

"Do the police know?"

"We haven't told them."

"Look," he said, sounding serious, "Kit, I really think you and your friends should just drop it. You could get hurt."

I frowned. "We can take care of ourselves. I'll tell you all about it on Thursday between innings."

"Um . . . great! I'm really looking forward to this. By the way, how are you fixed for the weekend?"

"It depends what you have in mind."

"Spend the weekend at the farmhouse, walks in the woods, fires in the evening, polar-bear rug?"

"Sounds amazing! The only thing that might stand in the way is the recording I'm doing. Since it's at the studio's expense, I have to take time when they give it. That might mean Saturday or Sunday."

"When can you let me know?"

"Hopefully at the game."

"Okay. See you at 12:30."

"Patrick?"

"Yes, Kit."

"I had a really great time, too."

By the time I made a pit stop in the bathroom, Carolina seemed about ready to begin her dissertation. I leaned over to Susan and whispered, "Since you haven't said anything about Paul to the others, I'm assuming you want to keep it between us."

"I'm not in the mood to listen to Jackie say, 'I told you so.'"

"What do you mean?"

"She told me the week before I got married – remember when you guys took me to that strip joint? – that I shouldn't marry Paul. She referred to him as a peckerhead. It may just have been Jackie being ornery, but I don't want to hear it again. Not now."

"Okay. Mum's the word."

Carolina stood up to lecture us on the Crime World According to Graf. "Here's how the facts stack up." She rustled her papers and began telling us what we already knew.

Jackie, who'd sat down next to me on the sofa, leaned over and mumbled under her breath, "I feel like I should be taking notes for the exam."

Carolina went on for fifteen minutes, during which time Jackie and I amused ourselves by making rude comments and snoring noises.

"In short," Carolina summed up, "I think we can safely assume that Marion wrote something about what she found during her investigation in that March 20th journal entry."

"What about those missing February entries?" Susan asked. "And where the heck did Rex go?"

"Ay, there's the rub," Carolina intoned.

"Spare us the Shakespeare," Jackie responded.

"Okay, I've sat back and listened, and haven't added much myself," Susan said. "Even though we haven't been able to find out anything that amounts to anything, I feel certain that Jackie is right. Someone silenced Marion. Well, can't we just sort of write all these separate things on pieces of paper, put them on the coffee table, and see if any of them join up, or maybe just suggest something absolutely brilliant?"

While Jackie, Susan, and Carolina began writing everything we knew on slips of paper, I drew on all my memories of Marion: her kindness, her unwillingness to accept that people could be nasty to her on purpose, her tidiness . . . *Tidiness*. Something fell into place in my brain with a clunk that should have been audible.

If Marion had found something important, some kind of wrong-doing for example, what would she have done with the information? I should have seen it. I'd had the answer the previous evening at Marion's apartment and been too damn stupid to see it.

I broke the silence. "Guys . . ." I said, then stopped.

Carolina asked, "What, Kit?"

"Nothing. It's nothing."

I'd been about to tell them that I had an idea where else we could look for information that Marion might have collected, but decided to keep it to myself for the moment.

CHAPTER 16

—ııı—

M aybe it was childish not to tell the Babes what had occurred to me, but dammit all, I'd begun feeling like my old self again and that old self was a person who went her own way. So I decided that it would be a huge hoot just to dump the fabled journal entry right into their unsuspecting laps. Maybe I also wanted to find out first if my brainstorm was correct.

Meanwhile, they tried every which way to make things fit together and the best they could come up with was to see if there was anything to be discovered where Marion had worked. We had a good excuse to go up there, since the lab people had called Marion's mom, asking if someone wanted to pick up the stuff from her desk. Maybe there were clues in that.

"The police would have found anything if they looked through it," Carolina pointed out.

"Oh, please!" Jackie sounded disgusted. "They wouldn't know a clue if it bit them on the ass."

Since the meeting had ground to a halt anyway, and the next day started early for me, I hustled a thoroughly frustrated Jackie and Carolina out the door almost immediately, but Susan hung around longer, obviously avoiding going home.

"Paul said he'd wait up for me," she said apologetically after the small talk ran out. "I don't know what I'm going to say to him." She finally picked up her coat. "Our trip to City Hall was pretty much of a waste, too. I was really hoping you and I might come up with something significant."

Sue sounded so down, I relented and told her where I thought Marion's missing journal entries might be.

"Why didn't you say something to the others?" she asked.

"Because."

"That's the kind of reason my kids give me."

"So what?" I said. "I'll follow up my lead tomorrow, and if I come up with anything, I'll let you all know. Okay?"

"Couldn't it be dangerous?" Susan asked, sounding concerned. "You should take someone with you."

"Not on your life," I laughed. "After all, you're the one who told me I should forget that I'm blind."

My alarm screeched at me at 6 a.m. – about four hours too soon, judging by the way I felt. I climbed into the shower, turned it to cold, and jolted every semblance of stupor from my tired bod.

I combined Shadow's walk and breakfast in one trip by a visit to Novik's, which opens at 6:00. I often wonder whether the two of them have any life outside the bakery. To have fresh pastries ready that early must mean they get up around 4:00, and they usually don't leave until 7:00 in the evening. Tough life. After enjoying some coffee and a still-warm apricot Danish, Shadow and I headed back just in time for Steve, who pulled up as I was unlocking the street door.

On the ride out to the studio, he and I listened to the rough mix Nick had given me. Steve seemed genuinely enthusiastic, saying that it was good to play in a group where he felt like the weakest one rather than the other way around. "Do you have any plans to gig?"

Perfect opening. "As a matter of fact, I wrote a song for a cause a friend of mine is involved with, and they want me to perform it at a rally on Monday afternoon. You interested in playing? It doesn't pay, but we might make the evening news."

"Just tell me when and where."

I sat silently for the rest of the trip, going over that day's songs in my head, but also feeling rather smug.

The session turned out even better than the first one. I still can't believe what happened.

It didn't take us long to get set up since Nick had everything pretty well ready to go. The only fly in the ointment was Danny, who called to say he'd be late, something that gave me a bad feeling. While we waited, I showed Terry, Frank, and Steve "Not Just a House," Carolina's song. The ideas flew hot and heavy, and we were in the middle of playing over what we'd come up with when Danny noisily arrived – forty-five minutes late. Terry had suggested that we vamp out on the chorus *à la* "We Are the World," but add a guitar solo over the vocals as the song faded. When I heard the squeak of the wheels on Danny's amp, I cranked up the volume, tromped my overdrive box, and let him have it right in the face – musically speaking.

With no ending, the song eventually crashed and burned, and the four of us playing cracked up. Then everyone went strangely quiet as someone new entered through the control-room door.

Danny said, "Kit, here's someone who'd like to meet you."

I stuck out my hand. "Who?"

"Victoria Morgan."

"*The violinist?*"

"Hi, Kit. Nice to meet you," said the woman herself in a soft Midwestern U.S. twang.

Now I knew why the guys had frozen. Victoria Morgan was the *enfant terrible* of the classical music scene and had the world at her feet ever since this bizarre concert in London where some people got shot. It also hadn't hurt her career that she "looks like an angel and plays like the devil" – as a besotted reviewer had written in an article Gerald had read to me from the *Sunday Times* a few weeks earlier. Why did she want to meet *me*?

My hand was gripped securely by a smaller one with surprisingly long fingers. "I heard a tape of yours when I was in England –"

"I had a tape in England?" I interrupted.

"A friend . . . had it. His cousin in Toronto sent it to him." Her voice betrayed a momentary wisp of sadness. "Anyway, I was talking to some people last night after my concert. I mentioned your name and someone said they knew who you were."

"My big sister plays viola with the Toronto Symphony," Danny explained, "and I'd been telling her about our session the other day."

"Danny's sister got me in touch with him, and he suggested that I ride out this morning. I *love* the song you were just running through. Could I play on it? I've got a nifty little idea for a fiddle part."

I didn't know what to say. It was as if Beethoven had walked in and asked to play keyboards. "Um . . . yeah . . . sure," I stumbled. "You brought your violin?"

"Listen honey," she said, "when you have an instrument that's worth what this thing is, you take it to the bathroom with you." She laughed.

By the end of three hours, we not only had the instrumental tracks of Carolina's song completely recorded, but I'd also done an acceptable vocal track – amazing, considering how nervous I felt with Tory Morgan listening in. She was great, though, and didn't make us feel as if she was anything special. She has an absolutely bizarre sense of humour and swears like a sailor. After we finished "House," she overdubbed a background part for "Nothing without You." Most classical musicians can't begin to play this stuff worth a hoot, but Tory could switch gears – and styles – at the drop of a hat.

Arnie wanted to have his picture taken with her. Nick also insisted on getting a shot for the CD booklet of Tory and me listening to a playback. She slouched back in the producer's chair with her feet on the recording console. The woman knew how to make an impression.

Tory had to leave around noon. "I can't tell you how much I've enjoyed this," she said, as I accompanied her to the door to wait for the airport limo. Shadow, who'd spent the morning lying on a sunny spot in the lobby (and didn't have his harness on, so he was in "dog mode"), romped around the two of us like a fool. "Being on tour with only a publicist for company can be a real pain. By the way, are you thinking of recording 'Shot Full of Love'? That's my favourite song on your demo. It really struck a chord with me at the time. I think it would sound great with the musicians you have."

I shrugged. "That might not be a bad idea. I'll see what Nick thinks."

"I had no idea you were blind until Danny told me," Tory said in a more subdued voice.

"I wasn't when I recorded that demo you heard in England."

"Listen, you're going to be a star, and I'd like to give you some advice: stay in control of it all, otherwise the bastards will eat you alive. Remember that." She laughed ruefully. "You only get one kick at the can."

When her limo arrived, Tory put her arms around my waist, the top of her head barely coming up to my chin. "Thanks for letting me play. It was great. A real antidote to 'classical over-seriousness.' Send me a copy of the recording when it's done. I think it's going to turn out fabulously."

"You can play in my band any time," I responded, grinning.

Tory's laugh was unrestrained. "You never know, Kit. I just might ask."

I headed back into the control room thinking that, with heavy hitters like Tory behind my recording, it couldn't fail to garner attention.

After sending out for sandwiches, we added the background vocals to "Nothing without You" before knocking off for the day. Since it was still early, I decided there was no better time than the present to check out my theory as to the whereabouts of Marion's journal pages.

Here's what had occurred to me the previous evening. I'd remembered Jackie telling me about Marion being uneasy about what she'd discovered. Marion had always been organized, careful, *prepared*. Anybody who couldn't sleep if they didn't have at least four extra rolls of toilet paper in the house did not leave important things to chance. *Marion would have made a backup of the information she'd found, even if she wasn't aware that she was being watched.* I didn't think she would have been dumb enough to leave it in her apartment, either. So what would she have done with it?

I felt that Marion wouldn't have wanted to give it to us, because we would have asked what the whole thing was about. After Jackie made fun of her yet again, her nose must have been firmly out of joint. She wouldn't have come to any of the rest of us, either. We wouldn't have made fun of her, but she would have been hassled. No, I was willing to bet that she'd decided to work quietly, and then, when she had everything gathered, would have astounded everyone (especially Jackie) by single-handedly solving her mystery and having all the crooks thrown in jail. Nancy Drew wouldn't have been able to do it better.

She hadn't given it to us and she hadn't been ready to give it to the cops. Who then? Her parents? Too nosy, and they'd be worried when they found out what she was up to. It had to be someone Marion could be sure wouldn't ask any questions. With that thought, a name had floated into my mind.

I picked up the studio's phone and punched in Glynis's number. What I got was flowery flute and guitar music with birds tweeting in the background. "Hi! This is Glynis. Mr. Big-Bottom and I can't come to the phone right now . . ." Mr. Big-Bottom was her cat.

The moment I heard the beep, I said, "Glynis, if you're there, pick up the damn phone!"

The phone line clicked. "Kit? Is that you?"

"None other." I had to avoid idle chatter; Glynis would have had me on the line for hours. "Look, Glyn, I have a question about Marion –"

"Wasn't that just *awful*?" she interrupted. "Poor, poor Marion! I nearly died myself when I heard. I would have been at the funeral, of course, except that I met this wonderful man and he took me down to the Bahamas for a week, so naturally I didn't hear until I got back and by then it was too late. Still, I sent some flowers to her mom."

While she stopped to catch her breath, I shoved my question in. "Did you get anything from Marion, you know, about the time she died?"

Glynis's normal flow of bubbly inanities stopped like a cork being put back into a bottle of Baby Duck. "What do you mean?" she asked, sounding guilty – and to my mind, suspicious.

"I mean, did Marion send you anything? It might have come while you were out of town." Glynis remained mute. "Glyn, are you still there?"

"Y-yes."

"Is there a package from Marion?"

"Yes. A big envelope actually."

"Have you opened it?" I found myself speaking slower than usual, enunciating everything clearly, as if I were speaking to a child or a senile adult. In some ways I was.

Glynis began to speak faster, each sentence almost tripping over the last as the story rushed out. "Kit, you're going to think I'm so stupid and such a fraidy-cat, but I couldn't bring myself to open it. 'It's probably not anything important,' I told myself. Marion and I used to write constantly, you know. Isn't it nice to get letters from people? Even though she only lived a mile or two away, we'd write at least once a week. So when I got back, there was this letter from Marion, but I couldn't open it because by that time my neighbour downstairs had told me that Mar had been . . . murdered. I was so upset that it was three days before I could even look at the envelope again. At first I thought it might contain something about her death, but everyone said that horrible serial killer had done it. Now it's been so long. I don't know what to do!" she ended in a wail.

Lord give me strength! She probably would have dithered over the letter for another month. But to be fair, what'd happened to Marion probably scared Glynis silly. I was just glad she hadn't destroyed the envelope.

"Look, Glyn, are you going to be home for the next little while?"

"Oh, sure!" She sounded relieved. "I'm waiting for Matthew to come over. We're going to spend a quiet –"

"That's very nice, but I'm in a bit of a hurry. I should be able to get over to your place in about an hour and a half, and I'll come and take it off your hands. Okay?"

"Anything you say, Kit."

All the guys had split by the time I got off the phone, so I fastened on Shadow's harness, threw my guitar (fortunately in its gig bag) over my shoulder, and we headed off. Glynis's flat was over near St. Clair and Christie, quite a hike from the studio, and Shadow and I had to use just about every conveyance the Toronto Transit Commission possessed to get there: bus, LRT, subway, and streetcar.

Since I only knew where I was going and not what it looked like to get there, the trip was filled with me asking people questions at nearly every stop. How do I get down to the westbound subway platform? Is this the streetcar that goes to Christie? Stuff like that. It would have been better to take a cab, but I was short on cash, and besides, sometimes it's good to leap into the unknown.

Trouble is, when you're blind and people want to help, they grab you by the arm and literally propel you where you need to go. That's pretty disconcerting. Only once in the whole trip did someone take my hand, put it on his forearm, and let me hold onto that while he walked me to the LRT car.

"Thanks a lot," I said when we got there. "It's nice when someone knows not to yank me all over the place."

"I know," he said kind of sadly. "My dad tells me that all the time."

Every minute of the trip seemed like an hour. If Marion had come through like I hoped, I was about to get answers to an awful lot of our questions. When Shadow finally led me off the streetcar at Christie, my palms were sweating.

The majority of the houses in this part of Toronto had been built in the twenties. They're mostly square, rather ugly, and made out of brick. Many have been divided into duplexes over the years to provide extra income for their owners. Glynis's place was pretty typical in that respect.

I had some problems navigating the few blocks from the streetcar stop. I'd been to Glyn's only a few times to rehearse, and with my state of mind that afternoon, I guess I distracted Shadow. He's usually pretty good about remembering places we've been to – unlike his mistress. Finally, though, we walked up the steps to Glynis's porch and rang the second-floor bell. In typical Glynis form, she flew down the stairs to let us in.

As we walked back up, she prattled away. "Kit! I'm so happy to see you. Your hair looks really super! When did you get it done?" She sat me down on this fluffy sofa thing that reeked of lavender. "What do you think of my new futon? Matthew bought it last week. He doesn't care for my bed," she giggled mischievously.

"It's lovely, Glyn. Do you have that envelope?"

"Sure. Can I get you some tea?"

"I'd rather have the envelope," I said, trying to keep from screaming at her.

She tripped off to her bedroom to get it. Something hissed from the opposite side of the room. Mr. Big-Bottom, staking out his territory. My pooch couldn't have cared less, and, with a big yawn, curled up at my feet. With his harness on, not even a cat walking across his nose would move him. If I took the harness off, though . . . it was tempting.

Glynis came back, handing me a rather full business envelope. In typical Marion-fashion it had been sealed with tape to make sure it didn't open in transit. I slipped my left index finger under a corner of the flap, and with a silent benediction, tore it open. Inside I found another envelope which I handed to Glynis.

"Is there anything written on this?" I asked.

"It says 'Don't open this, Glynis. If something happens to me, get it to Kit or my friend, Carolina.' What does that mean?"

Bingo! I felt certain that, if the envelope didn't contain all the answers, it certainly was *something* important. I decided that now was not the time to open it.

"Don't worry about it, Glyn, and don't tell anybody about this!"

"Why?"

"Because we don't think Marion was murdered by the Back-Door Strangler, that's why. And if you say something to the wrong person, it could be very dangerous," I added. *There! That ought to keep her mouth firmly shut*, I thought, *for at least twenty-four hours.*

"Oh my God, Kit. You're joking!"

I shook my head.

"Kit, would you and Shadow stay with me until Matthew arrives?" She sounded as if she was going to start crying.

Feeling bad that I'd scared her, I told her more sympathetically that I'd stay – as long as Matthew didn't take all day getting there. Then I asked if I could use the phone to make a few calls and dialled Carolina first. Jackie answered. It sounded as if she was eating an apple.

"Kit! What's up?" she asked around a mouthful.

"Is Carolina there?"

"Nah. She has classes until 5:00."

"If you hear from her before then, tell her to get her butt home. I'm pretty sure I've got something interesting to show you guys."

"What?"

"You'll find out when I get there. I'll call Susan and tell her. See you around 5:30." I clicked off and dialled Susan. She picked up her phone after the first ring. "Sue, it's Kit. Can you be over at Carolina's by 5:30?"

"Sure. I left the kids with their grandparents for another day. Paul won't be home until 8:00."

"You sound pretty chipper. How are things with him?"

"*Much* better. I came home and sat Paul down like you suggested. We had the best talk we've had in months. I think I've finally made him understand how I feel. He's promised to turn over a new leaf, and we're going to discuss between us anything concerning our finances from now on. Afterwards, we made the most beautiful love." She sighed contentedly. "I feel great!"

"What are you going to do about the debt?"

"I agreed to ask my parents for the money, but only if it's in the form of an official mortgage, monthly payments, the whole nine yards. Thanks for helping, Kit. It means a lot to me. Now, what's this meeting about? Did you find Marion's journal pages?"

"I think so. Looking at it might upset the denizens, if you know what I mean, so I'm willing to take the scorn and ridicule if we open it at Carolina's and it isn't what I'm hoping it is."

"Oh, I get it. You can't talk. Okay. See you at 5:30. Do you want me to pick you up on my way in? It's quite a hike from Glynis's place to Carolina's, as I remember."

"And it's a lot easier for you to drive in on the Gardiner."

"It's no trouble, Kit."

"I promised Glynis that I'd stay until her boyfriend arrived. That's going to be a while, and you'll be battling rush hour. Get over to Carolina's while the getting's good. I'll see you there."

"Okay. Maybe I'll ask Paul to meet me downtown. We could grab a late supper. Stay at a hotel overnight, one with a big bed." Susan was giggling as she hung up the phone. I felt glad that things seemed finally to be on the right track for her.

I also took time to check my answering machine, mostly in the hope that Patrick had called. The only message was from Detective

Morris, and it wasn't good. "Hello, Kit. Ron Morris. Listen, I have some disquieting news. That guy from Housing your friend Jackie Goode was after has been reported missing. Do you know anything about it? Please call me if you do."

I replaced the handset on the phone with a sinking feeling, then brightened. It sounded as if Morris was finally getting off his butt and taking us seriously. Maybe now I had more potential ammunition in my shoulder bag, too.

While we waited for Glynis's guy to show, I got treated to three cups of peppermint tea, some shortbreads, and several of her new songs. As I sat listening to her pure soprano, singing of simple things, good things, I forgave Glyn a lot of her faults. The world's a better place with people like Glynis Johnson in it – even if she can be pretty trying at times.

Matthew *finally* arrived at 4:50 and barely had a chance to shake my hand before I was out the door. Damn! I hadn't wanted to be late for this meeting. He asked if I needed any help. "After all, it's getting dark outside."

"Don't worry," I answered as I headed down the stairs. "I'm not scared of the dark." Once on the sidewalk, Shadow and I turned left and double-timed it down the street towards Christie, where I'd catch a southbound bus to the subway.

Right near Christie, there's an old streetcar yard. We were clicking along smartly when I noticed hurrying steps behind me. I squeezed to the left against the wooden fence that surrounds the yard, figuring I'd let whoever it was get past me.

Next thing I knew, someone pushed me square in the back and I fell hard to the ground with the wind knocked out of me.

CHAPTER 17

I got all tangled up with Shadow and my guitar as I went down, and, unable to take a breath, I couldn't holler for help. The person who'd hit me started yanking at my shoulder bag, but the strap's pretty thick, so it didn't snap and I wasn't about to let go. I struggled to my knees, trying to keep from being pulled over backwards and all the time dreading another punch, probably to my head this time. Shadow let out one ferocious bark as he tried to lunge at my attacker. I must have been really out of it, because I was holding on tight to his harness and he couldn't get by me.

My bag was yanked again, and this time I felt the thief's hand slip inside it. That was when I finally let Shadow loose. He knocked me sideways as he leaped, and I heard an agonized scream as he reached his target. From somewhere to my right I heard a voice shouting, "Hey! What's going on over there?" Shadow let out a yelp and I heard pounding feet as the thief took off down the street.

I sat there on the sidewalk, feeling sick and dizzy. Hurrying footsteps came from all directions as people from the adjacent houses poured out to see what was going on.

"Hey lady, are you okay?" someone asked.

"My dog! Is my dog all right?"

"Sure, sure. He took off after that creep. I think the guy kicked him."

"Here he is, coming back again," a woman's voice said, "all safe and sound."

Voices chimed in all around us. "That dog's a real hero." "Did you see the way he took off after that lowlife?" Did you see the chomp he took out of the guy's arm? I bet that clown's feeling it now!"

Shadow bounded into my arms, and I almost sobbed with relief. When I'd heard him yelp, I was sure he had been stabbed or something. "I never would have forgiven myself if you'd been hurt," I told him.

Someone helped me to my feet, and I dusted off my knees. The left leg of my jeans was torn and I'd scraped up my knee pretty badly, too, but fortunately Shadow had broken the worst of my fall. Otherwise things might have been a lot worse. Unzipping the Telly from its bag, I checked for damage. There didn't appear to be any. Okay, so far so good. Then it hit me. I swung my shoulder bag around and felt wildly in it for Marion's envelope. Christ! *It wasn't there!* It hadn't just been some mugger out for easy pickings. What was I going to do now? So close. So close!

"Did anybody see the guy who did this?" I asked.

When I received a chorus of "noes," my heart sank. Then the soft voice of an older-sounding man came through. "I saw it all from my porch, young lady. That man should be strung up for what he did to you! Imagine! Mugging someone who can't see. What is this city coming to?"

"Can you describe him?"

"I don't see too good any more, but he was taller than you, around three or four inches maybe. He had on some kind of jacket with a hood."

"Was he white, black?"

"I'm pretty sure he was white, but, like I said, I can't see too good."

They all wanted to call the cops, or take me to the hospital to have my knee looked at, but I kept insisting I was okay and already late to an important meeting. I can't tell you how low my spirits were as I hoisted my guitar onto my shoulder and prepared to set out again. Just then someone came running up.

"Excuse me," a kid's voice asked. "Is your name Kit or Carolina?"

"Kit. How do you know my name?"

"The man who tried to rob you dropped this when your dog bit him." The kid handed me Marion's envelope. "It was on the sidewalk."

"Thank God you found it!" I said gratefully, stuffing the envelope down my shirt for safekeeping. They'd have to get my clothes off before they'd get the damn thing now.

"It's important, then, lady?"

"You don't know how important."

The people insisted on calling a cab for me, a good idea which I gratefully accepted, especially since I didn't know where my attacker had gotten to. No sense giving him a second chance. During the drive over to Carolina's, I got the shakes, a delayed reaction to what I'd gone through, I guess. My nerves were in better shape by the time I got to Carolina's door, but my knee had stiffened up to the point where I was having trouble walking, and I still felt pretty wobbly in general.

Jackie answered the bell. "Well, well, look what the cat dragged in. You look like death warmed over." Then she spotted my knee. "Oh Kit! What happened?"

"I had a bit of an altercation on the way here," I said, handing her my guitar followed by my jacket. I also asked if she'd take off Shadow's harness for me because, with my shaking hands, I didn't think I could do it.

Everybody was waiting in the living room and jumped up all full of concern as I hobbled in. I sat down heavily on an overstuffed chair and assured them I was all right, just a little stiff. It was almost comical how my friends fell all over themselves trying to get my wounded knee cleaned and bandaged. Only Edward did something really intelligent by offering me some of his best Scotch. I felt less likely to pitch forward in a dead faint after a few swallows.

They were all outraged when I told them between sips what had happened.

"You can't go anywhere in this city any more," Carolina said indignantly.

"It wasn't a random attack, C," I said. "The person who jumped me was after this." Reaching into my shirt, I pulled out the envelope.

Susan ruined my big surprise by blurting out, "Is that the letter from Marion?"

Pandemonium ensued anyway. It took at least twenty minutes to explain how I had come up with the idea about the existence of the letter and where I might find it. Edward proclaimed me "a bloody genius." I blushed and took all compliments with tremendous grace and dignity.

"Kit, that was quite bitchy of you not to tell us yesterday evening!" Carolina said good-naturedly.

"Leave it to Glynis to screw things up!" was Jackie's take on it. "We could have had this thing settled long ago if she weren't such a baby – *and* assuming it's not something dumb like Marion's Christmas list. I would've looked at it first."

Carolina also thought I'd behaved stupidly, especially when she found out that Susan had offered to go with me and I'd refused to let her. "And you're always going on about how Jackie takes chances! You were just lucky the thief didn't have a knife or a gun."

Since I'd found the letter, everyone asked who I thought should have the honour of reading it. Jackie tends to forget to read out loud when she gets to sections that catch her interest, which would have been intolerable on this occasion. Even though C stops to look at sentence structure and wording, Susan didn't think she could handle the job, so Carolina it was.

I felt surprisingly nervous as Carolina slit open the envelope. Jackie might well have been right about the possibility of the letter being useless.

It wasn't.

"One of the sheets looks like a photocopy of the page from Marion's journal all right. It was still attached to the journal when she made the copy. There are some other papers and a couple of computer disks, as well. Kit, this is absolutely amazing!" she added. Carolina began reading in a slow, steady voice, managing to keep her emotions under control.

"'I still don't believe that what I've discovered is true! People just *can't* be so wicked. And why did they all do it? For money! Everyone did this for money. Even Doc S! I still can't believe that he was involved in this. *That* makes me really sad.

"'I have a few more loose ends to tie up before I can lay out my evidence to the police, but with any luck that should only take a few days. I've wanted so much to talk to someone about this, but I can't. I almost told Kit the other night, but she seemed so weighed down by her own cares and Carolina's bothering her about some song she wants written.'"

Carolina paused when Jackie snorted derisively, then said (with a pointed glare in Jackie's direction if I knew Carolina), "There's more soul-searching stuff before Marion gets to the point. Do you want me to read it?"

"No," Jackie answered, unperturbed. "Cut to the chase."

When Jackie's comment went unchallenged, Carolina said, "Okay," and started to read again.

"'I've been wondering the past few days if my finding out about this was completely an accident. If *I* had done something like this, I would certainly have made darn sure that I got rid of all the evidence, but it's almost as if Doc Sloane *wanted* someone to find out. I'm hoping that he felt ashamed, guilty . . . something! Why else would he have left the original test results on his computer? Granted, I shouldn't have been poking in those files, but I was only cleaning up after him yet again, and he knew I did that. Those test files should have been archived long before. How was I to know that they were more than his usual sloppy record-keeping? Now he's dead and he took his guilt with him, unresolved. He never got the chance to do the right thing. That's the saddest part of all.

"'So for the past week two weeks I've been digging around, and I kind of wish that I hadn't. Now the burden is squarely on my shoulders, because if I keep quiet, then I'm as guilty as they are, but if I tell the authorities what I know, then all hell's going to break loose. Doc S's name will be mud, and a lot of people will go to jail. That's a large burden to bear.

"'The results of the environmental tests done on the soil at the Riverside Project were falsified. If the true results were known, the project would have been stopped cold or at least severely cut back. Advantage Developments, the people bankrolling everything, have sunk way too much money into it to be able to survive, financially speaking, if the project gets scuttled. So they got to Doc S, and they got to Reynolds, who knew about the original results of the tests, and they paid them off. Reynolds got cash and Doc S got the loan he needed to keep his business afloat.

" 'There's something terribly wrong with the land where the public housing will be located in the Riverside project. They don't care. They figure they've buried the real results of the soil tests. Now they can build the entire project and make their filthy money and everything else can be damned. It makes me so angry!

" 'I'm going to do something about it – as soon as I have conclusive evidence. I'm hoping that Judy will be able to give it to me. She *must* know something, since according to Doc S's notes, she did the first tests on those soil samples before he took it over. She can't have missed something *that* obvious. I'll make Judy tell me what she found, and then I'll get her to go with me to somebody in the government.' "

We sat silently as Carolina finished reading, then she added, "There's a note to us at the bottom of the sheet. It says, 'I'm a little nervous. I don't think anyone knows what I'm doing, but if they did, I could be in danger. I've decided to send this to Glynis since I know she won't get on my case. I suppose I'm being melodramatic, but who knows? Something could happen, and I just don't want these people to get away with what they're trying to do. By Friday, it won't be my problem any more. I'll have all the hard evidence I need, and I'll dump it in somebody else's lap. If you're reading this, guys, it means I underestimated the whole thing. I suppose what I'm doing is stupid. Jackie probably thinks it's *really* stupid. You all say I never cause any trouble, that I can't stand up to anyone, and yet here I am with this, and I'm going to end up causing more trouble than all of you combined *ever* have. Surprise!' "

As Carolina stopped reading, I don't think there was a dry eye in the house – except for me.

I guess I'd been stunned a lot more by the attack than I originally thought. It wasn't until I'd started to relax in the safety of Carolina's home that something that should have leapt out at me the moment I found out the attacker had been after Marion's envelope began gnawing at my consciousness. Only two people – three if you counted Matthew (which I didn't) – had known why I'd gone over to Glynis's that afternoon. Glynis I dismissed out of hand, but I felt faint and my hands had begun to shake as I thought about the other.

Sweet Sue leaned over and said into my ear, "Kit! Are you okay? You look as if you've seen a ghost."

I couldn't stay in Carolina's house a moment longer. An idea, so awful in its implication that I felt soiled even considering it, suddenly seemed to me to provide the only possible answer to several of the questions we had about Marion's death.

"I think Kit's sick," Susan said to the others.

I started to get up. "I'm all right. I just need some air."

Carolina grabbed my shoulders, forcing me back down. "Kit, you're shaking. This is probably a delayed reaction to what happened to you at Glynis's." She laughed, attempting to lighten the situation. "I don't want you to fall and bleed all over our rugs!" She handed me the tumbler of whisky. "Here, have another slug of this."

I took a sip, but it didn't make me feel any better. Nothing would at this point – except finding out that the idea eating a hole in my brain was totally and completely wrong.

"I guess I'm not in as good shape as I thought," I said. "Would somebody drive me home?"

"I think we should take you to the hospital," Carolina said.

"Carolina, I'm only a little wobbly, that's all. The guy didn't hurt me except for my knee. I just need to rest."

Susan got up. "I'll take her home. I'm supposed to meet Paul at 8:00 anyway."

All the way back to my place I sat squeezed in the corner of my seat, holding my dark thoughts to myself. Susan was still bubbling with happiness over her reconciliation with Paul. When we pulled up in front of the apartment, she wanted to help me up the stairs, but I convinced her that I could make it under my own steam.

I made a beeline for the bedroom, not even stopping to take my guitar off my shoulder. Rummaging around in my night table, I found the handy little gadget my dad had given me for my birthday two years earlier: a talking phone directory. About the size of an electronic organizer, it's one of those computerized wonders that's supposed to make living easier for us blind folk. *That's probably why I don't use it much*, I thought with a derisive snort. Tonight, though, it would be indispensable, since I couldn't ask my friends to look up the number I needed.

I typed "marion 2" on the tiny keyboard, and its tiny mechanical voice gave me a phone number. Quickly dialling it, I waited impatiently while the phone rang five times before someone answered.

"Hello?"

"Is this Tony?" I asked.

"Yeah. Who's this?"

"It's Kit Mason. We met at Marion's memorial service."

"Oh, Kit! Hi. What can I do for you?"

"I need you to answer some questions for me if you can."

"Okay. Shoot."

This had to be handled delicately, since I had no idea how close Tony and Marion had actually been. "Did Marion speak to you about any of her other . . . any other men she, ah, had been involved with?"

Tony sounded a bit wary. "Why do you want to know that?"

"I'm sorry, but I can't tell you right now. Did she say anything?"

"Well . . . yeah. But I don't think you want to go all the way back to the first time she did it with someone, do you?"

"I was thinking of something more recent."

"How recent?"

"Like the beginning of the year . . . say, January."

"Oh! You mean right before I met her." He sounded more friendly. "Sorry. Can't help you there. We didn't talk about stuff that close to home, if you catch my drift."

"Damn! Well, thanks anyway, Tony. Sorry to have –"

"Say, you just jarred something loose in my pea brain. Marion did say something that might mean something to you. It was one night shortly after we met. Marion made some comment about meeting guys at her health club."

"Can you remember exactly what she said?"

"Let's see . . . She said that she should have known better than to get involved with the wrong person – especially if she met them at her health club. I supposed at the time that she was just teasing me. Could it mean something else?"

My heart beat a little faster. "It might. *Could* Marion have been involved with someone else at the club?"

"I wouldn't know. I only started working there in late February. We met my first day on the job. After that, I'm sure it was just me."

"Did you tell the cops about this?"

"No. I just thought of it. Truth be told, they really pissed me off when they were questioning me. I didn't want to tell those jokers any more than they asked, which I guess is pretty stupid. Anyway, once they realized that I couldn't have done it, they completely lost interest, and I wasn't about to say anything to rekindle it."

"Is there anybody at the club who would know about Marion?"

"Sure. Little Joey. He checks people in and out of the place. Believe me, if there's anything you want to know about anybody at the North Toronto Health Club, ask Joey Romano. He's there by 6:00 every morning. Tell him I said you should talk to him."

"Thanks, Tony."

"No problem. Call me when you can let me know what this is all about. Okay?"

"Sure thing," I said.

I hung up and remained sitting on my bed as I thought about what Tony had said. Half an hour later I was still there when Shadow came in to ask if I would take off his harness. No matter which way I looked at it, the puzzle pieces only fit together one way. But that way meant a betrayal so deep, so awful, I couldn't imagine what blackness lay at the bottom of it. The course I had to follow was clear. If I just walked away, I knew I wouldn't be able to face myself. Marion's words came back to haunt me.

I took the guitar off my shoulder and leaned it against the dresser. Shadow's needs came next, after which I stripped off my own clothes and threw them in a heap on the floor. Who cared if I tripped over them? I went into the bathroom and turned the shower on full blast, letting the water stream over my head so it would wash away the tears.

I finally gave up trying to sleep around 5:00 a.m. The weather outside promised a reasonable day, so I rousted out Shadow, gave him a quick breakfast while I sucked back two cups of coffee, and we hit the road at 5:20. It's maybe five, six miles from my place up to Yonge and Eglinton, where the health club is located, and I'd decided to do it on foot. Perhaps I was only trying to postpone the hour of reckoning.

Joey Romano turned out to be what I expected, part father-confessor, part confidant, all gossip columnist. I figured I'd better be careful what I said to him, since I couldn't be sure whether he'd want to protect somebody if he got the wind up as to why I'd come – or whether he'd broadcast it all over town. Our conversation was punctuated by the arrival of several early-morning exercisers, almost all of whom had something to say to the talkative little desk clerk.

"Sure. I remember Marion. Nice girl. Always smiling. Too bad what happened to her. There are some real pigs in this world."

I leaned on the counter over which Joey presided. "We're trying to find all the people who knew her, so they can come to a little do we're planning, kind of like an Irish wake, you know?"

"Am I invited?"

"Of course," I said. "Tony said you knew everybody here and I thought you could fill in some blanks we have in our list of Marion's friends."

"Well, besides Tone and me, she didn't really talk much to anyone."

I decided to take a flyer. "Really? I remember Marion telling me about some blond guy she met here in January, before she got together with Tony, that is."

"Let's see . . . blond guy . . . blond guy. Any idea, ah, what he looked like? Besides blond, I mean."

"Yeah. Marion said he was tall, about six feet, good-looking, nice haircut."

"Hmmm . . . I think I remember someone like that. Marion seemed to know him already. Came as the guest of one of our members. Yeah, now I got it! I went into the weight room one evening, and there the two of them were, laughing and carrying on, like they knew each other *real* well. Our Marion was flirting something awful, and this guy was making all these comments, double whatchamacallits, you know? Lots of touching they didn't need to do. Didn't surprise me they left together that night. You see a lot of that around here. He came twice more, if I remember correctly."

"When was that?"

"First time was the middle of January, I think. Then he was in again about a week later."

"And the other time?"

"I didn't see him exactly, but Marion stopped by on her way out one evening and asked if her friend had been looking for her. I was about to say no, when she said never mind, she could see his car pulling up out front. She went out the door and that was that."

"The date, Joey. When did it happen?"

"Maybe a week before she was, you know . . ."

I held my breath. "Do you remember the guy's name?"

"Don't think I ever heard it," Joey said and my shoulders sagged. "But I might be able to get it for you," he added quickly. I had to wait while he spoke to a few members who had questions, but eventually he went to his desk and made a phone call. Coming back to the counter he told me, "Okay, Little Joey comes through again! I called the member who brought that guy in and got the name for you."

The name he gave me was almost an anti-climax when he said it.

I left quickly after thanking Joey and promising to get in touch about the wake. A short walk got me to the mall at the corner of Yonge and Eglinton. I found a pay phone and called Carolina's.

"Kit! You're up earlier than I expected. How are you feeling? I have to tell you, you didn't look in the best of shape last night."

"I'm worse this morning," I said and outlined what I'd discovered.

"Sweet Jesus," Carolina said in a shocked whisper. "What are we going to do?"

"No matter what we do, I dread the outcome."

"Look, Jackie and I will drive up and get you. We need to talk."

The whole time I waited for Jackie and Carolina to arrive, two words tripped round and round my brain like a demented carousel: Paul Quinn, Paul Quinn . . .

CHAPTER 18

—ᨳ—

Carolina, Jackie, and I spent our most joyless morning ever. Since it was nearby, we drove over to the ball diamond at Davisville and Mount Pleasant where the Ruthless Babes play most of our games, and held our council of war in one of the dugouts. Carolina said that the big old trees surrounding the park (something to watch out for when chasing errant fly balls) were just beginning to show some green. I remember eagerly looking forward to that at one time, knowing ball season was then only a couple of weeks away. It was an especially bitter memory that day.

"Look," Jackie said, "much as I'd like to find one, there's no way to tell Susan without hurting her real bad."

"You're *sure* about all this?" Carolina asked me for the third time.

"Yes," I told her wearily. "I spent the entire night going over it all, and the answers always came out the same. What I found out this morning merely confirmed it. How did the murderer know so much about Marion, what she was doing, the fact she kept journals, the route she ran every day? How did they find out about Jackie? Or that I had that page from Marion's journal? All that information could easily have come from Paul!"

"*If* Marion was involved with him," Carolina persisted.

"Oh, C, give it up!" Jackie sounded fed up with Carolina's fence-sitting. "Fact #1: the cops said Marion had been seen with a blond man. Paul's blond. Fact #2: the guy at the health club saw them leave together one night and, hard as it is to believe, they were acting real chummy. Fact #3: Marion told Tony that she'd been involved with someone she met at the health club. Who else had she met?"

"But I just can't believe Marion would do something like that to Susan!"

"Like it's any easier to believe that Marion was into bondage and discipline!"

"Maybe it wasn't Marion as much as Paul," I ventured.

"Yeah! I tried to tell Sue about the bastard when they were still engaged, but she wouldn't listen."

"Maybe it was your choice of words, Jackie," I commented dryly. "Nobody likes to hear their fiancé referred to as a 'peckerhead.' "

"What did you try to tell Susan?" Carolina asked.

"It's like this," Jackie said slowly. "Paul made a pass at me."

"He *what*?" I said, totally shocked. Jackie? Paul generally went out of his way to be obnoxious to her – and vice-versa. "What happened?"

"Remember the night Sue's folks had that barbecue and you pushed me into the pool? I went into the upstairs bathroom to get some dry clothes on, and the next thing I know, Paul walks through the door. I didn't have a stitch on. He gave me the slow once-over and said, 'Jackie, that's quite the little bod you've got there. Does it work as good as it looks?' I didn't know whether to laugh or deck him. I wound up booting his ass the hell out. And Susan always went on and on about what a gentleman he was! Look, couldn't Paul have come on to Marion? From the moment he showed up back in university, he pretty well ignored Mar, and I got the feeling she adored him from afar. Maybe back in January, by a quirk of fate, he saw her working out at the health club – she was lookin' pretty good, remember – and he just put the make on her, and for naive, romantic Marion it was too much to resist."

"After finding out how little we *really* knew about her, I guess I can see that happening," I said.

Carolina sounded glum. "Me too, unfortunately."

"Okay," Jackie said, getting to her feet and striding up and down the dugout. "How do we handle this? We can't just sit Sue down and say, 'By the way, Kit's found out your husband was banging your good friend and had something to do with her murder.'"

"Stop pacing, Jackie!" Carolina said. "It's distracting. You seem to have forgotten that we don't know positively whether Paul had anything to do with Marion's death, or, for that matter, whether Paul and Marion actually, um, had an affair. And we must be positive before we tell Susan. Think of the needless harm we would do otherwise."

"Only one way to find that out," I said. "Ask Susan how much she's told Paul, especially whether she told him about my reason for seeing Glynis. That would be the kicker. Only Susan knew what I was up to, and yesterday she said she was going to call Paul after she got off the phone with me. She either told him then . . . or *she's* involved in this whole mess."

Both my friends said at the same time, "That's ridiculous!"

"My sentiments exactly. If it looks like a duck and quacks like a duck . . ." I shrugged. "It's *got* to be Paul."

Jackie stopped in front of me. "Care to do the honours?"

I stood up slowly. "Might as well. After all, I'm the one who started this."

Shadow had gone out to sleep on the nice warm infield, so we collected him and went off to look for a phone booth. My heart was pounding as Susan's number rang four times. She wasn't home, so I left a simple message. "Sue, a few things have come up. Could you call me or Carolina as soon as you get this? It's now almost 10:30. Give us forty-five minutes to get back to my place, okay? It's important."

"Thanks for bringing me into this," Carolina said after I hung up. "I thought *you* were going to handle it."

"What if I'm out with Shadow? Oh shit!" I stopped halfway out of the phone booth. "I forgot Patrick's taking me to opening day."

"So?" Jackie said.

"I just told Susan to call me. I can't go to the ball game now!"

"Opening day? Luxury seats? And you don't want to go?"

"Jackie's right," Carolina said. "Why shouldn't you go to the game? It might do you some good, too. You know if you sit at home, you'll just stew about this all day."

"Yeah," Jackie chimed in. "Didn't Susan say she and Paul were going to stay at a hotel last night? Who knows when she'll get your message? Go to the damn game. If she calls while you're out, we'll stall her. C'mon, stuff that fleabag of yours into the car and we'll drive you home."

We had only gone about a dozen steps when Jackie stopped dead right in front of me. Shadow had to really lean on the brakes. "Holy shit!" she said. "Look at this!"

Carolina pushed by me. "Now what?"

I grabbed Jackie's shoulder roughly. "Would you mind telling me what's going on?"

"They've got the Back-Door Strangler," she said. "He was in a shootout last night in Montreal. It's all right here in today's *Sun*." I heard the sound of someone dropping coins into the dispenser of the newspaper box. "I don't believe it!"

"Now what?"

"Carolina Graf just bought a copy of the *Toronto Sun!*"

"The *Globe* box is empty," Carolina pointed out dryly.

I was sitting on the front step of my building, head in my hands and feeling very sorry for myself, when Patrick walked up. Even though my discovery had brought us a giant step closer to understanding what was going on, it could bring me no joy. I'd rather we'd found out that we had been totally wrong in our surmises about Marion's death.

Susan would survive this. We all knew that. Beneath her suburban exterior beat the heart of someone with a lot of strength. Yeah, she would survive it – but it would take her a long, long time to recover. I supposed I should have felt lucky they don't shoot the messenger any more.

"Why the glum look, Kit?" Patrick asked, sitting down next to me after giving me a kiss on the forehead. "It's a beautiful day, we have great seats for opening day, and the evening is wide open. What more could you want?"

I blew out a long breath. "The shit hit the proverbial fan this morning. We just found out the husband of one of my friends was probably having an affair with one of my other friends, and . . . Oh hell! You don't need to hear about all this."

"Wow! No wonder the hangdog expression."

"It's been a bad morning," I answered sourly, shaking my head. "I feel pretty damn guilty, because it was me who found out about it."

Patrick helped me to my feet. "Well, I, at least, want to see the game. C'mon, Kit, it won't do you any good mooning around on the front steps. You can tell me all about it on the walk over to the ballpark. It'll help if you just get it all out. Then watch, a few homers and you'll forget about it. You'll see."

He was right, I did feel a lot better by the time we got to Front Street and bought a bag of peanuts on the way into the SkyDome.

But I didn't feel any less guilty.

Patrick and I were pretty disappointed that they didn't open the roof of the SkyDome. The day had turned positively balmy and certainly warranted it, but the Toronto fans have become real wusses since they got their mega-million-dollar playground. The real fans used to look forward to going down to Exhibition Stadium and freezing their butts off on opening day. They even had snow at the first one. Now you sit indoors and can suck on a Perrier and eat sushi while watching the game on the field. Or you can get a room in the hotel overlooking the field and play your own games. One time a couple put on a better show in their room than the one going on at field level, but the killjoy hotel management put a stop to that. Now you have to sign a special waiver saying you won't do anything naughty with the curtains open during a game. What is baseball coming to?

I'd never sat in the club seats, the fancy ones just above field level where you get extra-wide chairs for extra-wide bottoms. Patrick's seats were in the first row, dead behind the plate and close enough to hear the chatter on the field.

As usual, I'd brought my trusty radio and sat with the headphones hooked over my left ear so the Jays' broadcasters, Tom and Jerry, could whisper sweet statistics to me. These guys are real pros and a pleasure to listen to. With them, you don't need eyes to be able to see the game. With my other ear, I could listen to Patrick and hear the crack of the bat and the thud of the leather for real. In a way it's a waste of money for me to go to a game, but I like to be there, feel the excitement, the buzz of the crowd when something special happens.

"Enjoying yourself?" Patrick asked between the first and second innings.

I had decided to try my best to enjoy the day. Besides, it wasn't fair to bring Patrick down because of my problems. "Sure am. These seats are great! You can hear everything on the field. Do you notice the way the pitcher's popping the leather? He's got great stuff today."

Patrick didn't answer immediately. "You don't miss a lot, do you?"

Susan's face popped into my mind, but I forced it back into the darkness. "Why should I?"

Surprisingly, I eventually found myself honestly able to enjoy the game – with one exception: the guys behind us. You occasionally meet some real ignoramuses at ball games, but these yahoos stretched the definition. First of all, they fancied themselves Baseball Experts. You know the kind: no matter what anyone does, it's wrong. The manager can't manage, the players can't play, the groundskeepers can't groundskeep. When one of the Jays' big sluggers hit the season's first homer, I jumped to my feet and danced around. One of the bozos behind me snarled that I was blocking his view. A few bad innings later, the Jays scored the go-ahead run and again I jumped up.

"Sit down! We can't see," Bozo 1 snapped.

"Yeah," Bozo 2 chimed in. "You want to do that, go to the fifth deck. We paid a lot of bucks for these seats."

I turned and said, "C'mon you guys. Lighten up! Get into the game. Haven't you ever heard of rooting for your team?"

I distinctly heard "piss off, bitch," and the next thing I knew Patrick was in their faces.

"You got a problem with something the lady said?" he asked loudly.

Not wanting this to escalate further, I hurriedly got my butt back in my seat. Patrick remained standing, glaring I supposed at the clowns behind us. He eventually sat when they didn't respond.

Leaning over, he said in a low voice, "If one of those idiots opens his mouth again, I'm going to chuck him over the railing."

"It's not important. I've had plenty worse things said to me before. I can take it; I'm a big girl."

"I don't like hearing anyone talk to you like that. But if you want me to let it drop, I will."

I think the two guys came to the SkyDome to drink beer, pee, scratch themselves, and talk business, and while they were doing that someone entertained them with a ball game. They were off for one of their numerous washroom breaks, when Patrick helped me up to do the same, getting me as far as the doorway to the ladies', where I had to take over with my accursed collapsible cane. After that I stayed firmly planted in my seat no matter how much I wanted to get up and cheer. I didn't want any more hassles.

The game ended victoriously for the good guys, and Patrick and I waited until the worst of the crush had fled the premises before making our exit.

"What time is it?" I asked when we'd reached Front Street.

"A little past 4:30. Want to stop some place for a drink?"

My guilty conscience had been pricking at me on and off during the game, but I figured that, if Susan didn't get an answer at my place, she'd phone Carolina's. In any event, despite my words that morning, I would have been glad to have the others handle this mess. I squeezed Patrick's hand and answered, "Sure," to his invitation. "But we have to make it quick. I'm expecting a call."

We stopped at a place up the street from the SkyDome and had a couple of beers and shared a plate of nachos. After chatting about the game, I told Patrick about my surprise guest at the session the day before. He only vaguely knew who Tory was. "I'll play the rough mix of the song for you when we get back to my place."

"Yeah, ah, sure. I'd like to hear it."

"You're a million miles away. What's bugging you?"

He sighed. "Nothing. Work. A bunch of little things. Sorry. I shouldn't be sitting here stewing, not with a beautiful lady to distract me." He leaned over and kissed my neck. Tingles skittered up and down my spine, making me forget about obligations and begin calculating the distance to my apartment.

We left the bar about 5:30 for the walk back to my place. As we went through the doorway, somebody bumped me hard as they tried to force their way around us. I got slammed into the railing and almost got pitched over.

"Why don't you watch where you're going!" I snarled as I straightened up.

A blast of beery breath assaulted me. "Well look who it is . . ." The familiar voice died suddenly. "You're blind!"

"Yeah, so what?" I wasn't in the mood for an embarrassed apology from one of the bozos who'd tried so hard to wreck the ball game for me.

I didn't get one.

Old Beer-Breath turned to his buddy. "Can you beat that, Chuck? The bimbo's standing in front of us for most of the game, then gives us lip when we ask her to sit down. And she can't even fucking see!"

While the guy spoke, I could feel Patrick next to me, his muscles tensing. "Are you going to apologize to the lady?" It came out very softly, almost gentle, but the intensity behind those words sent a shiver of a different kind down my back.

Chuck egged on his drunken friend. "Hey, Vinnie, let's show this guy how you like to apologize."

Oh Christ! This is not what I needed. From the way Chuck spoke, his bud must be a behemoth. Patrick wasn't small, but how well could he handle two guys? Inside the bar, music thundered out of the sound system as the post-game revelry continued. Where were the bouncers when you needed them?"

I took Patrick's arm. "Patrick, ignore them. I have to get home."

"Yeah, Patrick," Vinnie jeered, "take the blind bitch home. You're lucky she can't see how ugly you're gonna be if you don't."

Now I was mad. "I don't have to be able to see to know what a moron you are! Why don't you just piss off before I call the Humane Society and have you put out of your misery?"

"*Eat shit, bitch*!" Vinnie said and pushed me.

That did it. With a swift movement, Patrick stepped between us and I heard two or three muffled thuds, followed by a whoof of air and the *sproing* of something big bouncing off a street sign.

I reached out for Patrick, who, surprisingly, still stood in front of me. "Are you okay?"

From the sidewalk came the sounds of Chuck presumably helping up his friend. "You sonofabitch!" Chuck screamed. "Look what you done to his nose! You're gonna pay! Get him, Vinnie!"

The two rushed forward, and I got pushed back hard against the corner of the door, banging my head. More sounds of struggling in front of me. This time I definitely heard fists meeting flesh. Someone bounced off the sign again.

"*Somebody help us*!" I screamed, beside myself with fear. I saw a bar fight once where someone almost got killed, and I couldn't do anything to help Patrick except yell.

The fight ended before I could fill up my lungs again, the air suddenly still, except for a soft moan from somewhere out by the street.

Patrick said, "C'mon, tough guy. Get up!" I heard the sound of someone being kicked. "I said get up!" Another kick, followed by a moan.

I stumbled down the steps. "Patrick?"

He was quivering with tension, rage, I don't know what. As I reached out, though, he seemed to deflate as if my touch drained all the anger away.

I asked, "Are you all right?" as several people noisily piled out of the bar.

He didn't answer as he turned and pulled me tightly against him.

Somebody came up to us. "What happened?"

Another voice from the growing crowd. "That guy over there pushed the lady. Her boyfriend just stepped in to protect her."

"What kind of condition are those two in?" the first voice asked.

"They'll live," someone else said and several people laughed.

"Do you want to press charges?" the man asked me.

"No. Why bother?"

"Look, I'm the manager. We don't like fights around here. Here, take my card. Next time you're in the area, drop by and have dinner on us."

"Thanks," I said, holding out my hand for the card.

"Are you blind?" the manager asked in a shocked voice.

"Everybody seems to be asking me that lately."

His voice sounded rough as he turned and said, "Get those idiots on their feet and out of here!" He turned back to me. "I can't believe somebody could be so low! I'm real sorry about this."

"It's not your fault."

I took Patrick's hand and had to start leading him away. He moved like a zombie. We walked up to Queen Street and turned left. Patrick hadn't said a word.

"Is everything okay?" I asked in concern.

We walked several more steps before he answered. "I could have killed those two guys."

"Yeah, I know what you mean! I was really mad, too."

"You don't understand. I could easily have killed them. That would have ruined everything."

"It sure would have put a crimp in their evening, I can tell you!" I said, laughing.

"I can't afford to lose it like that. I lost all control back there. I could have killed them . . ." Several more steps. "Thanks for handling things. I didn't want to say anything."

"Why not? You had every right to be spitting mad."

He sighed. "I should know better than to get into brawls outside bars. I don't like losing control like that."

"It's over now," I told him. "Why don't you just forget it?"

I pulled Patrick against me and, as we continued down the street, I tried lightening up his mood by bouncing my hip off his in time with our steps.

Shadow was overjoyed to see me, and I felt the same. I'm not comfortable going anywhere without him, and I'd been forced to do that a lot lately, but ball games aren't the place for bear-sized dogs. I crouched down in front of him, and he slobbered a welcome-home all over my face.

"Did you miss me, old boy? Sure you did. Would you like some walkies before dinner?"

The only phone message was a click. If it had been Susan, then she would have called Carolina after missing me. There would have been a return message if they needed me, so I figured it was safe to go out. We only used a leash on Shadow. That way he could move around more freely and just be a dog. Patrick's mood improved gradually as we walked, and by the time we got back to my building, he seemed to be feeling a lot better. All during the walk, I was very aware of his physical presence. Something like an electric current buzzed between us as we held hands.

When we got upstairs, Patrick asked if he could use the phone to check in with his office. He then had a few calls to return, so I took the opportunity to feed Shadow. Hearing the sound of Patrick's voice in the background, and knowing we were alone, the electric current built to a dangerous level. After slipping the security chain on the door, I moved up behind him and put my arms around his waist. He absentmindedly patted my hands with one of his and kept on talking. When my hands slid lower, he stumbled over a few words.

"Just a minute," Patrick said into the phone, then turned around. "Please, Kit, this is an important call."

I pulled his shirt out of his pants.

"Not when I'm on the phone! Besides, I didn't think we had enough time for this."

"What I want isn't going to take much time."

"Kit, why don't you go into the bedroom? I'll join you as soon as I'm off the phone. Okay?"

Feeling miffed that Patrick hadn't immediately hung up, I headed for the bedroom, leaving a trail of clothes to mark the way. When I got to the bed, I rummaged around in the drawer of my bedside table for a condom. My search also turned up one of those tiny perfume sample bottles. The contents had a nice musky smell, so I put a bit on my neck and other appropriate places, then lay back on the bed to wait. I was ready.

Patrick wasn't, though. His call sounded as if it had taken a turn for the worse. "We need to get something straight here, buddy. We had a deal. You can't start changing the rules in the middle of the game! I've stuck to my end of the bargain and I expect you to do the same." I couldn't believe the amount of anger in his voice. "Look, you knew what was involved before we got started! I'm a dangerous man to cross! Keep pushing and you're a fucking dead man! *You hear me?*"

He slammed my phone down so hard I thought it might be broken.

"Patrick?" I called. "What's wrong?"

He stomped to the doorway of the bedroom. "I'm sorry you had to hear that, Kit. In my business, you often have to deal with idiots, and sometimes I just don't have the patience for it." He came over and sat on the bed. "What happened to your knee? I noticed you were limping a bit."

"I fell down yesterday," I answered distractedly. All kinds of bad thoughts were crawling around inside my head. That didn't sound like any business conversation *I've* ever heard. "What kind of business are you in?"

"I told you: investment counselling." Patrick kissed my stomach, then my breasts, and finally my lips. "Now, what was it you wanted to do with me?" he breathed. When I didn't answer, he pulled away. "Did I say something wrong? You've gone cold on me."

The passion had all seeped away. Things had happened in the past hour which left me terribly confused: the vicious fight outside the bar, and the fact that Patrick had totally withdrawn afterwards. But then he'd seemed all right while we were out walking Shadow, as if something awful hadn't just happened. Two minutes after one of the most violent phone calls I'd ever heard, he was back to being his usual tender self again. I was suddenly aware of how little I knew about this man.

And a sentence echoed in my head: *I could easily have killed them.*

"Patrick, I'm scared."

He didn't ask why.

CHAPTER 19

P atrick's voice was cold. "So what do you want to do now?"
The ringing of the phone spared me from answering. Reaching over to the bedside table, I sat up and put the receiver to my ear. "Yes?"

It was Carolina. "We tried to hold off calling as long as we could, but the shit's really hit the fan. I've just sent Jackie over in the car to get you. Can you be waiting downstairs in fifteen minutes?"

"Yeah, uh, sure. What's happened?"

"I'll let Jackie explain on the way over. I have to run, Kit. See you soon."

As I hung up, Patrick asked, "What's the matter?"

"Problems with my friends. Look, Patrick, I have to go out."

"That works out okay, because I have to go straighten out something at work."

He still sounded distant, and I could tell I'd really pissed him off. Well tough. He'd scared the crap out of me with his schizoid behaviour.

"Should I give you a call later?" he asked.

"I may be out pretty late if this is as bad as it sounds."

"I'll be up late, too, by the looks of it." He put his hand on my right shoulder. "Look, I'm sorry our afternoon had to end like this."

Patrick's hand started to drift purposefully down towards my breast. I stopped its progress somewhere south of my collarbone. "Try me at midnight. I think we need to talk."

"All right." He got up, but stopped when he got to the doorway. "I'll call later." I heard him cross the living room and the apartment door open and shut. The sound made me feel pretty desolate.

In a very unsettled state of mind, I got dressed and went downstairs with Shadow to wait for Jackie.

During the crosstown ride to Carolina's, Jackie filled me in on what had been happening.

"Sue called Carolina about an hour after you would have left for the game. She was in a terrible state. Apparently Paul never met her at the hotel last night. As a matter of fact, she hasn't heard from him since that phone call she made yesterday."

"Really?"

"About midnight, Susan started phoning up all their friends, hospitals, the works. This morning she called his office, but they didn't know anything. The guy's completely vanished."

I slumped back into the seat. "Oh boy."

"You can imagine what Sue's going through. She's pretty near hysterical."

"Has she called the cops?"

We drove for almost a minute before Jackie answered. "No. We talked her out of it." The next part came out rather sheepishly. "Carolina told her that you knew something about it. She thinks that's the reason I'm coming to get you."

"Just great! That's a bit of a cop-out, isn't it?"

"Well it *is* true – in a way. What do you think is going on?"

"Maybe Paul was the person who attacked me yesterday evening and can't let Susan see him because of the chomp Shadow took out of him. That would be a dead giveaway. Or –"

"Don't even say it," Jackie said quickly.

Susan sprang at me the moment I walked into Carolina's living room and hung on my neck sobbing miserably. I patted her head and mouthed the words *What have you told her?* for the others to see.

"Susan only got here an hour ago, but I asked The Question," Carolina answered, paused, then said the words I'd been dreading all day. "She did tell Paul about you going to see Glynis – and why."

"Kit," Susan said, "what in God's name is going on? Where is Paul?"

"Sue," I answered gently, "why don't we sit on the sofa? This is going to take some time."

Jackie came in from the kitchen at that point with a tray of tea, and we eventually got our friend to stop crying and put a cup of the soothing liquid into her hands. I took a deep breath and began talking, trying to phrase the harsh truth as gently as I could. When I finished, poor Susan sat squeezed into the corner of the sofa, legs drawn up, in a state somewhere beyond tears, beyond shock.

Carolina came over and knelt in front of her. "Susan, dear, we know you're really hurting right now. What can we do to help?"

At first she was silent, but then changed her mind and said in a tired voice, "I want to be alone for a while."

"Why don't you come with me to the spare bedroom?"

When they left, Jackie said, "Well that was as bad as we expected."

"Her whole world has just collapsed. In many ways, Sue's even more naive than Marion was. Her marriage and her family mean everything to her. She's going to need a lot of help."

"So will Paul if I ever get my hands on him," Jackie growled.

About ten minutes later, Carolina came back in. "The worst is over, I think. Susan's having a good cry right now. She asked me to tell you that she'll be out in a bit. Kit, you handled that very well. Now, Jackie, what have you told Kit?"

"About what?" I asked, puzzled.

"Jackie and I decided to go over and see Glynis today."

"That's why Sue only arrived an hour ago," Jackie added.

"Glynis? What more could she know?" I asked.

"A lot more than we bargained for."

Carolina started talking. "Jackie and I naturally started discussing Marion when we got back here this morning. Glynis told you that Marion wrote to her all the time, and we also know the two of them could talk on the phone for hours. We thought it was very possible that Marion told Glynis about her indiscretion with Paul."

"Why didn't she tell me yesterday, then?"

"Because you didn't ask her," Jackie said, almost laughing. "We got her to give us another of Marion's letters she had. Want me to read it to you?"

"No," I said, feeling pretty stupid that I hadn't figured this out myself, "just summarize."

"As you suspected, it was Paul who started flirting with Marion at the health club. Mar kind of reciprocated, but didn't take it at all seriously. She wrote that, after all these years, she couldn't believe Paul was actually noticing her. He came back a few nights later and that's when things got out of hand. They went out for a few drinks after leaving the club. She told him about her collection of toys, you know, to sort of shock him. Next thing she knew, they'd gone back to her apartment and spent the rest of the evening, ah, using them."

Carolina jumped in. "Marion says over and over in the letter what a wicked, horrible person she was to have done this to one of her best friends."

"That's kind of like closing the barn door after the horse has escaped," I pointed out.

"Not to make excuses for her, but Marion suffered over this, Kit. She beat herself up pretty badly."

"Paul seems to have had some trouble accepting her decision, though," Jackie said harshly. "He showed up at her door a few days before she was killed. Was he looking to pump her for information, or just to pump her?"

"This is nothing to joke about!" Carolina snapped.

It was at that point that Susan came back into the room. Her footsteps sounded like someone sleepwalking. The room went deadly silent.

When she spoke, her voice seemed as if it had been strained through a dozen layers of gauze. "Regardless of what's happened, I still want to help." She sat down next to me again and patted my hand. "Kit, I know how hard this must have been on you. Thanks for being so gentle."

I still felt like a heel.

Jackie asked, "Did you hear what we were talking about just now?"

"Yes, a bit of it. I've been doing some thinking. A number of things Paul has said and done recently have fallen into place. First, he lets me trot off to be with you guys whenever I want – with nary a complaint. *Of course* I told him everything that was going on. He didn't even have to ask most of the time! Paul knew that Jackie was asking questions about Marion's death. He knew Kit was going to look for Marion's journal pages yesterday. He would have known all about Marion's routines and journals and everything because of getting . . . mixed up with her and things we've all said about her habits over the years." She hesitated, then said with a spark of anger in her voice, "I told him everything he needed to know!"

"Don't you dare feel guilty about anything, girl! That bastard played you for all you were worth."

"But I keep coming back to it: Paul with *Marion*? How could something like that have happened? And how could he have gotten involved in her *murder*? The whole world's going crazy!"

"Let the cops worry about it now," I said, getting back to the main agenda. "We should call them. Or have you already done that?"

"No." Jackie said.

"Don't you think it's about time we let Morris know what's going on?"

Silence, deafening silence.

"Jesus Christ! You can't possibly be contemplating what I think you are!"

More silence.

"Look at it from another angle, okay Kit?" Carolina said. "These people aren't going anywhere. They can't – unless they want to hide out in South America. They have a huge investment in this property, and we have no idea what other cards they may hold. But I think it's safe to say that we have them by the, ah, balls." She sounded pretty smug.

"And who knows what government people they may have in their pockets besides Rex at City Hall?" Jackie added.

Carolina continued, "It's my feeling that we should find out as much as we can before we go to the police. The more we have on these people, the less chance they have of wriggling out of this. So far we have only Marion's notes saying that the people connected with the project suppressed the tests. *Nobody* has any *proof* they killed

Marion. Look, Kit, none of us wants to risk the chance that they might get away with it. Without concrete evidence, and with the best lawyers money can buy, they just might. Tomorrow, we have to see if there's any chance of getting hold of the documents that Marion talked about. *That's* the kind of hard evidence we still need."

Susan spoke up. "I doubt if those documents exist any more. They would have gone through that lab with a fine-tooth comb after they silenced poor Marion. Maybe she told Paul what she had seen." She stopped, then spoke again, obviously near tears. "How could Paul have gotten mixed up with such *terrible* people?"

"That's a question only he can answer," I said.

"And I can't wait to hear the answer," Jackie growled.

"We have our rally on Monday and the support of a number of community groups, a few council members, et cetera," Carolina said distantly, sounding as if she was thinking out loud. "The media will be out in force. If we can supply those people with hard data and proof of what Marion says about the testing, we will have won. It's the perfect forum."

"I don't like it," I said stubbornly, feeling like the voice of reason trying to be heard over the roar of a hurricane. "We're up against dangerous people, and you make it sound like a game of one-upmanship! We're just a bunch of bumbling amateurs."

Jackie snorted. "Yeah, but the bumbling amateurs have done pretty well in the last twenty-four hours – led by K. Mason, I might add."

"I say we hand over all this information to the pros and let them get the evidence they need to get these guys."

"I want to see them stopped," Susan said. "Otherwise all this heartache has been for nothing. But I don't know if we –"

"And I say," Jackie interrupted, her voice suddenly deadly serious, "I want nothing to do with them, do you understand? Nothing! If you go to the cops, you do it without me!"

All three of them started talking at once, and I had the feeling they'd completely ignored everything I'd said.

"Have you all lost your minds?" I cried, waving my arms around. My teacup went crashing to the floor and everyone stopped talking. "That's it! I'm through. Somebody call me a cab."

Carolina said, "Kit, won't you stay and talk this out?"

"Talk about what? You all have your minds made up. I'm going home."

"Then I'll drive you," Susan said. "I want to stay with my parents tonight. The kids are there anyway."

"C'mon, Shadow. Let's go!" I didn't even bother to put on his harness. Sue offered her elbow for me to hold, but I refused and walked right out the front door on my own. Shadow trotted next to me, totally perplexed.

When we got to the porch, Susan stopped. "Just a sec. I left something inside."

Oh, my transparent friends! I knew what was being said while I waited. "Sue, get Kit calmed down and see if you can get her to agree to keep her mouth shut. She's just a little hot right now." Well, to hell with them!

I was letting Shadow take a huge dump in the middle of Carolina and Edward's postage-stamp front lawn when Susan returned. "Let me get you home," she said quietly.

On the way, even though Susan tried her best to get me to talk, I refused. When she pulled up in front of my place, I immediately started to get out, but she grabbed my arm.

"Wait, Kit. I know you're angry with us, but can't we discuss this?"

I slouched back into the car seat. "Okay, discuss."

"You think we're doing the wrong –"

"Damn straight I do!"

"I'm worried about Jackie," she said.

That stopped me. With everything that had happened to her that day, the last thing Sue should have been doing was worrying about someone else. She had enough problems.

"Why Jackie?"

"You should have heard the way she was going on earlier, before she went to fetch you. She honestly thinks she's going to catch all these people herself. It's scary."

I relented a little then. Shadow was bouncing around in the back seat, confused by why we weren't getting out. I turned around and snapped, "Lie down!" before turning back to Susan. "I admit I was a little surprised by her outburst just before we left Carolina's, but you don't know the whole story."

It didn't take long to tell Susan what Jackie had told Carolina and me about why she left home.

"Poor Jackie!" she said when I'd finished. "Carolina mentioned that Jackie had told you two something, but she never got around to telling me what it was. A lot of things about Jackie make sense now. To think that she's carried that around inside her all these years. My God!"

"Is it any surprise she has such an allergic reaction to the cops?"

"Regardless, Kit, my gut reaction is that, if we go to the police, Jackie's going to walk. And if she walks, my bet is she'll do something stupid. We already know how dangerous these people are."

"My sentiments exactly." I shook my head and smiled tightly. "I'll admit that I was going to call Morris the minute I got upstairs, but I'll hold off for now."

"I think that might be for the best, at least until tomorrow. Marion mentioned that lab assistant, Judy. We can try talking to her, and then maybe we'll be able to get Jackie to see reason. Maybe it will be enough."

I reached out for Sue's arm. "Are *you* all right?" I asked. "I can't even imagine what a shock all this has been."

She laughed ruefully. "An understatement! I've known for a long time that something's been very wrong, but I tried to ignore it. I did think at one point that maybe it was something like an affair. I've kidded myself for ages about Paul, I guess. In some perverted way everything you've told me seems to make sense, but no matter how angry I am with him right now, I just can't help wondering where he is."

This wasn't the time to be *completely* candid. "You know Shadow bit whoever attacked me. It could have been Paul. Maybe that's why he's disappeared. He knows the jig would be up if he came home with a dog bite."

Susan's second laugh was ripe with bitterness. "The jig's up anyway. You know, if it had only been a matter of Paul sleeping with Marion, I think I could have taken that. Now it's going to be arrest, trial, and a prison term, humiliation. And a possible role in Marion's death! I can never, *ever* forgive him for what's happened. It's over between us, Kit. I have to face that fact and move on. Even so, I keep thinking that Paul's out there somewhere alone and afraid and with no one to help him." Susan turned in her seat. "Poor Shadow's down for the count. You'd better get the sleepyhead inside."

"Just remember," I said, "we're here if you need us."

"I know."

I didn't even bother to put Shadow's leash on, but simply crossed the sidewalk to my door, holding onto the scruff of his neck. It confused the hell out of him, poor baby.

My watch said 10:38 when I got up to the apartment. Even though I felt exhausted and should have gone straight to bed, I poured a glass of orange juice, sat down on the sofa, and flipped on the radio to pass some time until Patrick called – and to catch the latest on Toronto's all-news station.

Right after the sports and a few commercials, the announcer came on with "an update on the police shooting of Canada's most wanted fugitive." I was instantly all ears. "We go now to a live report from Montreal with our reporter, Lorne DeLong. Lorne?"

"The Montreal police have just concluded a news conference at which they announced that earlier this evening convicted serial killer Keith Harvey, the infamous Back-Door Strangler – also wanted for the recent murder of a jogger in Toronto – succumbed to wounds received in a shoot-out with police yesterday. I've managed to buttonhole Toronto Police Detective Ronald Morris who travelled to Montreal in the hopes of questioning the Strangler. Detective Morris, did the Strangler make any sort of deathbed statement?"

"Yes, but much of what he said was pretty incoherent."

"I'm assuming that you wanted to ask him about his most recent murder?"

"Among other things, yes."

"And . . .?"

"I'm not at liberty to say what he told us."

"Did he confess to killing the girl in Toronto?"

You could hear in Morris's response that he was pretty ticked off. "The man was a pathological liar. I don't think he *could* recognize the truth."

"But he did make a full confession to his other eight murders . . ."

"I was part of the original team that captured him. I heard those confessions first-hand. They contained the truth, yes, but they also were a mess of lies and half-truths, as well."

"Does this mean the ravine strangling case is now open again?"

"I'm sorry. I can't comment on that. Now if you'll excuse me, I have a plane to catch."

I pressed a button on the remote, and the room became silent. There was a lot to digest here, not least of which were the things Morris had alluded to. What had the Strangler told him before he died? Had he denied doing it? Either way, the police might now be much more interested in pursuing our line of reasoning.

Carolina's phone machine clicked in when I tried her; she'd probably gone to bed early. Well, she'd find out about the Strangler in the morning when they brought the *Globe and Mail* in from the porch. I decided not to try to run Susan to earth at her parents'. She didn't need this information at this point.

I had a message from Nick on the answering machine. "Kit, we've got some time early tomorrow morning, like 7:00? The next week is going to be awful, so it would really be good if you could grab it. Danny's free, too. Maybe we could do some overdubs. I also think you can do a better guitar solo on the song we recorded yesterday. Call the studio as soon as you get in. I'll be here till at least midnight."

It only took a few minutes to get everything arranged, although considering what had been going on, and the lack of sleep I'd had, I didn't know how much good I'd be. Nick said he'd pick me up at 6:00, then apologized for the rotten scheduling. "I told you to expect this from Arnie, though, didn't I?" he said laughing.

Ha-ha.

Even though I sat for another hour thinking things over, Patrick didn't call. I couldn't decide whether to be concerned or relieved as I crawled into bed.

Of course the phone rang just as I was almost asleep. "Yeah, what is it?"

"Kit? Had you gone to bed?" Patrick's voice, smooth as honey. "I'm sorry about calling so late, but I wouldn't have been able to sleep if I didn't tell you how bad I feel about what happened today . . . just a sec." I could hear muffled talking as Patrick covered the receiver with his hand. "Sorry," he said a moment later. "As you can tell, I'm still at the office. I hope your evening went better than mine. Did you, ah, get your friend's problems sorted out?"

"Patrick, can't this wait? I'm completely done in. Yes, we got a few things sorted out with one friend, but now the other two are off on a wild-goose chase tomorrow morning. I'm pretty fed up with them at the moment."

"You've always got me," Patrick said softly. "Listen, would you let me take you out to breakfast? I think we should talk, and the sooner the better."

"No can do. I have to be at the studio by 7:00 a.m."

"No problem! I'll drive you out there. We can talk on the way."

"All right," I said wearily. "Be here by 6:00."

"Great! I'll bring coffee and doughnuts."

Having agreed to let Patrick drive me meant calling Nick back to tell him I didn't need a ride.

"That's actually easier for me," he said. "I can grab a few hours' sleep here rather than driving all the way downtown."

I fell asleep thinking that at least *something* had turned out right that day, even if it wasn't for me.

—∞—

JACKIE GOODE. JACKIE GOODE. THE TWO words tripped around the man's brain like a short circuit. He threw his newspaper down beside him on the bench in disgust.

Am I getting obsessive about this?

No. It was simply wounded pride and vanity. He wanted to go out a winner.

And Jackie Goode would be his curtain call.

He smiled sourly. The city had been outraged when that woman died in the ravine. "Another Awful Death," the local tabloid had screamed in a bold-type headline – naturally accompanied by a full-colour picture of the body bag being carried out. Today's headline – "WRONG AGAIN?" – made reference to the rumours about what this Strangler character had told the cops before he died. He'd probably denied doing it, and the cops would now be checking his whereabouts when the murder had been committed. If they figured out the murder hadn't been done by the Strangler (a likely possibility), they would be forced to reopen the investigation –

something he obviously didn't want. Not that they could get anything on him. He'd done his job too well.

Small mercies – considering the fiasco of his next assignment.

With a tight look around his eyes, he took a deep breath through his nose and exhaled slowly through his mouth. Calm and an intense feeling of energy flowed through him, anger replaced by cold reason.

He knew that there was a big risk in taking Goode out. The cops might be keeping an eye on her after last week's botched attempt. But that only added zest. He loved outwitting them. Did they even know he existed? He pictured himself as a ghostlike vapour, coalescing next to a target, then evaporating once the job had been done.

The sun glowed warmly in the cloudless sky, and he began to realize he'd picked the wrong place to sit, even this early in the year. Later on there would be leaves overhead to provide decent shade. He decided against moving, however, because this spot provided the best view. He picked up his newspaper again and took out a pencil stub from his jacket pocket, as if he wanted to make a stab at the crossword puzzle. The sandblasted brick house across the street from his vantage point remained closed up. They hadn't even bothered opening the curtains yet. 10:30. Didn't anybody work any more?

The previous evening, he'd caught a break when he'd been on hand to see Goode and her friends going in. When she hadn't come out again, he had thought of quietly entering the house and doing her there, but decided that route was too risky. No, he'd wait until he got her in the right situation and take his chances then. It's not as if he'd never done anything like that before.

A young mother with a carriage pushed her way along the sidewalk, distracting his attention from the crossword. Nervously, he did a casual scan of the whole park, then the cars lining the streets around it. No one else sat discreetly watching the house. This was going to be too easy.

As he stretched, the door of the house finally swung open and Jackie Goode appeared, wearing faded jeans and a Blue

Jays T-shirt with a jean jacket thrown over her shoulder. She lit a cigarette and took a long, satisfied drag, then turned to speak to someone still inside. For a person who apparently feared for her life, Goode's brightly dyed hair – would you call it red, or orange? – made her stand out like a stripper at a church social. Was she going out of her way to make it easy to tail her?

Another woman stepped out onto the porch and turned back to lock the door. This one was physically more to the man's liking. Quite tall, very slender, with long, wavy hair lightly streaked with grey, she was strikingly beautiful. Her ankle-length print skirt and brown leather jacket complemented her good looks and showed she had real class – not like her companion. Walking down the steps, she pulled a pair of sunglasses from her shoulder bag, and, without slowing, flipped them on. Goode rushed to catch up to her long strides.

When they'd disappeared around the corner, the man slowly got to his feet, stretching lazily. Folding his paper and tucking it under his arm, he sauntered after them, crossing the street to the side opposite the two women, who chattered as they walked down to the streetcar stop. A fast glance around. Nobody else was in sight. Good.

He considered doing it right there, but he'd have to take both women out, and that didn't appeal to him. Then there was the problem of the getaway. He'd left his car several blocks from the park. No, better to bide his time and follow them. Sooner or later they'd be in a crowd. He'd move in behind them and slide the narrow blade of his special knife between Jackie Goode's ribs in just the right spot to catch her heart from the back. He'd be gone before she would even realize she'd been stabbed and was, in fact, mortally wounded. There would be very little blood, not much pain, she'd just quickly bleed to death internally. An opportunity would come up sometime during the day on Toronto's crowded transit system – as long as he stayed with them.

The fire-engine hair would make that easy.

CHAPTER 20

S omewhat bright and way too early next morning, with Shadow wedged into the back seat (and drooling all over my left shoulder), a coffee in one hand and a doughnut in the other, I got driven out to the studio by Patrick. My guts were in a turmoil. I wanted to talk to him about what I was feeling, but I didn't know where to begin.

You don't go into a relationship expecting the other person not to have any warts on their personality. At least *I* don't – especially after my wake-up call from that creep, Robbie. Maybe those drunks the previous day and the way they'd caused Patrick to go – I don't know . . . berserk? – hadn't been such a bad thing. Could he be the kind of man who'd get upset sometime and beat the crap out of me? This cowgirl was definitely not one for abusive relationships. Better to know that kind of thing right off the bat.

We'd been silent for most of the trip when Patrick finally spoke up. "Obviously you're still upset. I already told you I'm sorry for the way I acted yesterday."

"Patrick . . ." I stopped, trying to make sense out of the jumble in my head. "I guess the best way to put it is what I first said yesterday: you really scared me."

"Scared? How?"

"The way you acted; the way you were talking on the phone. I'm not used to that."

Patrick took his hand off the stick shift and patted mine. "As much as you try to make it seem otherwise, being blind *does* make a difference. Ah, ah! Hear me out. For all your outward bluster and hard-ass behaviour, you're really uncertain about yourself, and that's what's coming out now." He put my hand on the stick and covered it with his. "But to be honest, I scared *myself* outside that bar. I thought I had myself under better control than that!"

"You said you could have killed those two guys. I believed it."

Patrick sighed. "I was in the army when I first got out of school. That's what they teach you to do: kill people. That's what armies are for. I think I probably took that aspect way more seriously than I should have, and it's one reason I got out the first chance I could get."

"What about that phone call? Don't you realize you threatened to kill whoever it was you were talking to?"

He didn't answer for several seconds.

"Okay. I see your point. There are things in my life that drive me, goals I've set that I'm trying my damnedest to reach. I get intense, maybe too intense. What you heard on the phone was frustration. The person I was calling won't allow me to do what I want, what I *need* to do." He squeezed my hand. "Kit, I've been alone a long time. I know this is going to sound conceited as hell, but I was alone because I chose to be, not because I had to be. Maybe it's my fault you don't know much about me. I guess I have just dropped into your life, haven't I? All I know is . . . I'm really glad I did."

I was more confused than ever. Patrick's words sounded wonderful. It was the kind of thing every woman wants to hear. On the physical side, I'd never known a man who turned me on the way he did. Just *thinking* about Patrick made me tingle. But everything else had to be weighed against that. I felt as if I was in deep water, struggling to stay afloat.

The car bumped around as we pulled into the studio parking lot. "Here we are and it's only ten of seven." Patrick undid his seat belt and pushed Shadow's head into the back seat. "Give me some room, fella!" he said with a laugh. "Look, Kit, I'm sorry for everything. Sorry that I didn't keep my cool at the ballpark, or the bar, or on the phone. Sorry that I scared you."

I put my head back against the seat. "Oh, damn it all, Patrick, I'm so confused! I don't know whether I'm coming or going any more."

"Maybe I can help you find your way." A strong hand turned my head and his lips were all over mine. They stayed put for a long time. "There! Does that help?"

"I don't think we have a problem with that," I told him, shaking my head. "Time to be getting inside."

As I released Shadow from his back-seat prison, Patrick asked, "Can I come in and watch for a while? I don't have to be downtown right away, and I've never seen a recording session before."

I shrugged. "Sure, but I should warn you, it can be pretty boring if you're not involved."

As I held lightly to Patrick's right elbow, and Shadow romped around us like a damn fool, we crossed the parking lot to the studio. I felt only slightly better. Since the previous night, I had been feeling more and more that disaster surrounded me like shadows in doorways.

Overly dramatic? Who? Me?

I guess I was filled with a lot more angst than I realized, because the session hit stormy waters almost as soon as it began. Since the first one, Danny had been well-behaved, but that morning I saw what Nick had referred to about him – in spades. Now that this rally gig had come along, I wanted to get "House" completed, and we didn't have much time.

This was turning out to be one hot number, and Nick had caught the urgency in the way we performed it with the kind of edge you normally get only in a live recording. Danny and Tory had done some awesome playing. The best thing was the way he echoed her notes and rhythm in his part, something I hadn't noticed at the time, and it was a pretty cool idea.

The problems arose in Danny's and my own differing concepts of the song. Most of its ultimate effect would come from the lead vocal. I'd sung it rather gently, as wistfully as I knew how, but a lot of that nuance had been lost in the fire of our playing on the bed tracks. Danny thought the vocal track just didn't work.

"You sound like a goddamed lovesick cow with a sore throat!" He was sitting in the producer's chair – a bad omen.

"Sor-*ry!*" I snapped from where I was leaning against a wall, not feeling that good about my vocal in the harsh light of a second listen, but I wasn't going to let him know that. "How's it supposed to sound?"

"Angry. People are having their homes taken away, aren't they?"

"But a lot of my songs sound angry. Doesn't that get repetitive after awhile?"

"This song is the first one people will hear," he countered. "It's important that they remember it, or they won't listen to the others. And they *won't* remember it if you leave the vocal sounding the way it does."

"I don't agree."

"You're full of shit! Nick, what do you think?"

Nick sounded hesitant. "I, ah, think Danny has a good point, Kit."

"Great!" I said. "So now I'm an idiot who doesn't know what my own songs are about."

"Kit, be reasonable. You can't expect to always be completely objective about your own material and your own performance."

"Where does Danny get off telling me how my songs should go?"

Danny jumped to his feet. "Oh, give me a freaking break, Miss High-and-Mighty! You may think it's your demo, but we *all* have a stake in its success. Why don't you just give my suggestion a try – or are you afraid I might be right?"

I could have popped him in the nose. "Play the goddam track. I want to hear it again."

I stomped over and flopped down next to Patrick on the sofa placed between the recording console and the big window looking out on the studio.

"Is this what they call creative differences?" Patrick asked as the playback started.

"No, this is what they call a pain-in-the-ass sideman."

"Do you think he might be right?"

"Oh, I don't know."

"You're not sounding too convinced about your position."

"I'm not."

"I think you're just being hard-headed. What's this song about, anyway?"

"It's the song for the anti-Riverside rally next Monday."

Patrick didn't answer. I put my hard head back against the leather and let the sounds wash over me. Each smack of the kick drum from the speakers overhead thudded against my chest. Danny's and my guitars weaving around Tory's inspired violin line pulsated with urgency. Against this outpouring of energy, my vocal sounded . . . insipid. Shaking my head, I had to admit that Danny was right.

The song faded out and Patrick stood up. "Kit, could I talk to you out in the lobby?"

"Sure." As he led me out, I said, "Just a minute guys. I'll be right back."

As soon as we got through the door, Patrick turned to me. "I don't think it's a good idea to do this song at that rally."

"Why the hell not?" I asked, puzzled. "They're getting heavy media coverage. It will be great for my career."

"These things can backfire. You don't want to be lumped in with a bunch of crackpots, do you?"

"They're not crackpots. They're people who think something bad is going on."

"What do you mean bad?"

"The company behind the development is up to all kinds of hanky-panky."

"Oh really? How do you know that?"

"Give me a break, Patrick! I'm in the middle of a session! This is not the time to get into a philosophical discussion on urban planning."

"Does this have something to do with, ah, the death of your friend?"

I shook my head, trying to hold my mounting annoyance in check. "Yes. We think it does. Now is that good enough to get you to drop it?"

He pushed on nevertheless. "But why would developers want to kill your friend? That's crazy. And the public would think so if anyone ever said that. If you're part of all this, people will think you're crazy too."

"Whose side are you on?"

"The side that doesn't want to see *you* get hurt."

"I appreciate your concern, but be realistic. We're going to try for a recording deal in the States. They don't care a fig about some Toronto housing development down in New York or L.A."

"I just think you're making a mistake. You should keep your distance from this mess. Promise me you'll consider what I'm saying."

I shrugged.

"I've got to be going. Another early meeting, can you believe it? I'll call later." Patrick kissed me and I remained by the receptionist's desk listening to him walk to the door accompanied by Shadow who thought we might be going, too. "You'd better lock this behind me since the receptionist isn't here yet." When I walked over to the door, he pulled me tightly against him. "Kit, maybe you think I'm butting in where I don't belong, but I don't want anything bad to happen to you." His hands slid down to my rear end. "I'm going to think about you all day, you know," he breathed in my ear.

"Good," I answered, reaching for something just south of his belt buckle. I felt an immediate response. "You do that." I laughed, then pushed him out the door and locked it.

Served him right.

I corralled Shadow and got him calmed down, and we went back into the control room, where Danny sat pontificating on my stubbornness. He didn't shut up as soon as I pushed open the door, but maybe that was his plan.

"I don't care what she's capable of! If you think I'm going to work with that overbearing, pompous bitch –"

"Where's a goddam mic?" I asked loudly. "Do you want me to redo this vocal or not?"

The room instantly went silent.

"Now you *want* to do it?" Danny asked, flabbergasted.

I smiled sweetly. "Sure. You're probably wrong, and this way I'll get to say 'I told you so.'"

Nick led me into the studio, set up a mic, and handed me the cans. "Thanks, Kit. Danny was ready to walk."

I snorted derisively. "We can do without him."

"That's not the point. He's really into this project. At the risk of swelling your head even more, he thinks you're one of the most talented writers he's heard in a long time. And you've already nearly blown him out of the studio on guitar. You've got yourself a partner for life if you want, but you're going to have to work *with* him, not *over* him."

With that, Nick went back into the control room, the outer door whooshing shut behind him like an airlock on the Starship *Enterprise.*

Holy shit! Danny Kutcher thought I was that good? I'd done some asking around about the kid, and everyone I spoke to raved about his chops and musicality. You should have heard Steve go on about him all the way out to the studio for the second session. Danny Kutcher this. Danny Kutcher that. A number of stateside heavies had been after him to join their backup bands, and he'd refused.

The result of that knowledge on me was total lock-up when I tried to sing. What came out of my mouth sounded about as musical as a carpenter with an attitude pounding nails into a board. *Overly stiff* would be a generous description. We tried to punch in around the few good measures I managed to produce before giving it up as a lost cause.

Nick had come prepared for a possible choke from *moi* and had a "medicinal" bottle of Southern Comfort standing by. Even though it wasn't even 8:30 in the morning, I knew something drastic had to be done. A few healthy chugs and I was flying. I tell you, that vocal sounded so angry they had to tell me to tone it down when the dreaded F-word made it into one take. Forcing my voice made it sound even more croaky but also more close to the edge. Remember Lennon's singing on the Beatles version of "Twist and Shout"? He's right on the edge with that one. I was in the same place that morning.

A few more tries and a punch-in or two later, and we had a keeper. Danny to his credit didn't give me a bunch of I-told-you-so's. As a matter of fact, he gave me a hug and said, "I knew you could do it."

By the time the clock hit 10:30, we'd pretty well finished the overdubs for the song, except for the part that Danny, Terry, Frank, and Steve would have to sing. Nick came up with a neat idea: at one point have my voice be the lowest one in the harmony (I can sing pretty low), with the guys singing above me.

"Imagine: fours guys on top of one girl," I quipped. "I like the concept."

While waiting for Nick to get the mic set up on the guitar amp so I could redo my solo, I sat in a corner limbering up my fingers with a few licks. Call me dumb, but that day I felt that even half-snookered I could do anything.

Danny strolled over. "Nice stuff."

"It's not mine," I admitted. "It's a solo my teacher recorded with his band, The Orchids, for 'I Got My Mojo Working.' I enjoy noodling around with it."

"Who was your teacher?"

"I guy named Link Chamberland. My folks lived a few towns away from him when I was in my teens."

"You took lessons from Link? I wondered where you learned to play that way. I've never heard anything quite the same. He was supposed to be fabulous."

"The best. It was a real tragedy when he passed away."

As a result of that conversation, Danny drove me home after the session, and we spent most of the afternoon cementing our friendship. The rest of Nick's Southern Comfort *and* my Cloudberry Liqueur got knocked off while we talked music and listened to every one of my Orchids recordings. Danny made me play "Mojo" about a dozen times, and kept saying, "I can't believe this guy played like that in 1964!"

The awful combination of drinking in the morning coupled with too little sleep took its toll on me, because I crashed right on the sofa. Danny was long gone when Shadow, leash in his mouth, woke me up shortly after 7:00 p.m.

I spent the next hour kneeling on my bathroom floor doing liquid laughs into the toilet. Served me right. If I was going to be any kind of long-term success as a singer, I'd have to find a less debilitating way to get loose. My head felt as if the Province of Ontario was building a new highway through my skull and they'd found a lot of rock that needed to be blasted away.

Clearing my stomach went a long way towards improving my physical state, but that only allowed me to focus on the turmoil of my mental one.

With the good feel of that morning's session now a distant, pre-hangover memory, all the things that had happened with Patrick the previous day slapped me down again. The conversation we'd had in the studio parking lot had left me reassured, but only slightly. His erratic behaviour set off all my warning bells. I liked Patrick a lot. His lovemaking knocked my socks off – well, everything but my socks. But would it go farther? The answer at that point was a pretty solid no. I felt that what I needed most was a rock-steady guy – in and out of the sack – nothing more, nothing less. At least for the time being.

I hadn't gotten closer to any answers when Steve called to say he'd pick me up at 9:00 the next morning. Apparently Danny, after I'd fallen asleep, had talked Nick into an hour or two of time to finish the vocals for "House," then booked space at a rehearsal hall near the studio so we could work on our set for the rally on Monday. How he had the wherewithal to think so clearly was beyond me, if he felt anything like I did.

Shadow and I finally went out for his walk. Actually, he walked; I sort of shuffled along. Chicken soup and crackers was about all I could manage for dinner, and I had to eat that in the living room, because Shadow's snarfing of his evening meal sounded so revolting.

At 8:45 my downstairs buzzer rang. I croaked, "Who is it?" into the door panel, and Carolina's cheerful voice came over the speaker. "Your taxi's here, ma'am."

"What are you talking about?"

"Didn't you get our phone message? We're having a meeting at my place." Then she laughed uproariously, which was like sticking a drill bit in my ear. "We've had a *very* busy day!"

———

THE MAN'S TAILING OF JACKIE GOODE and her friend had so far been an exercise in frustration. First, the streetcar they had gotten on had been close to empty – an almost unheard-of occurrence on that route. The more people around, the greater the chance they wouldn't notice him. He'd taken a seat at the back and kept an eye on them from behind his paper all the way to the subway. They'd travelled on that as far as Finch, the northernmost station, where they'd piled into a taxi. In a mad scramble, he had pushed ahead of someone and hopped into the front seat of the next cab in the line.

His driver was a Sikh, and when he opened his mouth, the man had a tough time not laughing. "Where to, buddy?" The accent sounded like a combination of East Side and East India. The driver had obviously seen too many gangster movies.

"See that cab that just pulled out? Follow it."

With a big grin, the cabby slammed his car into gear and took off in hot pursuit. "You a PI?" he asked.

The man wondered if he'd made a bad choice. If the driver of the cab they were following had half a brain, it wouldn't take him long to figure out he had a tail. At all costs the women must not be made aware of his presence.

"Yeah, I'm a dick," the man answered, slipping into the part his driver seemed to expect. "If you don't mind my butting in, you're tailing that hack a bit too close. I don't want 'em to know we're here."

The cabby smiled again. "Right. You tell me how you want it done, my friend, and I will do my best." He eased his car back into traffic three cars behind the other cab. "Can I ask who we're tailing?"

"The tall dame. Her old man thinks she's fooling around, and I'm here to find out where and who with."

The two cabs drove past the north edge of Toronto, then east, finally ending up in one of the industrial developments that seep over city lines into what used to be farmland. The first cab finally stopped in front of an elegantly designed building of brick and smoked glass. A sign growing from the shrubs on the lawn said Sloane Environmental. The man had his driver stop in the parking area of another building down the road. From that vantage point he could see the tall woman get out and walk purposefully to the front door. The cab remained at the curb.

"What now, boss? his cabby asked.

"We sit and wait."

The wait turned out to be about fifteen minutes. The tall woman re-emerged carrying a cardboard box. The cab took off again and drove a short distance to a plaza. Both women got out and entered a restaurant.

"Pull up here and wait for me," he ordered, reaching into his wallet for fifty dollars. "I may be awhile. This more than covers what I owe. Don't take off. I could be in a hurry when I come out. There's another hundred for you on top of the cab fare when we're through. Got that?"

"Sure, sure. You can count on me, boss. I'll be right here. Count on me."

Goode and her companion were sitting in a booth in a back corner of the restaurant, heads together. All the tables around them were taken, so the man had to be satisfied with a table at the front, where he could at least observe them.

Even though he couldn't hear what was being said, they were obviously discussing something important. Jackie Goode, by the way she gesticulated with her hands while she spoke, was busy being aggressive, while the other woman, with her calming gestures, seemed to be trying to rein her in.

Eventually, a third woman joined them. He hadn't seen her before and wondered if she might be from the lab. She had that look. But she seemed very much on edge.

Goode started in on the new woman. More gesticulations, pointing fingers, very aggressive behaviour. The other continued to be the calming influence, her hand frequently patting the hand of the new woman, comforting, reassuring. Classic interrogation technique. Somebody knew psychology. For the next forty-five minutes he watched, hoping against hope that Jackie Goode would feel the call of nature. Once she went off to the washroom, she'd be an easy target. But even though she finished two bottles of beer with lunch, she never moved. By the time the three got up to leave, he was sure she had a bladder made of cast iron. The meal wasn't a complete washout, though. As they passed by his table, he overheard a key exchange.

Jackie Goode, in her buzz-saw voice, was saying to the mousy one, "Then it's settled. I'll meet you at 1:00 tomorrow on the Union Station subway platform in the Designated Waiting Area. Okay?"

The third woman looked worried. "I hope I'm doing the right thing."

"Yes, you are, dear," said Goode's companion. "You'll be able to sleep better, knowing you have done the right thing. And you can count on us. We'll stand up for you."

The door closed, cutting off their voices. The man dumped a few bills on the table and followed them.

The rest of the day was a total waste. Goode and her friend didn't return to the subway, and the man had to pay through the nose to follow them back to the house in Cabbagetown.

His cab driver didn't mind. The fare was enormous, not including the promised $100 tip.

The two women didn't leave the house the rest of the day. Through the low windows, he could see them from his park bench, sitting on the floor in the living room, drinking beer directly from bottles, clinking them together, often in exuberant toasts. He began to yearn to get things wrapped up. The Goode bitch wasn't worth all this effort. It was only because he had an almost pathological need to settle accounts that he didn't just pack it in. At one point, he almost decided to walk up to the front door and, when they opened it, plug them with the gun he had in the waistband of his pants. The only thing that held him back was the next-door neighbour, who bustled around in her garden until well past 6:00. He really didn't feel up to plugging her, too.

When people began arriving at the house shortly after that, he realized it wasn't going to be his day, and reluctantly left, frustrated and vowing to finish the job the next day – no matter what it took.

As he walked back to his car, he thought about calling his contact and telling them what seemed to be going on. From what he knew about his current employers' business, he was certain that the woman they had met that day might be someone who could do an awful lot of harm. Should he tell them, maybe make a little bit of extra money?

The man smiled and shook his head to himself. No, let them look after it themselves. Amateurs. He'd had them pegged from the beginning.

If they were found out he'd be long gone to one of the untraceable bolt-holes he'd set up many years ago in the event that something went horribly wrong. They'd try to do a deal with the cops. "We'll give you the murderer!" the poor saps would say, and when the cops came to look for him, they'd find nothing.

Tomorrow he'd settle the score with Jackie Goode and be off to enjoy the just fruits of his long labour. *Retirement sounds awfully good,* the man thought to himself as he started his car.

—∽m∽—

The ride over to Carolina's was absolutely awful. I found that, if
I squished myself into the corner where the seat met the door,
the motion of the car didn't bother me as much. Carolina chattered
away about how the Blue Jays had managed another dramatic
come-from-behind victory, totally unaware of just how bad I felt.
She thought I had my window open so Shadow could get some air
up his nose. I just wanted to be ready in case I had to puke. How
could I have been so stupid?

Waiting at one rather long light, Carolina was tapping the steer-
ing wheel in time to the clicking of the windshield wipers and
humming to herself when something suddenly dawned on me.

"Carolina, how come you're driving me?"

She stopped tapping. "Because I felt like it."

"But you don't have a licence. Hell! I didn't even know you
could drive!"

"I am doing a pretty good job, though, aren't I?" She laughed
delightedly. "Sometimes I surprise even myself!"

"What if you get pulled over?"

She started the car forward. "You know, Kit, sometimes you
worry too much. Besides, you're the one who told me I'm a stodgy
old fart!"

I groaned and rested my head on the door again.

Everyone was waiting again – including Edward who, thank the Lord, offered me no Scotch. I felt as if I'd never left their damn living room.

"Kit's kind of quiet tonight," Jackie said. "I wonder if she's suffering from post-coital whatsit."

She and Carolina cackled over that like a couple of hens.

I muttered, "Curl up and die," under my breath.

Sue came over and sat down beside me. "Don't let them bother you, Kit. I think they're just a little overly pleased with themselves right now." Her voice was a bit tired and slightly hoarse, but overall, Susan sounded surprisingly normal.

"Have they told you what they found out today?" I asked.

"No. They said we had to wait for you."

"Okay, Carolina," I said in a louder voice, "let's get this show on the road. It's getting *way* past my bedtime."

Carolina spoke for about fifteen minutes. Since the lab had called Marion's mom, asking her if someone wanted to come by and pick up her daughter's personal effects, they saw the perfect opportunity to head up there and do a little snooping. "If there was any evidence that might still exist, then it made the most sense that we would find it at the lab."

"Right!" Jackie added. "And Mar had already mentioned that someone named Judy, who also worked there, would know something."

"We discussed all that last time," I pointed out. "Obviously, from the way you're both carrying on, you've come up with something. What?"

"I decided to take the bull by the horns," said Carolina. "I went right in there and asked for Judy, saying that Marion had always spoken highly of her, and that I supposed she would be the person our late friend would want me to speak with. It worked like a charm."

"What about that manager guy Marion had been complaining about so much?"

"I turned on the charm, and he acted like a real pussycat, although I think that he may have just wanted to humour me so I would leave as quickly as possible." Carolina giggled uncharacteristically. "It was an *interesting* exchange."

"What the hell are you on about, C?" Jackie asked.

"Nothing," Carolina said brushing the comment aside. "When this Judy person came out with the things from Marion's desk in a cardboard box, I made some small talk about how this had been such a shock to all of us and must have been even worse for her, since she'd also barely gotten over the death of the owner of the lab. When the manager got fed up with the small talk and walked away, I dropped my little bombshell. Granted it was just a flyer, but I felt that, all things considered, it was worth trying."

"And what was your 'little bombshell?'" I inquired.

"I leaned forward and said right into Judy's ear, 'I know all about the soil tests.'"

Playing along perfectly, Susan asked, "What happened then?"

"You'd think that C had kicked her in the stomach from what I heard!" Jackie said with relish. "Old Judy crumbled like a house of cards."

"Care to translate?" I asked Carolina.

"Well, I obviously don't know the woman very well, but she is scared and ashamed and –"

"And worried as hell they're going to come after her next." Jackie interrupted.

I nodded. "So the upshot of all this was?"

"I invited her to lunch," Carolina said.

"You what?"

"Invited her to lunch. It was the obvious thing to do if we wanted to find out anything else. You didn't expect her to talk about it there in the lobby, did you?"

"And over your nice little lunch, did you get anything useful out of her?"

"We did the best we could, because obviously a restaurant isn't the best place to talk about something this touchy, but we also didn't want to give her time to think about her position and possibly get cold feet about talking to us. We took a calculated risk."

"A restaurant isn't any kind of place at all! How do you know you weren't followed?"

"Kit," Jackie butted in, "I think I'd have known if we had been followed. I watched as we left the lab and had my eyes open all the way from Carolina's place to the lab. I didn't see anyone. No one followed Judy, either, when she came. I'm sure of it. We were at a secluded table way in the back of the restaurant, and no one came near us. Like C said, we did the best that we could under the circumstances. Now let C talk and stop carping at her."

"Judy does know something and is scared," Carolina said. "Quite scared. Marion was right about her being the technician who began the testing. When she discussed some of the preliminary results with Dr. Sloane, he told her to hold off on the work. Two days later, he took over the testing himself, told her she must not have cleaned the equipment properly, or some such thing, which was the reason she'd gotten such skewed results, and that was the last she thought about it until Marion started quizzing her. Judy told Marion about those preliminary results and Marion was very interested. Judy says she got the feeling Marion already had a good idea what had happened.

"According to Judy, the Riverside Project had already gotten the necessary go-aheads from all levels of government by the time the shit finally hit the fan. Someone at City Hall discovered that an area – by accident or design – had been left out of the soil analysis that's supposed to be done when industrial land is redeveloped. The oversight was embarrassing, certainly, but everyone figured it was only a matter of form, nothing more. An old warehouse, one of those huge brick monstrosities, is smack dab in the middle of the neglected area. Judy says that if the few results she got are in fact accurate, there is a *huge* problem with contamination on that land. Sloane found nothing wrong when he repeated the tests, which is hardly surprising since it appears that someone bought him off."

Edward, who had sat back so silently I'd forgotten he was there, said angrily, "I knew something fishy was going on by the way they ramrodded this thing through City Council! Nothing surprises me about big business."

From what *I* gathered at the time, the Riverside Project hadn't been ramrodded through. It had been packaged beautifully and the politicians had fallen on it like starving wolves on a leg of lamb. The site had been nearly useless as a source of tax income for years. It was an eyesore made up of derelict buildings and brown fields. The proposed project promised substantial commercial development, residences, a hell of a lot of temporary employment, and better *public housing*. With all the homeless and thousands on the waiting list for subsidized housing, it was like manna from heaven to the government officials. Everybody came out a winner. They even named it cleverly to sound bucolic: Riverside. It wasn't hard to confuse the new development with Riverdale, one of Toronto's most vibrant neighbourhoods.

Then the problems started. People didn't want to leave Regent Park for new public-housing digs in Riverside, no matter how nice they were supposed to be. Committees were formed. With good PR, though, the developers should have been able to weather the storm. After all, they had the city and provincial politicians strongly supporting them.

"Did you ask Judy if she knows where things like the original soil samples and Dr. Sloane's notes went?" Susan asked. "That could tell us a lot."

"Here's where things get really interesting," Jackie said. "When the new management took over, whole file folders started to disappear mysteriously, and some of the people at the lab swear that computer records were changed. Judy alerted Marion to this about a week before she was killed."

"Based on that," Edward told us, "I did a bit of checking into the ownership of Sloane Environmental today. It's now one of those businesses that's owned by a numbered corporation, which is owned by another corporation, and so on. It will take time to find our way through the ownership maze, but I'd be willing to bet who we'll find pulling the strings at the other end: Advantage Developments, the people behind Riverside."

"Who owns Advantage?" Susan asked.

"Again, it's one of those conglomerates of faceless big players on the investment scene. I tried to do some digging before, without much luck. It has some well-known director types on the board. You know, retired politicians and the like, who show up at the odd directors' meeting, have their name on the letterhead, and do sweet bugger-all for a fat paycheque. The public face of the development is their chairman, Gregory Ewing, and Carolina knows him very well."

"He's the guy she absolutely slaughtered in that debate on TV. Bet he remembers her, too," Jackie said, laughing.

"Up until now, he's been a bit player. Somewhere Ewing suddenly got an awful lot of clout to put a project of this size together – or he's just the front man, which is more likely." The phone rang and Edward picked up the receiver. "Yes? . . . Thanks for calling back . . . no, it's a little more complicated than that. . . . You can? That would be no problem. I could be over in ten minutes. . . . Sure I will. Thanks John. This is great!" Edward replaced the receiver. "That was John Sherman, the committee's lawyer. He's going to tell me exactly what we need in the way of evidence to sew this thing up, and he'll draft a bombproof affidavit for that lab technician. He wants me to come over to his place right now. Carolina, do you want to tag along?"

"No," I said for her. "It sounds like we have a few more things to discuss here." Edward made his farewells and left. "Care to explain why you need this affidavit?"

"Like I said, Judy is worried. First there's the testing that obviously wasn't right, then Marion finds out about it. She's killed – by the way, Judy had also wondered about that before we told her what we know – and it isn't much of a stretch to surmise a few things about Sloane's traffic accident. She thinks she may be next."

"Do they know about her involvement in the testing?"

Jackie snorted. "No, and she thinks that's one reason Sloane told her to stand down and did the testing himself. She's as besotted with the guy as Marion was, and thinks he was trying to protect her."

Carolina said, "I told Judy that if she gave us the results of the testing she did, we would protect her and make sure that there aren't any legal repercussions. That's why Edward went to see the lawyer. All we need is to have *something* to give to the press to get an investigation off and running."

I didn't think I wanted to hear the answer, but I had to ask the question anyway. "Okay. Can we call in the cops now?"

"Well . . ." Carolina said, "not exactly. You see, we only talked to Judy today. We don't actually have the hard copy of her lab results yet."

"So send the cops for it."

"It's not as simple as that, Kit."

"I don't understand."

"We need to have some experts Edward knows at the university look over Judy's test results to see if they contain the kind of information we need to stop Riverside in its tracks. If the info's the real thing, then we all feel that the rally would be the best place to release it."

"Ah, yes, the fabled rally."

"Oh, Kit, don't be like that! Everyone has worked too hard not to enjoy the satisfaction of –"

"Screw the satisfaction! You make this sound like it's a game of one-upmanship! If we're right about everything, then these men are killers. The sooner the professionals take over, the better I'll like it."

"Kit, it's stupid to make any sort of move until we have Judy's files!"

"Then let's go over to her place right now and get it!"

"We can't . . ."

"Why the hell not?"

"Because we don't know where she lives," Jackie answered sheepishly, "and we never thought of asking."

As I trudged wearily up the last flight of stairs to my apartment, the past two days' happenings were a total jumble in my head. Was I doing the right thing by not forcing my friends to call in the cops? I also still hadn't decided what to do about Patrick. Mightn't it really be best to cut that off now? And on top of all this, I was trying to make my first recording. God! My life had been *so* empty three weeks ago!

The worst part, though, was that I'd caved in yet again about not going to the police.

"Don't worry, Kit," Jackie had said. "It's in the bag. I've made all the arrangements with Judy. She's meeting me tomorrow."

"And by then," I'd finished, "it will already be Saturday, so why not wait until the rally on Monday to release the information and call in the cops. Right?"

"I told you she'd see right through it," Carolina told Jackie.

"Well, why not, Kit? Jackie said. "We'll certainly get a lot of bang for our buck."

So it was decided. Jackie would get the files the next day, Sunday would be spent checking the facts, duplicating everything, getting the word out to the press that something huge was going to be announced, then the whole thing would be presented at the big rally – with K Mason and Band supplying the musical accompaniment. The idea stank, but I'd felt too punk at that point to object any more. And it *was* only two days.

What could happen in that time?

Susan had offered to drop me on her way out to the burbs. As we'd driven along Richmond, avoiding the worst of the Friday-night crush on Queen, I'd asked if she'd heard from Paul.

"No. Not a thing unless two hang-ups on the answering machine were him. The kids have started asking questions about their daddy, my folks are wondering what the heck is going on, and I just don't know what to say!"

"Level with your parents at least. Tell them you and Paul are going through a rough patch. As for the kids . . . I guess you could say Daddy's out of town or something. One thing's for certain, though . . ."

"What, Kit?"

"Paul's a dead man when I get my hands on him."

Susan pleaded. "Oh Lord, don't say that!"

I kicked myself for my insensitivity.

After fishing out my key and unlocking the door, I took off Shadow's harness, then checked for phone messages.

"Kit, it's Patrick. I'd really like to talk to you. Please call me whenever you get in. I'll be up very late."

He answered on the second ring. "Where were you? It's almost 1 a.m."

I frowned. "I didn't know I needed to check in."

"I didn't mean it that way. I was just interested. I thought you may have been recording again."

"Nothing so exciting," I answered. "Just my friends having yet another meeting."

"Did it concern that anti-Riverside group?"

"Yeah."

"So, are you still going to play at that rally?"

"Patrick, I thought you were leaving the decision up to me."

"I am."

He'd picked the wrong time to yank this girl's chain. "Then why are you bugging me about it again? I've got a hot band and a lot of people are going to be there. I'd have to be crazy not to perform."

Patrick's anger rose also. "You've got to be crazy to get yourself involved with these protesters! The Riverside developers are very organized, and people like that play hardball. If your band is that good, surely you don't need this rally to get a recording deal."

"But I *want* to play. Patrick, you will *not* talk me out of it!" I said hotly. "Why are you so worried? There won't be any Riverside Project to worry about after Monday, because the organizers are going to blow the whistle on them at the rally."

Silence. Then, "How are they going to do that?"

I realized I'd started to say something I shouldn't have. "They are, ah, going to have all the media there and a whole mess of people and it will be, um . . . very effective. In any event, I'm *going* to be there. End of discussion."

If Patrick was always going to tell me how to run my life, this relationship would be over pretty fast. Continuing to carry on like this over everything I wanted to do was going to make my decision about him a mighty easy one.

He didn't respond for a moment, then said reasonably, "Look, Kit, you're just getting more and more worked up over this. Why don't we just put it on the back burner for now?"

"I'm sorry," I answered, softening a little. "I'm tired and not feeling too well."

"Would you like me to come over and soothe your furrowed brow?"

"No. What I need right now is a good night's sleep."

"Then I won't keep you on the phone. Are you free tomorrow?"

"I have to rehearse. One of the guys is picking me up at 9:00."

"Call me before you leave, and your friend can give me directions. I'll pick you up when you're through, we'll go out for a bite to eat and have a real heart-to-heart. It's about time I laid my cards on the table."

"What's that supposed to mean?"

"You'll just have to wait until tomorrow." Patrick laughed. "Now maybe you'll know how I felt all day after that grope at the studio. Good night, sweet Katherine."

"It's Kit! You know I hate to be called Katherine!" I shouted, my anger flaring again – but Patrick had already hung up.

I fell into a confused sleep some time after 2:00 a.m, and I had one of those dreams when you're not even sure if you're asleep. The events of the past few days played endlessly in my head, a tape loop gone amok. Events became mixed together in bizarre combinations: Carolina and Patrick arguing over whether Marion was really dead; Danny turning out to be the power behind Advantage Developments; walking in on Paul and Jackie making love in a bathtub.

The most unnerving one, however, concerned me desperately searching for Patrick. Something dreadful was going to happen. I pushed my way through a silent crowd, alone and naked; Shadow had run off. Over and over I called out for Patrick, and even though he didn't answer, I knew he was somewhere nearby. With no other recourse, I began reaching out for the faces of those I passed, trying to find which one was him. Whatever I touched would appear, a cheek here, mouth there, as if I had partial vision. But no matter how many faces I swept my hands over, I couldn't find Patrick. As the crowd pressed in on me, I started running, my hands stretched out in front of me, crashing into and tripping over things. Gradually, contact diminished, and I had the feeling I'd entered an alley. A few steps brought me flat up against a wall. I spun around.

"Patrick! Patrick, where are you?"

The silent crowd surrounded me. I could smell them; the sound of their breathing filled my ears. They were waiting for me, waiting for me to fall asleep. Then they would attack.

"Patrick!"

I slid along the rough brick of the wall until I came to a corner, where I tried to squeeze myself as far in as possible, hoping that I wouldn't be found. The crowd surged forward.

"Stay away! I'm warning you. Get away from me!"

Panic scurried out from a dark corner of my brain, like a hundred thousand spiders crawling over my naked skin. I grew more scared, more incoherent, as I tried to make the unseen mass of humanity back away.

"*Patrick* . . ." I wailed, covering my face.

Hands gripped my wrists and wrenched them down. "I'm right here, Kit." It was Patrick, his voice coming from deep down in his throat like the purr of a lion.

I threw my arms around his shoulders, burying my head against his chest. "I was so scared. I didn't know what to do."

He spoke soothingly. "It's all right now. I'm here. I'll always be here for you."

Then I remembered. "Patrick! Let me touch your face. I can see you if you let me." I touched his cheeks, then his mouth, his eyes, his ears. Things would appear for a brief moment, but only as a shadowy outline that flickered and disappeared as my hands passed on. "I . . . I don't understand. It worked before."

"I'm sorry, Kit," he said with infinite sadness, "but you can never really see me." Patrick's voice too began fading, pulling echoes from the hopeless darkness as he repeated, "I'm sorry. I'm sorry . . ."

Pounding drums rose to fill the void, Shadow began barking in the distance, and I awoke with a snap, sitting up, once more in my own bed.

Someone was banging on my apartment door. Shadow, scourge of all would-be robbers, barked frantically. I reached out for the foot of the bed, where I keep my robe. Nothing. Groping around on the floor next to me, I found my jeans but no shirt. The banging on the door increased in intensity. Not knowing what else to do, I slipped into the jeans and grabbed a towel off the dresser. Wrapping it around my chest, I crossed the living room.

"Who is it?" I called out. "I'm warning you. My dog is a killer."

The answering voice sounded surprised. "It's Danny! Open the door, Kit." I did and he walked in. "Do you always greet guests this way? Killer dogs? Half-naked?" He said it lightly, but he seemed rather nonplussed.

If Danny was nonplussed, you can imagine what I was. "I'm sorry, um, Danny." I ran my hand over my face in an effort to banish my powerful dream from the waking world. "I was, um, asleep when you started knocking. I was having an awful nightmare."

"You're okay?" He sounded concerned.

I nodded.

"Well then, you better get something on, or are you going to rehearsal dressed that way?"

I smiled in spite of myself. "What are you doing here? I thought Steve was picking me up. Did I miss a phone message?"

"I told Steve I wanted to tell you some big news personally, and from what you just asked, yes, you did miss a message."

"I had sort of a busy night," I apologized.

Danny laughed. "Judging by the way you look, I can believe it!" He turned me around. "Now, you get dressed and I'll make some coffee. Do you mind if I play that tape of Link again?"

After taking a shower and finding proper clothes, I sat in the kitchen with Danny, sipping strong coffee, its familiar warmth driving away the last shreds of my dream as I told him about it.

"Sounds deeply psychological to me," he observed when I finished. "Freud would have a field day with it: running around naked, people chasing you, a boyfriend who keeps fading away. Heavy stuff."

"I'm a mess," I said glumly.

"Garbage! You've got everything going for you." He put his mug down on the table with a bang. "Aren't you going to ask about my news?"

"Okay. Tell me."

"Nick called late yesterday. Somebody at this rally has pulled some strings, and they want you to perform one of those acoustic "Live at Five" things down at that new FM station – except that they want us to play around 7:00."

"What?" Sitting sideways on my chair, totally shocked, I almost fell over backwards. Danny grabbed my arm and pulled me upright. "When?" I gasped.

"Tomorrow. You get to play your big protest song over the air-waves of Toronto. Me too – if you want some backup."

"You bet! Oh my God, Danny, this is absolutely great! I can't believe it!"

"You better. And we also better get to that rehearsal unless you don't mind sounding like an idiot on the radio. Would you like me to carry your amp down to the van?"

As we made our way out to the studio in Danny's noisy, broken-down van, I started thinking. What did Patrick know with all his worrying? Here was one of the biggest radio stations in Canada and they *wanted* me to play the dreaded protest song live from their studio. So much for Patrick's concern that being involved in Carolina's rally would harm my career.

The last person who'd done a personal appearance at the station had been Bonnie Raitt.

—⁓—

HE COULD ALMOST TASTE VICTORY AS a sweetness on his tongue. The situation was perfect: lots of people in a hurry to get to the ball game. Bucking the flow of the crowd at Union Station wasn't easy, and he jealously watched the ease with which Jackie Goode accomplished it up ahead. She stopped under the bright lights of the Designated Waiting Area in the middle of the platform. As she checked her watch, the man automatically checked his: 12:54. He hoped that the woman she was waiting for wouldn't be much longer. The crush of people going to the game wouldn't last forever.

He'd been sitting in his car, watching the house in Cabbagetown again that morning, hoping that Goode would either be left alone in the house or head out by herself, and things had been working out very well. Around 11:30 she'd appeared at the door, looking excited and more than a little smug. When she'd reached the corner, the other woman had appeared on the small porch and shouted after her friend to "come right back and *be careful*."

"Stop worrying!" Goode had called back. "This is going to be a piece of cake. I'll be back by 1:30 at the latest."

Not if I can help it, he had thought as he got out of his car and began following at a discreet distance.

Someone bumped into him from behind, jerking him back to the present, and as he turned to curse the clumsy oaf, he noticed with some surprise that it was the short, mousy woman he'd seen at the restaurant with Goode and her friend the day before. Her size and meek appearance seemed wildly at odds with the way she forced her way like a runty salmon through the streaming multitude. He used the opportunity, following in her wake to get closer to his target.

Stopping at a bench just behind them, he grabbed a copy of the morning's paper someone had left behind. He was close enough to hear their words.

"You're late," Goode said sharply.

"I'm sorry." The little woman held her purse nervously in front of her. "I'm not used to coming downtown on the weekend, and it took longer than I thought it would."

"Did you bring it?"

"Yes . . . yes, I did. Now you're sure no one knows about this?"

"Positive. We've taken precautions." Goode smiled evilly. "*You* weren't followed, were you? These people are fiendishly clever, you know."

The little woman looked around wildly, her eyes wide with fear. "You don't think they know?"

"Not unless you've been careless. Time is getting late and I have people to meet. Give me the goddam envelope!"

"Here. Take it. I wish I'd never seen it!"

"Look, lady, don't give me any pious crap!" Goode snapped as she snatched the envelope. "Tell me, if we hadn't confronted you yesterday, would you *ever* have stepped forward with this evidence? My friend died for this, you know."

The mousy woman looked thoroughly miserable, afraid to go forward, afraid to go back. She leaned towards Goode, with her garish red-orange hair. They made quite an odd couple. "Remember, you and your friend said you'd protect me."

"We will, as long as you do what we told you to. Go home, pack a bag, and find a nice motel out of town. Lock the doors and listen to the news. You'll know when it's safe to show your face in town."

The woman looked around wildly again. "May I go now?"

"No. Our lawyer wants you to sign this," Goode said, as she took a carefully folded envelope out of the front pocket of her jeans.

"What is it?"

"An affidavit you're going to sign, stating that these are the original lab reports on the tests you performed on those soil samples."

"But you said no one would find out where you got it from!"

"We did; but lady, the rules have changed. Think of it this way: you're going to look pretty good having come across with this when the shit hits the fan."

"But I might get sent to jail as an accessory or something!" the lab technician moaned.

"No, you won't!" Goode stuck a pen under the woman's nose. "Now *sign*, goddammit!"

She signed with a shaking hand, and Goode snatched the paper back, stuffed it into the envelope with the lab results, and finished with a disgusted shake of her head as a train thundered into the station. The man smiled: perfect timing, lots of people to cover up his attack. His thumb stroked the handle of the special knife in his pocket, as he slipped it into his hand. It would all be over soon, her heart punctured by the narrow blade. Goode had even worn a tight T-shirt, her ribs sharply defined against the fabric. Perfect. He'd be aboard the subway train she would never take, gone before she even realized she'd been stabbed. He could imagine the shocked surprise on the platform after she collapsed.

Jackie Goode, with the other woman clinging to her insecurely, stood to one side, as the doors of the train opened to disgorge another load of happy baseball fans. Icy calm, the man moved up behind Goode, his face a bland mask of indifference, and waited for the car to empty. Palming the knife, he removed his hand from his pants pocket and put it down against his leg. The car had almost emptied. Just a few more seconds . . .

The mousy woman pulled at Goode's arm. "Remember, you said you'd protect me. You said –"

The man put his thumb on the blade release.

Goode whirled, fury on her face. "No one protected my friend!" She rattled the envelope under the startled woman's nose. "But what's in here will allow us to slit their throats. Now go away and hide until this is all over!"

As Goode turned back towards the door, the man should have made his move.

Should have.

Instead, he froze momentarily, and his target stepped into the subway car. The doors were already sliding shut as the man recovered himself and ducked in. The train pulled out and the disgust on Goode's face was replaced by a grin of triumph as she slouched against the far door.

Jackie Goode had said something very interesting on that subway platform. If she'd spoken the truth, the people who had hired him were in big trouble, and people in big trouble were willing to pay big money to someone who could get them out of it. What was it to him to wait just a little bit longer before finishing her off? The man smiled with cold calculation. If he played his cards right, he could have his revenge on the girl *and* on that snot-nosed guy he'd had to deal with the past few weeks. His plan for the afternoon suddenly changed: he would get the envelope from Goode, then whack her. Was it a good trade not to kill her when he had the chance?

He settled into a seat as Goode took one across from him. Only time would tell.

CHAPTER 22

Just as Danny and I were about to leave, I remembered my promise to call Patrick about giving him directions to the rehearsal hall. He answered the phone after one ring, and I got the feeling he'd been sitting by it, waiting for me.

"How do you feel this morning?" he asked.

"Better, but I had a rotten sleep."

"Are we still on for later?"

"I guess so, but our rehearsal is going to run until at least 4:00."

"Can you tell me how to get there?"

"That's why I called. I'll put Danny on. He'll give you directions." I turned as Danny came up the last flight of stairs, having just taken my amp down to the van. "Get your butt over here! I need you to give some directions to my . . . to somebody."

I just couldn't pull the trigger on the word "boyfriend," and that bothered me all the way out to the studio. Was I trying to tell myself something?

The session went fine. We were in and out of Complete Sound before noon. After only an hour of rehearsing, the guys got the background vocals to "House" down in one take. One take! Wow! Nick had again stayed the night, done a lot of preliminary mix-down work, and simply dropped the new vocals into what he had. Fifty minutes later, it was done. The control room was incredibly quiet as the first playback of the completed song ended. All I could think was, *Holy mackerel! Did we do that? Wait till the people hear it! And Tory's fiddle playing!* Nick told us Arnie was worried she would forget to arrange things with her recording company, and he'd get hit with a massive lawsuit. I loved to see Arnie worry. He did it so well. It might be an idea to hire him to do my worrying for me.

Nick booted our asses out the door as soon as he'd made copies of the mix for everyone. Like a bunch of kids, we all piled into our vehicles and headed over to the rehearsal space, four vans in a row, with the same song blasting out of their stereos.

Carolina had told me the committee wanted thirty to forty minutes of music to warm up the crowd beforehand, then the big tune as the grand finale, and possibly an encore afterward. We figured we could manage that. Mind you, we'd be running mostly on luck and adrenaline with so little time to rehearse; even so, the band was going to be phenomenal live. The rapport we had in the studio carried over perfectly to the rehearsal hall. Danny talked me into doing "Mojo," complete with Link's solo, and it worked really well, even though Terry seemed to have the impression the song contained a drum solo. The rest of our set would be made up of the material we'd recorded so far, and the tune that Tory mentioned from that old demo tape of mine she'd heard in England, "Shot Full of Love." It was basically a cover version of the Juice Newton original, and had always been a favourite of the Babes, too. The guys were all familiar with it, so it didn't take long to pull the thing together. I decided to dedicate it to Tory at the gig.

We all felt we should have another tune in the bag in case we needed it, so I mentioned one of the first songs I'd written, back when I was eighteen, "You Can't Make Me Love You." I'd never found a way to do it that I thought worked with the sentiment of the lyrics. I tossed it out onto the floor, just to see what would happen, and the guys didn't disappoint. It was Frank's idea to give it a touch of that Memphis soul groove that sounds so good on a Hammond, and Terry thought we should make the feel just a little bit dirty, like a slow bump-and-grind. When the groove was really working well over the chord changes, I slung my guitar behind me, grabbed the mic with both hands, and started biting off and spitting out the lyrics of the first verse and chorus:

Don't stand there looking sad.
It's not like I said I wanted to go.
I just got caught off-guard by what you said.
I might feel it in time, this thing you already know.

You can't make me love you just 'cause you think I should.
I have to get there by myself or it simply wouldn't be any good.
Just because you feel a certain way, doesn't make it so.
Unlike passion and desire, which always rises like fire,
Real love just has to flow.

The arrangement was supposed to be all in fun, the complete opposite of what you'd expect the song to sound like if you read the lyrics, but suddenly I realized it was as if I'd been able to see twelve years into the future when I'd written the damn thing. It's meaning was *exactly* what I was going through at that moment.

I sang it with all the subtlety of a baseball bat in the face. Damn Patrick! Damn my friends who'd gotten this whole thing started!

My relationship with Patrick unreeled in my mind like a music video gone mad, and I felt as if my life was twisting agonizingly on the point of a very sharp knife. To be or not to be. I couldn't continue this way.

Near the end of the song, I spontaneously swung my guitar back around and whipped off a blistering lick that sort of summed up all the rawness of my emotional state. Danny picked up the meaning immediately, answering back with a series of notes that had a blues-tinged, pleading edge. And we were off in an exchange that lasted four or five minutes and left me totally limp at the end. The band loved it, telling me I was absolutely brilliant. I wasn't. I was simply pissed off.

"Hey, what's the female equivalent of testosterone?" Frank asked, "because Kit's sure got a bellyful of it today!"

The rehearsal broke up at 4:45. It had been really productive and the vocals especially were coming together. The guys' voices had a nice blend. Pulling together a forty-minute set in the time we'd spent was not too shabby. Nick, who'd dropped by for a while on his way home, informed us that he'd do the sound for the rally, good news as far as we were concerned. You don't want some idiot behind the board doing the mixing. Nick would also make sure they had a decent piano for the two songs Danny would play on it, although, considering the venue, it would have to be electric. Frank had decided to slug his Hammond B3 to the gig, since he lived nearby. ("Hell, I can almost roll it down the street!") By the time we finished, everyone felt completely done-in, and Terry, Frank, and Steve still had their regular Saturday gigs to go to. But they said it had been worthwhile and they'd see me at the rally on Monday.

Patrick had arrived about 3:45, and sat silently in the corner while we went through the set one last time. Then Danny and I ran down the two numbers we were performing on the radio the next day. "House" sounded really different with only two acoustics, and regressed to being more wistful than angry, but Danny pulled off some nice bottleneck licks, which gave it an interesting slant. On "Nothing without You," I took the solo, but because we'd done so much playing already, my hands felt really tired and, consequently, sluggish.

At the end of the song, Danny said with a laugh, "Stick a fork in her, she's done."

"Toasted," I confirmed, as I wiped my guitar down and put it away. Then I stretched, taking a deep, satisfied breath. "Patrick, do you know who won the ball game?"

"Red Sox," he said distractedly.

"Sorry you had to wait so long. Let's get out of here, but we'll have to stop back at my place for Shadow. My downstairs neighbour has been dogsitting all afternoon."

We packed our stuff, and Danny said he'd take my amp with him, since I wouldn't need it until Monday anyway. "See you tomorrow at the station," he said and gave me a peck on the cheek. "Great rehearsal."

"Great," I agreed. "Tomorrow at 6:00."

Patrick had emptied some stuff from the tiny trunk of his sports car, so he'd have room for my two guitars, which he loaded silently while I got myself strapped in. He hadn't said anything since his two-word answer in the rehearsal hall, and I began to wonder what the hell was eating him. An ugly thought crossed my mind as he got in next to me.

"Patrick, are you married or something?"

"Huh?" he said as if waking up. "What the hell are you talking about?"

"You're right out of it. Something's obviously really bothering you, and you said last night you wanted to lay your cards on the table. It just got me thinking."

"That I'm married?"

"You've told me next to nothing about yourself. I thought maybe you've been keeping something from me – something like a wife."

The engine roared to life, and he quickly pulled out into the late Saturday traffic. As we drove, I got more and more apprehensive. He finally reached over and patted my thigh.

"No. I'm not married, and I don't run around. There are no skeletons like that in my closet." I squeezed his hand with my legs, more as a prompt than anything. "I did some thinking on this problem you have with that rally and –"

"*I* don't have a problem! *You're* the one who has the problem with what I'm doing."

"Okay, okay. It's just that this whole thing is making me really . . . uneasy." He floored the car and I assumed we were getting on the 401. During the next half-hour, as we sped downtown, Patrick quizzed me on what the Babes had been up to. It was good to have a disinterested party – make that someone who wasn't directly involved – to bounce my thoughts off, and Patrick pointed out things that began to make me really concerned.

"So what do you figure is wrong with the development site?" he asked at one point.

"Pollution," I told him. "The soil's all screwed up."

"And how did you find that out?" He sounded shocked.

"My friend Marion discovered it, and we've found some records she made before she was killed."

"How much more do you know?"

"That they didn't do a soil analysis on one section of the site.

Then the correct results were suppressed when they did. Jackie and Carolina made a deal with someone, and now we have the initial soil-test results, which the bad guys didn't know existed."

"Do you realize how dangerous that could be? From what you've said, these people are not the kind you fool around with. Plus, they seem to have known an awful lot about what you and your friends are up to. Doesn't that concern you?"

"No. We've cut off their source of information." I told him about Paul.

"Are you positive enough to gamble your lives? Kit, you need my help. You can't hold onto those soil-test results until your rally on Monday. They're way too dangerous! I know people around town, and I can make sure this information gets to the right people *today*. Do you know where these records are?"

"Jackie has them. She was going to meet someone to pick them up."

"Do you know where she is now?"

I shook my head. "No, but I can find out quickly enough," I said, groping for his cellphone. "How do I use this damn thing?"

Patrick took it from my hand. "Here, let me do it. What's the number?"

I got Carolina's voice mail. It has two minutes of recording time, and I used it up – twice. "Whatever you do," I said at the end of the message, "if you have that file right now or as soon as Jackie gets back, don't play any cute games. Get it all to the nearest police station. I think we've been pretty damn stupid to think we could do it any other way. I'll call back later."

As I handed Patrick the phone, he said quietly, "I thought we decided I was going to help."

"No, we didn't. The cops are going to handle this. They should have from the beginning. I felt that all along, and let myself get talked into doing something different."

"Kit, I know about these things!"

"So do the cops!"

Patrick didn't say anything for several minutes, then out of the blue he asked the wrong question. "Are you still going through with this rally? There doesn't seem to be much point now."

"Rally *and* radio appearance," I corrected firmly, and told him about Danny's news from that morning.

"I just want you well clear of this mess."

"Thanks for your concern," I said, "but I can handle the heat."

We pulled up in front of my building. "Want to come up? I'm kind of tired. We could order out for something and have our talk."

As I started to get out, Patrick grabbed my hand. "Kit, you said you wanted to know more about me, and I told you I'm going to lay all my cards on the table. Let's get Shadow. I'm taking you somewhere."

"Where?"

"*My* apartment."

He hauled out the guitars and we headed upstairs. I checked the answering machine: no messages. Damn! It only took a few minutes to get back down. Shadow watered the hydrant in front of the building and then piled happily into the back of the car.

I ruffled the fur on his neck. "How's my big guy?"

He told me, *Just fine, thanks*, with one swipe of his tongue.

Patrick got in and we headed uptown.

When he pulled into a driveway, a doorman opened my side of the car and lent a hand to help me out. "Good evening, miss. Good evening, sir."

"Good evening, Howell."

"Will you be requiring your car again tonight?"

Patrick said, "I'm not sure yet."

"Very good, sir."

The doorman expertly flipped my seat forward, and Shadow barrelled out unceremoniously, knocking him into me.

"Don't you have any class, you big oaf?" I whispered into Shadow's ear as I fastened on his harness.

My dog's nails clicked loudly as we crossed the lobby, sending echoes bouncing back from every corner. I envisaged marble floors and walls and ceilings.

A deep voice spoke as we got to the elevator. "Good evening, sir. A business associate called for you while you were out."

"Thank you," Patrick answered briskly. "Did he leave a message?"

"It's on your voice mail."

When we got into the elevator, Patrick took a key from his pocket, inserted it into the control panel, and the elevator took off like a rocket ship trying to make escape velocity.

"How high up do you live?" I asked.

Patrick's answer sounded preoccupied. "Um . . . penthouse . . . thirty-fourth floor."

The elevator slowed and a bell dinged discreetly as the door opened. We crossed a small lobby, he unlocked a second door, and we walked into an area which I could tell at once must be enormous.

"*This* is your apartment?"

"'Fraid so. It's got a whale of a view of the city down to the lake, floor-to-ceiling windows – not that you'd care," he added with a smile in his voice as he we waded through the carpeting.

"Patrick . . . why didn't you tell me?"

"I don't talk about it. A lot of women would date a troll if he had the bucks." He moved away. "Want something to drink?" His voice came from quite a distance. "Beer? Wine?"

"Whatever," I said distractedly. "Just what do you do for a living?"

"I already told you: investment counselling, real estate, that kind of thing."

"But on what scale?"

"Big enough, obviously," he answered as he handed me a glass of chilled wine. "C'mon over and sit on the sofa." I took Shadow's harness off, and he began wandering around sniffing noisily. "Let me check my phone messages. I'll be right back." Patrick left the room for about five minutes. When he returned, he sat down next to me and said, "I spoke to Arnie today. I offered to buy out his share in you."

"What do you mean?"

"I buy him out and I get you a recording deal. Hell! We could even put out the recording ourselves."

I was shocked. "You'd do that for me?"

"Sure. I believe in you."

"Blame it on my suspicious nature, but what's the catch?"

Patrick put his arm around me. "No strings. We head off for New York or L.A., whichever you think will give you the better chance. You know, scope things out. My job can be done from anywhere."

Words failed me. "You're willing to pull up stakes and go off where I want to?"

He stroked my hair for a moment. "Yes. I just want to be with you."

"But we hardly know each other!"

He went on as if I hadn't spoken. "How about leaving tomorrow night? We could hop a plane to Vegas, maybe the Bahamas for a few weeks –"

"Hel-*lo*! Back up the dump truck. I have to play on the radio, remember?" I turned away from him. "That's what this is all about, isn't it? You just don't want me to play at that rally!"

He pulled me back against him. "Kit, Kit, it isn't that way." He kissed my neck and said softly into my hair, "You don't need that rally for your career; you don't need Arnie; you don't even need that band. I can take care of it all."

I pulled away again. "Patrick, I appreciate what you're willing to do, but I don't want to be your Pia what's her name. You remember, she had no talent, but her loving husband financed everything? Do you understand? I want to make it on my own! Either I'm good enough or I'm not. I don't want things *bought* for me."

"I wouldn't be buying a recording deal for you. I'd be investing in your talent. Believe me, Arnie swung a pretty hard deal and that's because he thinks you're worth the bucks."

"Slow down! This is all moving way too fast for me. So you're suggesting that we just pack up and run away into the night?"

"Why not? I have the money. I've been thinking lately that it would be terribly romantic to just pick up and leave. Maybe go to France for the summer."

"*France*? Patrick, you're nuts!"

"Anything you want is fine with me," he said, then busied himself again with my neck and face.

Even though I was upset and not in the mood when he started in on me, things progressed quickly anyway. It was as if Patrick could switch on something inside me, and any hard decisions I'd made went right out the window. I felt like I was caught inside Robert Palmer's song "Addicted to Love."

We started on the sofa, and quickly moved to the floor. Eventually, we ended up on the vast acreage of Patrick's bed. I actually tried phoning Carolina at one point in the proceedings, although that was more because Patrick dared me to try, saying I wouldn't be able to concentrate enough to talk on the phone. He was pretty nearly right, though I didn't get a chance to put it to the test, since the line was busy. But it was really tough punching in the numbers.

At 9:00, we finally ran out of gas, and Patrick went to the study to make a phone call of his own. After he got off the line, he told me he'd like to take Shadow out for his evening walk.

"I should go too," I said from where I lay face down in the centre of the bed, trying to gather my wits – and resolve.

"No. You stay here." A chuckle came from deep in his throat. "You look too comfortable. Shadow and I have to have a talk anyway. After all, I hardly know *him*, do I?"

"I haven't agreed to anything yet, either," I reminded him. *And I don't think I will,* I thought as they left the apartment. Things had gotten way out of hand now. Maybe it was because Patrick was older or because he was a businessman – a very successful one, if this apartment was any indication – but he seemed to think I'd just be bowled over by his . . . offer.

Shadow had really taken to Patrick, and that was one thing I was glad about. He certainly hadn't felt that way about Robbie! It would be impossible for me to have any kind of long-term relationship with someone Shadow didn't get along with. But Shadow or no Shadow, I decided to tell Patrick that, at least right now, I just couldn't make the kind of commitment he wanted. I wanted to stay in Toronto *and* finish what I started. Would he be willing for us to go on like we had and simply let things follow their course – whatever that might be?

While the boys were out, I tried Carolina again. She picked up the phone halfway through the first ring.

"Kit, I got your message. Sorry I wasn't home. Edward and I were out doing a 20K run. Where are you? I've been trying your place for hours!"

"I'm with Patrick. Did you deliver that stuff to the cops?"

"No!"

"What do you mean no! *Are you guys crazy?*"

"I mean no we couldn't. Jackie hasn't come back. We don't know where the hell she is, and we're all absolutely frantic with worry!"

"Add me to the count," I said dully.

Patrick and I didn't have the chance to talk. I was dressed and waiting impatiently on a chair in the lobby when he and Shadow returned from their walk about half an hour later. I couldn't be anywhere but sitting at home, in case Jackie called or showed up. It was critical that she stop playing games and get that evidence to the cops. The more pieces of this puzzle we discovered, the more deadly the game seemed to become. Patrick had finally made me see that.

At least in the end I convinced Carolina to call Detective Morris and tell him Jackie was missing – if not the possible reason why. She and Edward (mostly Edward) were still clinging to the idea of the media shocker on Monday. Edward thought that maybe Jackie had run into trouble getting the lab tech to sign the affidavit he'd provided.

"And why is this affidavit so bloody important?" I'd asked.

"Well," Carolina had begun, "because we want to make sure we can prove it's authentic in case anything, um, happens to Judy."

"If it's *that* dangerous, didn't you stop to think that maybe *Jackie* might need a little protecting? You and Jackie and your goddam Nancy Drew games!"

I explained to Patrick what had happened, and he tried hard to talk me into staying. I explained again. Then he asked if he could stay with me, and I told him I really wanted to be alone. He pressed his case, but I remained firm. I'd decided not to be intimate with him again until we had everything out in the open. With Jackie God-knew-where, now just wasn't the time to get into that.

We got to my apartment door around 10:30. Patrick promised to be back at 5:30 the next evening to drive me to the radio station.

"If you hear from your friend Jackie, Kit, please call me immediately."

"I will." I gave his hand a squeeze. "I'm sorry about tonight. When all this is over, let's sit down and figure out where we're going."

I went up on tiptoes and kissed him lightly on the cheek. After closing the door, I stayed there with my back against it for a long time.

The night was spent dozing on top of my bed with the phone on my stomach. Carolina, who was out searching all Jackie's haunts, called several times to report the same result: no Jackie. Susan was pacing the floor at home, waiting for news about Jackie – or Paul. With each passing hour, we grew more desperate, fearing the worst. My two friends beat themselves up pretty badly, saying that they should have listened to me, that I'd been right about going to the police. I let them twist in the wind.

Towards dawn, I dozed off again, but my sleep was broken off abruptly by the sound of the downstairs buzzer. Thinking it might be Jackie, I shot across the living room, nearly tripping over Shadow.

"Who's there?" I said into the wall unit.

"Detective Morris. May I come up?"

He came up at a speed that indicated he'd taken the stairs two at a time and arrived at my door barely winded.

"Do you have news about Jackie?" I asked.

"I was hoping you could help me there."

I expelled the breath I didn't know I was holding. "In what way?"

"What's going on with you women? Ms. Graf calls me to say that she's afraid something has happened to Jackie Goode. Now, I don't have to be much of a detective to know she's not telling me the whole story. I figured you at least might give me the straight goods, no bullshit."

Since the opportunity had been dumped right in my lap, I seized it and did something I should have done days earlier: I told Morris everything.

He listened in silence, his racing pen my only accompaniment. When I finished, I expected an angry outburst. He merely sounded resigned.

"You've done the right thing by telling me, but I wish to God you'd done it sooner. I only hope your friend hasn't gotten herself killed."

"Can you do anything to find Jackie?"

"We put out an APB. That's the best we can manage under the circumstances. Do you know the name of this woman she was going to meet?"

"Judy something. Carolina probably knows her last name."

"Mind if I use your phone?" He punched in some numbers rapidly. "Brent? Ron. I want you to pick up that Graf woman and haul her ass into the office. I want to talk to her . . . What's that? . . . When? . . . You're sure? Positive ID? . . . Christ! Yeah, I'll be there right away." He mumbled "shit" under his breath as he put the phone down.

My heart was in my mouth. "It's Jackie, isn't it?"

"No. That guy you were telling me about from the Housing Department. Some people tramping through the woods up north found his car in the middle of a bog."

"And?"

"He was still in the front seat. Bullet in the head."

I was thoroughly preoccupied when I arrived at the radio station later that day. Probably I should have cancelled out. Something like a live on-air performance takes massive amounts of concentration, and all day long my brain had been chewing over just about everything *but* the music I was going to perform. Nobody had heard from Jackie in over twenty-four hours.

After asking if I'd had any news, Patrick had been sullenly quiet during the short drive over. He'd called three times during the day, concerned about Jackie's continuing absence, but our conversations had been short, because I didn't feel like tying up the phone in case there was any news. I knew how much he felt my connection with the Save Regent Park Committee was a bad idea – but tough. I had told him I was going through with it, and that was that. If he wanted us to continue as an item, he'd have to get used to me doing what I felt was correct. Besides, I knew more about the music business than he did. Right?

Patrick got me as far as the reception area, where he gave me a quick kiss and went back out to find a parking place. We'd left my unhappy pooch at home. I'd had visions of Shadow barking during the performance or knocking over a mic, one of those clumsy things he excels at.

Danny had arrived ahead of me and was busy chatting up the engineer and LC, the producer. Carolina and Edward came in shortly after – neither of them happy. The reason soon became apparent.

Carolina grabbed me by the arm, hustling me straight into the ladies' washroom. "Just what the hell did you think you were doing?" she hissed, still clutching my arm. "That detective had me down at the station most of the day!"

I angrily shook her off. "Back down, girl! Maybe you don't like it that I told Morris, but have you stopped to think that maybe I haven't liked what *you've* been trying to do? Did they tell you that Rex guy is dead? Somebody put a bullet in his head. And it's a good bet that all your screwing around may have cost Jackie her life, too!"

Carolina turned away and said quietly, "I thought about that all last night and all day today. Edward and I have driven to every place I could think of, trying to find her. Nobody's seen her; nobody's talked to her. She seems to have vanished off the face of the earth."

"I hope to God she hasn't vanished into a bog somewhere."

Carolina groaned. "Kit, what are we going to *do*?"

"What I did this morning. Let the pros handle it. We're in way over our heads."

"Deep doo-doo," she agreed.

Somebody pushed open the washroom door. "C? Kit? You in here?" It was Susan. "I'm on my way to the police station. Morris wants to talk to me. Any idea what's going on?"

"Morris came by my place this morning, looking for more information," I told her, "so I gave it to him."

Susan sounded shocked. "Everything?"

"Everything."

"Paul finally called last night." Susan's voice had a dead quality as if all her emotions had been cauterized, firmly segregated from everything she was going through.

"What happened?"

"I told him . . ." Her voice faltered, then she continued, "I told him he had to tell me everything that had been going on, that the time for lies was over if he wanted my help. So he did. Marion went to Paul to ask his legal opinion on what she'd found out about Riverside. That was about a month before she died and way after their little fling."

"A month? You mean she'd been on to it that long?"

"That's what Paul said. He also knew who these developers were, and realized that the information he'd been given by Marion was worth money. And he certainly needed that to bail himself out of the financial hole he'd gotten us into." She choked back a sob. "He sold Marion out to the Riverside people."

"Did Paul know they would use the information to kill her?" Carolina asked gently.

"No. He says he thought they were only going to try to get the evidence back. As a matter of fact, he's in denial about the whole thing. He still thinks the Back-Door Strangler murdered Marion." Susan stopped. Talking about this was obviously almost more than she could bear. "Paul was the one who got her out of the way when they searched her apartment and he told them where they should look for the information they wanted. The price for that little service was all the journal entries that named him as her lover – so I'd never find out. But that's not the worst part."

"I know. He should have gone to the police, but didn't."

"No, no, *no*! Even after Marion was murdered, he still told them about Jackie."

"In God's name, *why*?"

"More money," Susan said simply.

I shook my head at the sheer stupidity of a man I'd assumed was reasonably intelligent. "Do you know the name of the person Paul gave the information to?"

"No. He said he'll only tell the police – if they cut him a deal."

"That's his plan?" Carolina asked.

"Yes, and I don't really care. He didn't know what would happen when he told those people about Marion, but he must have when he told them about Jackie. He has to pay for that." Susan stopped for a moment to pull herself together. "He's arranging a meeting with a top criminal lawyer he knows. They're certain they can get a deal. A short prison term in exchange for the name of the person he gave the information to."

"Sweet Jesus . . ."

"He says that he got in over his head, that he made some stupid, stupid decisions, and he's deeply sorry for everything that's happened." Sue again snuffled back a few tears. "He's been so stressed out, I don't think he knew what he was doing, but he told me he still loves me and needs me. He just has to get some things straightened out."

"What are you going to do – about Paul, I mean," Carolina asked gently.

"Because of him one of my best friends is dead and another may be. And he weaselled the information that got them killed from me! What do you think I'm going to do?"

—∞—

THE SUBWAY TRAIN PULLED INTO BLOOR Station. The man had been carefully watching his target since he'd followed her on at Union Station. She'd only stared moodily out the window at the lights flashing by in the tunnel, her victory smile long gone. Each time they got to a station, she might look around for a moment or two, but once the doors closed again she'd go back to staring out the window. As soon as she'd got on the train, Goode had shoved the envelope down the front of her jeans and tucked her teeshirt over it. He sat there fingering the knife in his pocket.

The doors opened. A large number of people stepped off before even more began crowding in. Goode got up, and the man was immediately alert. Then she seemed to think better of it and started to sit down again. Just as he relaxed, she sprang for the doors, barely squeezing through sideways before they shut. The man couldn't move fast enough. He was trapped on the wrong side. He pounded them hard one time in frustration.

So close, *so close*!

He looked up. Jackie Goode stared at him from the other side of the glass, the tiny smile back on her face and a taunting look in her eyes. As the train began to move, she stuck up her middle finger and disappeared into the crowd of Saturday shoppers.

Bitch, bitch, bitch, bitch, *bitch*! Ever since he'd heard the name Jackie Goode, everything had been messy, sloppy, disorganized! How could he let the cow make such a complete fool of him? She made him look like a rank amateur!

Angry people make mistakes, he reminded himself. The man sucked a few deep breaths into his lungs and his heart rate backed down a bit. *Think!*

He went through everything, carrying on an inner conversation with himself. *All right, she's carrying something valuable. First, you have to let your contact know. Then you strike a bargain. Make them pay through the nose. Okay. But then comes the tricky part: she knows you're after her and she knows what you look like. What will she do? Where will she go? The cops? No, that's not the way she operates. The house in Cabbagetown? Not likely. If she was smart enough to spot you, she's smart enough not to go there. Where then? One of her other friends . . .*

At the next phone booth, he shoved in a quarter and dialled. It rang until the answering machine clicked in. "Leave a message."

"It's me," he said. "You got a big problem. Call me. I should be home by 2:00."

The phone was ringing as the man entered his apartment at 1:58. "Yeah?"

His contact sounded almost human for a change. "You left a message to call."

"Ever hear of a company called Sloane Environmental?"

The voice was instantly wary. "Maybe."

"Would it interest you to know that Jackie Goode met today with a woman who works there? They were discussing the contents of an envelope the woman brought with her."

A long pause followed before the voice asked, "What was in the envelope?"

"Does something about tests done on soil samples ring a bell?"

Through the phone, the man distinctly heard the sound of something shattering against a wall. "There was supposed to be no trace– You're sure about this?"

"Do you want the envelope?"

"Of course we do!" his contact exploded. "Where has Goode taken it?"

"I don't know. We got separated in the subway."

"When can you get it back?"

"As soon as we make a new deal." Saying that felt good! He'd been wanting to make the little piss-head squirm ever since the phone call when he'd forced him to take on the assignment of whacking Jackie Goode. And he could tell his pal on the phone was squirming real good now. "Seventy-five thousand, deposited immediately in my Swiss account, another seventy-five grand on completion."

"I'll have to clear it first and that will take time we haven't got. Look, you find Goode and kill her. Get that envelope. Make sure no copies were made. You must be pos-itive! Is that clear? Call me when you've got it and we'll talk money then."

"No, and be certain you'll see photocopies of whatever's in that envelope on every telephone pole from here to Vancouver if I don't get my money. Leave a message on my machine when we've got a deal." The contact started to say something, but the man hung up and didn't answer the phone when it rang again almost immediately.

Now to find Jackie Goode one last time. When he did, he'd slit her from throat to crotch and watch with pleasure as her life spilled out.

CHAPTER 23

—◆—

O ne thing seemed obvious to me. "Having the name of the person Paul sold that information to would go a long way to solving all our problems," I said to Susan.

"I tried to get him to tell me," she answered, "but he refused. It's pretty clear Paul's terrified of him. He was all set to make a run for it, and only came to me to see if I'd give him some money. It was everything I could do to get him to agree to call in this lawyer friend."

"Murkier and murkier," Carolina intoned. "I can't believe that I listened to Jackie over you, Kit. What was I thinking? Okay, Sue. I'm coming along with you to see Morris. You shouldn't have to do that on your own. There are more important things than Riverside. Edward will just have to do the interview for me. He loves the sound of his own voice anyway." She laughed tightly. "I am sorry we can't stay to hear you, though, Kit."

"I'm sure the station will be taping it."

"Suppose we meet back at your place later? Maybe Jackie will have surfaced by then."

Carolina's choice of words left me with a mental image I would rather not have had. I clung to her elbow as she led me back to the lobby, everything *but* the music I'd have to perform in a few short minutes churning around in my head.

My friends, blissfully unaware of the turmoil they'd caused, gave me twin pecks on the cheek, telling me to, "Break a leg."

"You must feel so betrayed by Paul playing you for information the way he did," I blurted out to Susan. "I feel just awful about this whole thing."

"Not as bad as I do," she responded, trying to sound light-hearted. "And if it's any consolation, that killer dog of yours took an almighty chunk out of Paul's arm. It apparently needed sixteen stitches."

I grabbed Susan and hung on tight. "Sue, I hope things work out."

"Maybe when things settle down, Aunt Kit and her dog can come out to the burbs to visit for a few days."

"I'd like that," I answered.

"Well, Sunshine," Danny said as my friends went out the door, "did you get your radio makeup all squared away in the wash-room?" I turned and gave him my best curl-up-and-die expression, and he added quickly, "Hey, sorry I asked!"

I shook my head, angry at myself. "It's not your fault." My legs felt wobbly all of a sudden, so I found a chair and sat down, rubbing my hands over my face. The mental cobwebs remained firmly in place.

Patrick finally strolled in as Danny was introducing me to the producer.

"Sorry that took so long. I figured the damn parking would be easy around here on a Sunday."

I didn't catch much of what LC told us about what we could expect, and without my being really aware of how it had happened, she soon had me on a chair, guitar in hand, mics at the ready, in one of the two studios at the station. Then she asked us to run down our songs so the engineer could get a read on the levels and balance the guitars with our voices. I could hardly play, let alone sing, and Danny started to freak out, thinking I was doing the Big Choke. We actually broke down in the middle of "Nothing without You."

He leaned over and put his hand on my shoulder. "Kit, are you okay?"

I was angry with myself for not being able to concentrate, and with my friends for piling all this shit on me just before I had to play the most important gig of my life. "Leave me alone!" I snapped. "I'll be all right. Worry about yourself."

Feeling a little better for releasing some of my anger – even if it was at someone who didn't deserve it – I counted in to the song again. This time I managed to focus more successfully. During the last verse, I nodded forward, using a little body English to add more emphasis to the lyrics, and bashed my nose hard on the mic. While I sopped up the blood with Danny's guitar cloth, Ted, the engineer, suggested I try one of those headsets the DJs use, which has the mic attached. Danny thought I looked hysterically funny with one earpiece on, one off to the side, and this stubby little mic in front of my face. Who cared? The jolt and the accompanying embarrassment had knocked me even more into the headspace I needed.

Just as we finished our run-through, Charley Austin, the Sunday afternoon DJ, came out of the studio next to ours and tapped me on the shoulder. I jumped a mile.

"Sorry, Kit. I, ah, forgot." He sounded embarrassed. "Look, I've got somebody on the request line who says she's gotta talk to you. Someone named Jackie? Says it's urgent."

"Jackie? I'll take it!" He led me into the control room, punched a button, and handed me the receiver. "Jackie?"

"Kit, thank God! It was just lucky I heard your name on the radio. I've been calling everywhere, and no one's at home."

"Where are you? We've all been incredibly worried. Are you all right?"

"I'm in a little trouble. Someone followed me yesterday. I'm not positive, but I think I saw him the other day at that restaurant. He got onto the subway at Union Station with me. I could tell by his reflection on my window that he was watching me. When we got to Bloor, I dodged out, and he got left behind in the car. God, you should have seen his eyes!"

"Where were you all night? Why didn't you call?"

"I got a little spooked and lay low. Today I got someone I know to look at the papers. They're dynamite!"

LC tapped me on the shoulder. "Are you going to be much longer? Charley will be through with the Stop Riverside interview portion pretty soon."

I put the receiver back to my mouth. "Look, Jackie. There's a lot more going on than you know about. We have to talk. That file you got from Judy is really dangerous."

"I know. Can you imagine what those people at Advantage are –"

"You don't understand! Oh damn! It's too hard to explain and I can't talk now. We're going on the air in a minute. How long will it take you to get over to my place?"

"About half an hour, forty minutes max."

"Great. I'll call Carolina and Susan and have them get over there right away. I'll be home as soon as I get done here. Whatever you do, *don't leave the apartment*! Wait for us there."

"What's going on Kit? You sound as if you're ready to pee in your pants."

"I am. Promise me you won't leave."

"Kit!"

"Promise!"

"Okay. I won't leave."

"Good. I'll be there in about an hour. Carolina and Susan will be there sooner." I handed the phone back to LC. "Is Patrick still out in the reception area?"

"No. I'm right behind you."

"Patrick! That was Jackie on the phone. She's all right!"

"That's great news! Does she have those documents?"

"Yes. Look, Carolina and Susan are down with Detective Ron Morris at Police Headquarters on College Street. Got that? Ron Morris. Could you call and tell them Jackie's going to my apartment, and she's got that evidence with her? Morris should go, too. We'll join them as soon as I'm done here." I smiled more out of relief than anything else. "Sorry, I get a little speedy when I'm excited."

Patrick kissed my forehead. "I love it when you're excited."

LC said, "C'mon. We're ready to go."

"Showtime," I told Patrick. "Wish me luck."

I sat down. My focus was back, the fire was stoked high in my belly. We played "House" first, since Edward had just finished talking about it in the interview. I had to be careful the song didn't get out of hand from all the pumping adrenaline. As we vamped on the chorus at the end, Danny, catching some of my fire, pulled off a few terrific licks and finished with an inspired burst of harmonics over my final chord.

Charley burst into spontaneous applause. "And that's only the acoustic version, folks. Now, Kit, your producer tells me that Victoria Morgan played on the recorded version. I didn't know she did this kind of music. What's she like?"

"Inspired and inspiring."

"What do you mean?"

"When somebody like that is playing with you, it's hard for your own playing to be commonplace. She gets you to dig a little deeper, play a little better."

"How did you talk her into performing on your recording?"

"I didn't. That's the really weird thing. She offered."

Danny butted in. "Tory offered because she thinks Kit's a major talent. She told me on the way out to the studio that, even though Kit will never sing at the opera, her voice has more emotional depth than a lot of famous singers she could name."

Charley said, "I'll second that."

I was flabbergasted. No one had told me anything about Tory's comment. Danny was a real sweetie to bring it up in the interview. I guess I'll take croaky emotion over technical fireworks and sweet vapidness any day.

"Tell me, Kit," Charley went on. "Is Tory as wild as we've heard?"

I knew he was trying to get something newsworthy and, remembering what she'd told me, I side-stepped the question. "I've only spent a few hours with her. She's terrific fun to work with, if that's what you mean. Really loose. Nothing like what you would expect from a classical musician." During the rest of the interview, Charley asked the usual musician-type questions: when I started playing; who my influences were. "Danny Kutcher," I answered, and we all laughed. "He's only one of the special people I work with. Everybody will have a chance to hear the whole shootin' match tomorrow afternoon at 4:00 at Riverdale Park. And let me tell you, this band really kicks some butt."

After a bit more chatter (he asked about my blindness, and I flippantly told him it was only a problem when I drive), we did our other song ("Nothing without You"), and then Charlie played the recorded version of "House," probably so everyone could hear Tory.

"I want you to know how much I've enjoyed this, Kit," Charley said, winding things up. "Things are pretty quiet on Sundays, but you and Danny have certainly livened up the joint. Will you drop by when the album's finished and play a few tracks for us?"

"Be glad to, Charley. It isn't fair that the weekday guys get to have all the fun."

After he broke to a string of commercials, Charley came over from his adjacent studio and thanked us again. "I really did enjoy it. You've got some fine material."

"We appreciate the chance you gave us."

"No problem. By the way, the station asked if I would introduce you tomorrow."

"That'll be great!"

"They don't let an opportunity like you slip by. I think they have it in mind to be the exclusive station for one Kit Mason. You know" – he slipped effortlessly into a phony-sounding radio voice – "you heard it here first on – Oops! Gotta run. The commercial break's almost over. See you tomorrow aft!"

Danny and I wiped down our guitars, while the engineer cleaned up his equipment. My watch said it was past 7:45 by the time we got back to the reception area.

LC gave me a big hug. "You were really super, honey. At one point, I didn't think you were gonna pull it off."

"You weren't the only one," I agreed.

Danny rested his arm on my shoulder. "You gave me a few bad moments in there, kiddo, but you came through. We were good."

"Thanks in large part to you, Danny. Sorry about snapping at you." I gave him a big hug. "Has anyone seen Patrick?"

LC answered. "He left the control room just as you started playing. I thought he was listening out here." She crossed the carpet. "Door's unlocked too. He should have told me he was leaving."

"Maybe he went to get the car," Danny said. "He was complaining about having to park so far away."

"Maybe," I agreed, but I thought Patrick would have wanted to be there for my performance, and I was a little hurt, until I realized that he knew we had to get back to my apartment pronto. *That* was why he'd left to get the car so early. Concern crossed my mind, though. The station was not in the best part of town. As the minutes ticked by, I began to get actively worried.

Where was he?

———◊———

THE MAN FELT MORE NERVOUS THAN he had in a long, long time. He tried convincing himself that it was just the usual tension, but he knew he was lying. Carrying out a hit in this place under these circumstances was ludicrous. He also knew he didn't have any choice. The girl could identify him, and that could wreck everything. Besides, she had to pay for that insult in the subway.

He never would have imagined his last whack job would turn out to be the toughest. You had to hand it to the girl, she'd given him a real run for his money. But now the chase was over. There would be no escaping this time. He smiled, but there was something hollow behind his expression. The best thing that could happen would be somebody coming through that door over there, telling him it was time to leave, the whole thing had been called off. But Rod Serling was dead.

It hadn't taken much to get into the apartment and secure the dog. Now, all he had to do was sit back and wait for the mouse to step into the trap. Pulling his three specially made, extra-heavy throwing knives out of his jacket pocket and opening them, he ran his finger down the razor-sharp edges of each. Perfect for what he had in mind . . .

There was no thought of subtlety any more. The cops wouldn't swallow it being an accident, so why waste time on that? Kill the girl, get the papers, take the body, and dump it later. Not having a body would make it hard for the cops. Not having the papers would make it impossible for the anti-Riverside group. He would be long gone. Things just might work out yet.

He only hoped the girl would show up soon. He didn't have a lot of time.

Jackie charged up the stairs to Kit's apartment. Christ! She could be such a worrywart sometimes! You had to make allowances, though, Jackie decided with a sigh. It's not as if Kit had always been this timid, and she *had* been coming out of her shell the past few weeks. So much had happened since . . .

Marion flooded back into her consciousness, and Jackie's expression tightened. To think that somebody could almost get away with what had been done to Marion. The cops hadn't even let them bury her yet! Jackie had an image of her friend's body lying in a darkened room somewhere, waiting . . . waiting for Jackie Goode to bring the killers to justice. She patted her belly where the envelope containing the files lay next to her skin, and smiled. She was about to give birth to a whirlwind.

Yesterday had been a real roller-coaster ride: finally getting the information she needed and then outsmarting that whacko in the subway. Jackie didn't kid herself that the danger from him was frighteningly real, but she was a survivor, if nothing else. It wasn't hard to make yourself scarce if you'd had as much patience as she'd had. Even so, it had taken all her willpower not to call any of the Babes the previous evening. Having somebody who wanted nothing more than to kill you was a pretty frightening thing to face, especially alone. It was quite possible their phones were tapped. Maybe she was being paranoid, but better safe than sorry. All she had to do was lie low and she'd be okay. Now she was rounding third and heading for home with the winning run and nobody could stop her.

Kit had sounded so bent out of shape on the phone, totally forgetting that she'd taken away the apartment key several months earlier. Lucky that Jackie had retrieved it from Kit's night table first chance she got. Reaching into the right pocket of her jeans, she pulled out her key ring and fitted the key into the lock. Funny . . . Shadow should be at the door making his usual almighty racket. She could hear him barking, but it sounded distant. Bet he'd gone into the bathroom to drink out of the toilet and managed to knock the door shut again. Poor baby! Maybe she'd give him a beer while they were waiting for Mommy to get home – if there was enough time to get the smell off his breath.

Jackie had a big smile on her face as she walked into the apartment.

The man had picked a chair in the corner to sit on, one that gave him a clear throw, but didn't allow someone to see him when they first walked in. The damn dog was creating an infernal racket in the bedroom, making it hard to hear anyone coming up the stairs. He thought of shutting the dog up, but decided against it. He liked dogs, and this seemed to be a nice one – not that he'd want to get too close if it were angry, and it sounded angry right now.

The night before, he'd almost been ready to admit defeat. The girl had been too smart to go to any of the haunts he'd been told about. His only hope was that she'd resurface before the rally.

The voice on the phone had seemed confident she would. "She's conceited. She'll want to share her victory with someone, probably one of her friends. But when she does show, you'll have to move fast."

"I'm ready."

Now he was waiting in the darkness. Waiting for Jackie Goode.

Jackie's smile lasted until she flipped on the overhead light. Shadow was in the bedroom. With all his clumsiness, she'd never known him to get himself shut in there.

A movement caught the corner of her eye. She barely managed to turn her head before she was hurled back, incredible pain erupting in her left shoulder. Though her body wanted to collapse, it couldn't. Turning her head slowly left, she saw a knife buried to the hilt, skewering her shoulder to the wall.

The voice that came from across the room was flat, devoid

of all emotion. "Didn't think I'd be here waiting for you, Jackie, did you?"

Fighting down nausea, Jackie turned her head again. In Kit's rattan chair sat the man from the subway. She'd been found. Stupid, stupid, stupid! Now gut-churning fear mixed with the nausea and pain. Those chilling eyes . . . Behind them lay only death. This was no game, no flipping some clown the finger in a subway station.

With a groan she lifted her right hand and reached for the hilt of the knife. As she touched it, a thud and another searing pain jerked her back against the wall. A second knife now stuck from her right thigh.

"It's no use struggling. I still have one more knife." Delicately grasping it near the point, the man held it up for her to see. "You're trapped. No way out. Don't try to yell for help. With one flick, this knife will be sticking from your throat."

"What do you want?" she groaned.

The man shook his head sadly. "I wouldn't have expected such a stupid question from you." He examined the knife blade closely for a few moments. "Where are the papers?"

"What papers?"

The man got up and moved across the room in six fluid steps. He held the knife against Jackie's throat. "Don't be stupid. You don't *have* to suffer."

She forced herself to look in the man's eyes. "If you slit my throat, I won't be able to tell you, will I?"

"Better answer," he replied softly and held the tip of the knife against her right eyelid. "You want to be blind like your friend?"

"N-no." The thought of sharing Kit's dark fate suddenly petrified her. Only one way out. She must tell him. If he had the papers . . . She fought the pain down, the rising tide of darkness threatening to overwhelm her. "They're . . . they're where I put them yesterday."

He moved the knife down her cheek, its razor edge cutting a delicate line through the flesh. "Even better." With a quick movement, he grasped the front of her jeans, slit them down to her crotch and removed the envelope.

Jackie's vision swam. She was suddenly fourteen again, fourteen and helpless. Anger welled up in her, uncontrollable in its ferocity. Almost without thinking, she spit full in the killer's face. The room was silent as the man stared back at her. Even Shadow had stopped barking. Jackie's gaze was drawn to his eyes . . . how could anyone look into their depths and not be frozen by what they saw? A total lack of emotion.

Pulling a handkerchief from his back pocket, the man carefully wiped himself off. "That was rather stupid, considering what I could do to you before you die."

As he opened the envelope, the killer turned away so he could use the overhead light to see what lay inside. Jackie gathered her strength, and, biting down hard on her lip to keep the pain inside, made a desperate move.

It was almost over. But the cruelty he'd always held back, tried to deny, was there, flowing through his body like fire. It would be etched in his memory forever, how the first throw had skewered the girl to the wall. Now the anger he felt towards his victim made him wish he had more time. Her end should be artistic – and lingering. Even though he'd been taught how to do that, he'd always held back. It made the man even more angry that in the end the little bitch had brought it out in him.

This reaction both fascinated and repelled him. When a job was finished, he'd always quickly gone back to being normal, blending in with the crowd. He'd partitioned one section of his life from another, forgetting his work as soon as he got home. He couldn't say, "What do I do for a living? I murder people. But don't let that put you off, I'm really an okay guy." With a force of will, he began to overcome his rage. Better get this done and get out. But first he wanted to see what he was getting paid a hundred and fifty grand for.

He pulled the papers from the manila envelope: five sheets bearing the Sloane letterhead, one legal form, and a handwritten sheet covered with notes and names. Interesting . . . Nobody'd mentioned anything about a deed.

The man turned back to his victim, holding the paper up to her face. "What does this mean?"

The knee of her free leg lashed upward and caught him totally off guard with a hard, direct hit to his groin. The force of the blow knocked him backwards, and he lay dazed and breathless from the excruciating pain. His knife had fallen near the sofa. In disbelief, he stared as Jackie reached up, wrenched the knife from her shoulder, then slowly sagged to her knees, the bloody weapon dangling from her right hand. The one in her leg was already out. He could see its handle, partially covered by her T-shirt, sticking out of her right-hand pants pocket. She must have done that while he'd been absorbed in the documents. How could he have done something as amateur as turning his back before she was dead? He deserved the kick in the nuts.

The man threw himself towards his third knife. The girl half dove, half fell on him, landing on his legs. He turned to parry the thrust she aimed at his chest with *his own knife*, and their eyes met. Gone was the fear, the deer eyes of the suffering victim. He saw only consuming hatred.

Easily knocking her arm off its swinging arc, he rolled quickly to the side, and the knife went skittering across the floor. He tried sliding across to it, but she was all over him like a demon, pulling his hair, her knees jabbing into his back, screaming at him in a banshee wail. As he stretched his arm out for the knife, she bit him hard in the ear, almost severing it. He yelled more from shock than pain.

She flipped herself off him, and, as he rose to throw himself to the side, their eyes met again. Squatting with her weight on her good leg, she held the second knife in one hand while steadying herself on the floor with the other. The left side of her body was covered with blood. Her face was blanched, as if the red flood came directly from there. He knew she was losing the battle against her wounds.

Victory could still belong to him. Goode's injuries were impairing her movements, and she was no match for his skill in hand-to-hand combat. He was straightening up, getting ready to attack, when she sprang forward like a missile. The knife, gripped tightly in front of her, buried itself deep into the base of his throat, severing the jugular vein. The force of her leap carried him over backwards, and she landed heavily on his chest.

The killer's eyes slowly glazed over as the blood fountaining upward from his neck mingled with her own. His body heaved in a massive shudder and then lay still. Overwhelming tiredness washed over Jackie. Her chest heaved from the exertion of that final desperate leap, and she realized she was fading fast.

Have to warn Kit, she thought fuzzily. *Have to make sure she keeps the papers safe.*

Thank God she'd been able to get the guy. If Kit had walked in with him there . . . She squeezed her eyes shut, trying to keep those thoughts out of her head.

She rolled off the man, groaning with pain as she hit the hard surface of the wood floor. She lay for a while, gathering her remaining strength, then slowly dragged herself forward to where the precious papers lay by the sofa. A rivulet of blood had reached them first, and one had already begun absorbing its crimson colour.

She lifted that one up and shook it, then slowly gathered the others. With the papers clutched in her hand, Jackie pulled herself painfully towards the apartment door, leaving a bloody smear in her wake. As she reached her goal, darkness finally engulfed her.

CHAPTER 24

I waited in the lobby, holding my guitar case, anxious to be on my way. Jackie and the others would be waiting at the apartment by now; the nightmare was almost over. I was just on the point of asking Danny to go out and look for Patrick, when the man himself entered and swept me up in his arms.

"Where've you been?" I asked. "I've been getting worried!"

"The pressure was getting to me. I had to listen from the car."

"How come you didn't come back in when we finished?"

"I wanted to get you flowers, but I couldn't find any place open. I'm sorry."

"That's all right," I said as he put me down. "Well?"

"Well what?"

"How *was* it, you oaf?"

"Okay," Patrick replied with a verbal shrug, then burst out laughing. "You were sensational! And you sounded good being interviewed, too. Very natural."

"So you admit that it went well?"

"Very well."

"And that I can handle my own business, that I know what I'm doing? Do you see now why I've been getting sore at you?"

"Yes, Kit, I see. I see that you're more than a match for me. I hereby capitulate."

"My, you're in a good mood."

"Life is good." He laughed again. "Do you have an answer to my question yet?"

"What question?"

"About running away with me."

"Patrick," I said, lowering my voice, "give me a chance to breathe! We can talk about this later. I have to get back to my apartment. Everyone's waiting. Good night, Danny," I called across the reception area to where he stood talking to LC. "See you at one o'clock tomorrow for the sound check. And thanks for everything, LC. It was great!"

Patrick had the car right out front. "Your chariot, my dear."

The drive back to my place lasted only about ten minutes in the light Sunday-evening traffic, but it seemed to take forever. Then, the entire city had decided to park on my block.

"Damn!" Patrick said in frustration. "This sure isn't my day for parking. I'll let you out here and go find a place. Okay?"

"No problem. Just point me in the right direction."

I grabbed my guitar from the back and he took me to the door. "I'll just be a couple of minutes," he said.

As I started up the second flight of stairs, I could hear Shadow barking hysterically.

"What the hell are those idiots doing to him now?" Then I realized that it didn't sound like the big goof was playing. He was upset.

I took that last flight two steps at a time, skidding to a halt at the top. From my half-open door, a hideous stench – excrement mingled with something else I couldn't identify – sent a chill down my spine. The door banged into something when I pushed, something that groaned. I put my guitar down and slid around the edge of the door. Reaching out, my hand touched wet fabric, a woman wearing a teeshirt. Jerking back, I realized what the horrible smell must be. Reaching out again, I found short, spiky hair, sticky with coagulating blood.

"Jackie? What's happened? Have you been *shot*?"

She groaned again when I spoke, and hit me in the face with a handful of papers. A mumbled phrase escaped her lips.

"What is it, Jackie? What are you trying to tell me?" I bent over, putting my ear right above her mouth.

Her slow, wheezing breath tickled my cheek. "The papers, Kit, hide . . . the papers. He mustn't get . . . them . . ."

Her voice trailed off, and her hand dropped back to the floor. I felt the side of her throat. Her pulse was slow and her breathing shallow. I pounded the floor in frustration. What in God's name had happened? If she was in *this* kind of shape, why did she still have the papers? I folded them swiftly, and without another thought, shoved them into the back pocket of my jeans.

Jackie needed help – and fast. Where the hell was Patrick?

An ambulance. Dial 911. Crawling over to the sofa, my stomach churned as my hands became sticky with the blood that seemed to cover the entire floor. The stench of it, mixed with urine and feces, made my head swim. The end table that usually held the phone had been knocked over, but I found the cord without much trouble. Following it, I discovered the phone underneath the sofa, but the handset uttered no comforting dial tone.

Shadow, hearing my voice, had set up an even greater racket from the bedroom. They must have locked him in there while they waited for Jackie. Thank God nothing had been done to him. I thought about using the phone in the bedroom, then decided I might not be able to control Shadow, given the state he was in.

"Damn!" I said explosively, then took a steadying breath. "Think, meathead! Gerald said he was going out. Nobody else must be around, either. Where were Carolina, Susan, and the rest of them? Okay. You'll have to go down to Guido's."

Where was Patrick?

As I felt my way back to the door, I finally heard footsteps on the stairs. "Patrick! Anybody! I need help! Something awful's happened."

A comforting voice answered. "I'm coming, Kit. Sit tight!" I held on to the door so Patrick wouldn't slam it into Jackie. He slid into the room and stood, frozen. "Jesus Christ! Is she dead?"

I felt her neck again. "No. She's still with us, thank the Lord."

"And what about the man?"

"*What man?*"

"There's a man about five feet to your left, and judging by the knife sticking out of his throat, I'd say it's a good guess *he's* dead."

As Patrick went over to check the dead man, involuntarily my hand went to my mouth. I must have just about put it on the guy. Patrick spent a moment examining the body. I heard the rustle of fabric. "He's dead all right."

"How badly is Jackie hurt?" I asked.

Patrick checked her over for a several moments without saying a word. I could hear the rustling of fabric again.

"Patrick, speak to me! How bad is it?"

"She has a stab wound in her thigh and a slit down one cheek, but her left shoulder looks the worst."

"We have to get her to the hospital!"

"Have you called an ambulance?"

"The phone's broken. I found it under the sofa. What are we going to do?"

"Just stay calm, Kit!" Patrick said sharply. "Let me think for a moment!" He walked around me to where the body of the man lay. "Okay," he began slowly, sounding more like he was talking to himself. "It'll save time if I take her to the hospital myself. I can use the cellphone in the car on the way. But first I'll fix up some kind of pressure bandage for the wound. It'll slow the bleeding. Why don't you wash your hands?" He got a dish towel from the kitchen and worked on Jackie's shoulder, while I scrubbed myself at the sink. "Help me lift her up," he said as I came out of the kitchen. "Do you know the fireman's-chair carry? That should be the easiest on her."

Even though we slid our arms as gently as we could under Jackie's back and knees, she groaned loudly as we clasped hands and lifted. He kicked the door open, and we started down the stairs with careful speed.

"I don't understand why Carolina and Susan and Morris aren't here yet. You spoke to them directly?"

"Yes. They said they'd be right over. Something must have held them up."

I shook my head. If I hadn't told Morris what was going on, the girls would have stayed at the studio and could have come right over. *That* brought me up short. Who knew what would've happened if they'd all been there?

Patrick had parked behind the building in the alley. He kicked the crash bars on the rear exit, and we moved into the cool night air. Removing the arm he had under Jackie's knees, he opened the door on the passenger side.

"Shift her over to me and I'll put her in the front seat." He got Jackie settled in the seat, then turned back to me. "The best thing for you to do would be to wait here for your friends."

"No way! I'm going with you."

"Kit, that's ridiculous. What good could you do at the hospital? There's not even space for you. Wait here. You can come with them later."

I stumbled my way around to the driver's side of the car and wrenched open the door. "If there's room for Shadow, there's room for me!" Patrick tried to stop me as I climbed in the space behind the front seat, but I shook him off roughly. "We're wasting time!"

"Have it your way," he said as he got in, started the engine, and eased his car down the alley to Queen, where we turned left. Accelerating rapidly, we turned right almost immediately, then left again a few moments later.

"Where are we going?" I asked.

"St. Michael's."

"Why didn't you take Queen?"

"Adelaide's quicker."

I kept one hand on Jackie's chest, so she wouldn't fall forward if we stopped suddenly. Her breathing seemed slightly improved, and her heartbeat felt no weaker. I began to feel less anxious about her condition.

"How does Jackie look?" I asked

"Her colour's a bit better. Did she tell you anything before I got upstairs? Anything at all?"

"She was out of it when I got there and she only mumbled something about hiding the papers."

"Papers?"

"Something like that. I don't remember too clearly what was going on. I was pretty freaked out."

"Think, Kit! It's important!"

"I don't remember!"

Jackie stirred and moaned weakly.

I stuck my head between the seats. "It's all right, Jackie. We're taking you to the hospital. Don't worry, they'll fix you up. Patrick, we should be there by now. What's taking so long?"

"I missed my turn while we were talking. I've had to go a few blocks out of the way because of these damn one-way streets. Hang on!" He gunned the engine and soon made several sharp turns.

Jackie gripped my hand hard as Patrick braked to a stop. "No, not here," she gasped weakly.

Patrick said, "I'll come around and lift Jackie out, then we'll go park, okay?"

"No. I'll help you get her inside. I want to be with her."

"Kit, it's not necessary. I can manage."

"I'm staying with my friend!"

As Patrick was walking around the car, Jackie shocked me by saying fairly clearly, "Kit, don't leave me alone. For God's sake, don't leave me alone!"

I gave her hand a squeeze. "Don't worry. I'm here for the duration."

Patrick opened the door and lifted Jackie. I climbed out and stretched the kinks from my back.

"No, not here," Jackie moaned again.

"Patrick, wouldn't it be better to get somebody out here with a stretcher?" I asked.

He sounded perturbed. "It's only a few steps."

I stumbled along behind them to the door anyway. As soon as we got inside, Patrick put her down – *on the floor*!

"Patrick, what the hell are you doing?"

"You wouldn't listen to me for a change, would you?" he snapped as he grabbed my wrist. "You had to come along. Now everything has turned to shit!" He began pulling me along.

I dug in my heels and yanked back. My hand slid free. "Have you gone crazy?" I shrieked.

Patrick let go. "Suit yourself. You can wait here," was all he said. He must have gone out. I heard the snick of a lock.

Call me incredibly slow, but it finally hit me. This was no hospital. It smelled all wrong: old, musty, disused, and it was very cold. Where had Patrick taken us?

His car started up and crunched slowly away on a gravel road or something.

"Patrick!" I yelled. My words echoed strangely, as if I were in a small room but right outside was a much, much larger one. I knelt next to my friend. "Jackie can you hear me? What's going on? Where the hell are we?"

Jackie's voice was weak, but still vibrated with anger. "He's going to kill us! I told you to . . . hide the papers. He must have found them."

"No, you're confused! That guy is dead. This is Patrick, the man I've been going out with. He wouldn't hurt you, but I don't know why he brought us here. We're supposed to be at the hospital!"

"Kit . . . Listen to me." Jackie took a few deep breaths and when she spoke again her voice sounded stronger. "This is Riverside. We're in an old warehouse."

I wanted to be able to deny it. Something flickered across my brain, disappearing again before I could grab it, but with a jolt in my gut, I knew she was right. "We have to get out of here."

"Can't . . . sitting ducks . . . outside." Jackie coughed, then groaned loudly. "God, it hurts!" She turned her head. "We need to find . . . place to hide. By the door is a box . . . Handle on . . . the side. Shuts off lights."

Good idea. In the dark we'd have a better chance. I felt my way back to the door. I found the box to the left, about head-high. Grabbing the handle on its right side, I yanked down hard, smashing my fingers on the metal case in the process. "Shit!"

Jackie said, "Okay . . . Lights are out. Open the box . . . Carefully reach into it . . . You'll find . . . long fuses."

"Yes. I remember what they look like."

"Jerk one out. He won't be able . . . turn lights . . . back on . . . But . . . be careful. Live wires . . ."

I carefully grabbed a fuse with my right hand, braced myself against the wall with my left and yanked. The fuse came free with a *sproing*, and I fell hard on my butt. The fuse skittered away. After getting my bearings, I cast around with my hands where I had heard it land, and found it about five feet behind me. As I stuck the fuse in my back pocket, my hand touched Jackie's precious papers. I'd forgotten all about shoving them there. And Patrick had been asking about them . . .

I crawled back to Jackie, finding her by her raspy breathing. "How do you feel?"

"Like shit. . . . Have any Aspirin?"

"You're crazy." I said, laughing softly. "Where do you think Patrick went?"

"Couldn't leave his car . . . where it was. Would attract attention."

"We can't sit here. Did you see anything when the lights were still on that might help us?"

"Not a lot. There's . . . empty warehouse . . . outside room."

"Can you walk?"

"No. Leave me here. Find . . . someplace to hide . . . Keep the papers away . . ."

Jackie had been speaking very slowly and carefully, apparently putting all her effort into staying conscious. Feeling around her left shoulder, I discovered the flow of blood had slowed because of the towel Patrick had tied around it back at the apartment. Obviously he hadn't wanted her to bleed to death before she could tell him about his goddam papers. It was pretty gross when my finger slipped into the slit the knife had made. I retied the towel a little more tightly. Jackie's leg was still bleeding pretty badly, but there was no time to do anything about it. I had to get us some place safe in a hurry.

"I'm not going to leave you."

Jackie didn't answer. I figured she'd passed out again, so it would be okay to lift her in an over-the-shoulder carry. She'd be quite a load, but I felt I could manage. Hell! I *had* to manage. Patrick could be back any minute.

I manoeuvred Jackie over one shoulder, but had to half drag her, because I needed a hand to feel my way. Shuffling carefully forward, I located a wall and followed along it to the door that led to the larger room. Then I stopped. I had absolutely no idea what was ahead of me.

"Hey!" I shouted, and the reverberating sound told me the room was BIG. "Think, Mason! Use your brain!" I said to myself. "You don't have a cane or your dog."

Shadow.

The thing nagging at the back of my mind finally broke free and surfaced. Somebody had shut Shadow into my bedroom, someone he had to know well – and trust. It couldn't have been the killer. Shadow would've eaten him alive. Jackie wouldn't have done it. It would've had to have been . . . Patrick, my shithead of a crooked lover! He hadn't been out listening to my radio performance in his car. He'd been clearing the way for the killer to wait for Jackie. Why? How did he fit in?

My cogitations were brought to a screeching halt by the sound I'd been dreading: footsteps approaching the outside door. At that point I did the scariest thing a blind person can do. *I ran forward with no idea of what was in front of me.*

By the time I'd gotten about twenty steps and still hadn't slammed face-first into anything, the outside door opened, and even though every nerve in my body screamed out *keep running*, I froze.

Patrick muttered, "Jesus Christ!" He tried the lights. "Goddammit, Kit! Where the hell are you?"

Hearing the anger vibrating in his voice brought me up short. This man was extremely dangerous. At the radio station I'd *told* him exactly where Jackie would be and then stupidly made sure she'd be alone. He'd tried to have her killed, and I had no doubt he wouldn't hesitate to kill both of us now.

But he'd also said he cared for me.

Patrick went out the door again, probably to get a flashlight. With tears burning my useless eyes, I shuffled my way slowly forward maybe a hundred feet, eventually reaching the opposite wall. I was sure by that point that the building was empty. It would only be a matter of time before Patrick returned with a light. Since there was no place to hide, he'd soon catch us in its beam like a couple of butterflies being spiked to a display board.

Anger blazed in me. I wouldn't give up. There *had* to be a way out!

My back ached under Jackie's weight. I wouldn't be able to carry her much longer. Turning left, I felt my way as quickly as I dared along the brick wall. I'd gone a fair distance when my hand discovered a railing coming from the wall at a right angle. After about eight feet, it turned and led me eventually to a flight of stairs.

Without a moment's hesitation, I started down. The cold air of the derelict building got a lot colder.

At the bottom I found a metal door, which grated noisily when I pulled it open. The air inside smelled even more of dust and neglect, but also of wood and cardboard. With one hand out in front of me, I carefully shuffled forward another ten feet and came to a stack of cartons.

Praise the Lord, my prayers have been answered, I thought. *Cover.*

Despite the fact that I slipped Jackie as gently as I could onto the concrete floor, she groaned loudly. I slapped my hand over her mouth, because I could now hear careful footsteps on the floor above. Dickhead must have returned.

Moving as quickly as I dared, I again shuffled carefully forward, hands waving in front, and soon discovered a corridor extending out into the room, lined with piles of cartons, crates, and steel drums. I could get no idea how big the room was, because I didn't dare make a sound to use my echo-location abilities. But I wasn't about to complain. Better junk, than more emptiness. Hoping I was heading in the right direction, I moved a little more quickly back to where I'd left my wounded friend.

"Jackie!" I said softly into her ear. "Are you with me?"

Her voice came out more like a sigh. "Yeah . . . I guess so . . . I hurt, therefore I am."

I grinned despite myself. Severe injury seemed to bring out the humour in her. "I've got us down into the basement. I think Patrick's upstairs. At any rate, I can only hear one set of footsteps. Are the lights still off?"

"Yes. Unless I've gone blind, too." She shuddered.

"Cold?"

"Yes, but it's not that. The guy . . . the one I . . . He wanted to make me like *you.*"

"What do you mean?"

"Blind."

"Make you blind? How?"

"With his knife. He . . . touched his knife to my eyelid." Her hand reached out and gripped mine hard. "Oh, Kit! I never understood before . . . what you've gone through."

Her words meant a lot, but this wasn't the time to go into all of this. Sooner or later Patrick would decide to come down the stairs. Jackie was obviously thinking the same thing. "Kit, there's a lighter in the left . . . front pocket of my jeans . . . Hold it up high . . . so I can see."

I did as Jackie requested, and even walked a few yards in each direction to spread the meagre light further, then scuttled quickly back to her. "So?"

"Boxes, steel drums . . . floor-to-ceiling junk. We're in a long aisle with corridors leading off in either –" She stopped and took in a deep breath, followed by a groan of equal intensity. It was obvious Jackie was having more trouble speaking.

"Do you see a place we can hide?"

"No . . . not from here, but . . . get me down . . . one of those corridors. I'm sure . . . there's something."

Grabbing Jackie gently under her good arm, I dragged her down the aisle in front of us a few feet at a time. Each time I paused, I relit Jackie's lighter, so she could look around.

The first two times I did it, nothing, but on the third try, Jackie said, "Hold . . . the light . . . a little lower. Yeah. Kit . . . feel . . . with your hands . . . just to . . . left. See? There's . . . space . . . in back of . . . metal drums . . . sure . . . of it."

I knelt by her side. "Jackie, you sound awful. How bad is it?"

"You mean . . . my . . . bleeding to death? Doing . . . nicely . . . thanks. Look . . . Kit –"

"No! End of discussion. Okay?"

I don't think I'd ever felt so helpless – or frustrated. Jackie couldn't go much longer without medical attention. I didn't need eyes to see that. And the longer we stayed down here, the worse our chances were. To get to help, I had to get past Patrick and anybody he might call in to help him. A pretty tall order for someone like me. Unless . . . Hmmm . . . Having a place to hide gave me an even chance. It could be better than even, if I could get whatever light he had away from him.

The first thing was to get my friend under cover. I was another matter. I wanted Patrick to find me – but on my terms.

"Jackie, this may hurt. Can you handle my moving you again?"

"You . . . don't mind . . . if I pass . . . out?"

"Be my guest. I'll be a gentle as I can."

By turning Jackie on her good side, I managed to carefully drag her through a space between two of the drums. Behind lay an area about six feet square, and by shifting a few of the drums, I felt confident she wouldn't be easily discovered.

Kneeling, I put my mouth next to her ear and whispered "Jackie, are you conscious?"

She nodded feebly. "Been trying . . . not to . . . cry out."

I smoothed her hair back. "Sorry if I've been rough, but I had no choice." She nodded her head again, and started shivering, whether from the cold concrete or shock, I didn't know. I took off my jacket and spread it over her, carefully tucking it in. "I'm going to go away for a bit. I'm sure Patrick has a flashlight, and I have to get it away from him. Don't make any noise if you can help it. I'm not sure how well I've got you hidden. Do you understand?"

Jackie nodded. "Careful . . ."

Footsteps on the stairs. I wormed my way through some more barrels and came out in another corridor running parallel to the first. I needed to find the right kind of cover quickly, but I had to be absolutely silent doing it. As he entered the room, I froze again.

"Kit! Please come out. I promise I won't hurt you. We need to talk."

I didn't answer and he started down the first corridor, passing Jackie's hiding place without any hesitation. I breathed easier.

Every time Patrick moved, I used the sound of his footsteps to mask my own. Separated by a wall of junk, we proceeded down our respective corridors, he looking for me, me frantically feeling the cardboard, wood, and metal drums for another place to hide. I was saying constant prayers he wouldn't shine his flashlight between things and spot me, and that we wouldn't come to the far wall too soon.

We'd gone maybe thirty feet, when I nearly tripped over a board. It felt like a piece of an old pallet. I smiled as I picked it up.

Patrick said, "I can hear you, Kit. Let's stop playing games. You know you need help."

The board made me feel more confident. I called out, "Don't be so sure."

He immediately moved more rapidly, and I realized that cockiness could put me in a lot of danger. Feeling around wildly, I discovered a narrow space between some stacks of cartons. Throwing my weight into it, I managed to move one of them about eight inches more. I quickly wormed my way in, rearranged things as best I could, and crouched down to wait, barely breathing. With that sixth sense blindness has given me, I felt, rather than heard, Patrick sneak past.

This stupidity was only wasting time. I needed to take the offensive or Jackie would bleed to death before I could get help. Besides, Patrick might have used his car phone to call for reinforcements.

My mind was also filled with the most horrible, confused thoughts. I'd been set up right from the beginning. Patrick must have been using me all along to get information. I knew what Susan meant when she said she felt soiled. Barely an hour ago the bastard had said he wanted to *run away* with me for Christ's sake! I squeezed my eyes shut. How could I have been so blind?

But Patrick was not going to get away with this, and I was going to have to be the one to stop him. First, though, I needed to get that flashlight out of the equation. The stacks of cartons gave me an idea, pretty risky but possible.

Taking a deep breath, I edged into the corridor again. No shout. No rushing feet. Okay. Pushing with my hip, I widened the space between the cartons, but also edged one stack out a bit. That done, I went back into my hiding place and felt around for a way to climb up.

The cartons were about three feet square, and whatever was inside seemed to be strong enough to keep them from collapsing under my weight. Carefully, I started climbing, hoping all the junk that separated Patrick and me would deaden any noise, hoping I wouldn't drop the board I'd found. With my ears cocked for approaching footsteps, I inched upwards, every iota of concentration focused on moving silently. Dust and dirt cascaded into my face every time I reached up, and twice I had to pinch under my nose to keep from sneezing. The board made things even more difficult, but I wasn't about to leave my only weapon behind.

By the time I got to the third layer, things had gotten decidedly more rickety. But with a feeling of relief, my hand found nothing more. Good. Another layer would probably have put me too close to the ceiling and toppled the whole pile. Even though I should have been shivering from the dank, chilly air around me, sweat trickled down my forehead as I slowly eased myself onto the swaying stack. After lying there for a few breaths, I carefully sat up and felt for the ceiling, which I judged to be not much more than four feet above. What I found wasn't the ceiling, but an unexpected bonus: a pipe of some kind, hanging from the ceiling. The sprinkler system?

Judging by some crashing off in the distance, Patrick had begun to get frustrated. All the better for me.

"Hey, Patrick! Want those papers?" I yelled. "I'm ready to make a deal." My voice died in the stacks of cardboard and wood.

His answer sounded pathetically eager. "Did you remember where they are?"

"Yeah. I had them all the time. Silly me!"

"Why didn't you say so? You could have saved us all a lot of trouble. Your friend could have been at the hospital by now."

"Seems like there's an awful lot you didn't tell me, too." I fought hard to bite back a more caustic remark.

"Kit, you don't understand. I wanted to explain things. I tried. We could have been on a plane out of here tonight. Remember?"

"What do you mean?"

"I wanted to spare you this. I didn't know . . . I would fall in love with you."

"What?"

His voice came from a different direction now. I knew that Patrick's bullshit was only an attempt to keep me talking so he could sneak up on me. The walls of junk, while they muffled any noises I made, also made it tough to tell where his voice was coming from. It was crucial that I know precisely where he was before I made my move. I'd have only one chance, and if I blew it, Jackie and I would die. This was hide-and-seek for grown-ups. Patrick was stalking me, and I was sitting in a tree waiting for him to walk by. I longed for my mother to call me in for dinner.

A roaring bang jerked me to my senses. The sound of moving boxes was followed by "Goddam rats!"

Great! Patrick had a gun.

"Kit, I told you how much I care about you and that's the truth.

Please give me those documents. I promise I won't hurt you. I couldn't hurt you. I'll just take them and leave."

He had to be kidding!

Patrick was at the far end of my aisle now, moving in my direction. If he raised his flashlight, I'd have no way of knowing. I'd be worse than a sitting duck. Every time I barely twitched a muscle, the stack of boxes trembled. I held my breath and chanted to myself, *Keep the flashlight down! Keep the flashlight down!*

"You don't know what I've been going through, Kit. I never wanted to hurt anyone. Things just got out of hand. And I *certainly* never wanted to hurt you."

You fucking idiot! my brain screamed. *My friend is dead because of you! Do you think I could feel anything but hate for you now?* My throat burned with the effort of keeping my emotions from boiling over.

Patrick talked on. "But things had gone too far. Believe me, I would have done anything to stop this. First your friend Marion started meddling. We made it as difficult as we could for her, but she ploughed right on. Like your friend Jackie. Like you. None of you ever gives up. You tied my hands. My investors expect to be protected, and I couldn't let this deal collapse."

I couldn't control my anger. "You set me up from the beginning!" *Fool! Don't help him find you!*

Patrick immediately stopped moving. I squashed myself flat as I could, held my breath and hoped.

"No, Kit," he said. "Paul Quinn mentioned you one day. His wife had been telling him about the companion ad, and quite frankly, you sounded very intriguing, so I called up."

The fact that Patrick honestly expected me to believe such bullshit made me more angry than anything so far. Did he think I'd leap off my stack of cartons, fall into his arms, and we'd race away into the sunset to live happily ever after? Regardless of why he originally answered the ad, our relationship had been perverted by who he was. Jackie had been attacked and would die unless I could do something, and it was due to him getting the information from me. I told him everything he needed to know – just like poor Susan with Paul. Boy, did I know how she felt!

"Meeting you changed me," Patrick continued. "But I'd set things in motion that couldn't be stopped. Isn't there anything we can do? Is it too late? You were the best thing that has happened to me in a long time."

He walked by right below me, but I couldn't react. I felt as if he'd stuck a knife in my heart and twisted it round and round. No matter how much I wanted to deny it, I'd begun to have strong feelings for him. Patrick had been a big part of my escape from the cage I'd built around myself.

But his little monologue had backfired. With a chill, I suddenly realized that he'd revealed *his* true intentions. He'd said I was the best thing to happen to him in a long time.

Was.

That one word let me know exactly where I stood. The frigid wind that had blown through me so many times in the past returned again in its full winter fury. Forget my friends, everyone Patrick had harmed, everything else! I wanted to do this for *me*!

Quietly, carefully, I sat up and wrapped both hands firmly around the sprinkler pipe. With one foot, I slid my board over the side. It fell to the floor with a satisfying clatter. Bracing both feet on the rear side of two cartons, I waited as Patrick raced back. I could hear his breathing, feel his presence below me as he stooped to pick up the board. But he was a little off to the right.

Come on! I screamed at him in my head, *Move forward! And whatever you do, don't look up!*

I hung suspended from the pipe for several wildly thumping heartbeats. Finally he saw the boxes I'd moved and stepped forward to the spot in my mind marked "X."

Mentally thanking the manufacturers of my rowing machine, I snapped both legs straight and sent my heavy load crashing down on his head.

After the initial rumble of falling cardboard, silence descended again like an enveloping blanket.

"Patrick?"

No answer.

I remained hanging from the pipe for an additional ten seconds before swinging to an adjacent stack of cartons and climbing down to the floor. With luck I'd knocked Patrick out. Hell, I hoped I'd killed the bastard. Using my foot, I felt around until I found his body. I gave it a questioning shove. No response. As I turned to make my way back to Jackie, a hand grasped my ankle and gave a twisting pull. I fell like a stone, but fortunately didn't hit my head. Using my free foot I lashed out and repeatedly connected hard with something – hopefully Patrick's face. When his hand released its hold, I scrambled away crablike about fifteen or twenty feet before stopping with my back against some crates.

Patrick got up slowly and immediately tripped over something. Good! No flashlight, but had he lost the gun? I slid forward, keeping track of him by his breathing, not fearing him as much now.

Inching along, I came to one of the cartons I'd knocked down. I swept my hand in an arc along the dusty floor around me, searching for my piece of wood.

"Kit? I know you're nearby. Can't we work something out? There's a lot of money in this. You may hate my guts, but I could give you enough to start your own damn record company if you want. How would that be?"

While he spoke, I moved forward a few feet and stopped no more than a yard or two away from him. He was in my world now: enveloping, black, impenetrable darkness. And although he didn't know it yet, gun or no gun, I had him where I wanted. I swept my hand out again and found what I was looking for: the board. But Patrick was standing on the other end. I was about to pull it out from under him, hopefully sending him for a loop in the darkness, when he stepped off.

"Okay, Kit . . . you win. Just give me time to get to the airport before you call the cops. After all, we did mean something to each other, didn't we? Would that be too much to –"

I couldn't stand listening to any more of his shit. I stood up, and with my best home-run swing, smashed the side of the board into Patrick's head.

EPILOGUE

—◊—

A month has passed and not a day goes by when I don't feel like I've got salt in my soul, you know, that gritty feeling when you think about certain things you'd rather not think about. What surprises me, though, is that I'm not more bitter. After all, I got dumped on pretty good. Even when everything went down, I didn't retreat into my safe little cocoon, though. I *never* want to be back in that place again. Life is much too short to spend it all indoors – mentally speaking. Mary Chapin Carpenter did an album a few years back called "Shooting Straight in the Dark." I guess that pretty well sums me up.

I didn't kill Patrick – although it wasn't long before I found out that wasn't even his damn name. (Should have expected that!) No matter how much I loathed what he'd done, what he stood for, I wouldn't have wanted that on my conscience – most days. There'd been too much killing already.

I'd tied him up with my shoelaces, scuttled back to Jackie, and found that she had passed out again but was still breathing. As much as I didn't want to leave her, I had to get help. A police cruiser discovered me wandering the streets about a block away from the warehouse, and my physical appearance – apparently I was covered in blood – convinced them pretty quickly that something was definitely amiss. It didn't hurt to mention Morris's name early in the conversation, either.

Patrick had never called the police station, of course. He'd simply used the time I was playing on the radio to swipe my keys from my jacket, get over to the apartment, and let his hired killer in. That was probably how he knew about the back door out to the alley, something I didn't twig to at the time. Fortunately for him, I hadn't thought of getting Guido to help with Jackie.

Anyway, you can imagine the reaction of my two friends when they eventually walked into the apartment. Sue says that Carolina's hair is noticeably greyer because of it. They were certain Jackie and I had been murdered.

We almost lost Jackie anyway. By the time they got her to St. Mike's, she was hanging on by sheer cussedness. Ironically, it was the cold of the warehouse that saved her, slowing down her heartbeat. It took the doctors several hours in the operating room and about ten gallons of blood to get her back in working order. Now she'll have to spend the entire softball season on the DL, and that's made her even more intolerable than usual. But we'll take an intolerable Jackie any day over not having her around at all.

Morris, with Carolina and Susan in tow, met us at the hospital, and I told them everything that had been going on before handing Jackie's precious papers over to the detective. The bastard, after taking one glance at them, refused to say anything and started to hot-foot it out the door.

"Hey! Wait a minute, buster!" I shouted, no doubt attracting dirty looks from every nurse on the floor. "You owe me big-time for that! You can't just walk out of here without explaining what's so damn important about those papers."

"You're right," he conceded, then made a big show of taking me into a vacant room, leaving Carolina and Susan out in the waiting area. He probably wanted to teach them a lesson for not co-operating with the authorities. "We've suspected something was going on with that Riverside deal for some time," he said.

"Why? I thought nobody knew about this soil-test stuff but us."

"Rumours on the street. Insubstantial stuff we couldn't confirm. These lab reports are going to bust this thing wide open, and also secure us a warrant to look into a few other things." Morris chuckled. "By the way, it turns out that man you slugged is the CEO of Advantage Developments, David Donaldson. How did you get yourself mixed up with him?"

That brought me up short. "He told me his name was Patrick – and you don't want to know how I met him."

"Patrick is his middle name, I believe."

"And he's the main person behind Riverside?"

"Absolutely, and that basement where you KO'ed Donaldson is apparently stuffed to the gills with toxic chemicals. There must have been illegal dumping out of there for years. You realize from these test results what a cesspool the ground around the warehouse is. And who knows how much they sent out from there to be illegally dumped other places? Besides being involved in at least two murders and one attempted one, he's broken probably every environmental law on the books." He paused. "But for the present, you have to promise not to open your mouth about this to anyone, not even your friends. I don't want anything to go wrong with this bust. There are more things going on than I can tell you about at the moment."

"Does this have something to do with Paul?"

"I'm not at liberty to say, although he is downtown singing a very interesting tune right now."

"What about him?"

"Prison for sure, but his clever lawyer will probably cut a deal and get him off with a minimal sentence. Leave all this to us." He patted my shoulder. "Thanks for believing that we could do the job. Now, go home and try to get some sleep." He stopped at the door. "Oh, by the way, we listened to your performance on my office radio. I'm impressed. You're good."

The story, considering how big it was, broke surprisingly slowly. The cops tried to keep a lid on it for as long as they could while they got everyone involved tied up good and proper, before the media could go to work. Not a thing was in the paper or on TV the next morning, other than the murder in my apartment. (You should have heard Mrs. Novik go on about *that*!) Over the next few days, word began to trickle out, but it wasn't until they arrested two mob bosses the following Wednesday that the media went absolutely berserk.

The real reason Morris had been so excited was that the cops had heard rumours, all right – rumours about money laundering, as well as illegal toxic-waste dumping, and hadn't been able to take it further because Advantage Developments had been such an effective front. The respect and backing the company had garnered from the city and provincial governments made it impossible to do any high-level snooping without something a lot more substantial than innuendo from the street.

With the evidence Marion had dug up, the cops got warrants and searched the offices of Advantage Development and Patrick's apartment, where they'd apparently turned up all kinds of interesting things – like the deed for that warehouse we'd been in. It had the names of the two Mafia bigshots they eventually arrested as owners. The cops had been after those slippery characters for years. It was hailed as a major coup for Toronto's police. Word from the trenches was that the deed had been Patrick's insurance policy against his backers. No wonder Patrick's crew had been willing to take such big risks to shut down our little investigation! He was well aware that their blunder put *him* in danger of being found floating in a bog up north somewhere – just like Rex.

Morris's kisser was on the idiot box almost daily. Then some "high-level source" leaked that most of the legwork had been done by four amateur sleuths, "friends of the dead woman whose moral courage started this all." You can imagine what happened. It didn't take much in the way of reporting skill to put names and faces to the "high-level" hints. Suffice it to say we all headed for the hills, and are thinking of getting unlisted phone numbers. Jackie suspects Morris, of course.

All during that time, Edward was after me to tell him everything Morris had said in our little heart-to-heart at the hospital.

I finally got fed up and told him off. "All you need to know is that the Riverside Project is dead. And they ain't never gonna get it started. You've won, so be satisfied with that."

Edward knew better than to push his luck with me. Eyes or no eyes, I'd whip his butt . . .

He also went ahead with his now rather lame rally without Kit Mason and her band. I was in no shape physically or mentally the morning after I flattened the man who'd told me I meant the world to him. I couldn't get up the energy to do anything except walk Shadow. Here I'd been agonizing all along about how awful it must have been for poor Susan, when all the time the same thing had been happening to me. Talk about salt in your soul . . .

The disappointment of the guys in the band when the rally appearance got cancelled surprised me. They really wanted to get out in public so we could strut our stuff. Danny appeared at my door that evening and we talked far into the night about where this whole recording project was going. We ended up writing a hurtin' song together: "I Used to Have Wings," and it's a great one. The little so-and-so really knew how I felt and I appreciated his company more than he might realize.

Putting the finishing touches on the recording the past few weeks, we've all become really close, especially Danny and me (he calls me his big sister – ha!). Next week we're all doing a showcase the radio station arranged at a local club. A lot of heavy hitters from the recording industry have promised to show up. Arnie has also offered to be our manager. He used to handle some successful local bands before he built the studio, and he has the kind of pinchy-penny attitude that can really work in an artist's favour. Where managers too often blow it is in the financial department. No worry there about old Arnie, except that he'll probably want to sell us those crummy studio amps of his.

Paul *did* cut a deal with the cops. He gave them what they needed to put Donaldson and his cronies behind the eight ball for Marion's murder. Even so, Paul will go to the slammer, but only minimum security and not for long enough, either. Susan, however, has stuck by her decision to cut her losses, and that's been really tough on her and the kids. We're all doing our bit to get her through this. Her parents helped a lot by paying off the rest of Paul's debt so she won't have to lose the house.

Oh yeah, that bastard Paul *did* tell "Patrick" everything he needed to know to make himself irresistible to me. Big surprise there. I wonder if Paul even mentioned what I enjoyed in the sack. After all, we had messed around a few times back in university before he met Susan. That's almost too disgusting to contemplate. At least "Patrick" actually owned that house in the country that he took me to.

Sue and I have spent a lot of time together lately. I really enjoy being around her kids and her littlest one, Caitlyn, loves her "Uncle Shadow" and his horseyback rides. It's going to be a long time for both of us to get over everything that happened. I row the Great Lakes in the late hours of the night when things become too black for me to handle.

Jackie's become more mellow. She's actually letting her hair grow out, and in its natural colour, too – for the moment. With her, you never know. Her convalescence has kept her at a pretty low ebb. The most noticeable damage is the scar down her cheek, but she actually likes the effect. It's the shoulder wound that's going to be the long-term problem. The last couple of weeks she's been going on about becoming a private investigator. I don't know if our nerves could stand it. Carolina and I also think she's got the hots for Danny. We noticed Jackie's been hanging around the studio a lot, pretending she's our "gofer." Sooner or later she's going to jump him. C's dying to see what happens. But who knows? Over the last little while I've been thinking I may give her a run for her money.

And what about the guy Jackie killed in my apartment? She doesn't talk about it much. I can't imagine what it must have been like. The cops weren't able to find out much about him other than basic stuff like his name, Bob Brawley. What an innocuous name! None of the guy's neighbours knew him, and he went through life with no one asking questions or noticing him especially. Morris told me there are a handful of specialists like Brawley who make their very successful livings hunting people who are in delicate circumstances, and the cops don't catch them too often, either. His *very* off-the-record opinion is that Jackie performed a public service, although he'd never tell her that. I've been trying to decide when would be the best time to inform Morris of Jackie's possible career change.

We buried Marion three weeks ago. It took a few days to get the medical examiner to release her body. Ron Morris was a big help there. The examiner had some ridiculous problem with a couple of odd bruises on her body and wanted to conduct further tests. Fortunately, Marion's parents kept the graveside service simple and to the point. Afterwards, the ball club got together and had a major-league Irish wake in her memory at the Bow and Arrow, the Babes' usual after-game pub. The management was great and let us use their upstairs room so we could do our crying (and laughing) in private. People need to say goodbye in their own way, and we all felt most comfortable with this. Marion would have loved it. And we did invite Little Joey.

Let's see . . . what else? Oh yeah, Carolina dumped Edward. She got fed up with him trying to mould her into the person he wanted her to be. She's thinking of a hiatus from her university toils next fall and has moved back into the family pile in Rosedale – but that's only until she figures out what she wants to do next. C even went out on a date last week with a guy she met in a supermarket check-out line! We still can't believe it. She's decided to enter the Canadian International Marathon next fall. Edward's telling everyone it was originally his idea and she'd been refusing to do it. Jackie says that, if Edward was so interested in the marathon, then *he* should have entered it.

I suppose I should say something about Patrick. No matter what his name may be, I still can't think of him as anyone but Patrick. When the story broke, the public outcry against the people responsible was incredible. The indictment "threw the book" at Patrick, and that book ricocheted off a lot of other people: two city councillors, Reynolds in Housing, the two crime bosses, of course, the manager of Sloane Environmental (which the bad guys had controlled even before Doc Sloane's death), and the list keeps growing. Patrick, as the main man and someone who the judge strongly suspected might take it on the lam, had his bail denied, so he's currently rotting in jail along with his lackey, Gregory Ewing, the person everyone *thought* was running Advantage Developments. The two of them are sharing the rap for Marion's murder, with Paul testifying against them.

Patrick caught me by surprise one afternoon a week ago when he phoned from jail. He was lucky to get me. At the time, I was sitting on the last of the boxes in my living room, eating an apricot Danish – a going-away present from Mrs. Novik. I'd found a new apartment near Yonge and Davisville (all the more important because I could be closer to Davisville Park and the Bow).

I couldn't stay where I was any longer. No matter how much everyone scrubbed, all I could smell in my apartment was blood. Maybe that's just my overactive imagination, but I also knew that none of us could ever feel comfortable there again. Jackie wouldn't even set foot in the place.

Anyway, when I heard Patrick's voice, I was too stunned even to think of hanging up. All the pain I'd been trying to bury during the past month rose up from its shallow grave to haunt me again.

He said he'd called to tell me how sorry he was for everything that had happened.

"Patrick," I said, finally locating my tongue, "you're responsible for all the terrible things that happened to me and people I love. How can you have the *balls* to call me? Do you think I ever want to hear your voice again?"

He laughed. "I'm the eternal optimist. I could plead temporary insanity, I guess."

"Permanent is more like it."

His voice got that gentle softness I remembered with such an ache. "I sincerely wish this could have turned out differently, Kit. You're a special person."

"Ain't life a bitch," I said quietly and hung up.

So I'm sitting here on the bleachers at Davisville Park in the May sunshine, a sweet-smelling, gentle breeze barely rustling my hair, listening to the Ruthless Babes playing in yet another softball season. Shadow's lying in the cool shade underneath, having a siesta. I bought one of those pocket tape recorders last week so I could keep an audio diary. It's a kind of therapy for me, too, I guess.

I've been trying to finish up before the game begins, but Jackie just came over and she's been going on and on about not being able to pitch this year. She probably thinks I'm an idiot to be dictating all this garbage into a tape recorder. "Right, Jackie?"

"Right, sports fans. This girl's definitely got some major screws loose."

"Hey Jackie?"

"Yeah?"

"Piss off."